Praise for *The Lost Americans*

"*The Lost Americans* is a gripping, page-turning tour de force. Christopher Bollen isn't merely a great storyteller—though he is. He is also a brilliant stylist who, once again, has given us a literary thriller where the action never flags and character and atmosphere never are slighted."

—Chris Bohjalian, #1 *New York Times* bestselling author of *The Flight Attendant* and *The Lioness*

"A terrific novel, rich in character and wonderfully atmospheric, with a propulsive plot packed with nerve-racking peril and satisfying twists and reading enjoyment on every single page. I loved it."

—Chris Pavone, *New York Times* bestselling author of *The Expats* and *Two Nights in Lisbon*

"*The Lost Americans* is a perfectly taut thriller. A deeply atmospheric portrait of Cairo in all its beauty and decay, the novel pulses with energy. Bollen orchestrates a vivid and gripping reading experience."

—Emma Cline, international bestselling author of *The Girls*, *Daddy*, and *The Guest*

"Uncharted territory . . . gripping and genuinely moving. While *The Lost Americans* begins in the heady mood of a fish-out-of-water adventure, the ending is sobering, shocking, and, I suspect, all too realistic."

—*New York Times*

"Bollen is a modern master of the Highsmithian literary thriller. His previous book, *A Beautiful Crime*, was a Venice-set caper about lovers turned con men, a mystery that tapped into the Floating City's labyrinthine nature. Here, he flies readers to Cairo to uncover a mystery about an American defense contractor who'd reportedly died by suicide and his increasingly suspicious sister working to understand what really happened."
—*Electric Literature*, "Most Anticipated LGBTQ+ Books of Spring"

"A gripping thriller with lingering emotional effects. . . . Bollen takes real risks with the story, making it more haunting than the reader may be prepared for. The scarcity of civil rights in contemporary Egypt is captured to shadowy effect, extending to the targeting of gay citizens like Cate's guide and driver, Omar. . . . Cut from the same mold as Robert Stone's great political thrillers with its international intrigue, darkly atmospheric setting, and compromised characters." —*Kirkus Reviews* (starred review)

"A bold plot twist bolsters the story's gritty realism, revealing that the villainy behind Eric's death shields a lot of human complexity. Bollen, known for setting thrillers in alluring locales, skillfully captures Cairo's beauty and palpable tension, and Cate and Omar's courage in facing hard truths gives this memorable thriller extra frisson."   —*Booklist*

"Summer is the time for murders set somewhere interesting: Christopher Bollen is the master of these. His latest, *The Lost Americans*, is a treat."
—Zadie Smith, *The Guardian*

"Sharp new literary thriller."   —*Vanity Fair*

"We're in Graham Greene territory in Christopher Bollen's *The Lost Americans*, which takes place in Cairo. . . . *The Lost Americans* is a sensitively written, keenly observed, hauntingly sad thriller that will make you want to weep with frustration: for the brief, broken promise of the Arab Spring, for the betrayals that take place within families, and for the ugly business of war, which is always booming."   —*Air Mail*

"*The Lost Americans* is a delicious jigsaw puzzle of a novel, one that evokes the allure of far-flung travel and the complicated fantasy of trying to disappear into a place that is not your home." —*Departures*

"*The Lost Americans* is a thrilling and engaging novel that will keep readers on the edge of their seats from beginning to end. Bollen's skillful storytelling and richly drawn characters make for a deeply satisfying reading experience, and the novel's exploration of themes such as power, corruption, and identity make it a thought-provoking addition to the mystery and thriller genres. Highly recommended for fans of smart, atmospheric fiction that will keep you guessing until the very end." —*Bookish Buzz*

"*The Lost Americans* is engrossing, expertly conceived and executed, but it's also disturbing—as it should be. It solidifies Bollen's stature of a literary crime writer—for many readers, the best kind."

—Peter Handel, *CrimeReads*

"Bollen's novels are always stylish and smart, with twists of international intrigue and a sharp eye for social commentary, and *The Lost Americans* is certainly no exception."

—*Town & Country*, "Must-Read Book of Spring"

"*The Lost Americans* is a well-conceived, extremely evocative thriller that respects the reader's intellect." —*Crime Fiction Lover*

"You don't want it to be finished when you turn the last page because getting there was so gripping. . . . Bollen is a masterful writer. He didn't invent literary suspense, but he's one of the best at it."

—Timothy Jay Smith, *Lambda Literary Review*

"Bollen's depth of characterization keeps the intensity at fever pitch throughout this riveting novel." —*Brooklyn Digest*

The Lost Americans

ALSO BY CHRISTOPHER BOLLEN

A Beautiful Crime

The Destroyers

Orient

Lightning People

The Lost Americans

A NOVEL

Christopher Bollen

HARPER PERENNIAL

NEW YORK • LONDON • TORONTO • SYDNEY • NEW DELHI • AUCKLAND

HARPER ● PERENNIAL

A hardcover edition of this book was published in 2023 by Harper, an imprint of HarperCollins Publishers.

HarperCollins books may be purchased for educational, business, or sales promotional use. For information, please email the Special Markets Department at SPsales@harpercollins.com.

FIRST HARPER PERENNIAL EDITION PUBLISHED 2024.

The lines from "Trying to Talk with a Man," copyright © 2016 by the Adrienne Rich Literary Trust. Copyright © 1973 by W. W. Norton & Company, Inc., from *Collected Poems: 1950-2012* by Adrienne Rich. Used by permission of W. W. Norton & Company, Inc.

Library of Congress Cataloging-in-Publication Data has been applied for.

ISBN 978-0-06-322443-8 (pbk.)

23 24 25 26 27 LBC 5 4 3 2 1

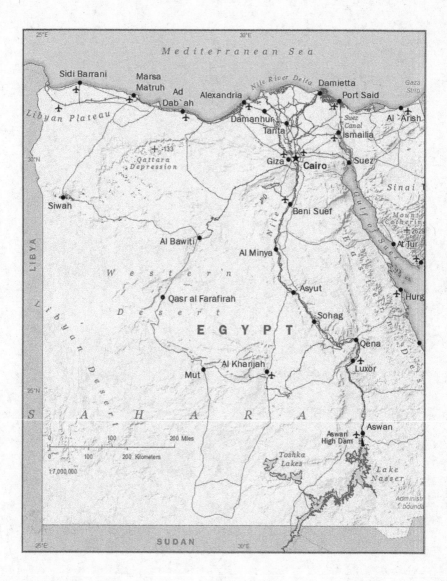

FOR MY SISTER

There is a point of no return, unremarked at the time, in most lives.

—GRAHAM GREENE

Out here I feel more helpless
with you than without you
You mention the danger
and list the equipment
we talk of people caring for each other
in emergencies—laceration, thirst—
but you look at me like an emergency

—ADRIENNE RICH

I have told my sons that they are not under any circumstances to take part in massacres, and that the news of massacres of enemies is not to fill them with satisfaction or glee. I have also told them not to work for companies which make massacre machinery, and to express contempt for people who think we need machinery like that.

—KURT VONNEGUT

The Lost Americans

CAIRO

D id he know, that last afternoon, as he wandered the tangled
streets of Cairo's Garden City, that he'd never make it home
again?

He must have suspected it, for that was the point of the errand
he was running. Eric Castle, three months shy of forty, an expert
in explosives, more than a little drunk, staggered across the road
and nearly got mowed down by a careening Peugeot. This was
the way in Cairo: every step felt like a near miss. Still, the walk
through the decaying neighborhood of grand, neglected mansions
and rifle-guarded embassies gave him a chance to think. Or, at
least, to defog his brain from the five whiskeys he'd consumed to
chase away the terrible thoughts in the first place.

It was sticky for early November, the shade warm and thick
with flies, and Eric had to watch his steps carefully with the alcohol copiloting them. The trees in Garden City could trip up
even a sober person. He had never seen city trees growing so
wild and unchecked. They were more like isolated storm systems,
great twisting cyclones buckling the pavement, while their arms

smashed through front gates and supplied a steady rain of bark and bird droppings. The cars parked along Al Bergas Road were draped in bolts of striped canvas, and judging from the debris collected on these covers, the cars hadn't been moved in some time. They reminded Eric of the motorboats tarped and left to rust in driveways back in his native Massachusetts. Feral cats slept on the car hoods, oblivious to the traffic. When the sidewalk crumbled away, Eric was forced to walk in the street.

By now, his ears should have grown accustomed to the loudness of Cairo. He had been stationed in Egypt once before, a few years back when he was working for a different company. On that trip, he'd been given a room with a view of the Pyramids. "I'll take your word for it," he'd joked to the hotel manager, for only on the last morning could he make out the blurry shape of those wonders in the distance, through miles of yolky smog. But Eric had been like a child at that window, standing on tiptoe to catch a glimpse of something so ancient and miraculous. On this trip, his company had booked him into a bland economy hotel. His room had no view, only a half-moon balcony overlooking an alley that offered a wormy breeze at night. Eric had been in Egypt for six weeks, and it was likely his assignment would extend for another six. Too much work to leave. Too many explosions to stage-manage. Unless his bosses got rid of him. Lately, when he had trouble sleeping, he sat out on the balcony in his underwear, drinking down mini-bar bottles and counting his mistakes.

At the next intersection, Eric spotted a lull in traffic and ran in a clumsy diagonal across four lanes. On the opposite side, old men in blue robes lounged in a throng of mismatched chairs—plastic patio furniture next to foam-chewed office swivels (chairs in Cairo were like pack mules, worked until the moment their legs gave out). The *bawabs* practiced their English on this sweaty foreigner. "Hello? American? USA? Hello!" Eric responded in his slurred attempt at

Arabic. "Welcome," the oldest man replied, insisting on English and on comedy, "Welcome, my friend, to freezing Alaska!"

Eric had been sent overseas to a lot of awful places. Some declared themselves as awful upon touchdown. Others took a few days to reveal themselves as such. Some were awful only because of the work he performed there for their leaders. But Cairo was the opposite of awful. He wouldn't miss the traffic, the streets a sick ward of engine ailments, the incessant honking a kind of religion that sensed the devil lurking in any pocket of silence. But at the same time, the city kept opening up to him, kept blooming, loving him back, and he would miss the stray, beautiful fragments of forty-six centuries that whirled around him at all hours. That morning, sipping his second whiskey, he'd booked a flight back to the States, leaving in two days. He hadn't told anyone about this plan, and he wasn't even sure he was going to use the ticket. Go or stay. Escape or face the consequences. It depended on the trouble ahead.

Halfway down the next block, Eric paused in the shade of an overgrown eucalyptus. He closed his eyes and felt two sweat beads race each other down his spine. There was a chance everything would be fine, that nothing bad would happen to him. He was probably overreacting, growing paranoid for no reason. He'd definitely been drinking too much since his return from the desert. His thoughts, which always ran too fast, kept tripping over themselves and falling into the darkest holes in his mind. Still, even standing here with his eyes closed in the middle of busy Cairo, he felt the fear for his safety returning. He snapped his eyes open and continued marching toward the post office. An insurance policy, that's what he was sending off, the smallest red flag mailed back home just in case the worst happened to him. He could easily laugh it off later if it proved unnecessary. "It was a joke! You didn't think it was funny? Oh, forget it. You've really lost your sense of humor."

Outside the post office customers mobbed the front entrance, trying to push their way inside. It was almost three o'clock, the hour the post office closed, and the mere idea of waiting in that tight fist of bodies nearly convinced him to abandon the plan. It was a foolish errand anyway, fueled entirely by paranoia and alcohol. His fear the past few days suddenly seemed ridiculous to him. "You're going to be fine!" he muttered aloud. A passing young woman in spandex workout clothes and a pink headscarf eyed him nervously, clearly unconvinced by his own declaration. Eric shuffled backward, on the verge of turning around, but committed to the errand and added himself to the crowd of waiting customers.

He wondered what his sister, Cate, was doing at this very moment in New York City. He always pictured her in a similar mosh of bodies—on a subway or in a club, Cate squashed between strangers by choice, a lover of crowds. He and his younger sister were such opposite creatures, and yet they had somehow been raised on the exact same diet of satellite television, junk food, and abandonment issues in their mom's mildewed cottage in the Berkshire Mountains. The last few years had pushed them even further apart. Still, when you're alone and panicking on the other side of the planet, who else can you reach out to than the person who knew you first?

Once inside the post office, the semblance of a line emerged, as if shaved into shape by the narrowness of the doorway. One clerk, hoping for a little baksheesh, waved excitedly to tall, white Eric. "Sir, mister, here," he cried from the counter, "I take you! Right this way!" But Eric shook his head. Even with his life in danger, he would wait his turn.

The Cairo sun set early in November, the city awash in Saharan gold, all the concrete transforming for a single hour into a priceless material. Eric returned to the Ramses Sands Hotel a little after 4:30. He took the elevator to the third floor, smiling up at the surveillance camera hanging from the ceiling—first he offered it an innocent smile, but held for too long, it soured into the expression of a dare. He desperately wanted another drink and to crawl into bed and forget. But mailing the insurance policy wasn't his only errand that afternoon. After all, in two days he might be flying over the Atlantic, on his way home.

*   *   *

Later that night, when Eric fell from his hotel balcony, he went without a sound.

PART I

Greetings from Jamaica

Chapter 1

NEW YORK CITY

ate took the crosstown bus through the autumn golds of Central Park. The rain drummed against the bus's roof, rising and fading like rounds of applause. For a moment the downpour was so heavy and unrelenting, she couldn't see the office buildings crowding the sidewalks or hear the voices of the men arguing at the grip bar next to her. The rain had lapsed by the time the bus deposited her on the corner of York, and she dodged the dripping awnings and drooling umbrellas as she snaked through the Sunday foot traffic. She kept reminding herself to walk slowly—that killing time had been the sole motive for spending the afternoon out of the apartment. But after eighteen years of living in Manhattan, Cate's default pace was set somewhere between late-for-a-dinner-reservation and trailed-by-plainclothes-police. She waited until the daylight began to dim on the east side before entering her building. In the lobby, she gave a frail wave to the doorman.

"Is the coast clear?"

Even the weekend doorman knew the answer would sting. He looked down at his screen and nodded. "He left with the piano about an hour ago. He brought two helpers, but they still managed to scuff up the hallway. I hope the co-op board doesn't notice."

"Thanks," Cate said, and hurried into the stairwell to absorb the blow alone. That was it, then. Luis had taken his last belonging. He'd moved the rest of his stuff out the week before, but he needed expert hands to extract his beloved 1907 Steinway upright, and Cate had agreed to make herself scarce while he took it. She climbed the stairs to the second floor and trudged down the hall to her apartment. As she threaded her key into the lock, she steeled herself for what awaited inside—or rather, for what didn't. A part of her held out hope that she might find a note from Luis on the kitchen table, or even Luis himself sitting at it. But he'd already taken the table when he moved. The kitchen table. The chrome bell lamp. The gaudy bamboo-framed mirror they found last summer in the trash near the Morgan Library.

Cate had to ram her shoulder against the door a few times to prod it loose from the frame. "Prewar," she muttered. That had been their favorite curse word for the two years they called this apartment home—uttered when wall sockets blew black smoke or the bathroom ceiling rained shards of plaster or the gas oven asphyxiated families of mice on the baking trays. To be fair, they'd been warned. "Prewar!" the rental agent had crowed the day they visited the open house. Midtown East, *Far Midtown East,* had been an unfamiliar pocket of Manhattan for both of them—a quiet, black-hole neighborhood in the center of the overcrowded universe where the office buildings went dark at sunset and all the restaurants shuttered by 9:00 p.m. Yet it had felt pioneering to try an untested part of the city, and it was far cheaper than the youth catacombs of downtown tenements. "Prewar! Prewar!

Authenticity in every corner! You won't find character like this in the East Village!" The broker had been right. Even in its post-war decline, Cate loved the place. There were still three months left on the lease, and Cate had to figure out a way of covering the rent all by herself. Only a month before, she and Luis had been planning to spend New Year's in the Caribbean, just long enough to wash another Manhattan winter off their skins. Now she would spend that week packing boxes and hunting for a cheap studio sublet.

Inside the apartment there were no surprises, only a rectangle of carpet-thick dust on the floor where the black upright had stood. Luis had been so proud of that piano; he'd rehabbed it himself. Ironically, the only time he'd been able to play it was the first night they moved in. Within an hour they'd incurred four noise complaints and an irate call from the rental agent. "You didn't tell me you had a piano!" she snarled, as if they were harboring a fam-ily of refugees. The building allowed dogs of all sizes, up to five cats, and an unlimited number of children. But it drew the line at musical instruments. For two years the piano sat in the corner, as tempting as a loaded gun left on a coffee table, just begging to be played with. Cate wondered whether Luis was sitting at its bench right now, *finally free of her and that building.*

On the bedroom nightstand sat two framed photos: one of Cate and Luis on a Washington Square Park bench not long after they met, and the other of a teenage Cate with her older brother (show-ing off his college muscles in rolled-up sleeves) and their reed-thin, chronically-zoned-out mother. That second photograph had been placed on the nightstand as a decoy. It was meant to give Luis the impression that he wasn't the only source of stability in her life, that Cate belonged to a tight-knit family in not-faraway Massa-chusetts. As she entered the bedroom, she noticed that Luis had taken the photo of them on the park bench, removing even that last trace of himself. All that remained was Cate and her tight-knit family, as if that family hadn't unraveled years ago.

*   *   *

For the past week, Cate's survival strategy for weathering the breakup had been to keep busy. Thankfully, New York City was the great white shark of distraction, and she only needed to slip from the lonely raft of her apartment to be devoured by it. Her days were already covered. She worked in fundraising at a small nonprofit art space called Upper East located in a renovated town house in the East Eighties. Cate had been late finding a career, too busy in her twenties cultivating the impressive résumé of a personal life (partyer, nightlife fixture, girlfriend of, never home before 5:00 a.m., her daylight hours consumed with the delicate art of piecing together her mind and body from the previous night). Cate owned the city in her youth—she discovered she had a talent for being young, or maybe recklessness had been her gift. Yet with each advancing year she'd begun to feel less like one of the city's glittering conquerors and more like a guest who had overstayed her welcome. She often thought of those elaborate chalk drawings that artists used to draw on Lower East Side sidewalks, gorgeous fluorescent monsters that became staples of the neighborhood before the next rain washed them off. Everything vanishes, especially here. It was a lesson that Cate kept needing to relearn.

She'd started at Upper East five years back. The tin cup was New York's oldest instrument, and it turned out that Cate played it particularly well. She rattled it at wealthy art patrons, singing songs of love or guilt or eternal status points, whatever motive might convince the rich to cough up a sizable donation. The job was hardly a passion. But to her credit, she kept afloat a small, scrappy art organization whose offbeat exhibitions attracted enough foot traffic and social media likes to validate the effort. She usually left work around 7:00. It was nights that posed the biggest threat to her sanity in the wake of Luis's departure. To her own amazement, at age thirty-seven, Cate had managed to spend every evening out, conscripting a myriad of friends to participate in a grueling marathon of dinners, cocktails, openings, Brooklyn house parties, concerts, and one fizzled attempt at an after-hours club.

On Monday morning she awoke to the heavy-metal soundtrack of garbage trucks. Collection started early in Far Midtown East. A tiny meteor pulsated behind her right eye—the residue of attending a stranger's birthday party in a Chelsea loft the night prior. Assessing the pain, Cate was grateful to be spared a more debilitating headache in the lottery of five-vodka hangovers. Nevertheless, *Back to this*, she thought with the revulsion of an organism regressing to an earlier stage of development. *Back to hangovers and dry mouth and waking up alone, wondering whether my purse made it home with me.*

Her phone was vibrating on the nightstand, the ringer turned off. For a second Cate worried she'd overslept for work. But, no, the garbage trucks started at seven. The call had gone to voice mail by the time she grabbed the phone, and she found she had two missed calls. Both were from her mother's landline in the Berkshires. Her mother would never call her this early, let alone twice. Before Cate could convert that oddity into dread, the screen lit with another incoming call.

"Catelin?" The voice belonged to her stepfather. Wes Steigerwald was the only person who called her by her full name. She assumed it was his attempt to fast-track an intimacy that had never grown naturally between them.

"Hi, Wes," she replied warily. "What's up?"

"I hate to call you like this," he said, stumbling, leaving awkward gaps between his words. In the background Cate heard a faint shriek, as if a teakettle had been left whistling on a stovetop. "Joy should be the one to call, but she can't. So I'm doing it. I don't know where you are in the city right now. Are you at home? Maybe you could find a—"

The sound wasn't a kettle. Cate closed her eyes. "Just say it."

Chapter 2

THE BERKSHIRES, WESTERN MASSACHUSETTS

Eric's body was found in the alley behind the Ramses Sands Hotel at 7:00 a.m., local time. A hotel porter had been dragging out laundry bags for collection when he spotted a vagrant sprawled on the pavement. Then he noticed the man's clothes—a yellow T-shirt and black jeans—and ran over to him, thinking he might be a tourist who had fallen and hit his head. Eric Castle had fallen, but from the height of three floors. The balcony doors to his room had been left open, the white curtains billowing out and climbing up the outer walls like plumes of smoke. Twenty minutes after the discovery, the hotel manager, a Mr. ElBaradei, led Cairo police to room 3B. The lead detective stepped onto the half-moon balcony, peered over the edge, and saw Eric's body lying directly below the drop. According to the hotel's night operator, Eric had been alive a little after 11:30 p.m., when he'd phoned down asking not to be disturbed. An initial estimate suggested that he had been dead for several hours, quite possibly since the previous night. No one had heard or seen the fall.

That was all the information that the American embassy in Cairo could provide when they called Cate's mother that morning, waiting for first light on the East Coast to break the news. Wes had relayed those grisly details to Cate and, in the warble of a question, added, "They said they'd call back when they knew more?" He seemed to be asking Cate to confirm that the embassy would indeed call back. "I'm so sorry, Catelin," he blubbered, "I'm so so sorry."

Sorry. The word made no sense to her in the moment. Likewise, the words *fall* and *Cairo* failed to cohere. Yet she was already climbing out of bed and grabbing for clothes in the speed and imprecision of an emergency. An hour later, driving a rental car up the FDR, heading north beyond the redbrick fortresses of Bronx housing projects, Cate tried to recall the last time she and Eric had communicated. A text in September? A group family email in August? She had no idea that he was even working in Cairo. They weren't friends on social media because her brother had always refused to join. He claimed that too much personal information was a liability for his job. Better, he said, to be a smiling blank, with no accessible backstory of friends and interests. A smiling blank. That's what he'd been to her these last few years as well.

They hadn't always been so distant. Growing up in the flowering mud fields and knee-deep snow of Western Massachusetts, Cate and Eric were practically inseparable. Their childhood home was the definition of troubled, a yellow house isolated in the woods, miles from neighbors, the thick, thriving hemlocks and oaks providing free, high-quality soundproofing for their father's manic rages. Cate and Eric were pretty much left to fend for each other. That bond lasted through high school, two grades apart at Monument Mountain Regional. The school was a featureless beige-brick building that could have been mistaken for a grandiose highway rest stop, and in hindsight its bathrooms, vending machines, and parking lot provided the most fertile memories of Cate's years there. The Castle siblings hung out with the same groups of friends and held near-identical grade-point averages (oh, the promise of a B-minus, ready to set the world on simmer). And yet their ideas of life beyond age eighteen couldn't have been more incongruous. It was as if she and Eric had been sent to separate rooms to concoct a slapdash notion of what adulthood looked like and emerged an hour later with shockingly incompatible visions.

When Cate thought of her brother's job, she pictured black death machines in the desert, refusing to wilt in 120-degree heat. Tanks, field guns, howitzers, missiles, weapons with long, lean barrels that swiveled like apocalyptic weathervanes. After college Eric had landed a tech job in Nashua, New Hampshire, at one of the biggest private defense firms in the Northeast. The company turned out to be a chief supplier of international arms. Cate made her disgust clear. When her outcry fell on deaf ears, she tried to accept Eric's choice of a career, even briefly romanticizing it among her New York friends, the way others bragged of an uncle in the Mafia or a cousin busted for drug smuggling in Thailand. "My brother is an arms dealer." Except Eric wasn't an arms dealer. He didn't sell the merchandise. He never lunched with generals or made deals in airport business lounges. She wasn't even certain Eric owned a suit. His specialty was the blue-collar field of maintenance and repair. For weeks or months at a stretch, her brother was deployed to various foreign military outposts, serving as the fix-it man for technical glitches, the spare-parts replacer when a mainframe shorted out, the grease monkey on call when, for example, your short-range ballistic missiles weren't efficiently incinerating minority groups in the dead of night. Even on the day of his death,

Cate couldn't resist the habit of self-righteousness. She had been ashamed of her brother's profession. And the worst part was that he had known it.

They fought through their twenties, especially whenever they sat within two chairs of each other at holiday gatherings—Cate on the side of human rights and world peace (admittedly vague on real-world solutions), and Eric with his encyclopedic knowledge of regional hostilities and the inventories of government arsenals. Despite their squabbles, they still managed to forge an enduring friendship, albeit one at far range. When Eric got married to a baker in Nashua, Cate drove the four hours to stand among five smiling strangers in matching peach taffeta. Eric would call her one evening each week, and they perfected a cheerful sibling banter not unlike two beginners in a foreign language class—they spoke primarily in the present tense and kept to innocuous topics like food and weather. Despite knowing zilch about the intricacies of her brother's job, Cate still occasionally managed to harangue him about his safety overseas. "Don't worry about me," he replied. "Tell you what, I'll send you a postcard so you know I'm still alive." She assumed he was joking—*Who sends postcards anymore?*—but sure enough, they started trickling into her New York mailbox, one every few months. Never a text message from Eric, only auntly postcards with exotic stamps quilted on the backsides. Oman. Israel. Bahrain. Saudi Arabia. Places she would never visit. Eric always chose pictures of desert sunsets, and she would tack them up on her refrigerator, a rumbling cold storage of Middle Eastern suns.

Then, out of the blue three years ago, Eric divorced and moved back to the Berkshires. He accepted a job at a smaller "boutique" defense firm called Polestar, whose headquarters was located in a suburban office park in the town of Pittsfield. More surprises followed. Cate learned that Eric had started dropping by their mother's house to talk and help with chores. Neither Cate nor

Eric had ever been fond of their stepfather or his *aw-shucks* earnest Scout-leader routine. In their teenage minds, their first bad father hadn't underscored the need for a good one so much as exposed the redundancy of the entire position. Their joint aversion to Wes Steigerwald eventually filtered down to a half sister named Willie, born the very year Cate moved away for college. Neither Cate nor Eric had ever mustered much interest in the girl. But Eric's return home brought about all manner of unexpected reunions. He began taking Willie camping in Vermont in summers and went on weekend hunting trips with Wes during bear and turkey season.

Cate could pinpoint the exact day of their falling-out. It was Thanksgiving the year Eric moved back. Cate must have agreed to come home for the holiday—or, more likely, her brother just assumed she would make her annual begrudging appearance. When Cate's new boyfriend invited her to join his parents in Washington Heights, she didn't think twice before accepting. Eric called her up that chilly Thursday morning to reprimand her about abandoning her own family. "It's so like you," he hissed, and Cate thought, *No, it's so like us, old us, before you moved back and decided to reinvent yourself as the model son.* She felt betrayed by Eric's eagerness to reassemble a family from the junkheap of their childhood—at least without consulting her first. Running away had been the last quality they'd shared. He proceeded to lecture her on the importance of repairing her relationship with Wes and Willie and spending *meaningful* time with their mother, who was slipping further into the mental abyss. "Come home!" he cried. "We're your family. Get to know us!" In that moment, Cate experienced an inexplicable pride in being the last Castle holdout, the prodigal child who didn't need to return. "I'm glad you're reconnecting," she replied in a tone that did not suggest gladness, "but I'm not interested in appearing on command simply because you've decided you want a family again. I'm happy in New York with my new boyfriend. Come meet him.

His name is Luis. I'm spending Thanksgiving with *his* family." A week after that call, Eric had been sent to Beirut for work. Cate waited for a desert sunset to appear in her mailbox, but no postcard ever arrived. Now, as she sped through Connecticut, the autumn light spilling like cold white wine over the leafy fields, she couldn't fathom why she'd been so proud to stay away.

Eric had opened the balcony doors. He stepped out. He fell over the railing, plummeting to his death in a back alley in Cairo. Was he half asleep? Drunk? Had he gotten tangled up in the curtains? All those possibilities seemed improbable to her. Her brash, handsome brother could assemble warheads with his eyes closed, but couldn't navigate a hotel balcony? There had to be some mistake.

Her phone buzzed. When she answered, she heard the whine of the screen door and the staticky white noise of her mother's front lawn. It was Wes on his cell phone.

"Sorry to bother you," he said in a whisper.

"I'm an hour away."

"I wanted to let you know—"

"Wes," she interrupted, trying for a kinder tone, as if a few warm words might make up for twenty years of stepdaughterly chill. "Are they certain the man they found is Eric? Who identified him? Couldn't there be some mix-up with another man in his work unit? Because I just can't imagine that Eric would fall over a balcony."

"We've heard more news," Wes said. "One of Eric's bosses in Pittsfield called. He's spoken to some of Eric's colleagues in Cairo. I wanted to warn you."

"Warn me?"

"I figured it would better if you knew the situation before you got here. For your mother's sake." Wes paused. As Cate waited for him to continue, she nearly missed the highway turnoff at

Waterbury that would take her north. She whipped the rental car across three lanes, the tires grinding over rumble strips, a rock concert's worth of honks and flashing headlights chasing her over the viaduct. "There's no good way to put this. Eric's boss says there's evidence that his fall wasn't an accident. His boss says it looks like Eric might have jumped."

"Jumped? Like deliberately? Like"— the word wouldn't detach from her tongue —"suicide?"

"Polestar is telling us it looks that way."

Her rejection of that news was instantaneous. Eric might have been depressed, might have been drinking too much, might have been a lot of things she couldn't begin to name, but she was certain her brother wouldn't jump off a balcony on a business trip in the middle of the night. Not without sending a message home first. A message to *her*, at least.

"How did they reach that conclusion?" she demanded. "That's bullshit! You need to call Polestar back and tell them they're wrong. It had to have been an *accident*." Two minutes ago, Cate had refused to believe in accidental falls, but now she was determined to embrace that version of events. Accidents were blameless evils; suicides possessed long fingers that pointed at the living. "Mom can't think it's suicide, can she?"

"Joy isn't doing too well no matter the cause. I thought it best that you knew so you'd be prepared. We'll see you soon, Catelin?"

Cate focused on the highway as it angled north through the luckless gas-station towns of Litchfield County. Ten miles before the Massachusetts border, she pulled onto the shoulder and broke down while cars whizzed past. When she finished crying, she used the rearview mirror to wipe her eyes. If age is a painter, adding fine lines brushstroke by painstaking brushstroke, grief is a sculptor, jamming its thumbs into the clay of the face, hollowing out the eyes, gouging the cheeks. She looked as beaten as she felt.

*   *   *

The line that separated Connecticut and Massachusetts wasn't imaginary. You could feel the shift between states, the tires running over a smoother grade of asphalt, the wheels whistling in a higher key. The shadows of migrating geese streaked across the road like comets. Cate rolled down the windows to take in the sugary smell of the pines. Up here, the trees were nearly naked. The brightest colors—the blood reds and phosphorescent oranges—already blanketed the ground. Autumn leaves were Berkshire's gold, the reason for the seasonal surge in sightseers who packed the bed-and-breakfasts and whaled through the valleys in giant tour buses. Cate's tiny village of New Marlborough didn't draw as many visitors as Rockwellian Stockbridge or blue-blooded Lenox, but it managed a respectable autumn trade with its apple-picking farms and two antique shops. New Marlborough was *real* country, not bucolic suburbs masquerading as hinterlands. Locals stopped talking when a commercial airplane flew overhead and waited until the invasive species passed. Still, the town was stocked with plenty of rich sophisticates inhabiting the grander houses on weekends, some of whom might have been Cate's neighbors in Manhattan.

She turned onto Foxglove Lane. On one side of the dirt road sat a renovated eighteenth-century farmhouse. Cate had spent the first twelve years of her life in a sunflower-yellow ranch house that straddled this property's back pasture. After her parents' divorce, her mother had sold the house to their wealthy neighbors, and the three remaining Castles moved a mile down Foxglove to a rustic, semiwinterized cottage that had no business serving as a container for two feral teenagers. The wealthy neighbors who had bought their house swore they were going to renovate it, but six months later they tore it down and replaced it with a tennis court. Some nights, as teenagers, Cate and Eric would slip past the chain-link fence and tour the ghost of their former home—the bedrooms in the deuce courts, the pantry kitchen at the baseline, the liquor cabinet by the net, conjuring for each other the tiniest domestic details, like the crooked handle on the silverware drawer or the watery light that swam through the foyer window in the mornings. They knew the blueprint of that home with the intimacy reserved for children who had hidden, crawled, and took their first steps inside of it. But neither of them had been sad to see the house demolished. One less reminder of their father the better.

The roof peeked above the bend. Cate pressed the gas, and the rest of the battered two-story cottage rose into view, its mildewed siding the color of freezer-burned meat, the windows blinded by fistfuls of dust. Laundry lines bowed across the lawn, flapping bathmats and towels. Her mother's property consisted of sixteen acres of meadows and woods, and yet the house was crammed by the side of the road as if clinging to the last thread of civilization. When her stepfather entered the picture twenty years before, Cate thought he'd at least fix up the house and yard. Wes was employed as the "director of facilities"—euphemism for groundskeeper—at a nearby coed boarding school called Brightwell. But it turned out that Wes didn't like to take his work home with him, and the Castle house continued to lose its lifelong battle against weather, insects, and mold.

Cate hadn't been home in nearly a year, not since last Christmas. As she pulled into the gravel driveway, she noted a few improvements: the gutters were no longer peeling off the roof and a new woodshed housed an orderly Jenga of logs. These enhancements must have been Eric's good-son handiwork. She climbed out of the car, collected her bag from the trunk, and stared up at the cottage. There was no place lonelier than a former home. The screen door let out its shriek of welcome, and Wes stepped outside, his eyes washing over her before he picked up a twig on the lawn. Wes had quit cigarettes a decade ago but suffered the curse of the long-term smoker, an uneasiness with idle hands.

Cate walked toward him, unsure how to broker a meaningful conversation with a man whom she'd spent half a lifetime avoiding. She stuck to the simplest fact. "I made it."

"You did," he agreed. Cate studied him, taking in the toll of what a year had done. His face looked thinner, cleated with its bony nose, which tilted to the left as if pushed at the tip by an invisible finger; his reddish hair was dusted gray. Wes Steigerwald's eyes were his only stunning feature. They were a glacial blue, the rare kind of glowing eyes that reminded you of the miracle of human sight. (The Castle eyes were all a dull, miracle-free brown.) Cate had witnessed supermarket clerks and cashiers stop to admire Wes's eyes, blushing as they did so, as if confused by their sudden attraction. It was because the rest of Wes was so plain that his eyes stuck out as extraordinary, like coming across two sapphires in a pile of leaves. Cate was certain those eyes had been the twin seducers responsible for persuading her mother to remarry and bear a third child in her mid-forties. Cate was about to ask about Willie when she noticed the disturbing sunkenness of her stepfather's chest.

"My doctor has me on oxygen," he said. "It's nothing serious. Just breathing issues at night." He lurched off the porch and extended his arm. For a second, she thought he might give her a hug, but his hand went for her bag.

"No, please. I can carry it. I'm sorry about the oxygen. Mom didn't tell me."

"It's not serious," he said dismissively.

"How's Willie?"

"Heartbroken. But I wouldn't let her come home today. She's just finishing her midterms, and it all seemed . . ." Willie had started her freshman year at Smith College, a two-hour drive away. Their mother had finally reared a golden child on her third try, the pride of the family, a graduate not of Monument Mountain Regional like her half-siblings but of Brightwell Academy. "To be honest," he said, "I only told her fifteen minutes ago. It's been hard, making these calls, breaking the news over and over." His voice began to break.

"Of course," Cate said. A part of her wished they had hugged. She clambered onto the porch and asked quietly, "How's Mom holding up?"

Wes bent his head. "Not good."

"It wasn't a suicide!" Cate blurted. She realized she'd been waiting to scream this fact for the past hour in the car. "I don't care what Polestar told you—they're a criminal weapons company. They're monsters. We shouldn't trust a word they say."

Wes blinked in defense, as if Cate were somehow blaming him. "I don't know how any of this could have happened. I'm sorry that I . . ." He was struggling to find the right words. "I can only repeat what they told me. I spoke to a nice woman earlier, an attaché at the embassy in Cairo named Elizabeth Skyler. But she hasn't called us back. And Polestar seems to be actively trying to get answers on—"

"But you could have defended him as soon as they accused . . ." Cate realized that she was, in fact, trying to blame Wes. She wondered whether her stepfather had ever once stopped to question the ethical behavior of an arms distributor. "That company would say anything to make a problem go away. Who knows the danger they put him in over there? Eric didn't kill himself," she repeated. "I know my brother."

Wes opened the front door but didn't follow her inside. As she stepped into the mudroom, his voice rose hysterically behind her. "What more do you want me to do, Catelin? I'd ask the police for answers if I could, but which police? The town? The state? Eric's death wasn't in any of their jurisdictions. All I can think to do is wait for the embassy to call back."

In the mudroom, Wes's hunting gear hung on the walls. Packages from Amazon and FedEx columned in a corner. A glance at their address labels told her that her mother was back to caretaking for weekend country houses—collecting packages, watering gardens, stocking pantries, organizing propane deliveries, and playing all-around concierge to wealthy homeowners for extra cash.

Cate found Joy in the kitchen hunched on the window seat, her face sallow in the afternoon light. She still wore the yellow robe that she must have had on when she took the call from the embassy that morning. For a second Cate was scared to interrupt her, afraid to disrupt whatever temporary equilibrium kept her from breaking apart.

She sat down on the window seat, and after a minute, Joy wrapped her arms around her daughter. They remained that way, not so much crying as sharing the rise and fall of each other's breaths. The house was stone quiet, and Cate didn't break the silence by speaking. She hugged her mother. *Anything but suicide*, she thought, because that meant they might have failed him somehow. They had lost too much already. Cate would accept an accident. In the worst case, she would even take murder.

Chapter 3

THE BERKSHIRES, WESTERN MASSACHUSETTS

Cate spent the night on the wafer of mattress in her old upstairs bedroom, which technically now belonged to Willie. The walls were plastered in posters of nubile boy bands, Pride ribbons, and snapshots of fat-cheeked girls camping by a creek—the teenage leftovers that Willie had shed for her new life in the dorms of Smith.

Cate managed only brief snatches of sleep. For most of the night, she stared up at the ceiling, listening to the coyotes screaming in the woods and the beech trees creaking in the wind. She tried not to think of her brother's bedroom down the hall, or how they'd learned to conduct most of their teenage rebellion in silence to evade the ears of a new stepfather. Cate had lost her virginity in this room at fifteen, choosing almost at random one of Eric's close friends. In her mind, that experience, too, had been performed in silence, the boy's smooth body on top of hers, his shoulders bony and freckled, his black hair matted at his ears, the taste of beer on his lips, doubtlessly chugged for courage, the bright afternoon light pouring through the window, both amplifying their nakedness and making it hard for her to see what was happening in the shadows between their legs. It amazed her to think she'd taken that reckless chance. This house could never be depended on for privacy. It had been built as a seasonal hunting cabin a century before; there were gaps in the floorboards, and half the rooms lacked proper insulation. The walls shivered when the stairs were climbed. Every sound was magnified, every word overhearable. Even now, Cate didn't need to hold her breath to summon the sound of Wes's oxygen machine murmuring from the downstairs bedroom, lapping like waves on a distant shoreline.

She woke to yellow light, somehow managing to catch the last hours of sleep. Downstairs Wes was thanking someone for their call. Cate jumped from bed and grabbed her jeans off the chair. She was trying to beat the sound of him saying goodbye, sprinting down the steps and into the kitchen. Wes stood by the refrigerator, his body lassoed first by the landline's curly antique cord and a second time by a thin tube that carried oxygen to his nose. A portable, blinking tank sat at his feet like a futuristic pet. She was too late. Wes was untangling himself from the cord to return the phone to its hook.

"Cate, please!" her mother cried from her perch at the table. Cate glanced over, relieved that Joy had at least dressed for the day in chinos and a Smith College MOM sweatshirt. The tabletop was covered in old snapshots of Eric. "You can't run around here half naked!"

Cate looked down at the T-shirt and stringy red underwear that, admittedly, under normal circumstances, had she not been racing to intercept a call from the Cairo police or the American embassy, would have been inappropriate. She quickly slipped on her jeans. Her mother had adopted a far stricter parenting style in raising Willie than she'd ever employed with her first kids, and as a result, now in her thirties, Cate was retroactively treated to sermons about her cursing and bad posture. "It's the city where you learned those bad habits," went Joy's customary refrain—as if New York City had been a disaster of a finishing school. Today, though, Cate was committed to acting like the daughter her mother wanted. "Sorry, Mom," she offered sheepishly.

Wes held up a pad of paper where he'd scribbled the attaché's name—Elizabeth Skyler—along with a phone number and an email ending in @usembassy.gov.

"Was that the embassy in Cairo?" Cate asked. Wes nodded as he placed a pan on the burner. She considered warning him about turning on a gas stove near his oxygen tank. But before she could, he clicked on the flame, and the kitchen didn't explode.

"Want some eggs?" he asked.

"No. I want to know if you told the embassy that we don't believe Eric killed himself. Did you ask about a police investigation? Did you remind this attaché that Eric wasn't a tourist but was working with Egypt's military? Did you tell her he wouldn't have—"

"Cate!" Joy cried again. "Stop! Wes is doing his best. I asked him to handle the calls."

"I'm sorry!" Cate shouted in defense. Then she modulated her tone and repeated the apology to her stepfather. "I'm sorry."

Wes cracked two eggs in the pan. "A lot was discussed. Ms. Skyler assured me they're monitoring Eric's case carefully. Apparently, there's a lot of red tape in sending a"—Wes stumbled for a euphemism, as if searching for the dullest knife in a utensil drawer—"a deceased foreigner back to his home country. *Repatriation*, they call it. First, the Cairo police complete their investigation, and that includes an autopsy. Ms. Skyler explained that since Eric died on foreign soil, his case must go through their laws and procedures, and the US government can't just step in—"

Cate spun around to her mother. "Mom, you don't think it's suicide, do you?" They had already gone over this heart-grating topic the night before and unanimously agreed that Eric hadn't shown signs of depression and wouldn't have taken his life. But Cate felt the need to reinforce that conviction in the minds of her mother and stepfather. Their meekness made them easy prey for Polestar's powers of influence. And perhaps Cate also needed the reassurance.

Joy shook her head, her lank, gray hair splashing against her shoulders. "Of course I don't believe that! Eric didn't intend to jump, I know that in my heart. It was either a terrible accident or . . ." But she wouldn't put the alternative into words. "He couldn't phone much when he was overseas, but he called to check in . . . when was it?" She consulted Wes's face. "Three weeks ago?" Wes nodded in confirmation. "He was just about to fly to the desert." Her voice turned high and thin. "He sounded perfectly normal! He wasn't upset! Nothing was wrong!"

"You see," Cate said, and squeezed her mother's hand. As if a call home to parents served as a conclusive indicator of a person's emotional well-being. As if Cate hadn't fictionalized the existence of an imaginary Cate, full of positivity and early bedtimes, in her calls from Manhattan all these years.

"I remember thinking he sounded cheerful," Wes chimed in, as if wanting to add to the delusion of an exceedingly unsuicidal Eric in Egypt. "Happy even!"

Cate looked over at Wes. "Did the attaché mention why Polestar jumped to the conclusion of suicide? Or are we just supposed to go along with their opinion and not ask any questions?" She hadn't meant it as another dig at Wes's limp handling of the situation, but he looked up from the stove with hurt. "Sorry, I wasn't trying—"

"You can ask Polestar all the questions you want," he replied in a wounded tone. "They're coming to the house today at two o'clock. I'm afraid that you only woke up for the last call I fielded this morning." He unhooked the oxygen tubes from his nose and carried the eggs over to Joy. He whispered "Eat," and kissed her on the top of the head. Cate felt sandbagged with guilt for the slight.

"I have to go pick up the dog," he announced, and Joy instantly moaned, "Oh, don't bring that thing here!"

"What dog?" Cate asked, thankful for the change in subject.

"Eric got a Doberman puppy a few weeks before he was sent to Egypt," Wes said as he grabbed his car keys. "Bad timing. His neighbor was watching her, but, well, he doesn't want to anymore." Cate didn't know about the dog, but she knew very few of the milestones that dotted her family's lives for most of the year.

Joy sighed. "There's no room for a puppy in this house."

"I'll keep her in my office until we can find a home," Wes promised, referring to his renovated toolshed on the other side of the lawn, his reclusive pegboard kingdom away from the Castles. He gazed at Cate before he left, his mouth twitching as if trying to sculpt words that would bring a truce. "Eric was crazy about that puppy. He was excited to get home to her. I'm on your side, Catelin. He had too much to live for. He wouldn't kill himself."

Cate took the seat next to her mother and waited until Wes's truck disappeared before pledging to be a kinder stepdaughter. "I will try harder. Old habit."

"Wes is grieving too," her mother replied. "He and Eric had grown close these past few years. You forget that."

"Do eat something, Mom."

"Blah." Joy pushed the plate of eggs away. She never ate, never took care of herself; why would she start on the day after her son's death? Cate's eyes fell on Wes's oxygen machine by the counter. It still looked like a bomb, a suitcase abandoned in a terminal waiting to explode. In truth, it was a kind of explosive device waiting to go off. It meant her stepfather might not be around much longer to push meals on Joy and kiss her head, to keep her protected and fastened to the world.

"Is Wes okay? You didn't tell me he was having lung problems."

"It's only been since August," Joy replied. She tapped her nails on the table, five unlacquered moons with dirt nimbuses. "It's from smoking. Although who knows what fertilizers and insecticides he'd been breathing all those years at Brightwell." For decades Wes had been the school's overworked, underpaid groundskeeper, the man in charge of its brochure-grade acres of velvet-green lawns with stables and an artificial lake, and he'd persisted in that job past his body's expiration date because of the free tuition it offered Willie. Wes had retired at the start of Willie's senior year. But early retirement in the Berkshires was a privilege reserved for the weekenders, not the lifers, and now, with Wes on oxygen and their daughter at an expensive college, Cate didn't want to imagine the state of their savings account. "His lungs are disaster zones," Joy said. "That's how the doctor described them. But we're praying the machine helps. He's supposed to be using it all the time, but, well . . . male vanity."

"I saw all those packages in the mudroom," Cate said, clasping her mother's wrist. The implication that she didn't like her mother working as a grunt for rich neighbors didn't need to be verbalized.

Joy returned to the task in front of her. "We'll need some pictures of your brother for the funeral." She examined a small grade-school portrait of Eric and slowly moved it across the table with her fingertips as if it were the planchette on a Ouija board. "Look at my precious boy."

Cate surveyed her mother's photo-album plunder. The snapshots were primarily of Eric as a child, with Cate occasionally serving as bumbling costar. Several photos were cropped with scissors: Cate and Eric sitting on living-room floors or at restaurant tables, leaning away from a person that Joy had sliced from the frame. Her father did appear in two photographs, in which his intrusion was impossible to expunge. In one, Jason Castle stood wearing a brown suit with a green tie. It was nearing dusk in the shot, and they were grouped in front of their old house, its sunflower-yellow siding glowing murkily in the background. Cate was a toddler hanging on her father's hip, while Eric in pajamas smiled widely, showing off his missing teeth. She knew this photo; she'd seen it dozens of times and had drawn her composite of her father from it. Jason Castle smiled widely in the photo too. He was handsome, almost stunning, with dark eyes, glossy brown hair, and a lean, muscular body. Both Cate and Eric had inherited their most attractive features from him: the sharp nose, the splash of olive coloring, the wavy hair, the lionlike curl of their lips. Cate's prettiness was due to her father, she knew that. But it was Joy who had saved her children from inheriting his cruelty. Jason had been a swindler, a very bad one, with a kind of perfumed charm that wore off after a few minutes in his company. In the end, the only people he successfully swindled were his wife and children.

It was inside that sunflower-yellow house that Cate had last laid eyes on her father. She had been twelve years old, and he had just taken a flashlight to the side of her mother's head. That proved to be Jason Castle's final act in their lives. Joy's temple still held a faint red scar from that attack. The last Cate had heard of her father, years ago, he had been drinking himself to death in Boston.

Her father still alive, her smiling brother in New England Patriots pajamas now dead in a foreign morgue. Cate felt a wave of panic cresting over her, like trying to enter a roiling ocean, and she stood up from the table so violently her chair toppled over.

"I can't, Mom," she said. "I can't go back there. I'm sorry."

Her mother looked up in alarm. "Back where?"

Cate pressed her finger on the sunflower-yellow house that had been torn down decades ago. "Back there."

*   *   *

The baby Doberman's name was Moose. She had a pointy, praying-mantis head, sharp eyes, enormous paws, and, in the Berkshire daylight streaming into Wes's toolshed, a coat more pewter than black. She reeked of urine and kept gnawing at the tender flesh of Cate's palm. Wes stroked her flank as Cate held her in her arms, and for a few seconds, softened by the benign tornado of a twelve-week-old puppy, their usual guard against each other evaporated.

"She's the absolute cutest!" Cate tried to hold the squirming puppy against her chest, as if it were the pure distillation of happiness, soft fur around a beating heart.

Wes snickered. "I told you. Eric just loved her. He was heartbroken to leave, but Polestar wouldn't let him off the assignment. Egypt is their biggest client, so they had to send their best workers." Wes began pinching clumps of dog hair off the sleeve of Cate's sweater. They had both changed into nicer clothes for the Polestar meeting. Cate could see that her stepfather had lost a worrisome amount of weight. His beige cords bunched at his waist like a brown paper bag around the neck of a beer bottle. She felt the urge to apologize to him and thank him for taking such good care of her mother. Eric had made peace with this man. Couldn't she bridge their differences too?

Wes knelt down to spread a ratty blanket on the floor. "Moose can stay in here, so your mother doesn't get upset. I'll put out a buffet of chew toys."

"Wes . . . ," Cate said as she lowered the puppy onto the blanket.

But then a different kind of peace offering spilled from her mouth. "It's important that we find out what really happened to Eric in Cairo. He was my brother." The tears started to well up at that simple declaration of siblinghood. "All I'm saying is, let's not agree too quickly with the story that Polestar is trying to sell us."

Wes gazed at her, his eyes the color of rivers on maps. "I wish I could fix this for us," he said, before nodding in acquiescence.

By the time the new-model SUV pulled into the driveway, Cate's mother was sitting at the kitchen table, a pitcher of tap water placed by her elbow. From her chair she eyed the coffee maker, and Cate jumped at the opportunity to be helpful. Wes was stowing his oxygen machine in the pantry, taking a few last inhales behind the door like an alcoholic sneaking sips from a bottle. Through the window Cate watched an older, wide-shouldered man emerge from the SUV. He had a mane of silver hair, and his arm was struggling to locate the sleeve in a leather coat. He was followed by a petite woman in a gray suit with extremely tan skin. She removed a cardboard file box from the back seat, her black braid, thick as a climbing rope, swinging down her back. Her heels were too high to navigate the yard—she wobbled on the gravel path, sampled the slick grass, and returned to the safer bet of the gravel. One hand was pressed gently on the box top, the way a person might carry a cake.

Wes hurried to the door just as the coffeepot overflowed. Cate was busy sponging up brown liquid and missed the initial round of introductions. She belatedly shook wet hands with Mark Rassier, vice president of Polestar's Air and Missile Division, and Theresa Alvarez, head of HR, over the kitchen island.

Mark and Theresa flanked Joy, offering their condolences at the very moment that she decided to move to the window seat. Cate searched the cabinets for the "good cups." Wes clapped his hands together and mentioned the looming rain. There was so much well-meaning blundering going on, such polite wrangling as to where everyone should sit and who wanted refreshments and apologies for the distance of the drive, that it was almost possible to believe that these tiny, graceless acts of kindness might change the outcome of the meeting.

"Thank you for your patience," Theresa said, after taking the chair that Joy had vacated. "As you can imagine, the information from Egypt has been evolving, and we wanted to wait to speak with you when we had a fuller picture." The HR rep was only a few years older than Cate, though the industrial tan and synthetic eyelashes made it hard to determine her exact age. Yet she possessed a formidable self-confidence. She made Mark, two decades her senior, appear shy and untested, his eyes fascinated by the infestation of ladybugs in the corner of the kitchen ceiling that Joy allowed to hibernate undisturbed through winter. Theresa refrained from coffee, but Mark accepted his cup. He took a sip, swallowed, and then realized it was his turn to talk.

"Eric might have only been an employee at Polestar for three years, but he was a vital member of our family." Mark recapped Eric's duties as a chief maintenance technician under Polestar's division of A&M. The predictable hyperbole followed. Mark made a fleeting reference to Eric's good looks, which Cate figured was an attempt to showcase the fact that Mark actually knew Eric by sight. He sidetracked into a speech about Polestar's $6 billion annual revenue and its impressive job creation in Berkshire County, and then tailored the speech for this day's audience by adding that the success of the defense firm depended on workers like Eric. "We're broken up about losing him," he said, his eyes venturing to Joy for the first time. "There was no report of any incidents or signs of mental instability on previous assignments. Everyone's liable to have trouble getting their sea legs in some of these countries. They aren't easy locales. But we never had concerns about Eric. If I'd had any clue to his frame of mind . . ."

Theresa broke in as Mark trailed off, as if they had rehearsed this verbal choreography on the forty-minute drive from Pittsfield. "First and foremost, we want to assure you that we're here for you, here *with* you. And let me clarify from the outset, this is not the time for you to be burdened with financial worries." Theresa gave separate nods to Joy and Wes. "We're committed to handling all the expenses of transporting Eric home from Egypt." She paused, as if anticipating a small chorus of gratitude. "Moreover, I'm personally working with the American embassy to expedite his return. We're lucky that Polestar is in such strong standing with the Egyptian government. We wield considerable influence and can cut through much of the red tape. Additionally, I hope you'll allow us to pay for the funeral costs. That would mean so much to Polestar as a gesture of our support."

"Do you know," Joy asked in a feeble voice, "when Eric will be back home?"

Cate and Wes shared aggravated glances. It was the wrong first question. It suggested an acceptance of the circumstances surrounding Eric's death.

"I can't give an exact date," Theresa replied. "No more than two weeks is my hope. Unfortunately, there is certain bureaucracy—an autopsy, the filing of a death certificate—that even Polestar can't sidestep. But if you can give me the name of your local funeral home, I can make all the arrangements."

Theresa dug through her purse for a pen, while Mark made a show of drinking his coffee. A moment of silence invaded the room. Cate tried to gather the words for her opening salvo. She didn't want to sound too hostile, but she couldn't locate a softer entry point. To her surprise, it was Wes who filled the quiet.

"You said yesterday on the phone that Eric might have committed suicide." He patted the table as if it were an animal easily spooked. "I should have challenged that conclusion right then. You see, Eric may have been *like* family to Polestar, but he *was* family to us, and we don't feel he would've taken his life."

Theresa didn't look startled by this small objection. Instead, she scrunched her forehead in the guise of compassion. "Of course. It's so hard to accept. Especially from a loved one. I wish we could have waited to tell you that news here today in person, but we didn't want you to misunderstand and hold on to false hope."

False hope? Cate gave a belligerent grunt, and Theresa and Mark turned to take her in. Her chance had come, and her tongue was still tripping over the words needed to defend her brother. She glanced at Wes, and he nodded in encouragement.

"I'm sorry," Cate snapped, more viciously than she'd intended. "Would you mind telling us how you've drawn that conclusion? The only thing we know for certain is that my brother fell from a hotel balcony, and somehow you've decided that he killed himself, without offering us any evidence or—"

"His death is still an open investigation," Theresa remarked as she removed the lid from the file box. "We were simply passing along the information that the Egyptian authorities provided us. We felt you deserved to hear it. Let me clarify, we aren't deciding anything in your brother's case. The Cairo police will determine the cause of death. All we can do is cooperate in their investigation and turn over everything in our possession." Theresa reached into the box and extracted a silver laptop. "But I agree with you, let's stick to the *evidence*." She studied their faces as she opened the computer. In a matter of seconds, the dulcet Berkshire friendliness of her voice had been lacquered over into one of cool professionalism. "Were you aware that Eric had a severe drinking problem?"

Cate eyed her mother and stepfather. Both tentatively shook their heads, an unconvincing jury. The truth was that Eric did drink. So did Cate. They were the children of an alcoholic father, and yes, they both consumed too much. But to admit that indulgence to Polestar in the wake of his death felt like a betrayal of his memory.

"He didn't have a *severe* drinking problem," Cate countered.

"We didn't know about his problem either," Theresa said as her fingers glided across the laptop's keyboard. "Drinking is a violation of our foreign assignment contract. We don't typically enforce it if it's a minor infraction—a drink here or there. Certain client nations, like Saudi Arabia, forbid it outright. Egypt is more lax, so Eric might have thought he could get away with it. For his Egypt assignment, he was regularly shuttling between Cairo and a military outpost in the Western Desert with a unit of up to six Polestar workers. We spoke to each one of them, and the consensus is that, in the week leading up to his suicide, Eric was exhibiting disturbing and erratic behavior."

"What kind of behavior?" Wes asked sheepishly.

"Signs of aggression, rambling incoherently, picking arguments with members of his own team. He had been discovered inebriated in his hotel room on multiple occasions and had even missed days of work. One Polestar tech described him as suffering hallucinations. He confided to a colleague that he felt paranoid and depressed. We believe he might have tried to stop drinking in the days leading up to his death and, according to one physician we consulted, could have been experiencing delirium tremens."

"Delirium what?" Joy squawked.

"A physiological response brought on by alcohol withdrawal. It would explain the odd behavior and the hallucinations." Theresa grimaced, like a nurse about to administer a shot. "I'm sorry to tell you this. I know it's upsetting. No one likes to think of a loved one suffering a disease of the mind." She trained her gaze on Cate as if she were to blame for the airing of these unpleasant facts in front of an elderly couple. "We do test our employees for drugs and alcohol, but we primarily rely on their word overseas. I think the testimony from his colleagues sheds light on Eric's state of mind that last night in his hotel room."

Theresa swiveled the laptop around so that the screen faced them. She cued up a live feed of a young man with a pixelated buzz cut, seated against a backdrop of murky night, punctured with occasional alien lights and noises. A motorbike whizzed by, and Cate realized he was sitting at a sidewalk table.

"Lucas, can you hear us?" Theresa asked loudly over the table, as if conjuring him from the spirit world.

"Yes," he replied, although his follow-up *Can you hear me?* was half eaten by the roar of a bus. Even through the digital glitches and dark chiaroscuro of an unstable connection, the man looked deeply uncomfortable. Whatever he was about to tell them, it would hurt.

"This is Lucas Keulks," Theresa continued, "a tech who's been in Egypt with Eric for the past month. They'd previously been deployed together in—"

"Emirates," Lucas said. "Ma'am, sir"—Cate wasn't sure whether he could see them bunched together around the screen—"I'm sorry about Eric. He was a friend. We worked together a lot. I wish I could have done something to prevent what happened." He wiped sweat from his face, and the screen briefly lost signal before recapturing him.

"Lucas," Theresa prompted, "can you give Eric's family an indication of his behavior in the days before he died?"

The young man grimaced as he nodded. "He was going through a rough time for about a week. Troubled. Not himself. He'd been acting edgy and nervous. Just not right in the head, you know, not the usual Eric. Like, he got into a fight with an Egyptian officer when we were doing test fires, which is about the last thing you want to do when you're working with the military. As I told the police yesterday, he'd been drinking a lot and was depressed."

Cate leaned toward the screen. "Hi Lucas, I'm Cate, Eric's sister. You say Eric was depressed. Were you surprised to hear that he might have killed himself? Did it seem like that degree of depression?"

"I would have stopped him if I'd known," he swore. "We were like brothers. I had no idea he was suicidal. So, yeah, it was a big shock."

"But he *was* depressed," Theresa emphasized.

Lucas's face seemed to melt, and his eyes darted around as if he were looking for a way to escape the screen's frame. After a moment, though, he reluctantly nodded. "Yeah. He was depressed. It can be hard when you're gone from home for so long. The conditions over here, even in Cairo, can take a toll."

"Lucas," Cate said, taking her turn, "you say he was worried and nervous. Could that have been because someone was out to harm him? I'm asking, could he have been paranoid for a reason?"

Lucas looked off at some invisible point of interest—maybe a person? Cate couldn't tell. "I mean, anything's possible. But in terms of a reason, not that I know of?" His voice rose in the form of a question. Cate felt intuitively that it wasn't the answer he wanted to give. "As I said, Eric was going through some problems mentally. You'd have to ask Mark and Theresa about specific—" The sound cut out and Lucas froze on the screen, his face reworked as a Cubist painting.

"Lucas?" Cate called. But there was no response, and Theresa turned the screen around to check the signal.

"Lucas, can you hear us?" She tried refreshing the screen. "Damn, I'm afraid we lost him." She shook her head and shut the laptop. "But what you just heard is indicative of the testimony we gathered from several of Eric's coworkers. I'm sorry to say it, but 'acting not right in the head' was a refrain repeated many times."

Cate narrowed her attention on Theresa. She despised this woman for her oily sincerity. It was easy to hate the deeply tan, those who insisted on turning themselves the color of a permanent vacation. "Suicide makes it more palatable for Polestar, doesn't it?" Cate snapped. "You sent Eric overseas, he's working there on your watch, and something frightens him the week before his death. You decide the answer is that he killed himself. How convenient that your explanation happens to relieve you of responsibility."

"Catelin," Wes murmured in an attempt to calm her. But Cate was not calm-downable. "No, I want to get this straight. My brother expresses fear in the days before his death in a foreign country, and your only evidence of suicide is testimony from a bunch of coworkers who happen to collect a Polestar paycheck. I understand why you'd *prefer* his death to be a suicide, rather than *you* failing to protect an employee who was clearly in trouble."

Cate was not a lawyer, but she knew that she had crossed into the terrain of legal accountability. On the other side of the table sat two people who had just offered to pay for her brother's funeral expenses. Cate had provoked them knowingly, but as she watched the soft folds of Mark Rassier's face harden, she was struck by a disturbing realization: these two executives represented a defense firm whose annual death toll probably yielded a figure somewhere in the hundreds of thousands, whose products didn't need to be advertised on television because their efficiency was on display every time there was a report of a missile strike on the evening news. Suddenly, it frightened her to watch Mark Rassier knead his knuckles at her mother's table.

"We have our men trained," he rasped, "to alert us if there are any unsafe conditions on the ground. We received no such warnings from Eric, not a flare of any kind. We checked his phone and laptop for indications of any threats. I assure you, ma'am"—his eyes skidded over to Joy—"we vetted his electronics and turned everything pertinent over to the police. There was nothing there, not a shred of evidence to suggest anything approaching foul play. Eric's last interaction was reported by the hotel operator. He called down from his room a little before midnight, asking specifically not to be disturbed. You can draw your own inferences from that final request."

Joy did not respond, and when Cate looked over at her, she saw her mother staring in a daze out the window, watching two cardinals peck in the dirt.

Cate turned back to Mark. "When can we see his phone and laptop? Maybe we can interpret his messages in a way that you can't. We knew him better than you did."

"When can you see his phone and laptop!" he repeated mockingly, unable to mask his irritation. "Those devices are encrypted Polestar equipment! You don't seem to understand the gravity of what your brother did for a living. He worked on vital security interests for an ally of the United States. Those devices weren't used for personal matters. There's material on them that would compromise national security. No, I'm afraid you will not be *seeing* his phone and laptop."

Theresa flashed a frown at Mark to curb his temper. "I was hoping to avoid showing you this," she said as she extracted a manila envelope from the box. Cate was expecting something more impressive than the flimsy sheet of white paper she pulled from its sheath. "However, in light of your doubts concerning our handling of Eric's case, it's best to present you with all the evidence in our possession. I'll point out that Mark and I have come here today voluntarily. We aren't required to share information with you. If you prefer to limit your contact to Ms. Skyler at the American embassy—"

"Please," Wes wheezed. "Don't misunderstand. We're upset and struggling to make sense of things."

Theresa slid the piece of paper across the table. "This is a copy of a note found in Eric's hotel room. No, it's not a suicide note in the traditional sense, but it's something he wrote into a work notebook in the days leading up to his death."

Cate drew the paper closer. The text was isolated in the center of the page, a few sentences scribbled on blue-lined paper. If Eric had written anything above or below this inch of text, it had been cropped out, leaving gulfs of white space. Nevertheless, Cate recognized Eric's handwriting from his postcards, the slanted, boyish melding of print and cursive.

It's sick to be taking advantage of those young men and women. I won't make any more excuses. Exploiting a crisis, paying for sex, and they have to take the money. What choice do they have? I can't stomach it anymore

"Where is the rest of it?" her mother cried. "This could mean anything. Eric could be talking about anyone! Where's the rest?" It broke Cate's heart to hear the keening-animal sound of her mother trying to defend her son.

"I'm afraid that's all we were given," Theresa conceded. She reached across the table to retrieve the paper. No one in the family tried to keep hold of it.

"Who gave this to you?" Cate demanded. She felt her face turning red, as if the implication of her brother paying for sex reflected on her and the rest of her family.

"The Cairo police," Theresa replied with an uncooperative smirk. "They found the note during their search of his room, and they felt this portion was the relevant material to share with us."

"How can we see the rest of it?"

"I suppose that would be a matter for the Egyptian courts?" she proposed in a tone of helpful insincerity, as if to indicate the futility of the endeavor. "Frankly, we have no reason to doubt the professionalism of the Cairo police or presume they're holding evidence back. They've been nothing but cooperative." Theresa took a sobering breath. "But to be clear, what this note suggests, in the kind of country where Eric was stationed, not a Western country, with its strict morality laws . . ." She didn't elaborate.

Cate saw right then that there would be no hope of gleaning answers from the police investigation. This note, if it did belong to Eric, transformed him from a potential victim to a depraved predator, a Western foreigner preying on their own population. It supplied the Cairo detectives with enough of a motive to draw the same conclusion that Polestar had, a suicide, and close the case. Mark and Theresa hadn't stopped by the house this afternoon to update the family, but to prepare them for the inevitable verdict.

"It seems like Eric was really struggling in his final days," Theresa whispered across the table. "I know it's not the news you wanted to hear."

Mark collected his coat from the back of the chair. Theresa shut the box lid. In another minute, the two were making their way on the gravel path back to the SUV.

Wes shook his head as he returned from the front door. "Did you notice, Joy, that Mark Rassier didn't remember us? Never mind that his two daughters went to Brightwell. I was just the groundskeeper. But we met Mark at the Polestar company picnic with Eric two summers ago. And he had no memory of us. Like we didn't spend half an hour listening to him talk about his daughters' college prospects. Like we weren't worth remembering, just nothing people."

Joy switched from the window seat back to her chair. Cate put her hands on her mother's bony shoulders. "I'm sorry, Mom," she said. "That note is bullshit. You know that, right? It doesn't prove anything."

Joy swiveled around so abruptly that Cate's hands were knocked away. "Don't you dare tell Willie about that note! Promise me. Not a word to her about that business!"

"Okay," Cate murmured, stung that her mother's first instinct was to protect her other daughter. She cleared the coffee cups from the table, carrying them to the island where Wes stood, gathering his breath.

"Thanks for backing me up," she said, touching him on the arm.

"They really stomped all over Eric's memory, didn't they? Polestar spun it all around so that he's entirely to blame."

"That's the job of a defense firm. They destroy people. But we shouldn't let them have the last word."

"You mean we need to get a lawyer?" Wes asked.

"Maybe," she said. "Yeah, we should."

Cate was putting on a show of determination, but in her heart, she already felt defeat. Out the window, the afternoon light was darkening toward dusk, and she envisioned her long drive back to the city with all its endless distractions and opportunities of erasure. Wes smiled at her, as if reading her mind.

"I hope you're staying for dinner?"

"Oh, I'm sure Cate wants to get going as soon as possible!" her mother groused, wiping her eyes. "She always escapes the first chance she can get."

Her mother was referring to those nights as a teenager when Cate sneaked out of the house, jumping from her bedroom window, once severely twisting her ankle in the process, until Eric taught her how to hang from the roof's edge to make a safer leap. Something about that memory stopped her cold.

"What floor was Eric's room on at the Ramses Sands?" she asked.

"Third floor, wasn't it, Joy?"

Cate shut her eyes. An impenetrable fog enveloped a death that occurred halfway around the world, blurring its details, making it impossible to perceive with any clarity. Cate didn't know Egypt. She couldn't picture its alleys and streets. But she knew her brother. She didn't care how drunk he'd been. If he had wanted to kill himself that night, he would have chosen to jump from somewhere higher than the third floor. Yet if the fall had been an accident or a murder, why hadn't anyone heard a scream? His death didn't add up, no matter how much Polestar or the Cairo police tried to force it into a simple equation.

Cate stayed for dinner and drove back to the city under cold November stars.

Chapter 4

NEW YORK CITY

I n the grind of midtown Manhattan, Cate tried to disappear into her life. She rose early, sweated through her morning run along the East River, and sat at her desk at Upper East long after sunset; nights fell early in November, like not-fully-earned rewards. Her apartment offered little comfort. There, alone, she was prone to crying fits, prey to too many memories of her brother in their childhood and not enough of them in adulthood. Going out at night didn't help either, the city's belligerent euphoria an affront to grief, alcohol too volatile an elixir. In the lingering confusion of who or what was to blame for Eric's death, she often put the blame on herself. She hadn't been a good enough sister—as if that could stop a man from falling over a balcony.

Cate made a point of staying at work later than her boss, Sarita Chakravorty, whose office darkened at around eight thirty. Fortunately, there was plenty to keep her busy—her job consisted of gathering money, and that was an assignment that never had a limit. The nonprofit had lost a crucial grant for its upcoming exhibition on seventeenth-century Chinese porcelain, which left Cate scrambling around the clock for donations, turning the taps on her network of human money faucets. The days streaked by in a blur of lunches, phone calls, and groveling appointments on plush sofas in Central Park living rooms. Yet Cate made a point of calling the house on Foxglove Lane each morning, increasingly relieved when Wes answered rather than her mother. Wes had secured a lawyer in Great Barrington to help them fight for answers. For the time being, though, they had to wait for the Cairo police to close their investigation and render a verdict. Until then, Eric's body remained in the limbo of an Egyptian morgue. It reminded Cate of waiting for the power to come back on as a kid after a storm pounded New Marlborough—it could take days, or hours, or weeks, no one could say. They were left stranded and at the mercy of a remote bureaucracy. But in this case, when the power was restored, nothing would ever be the same.

On the following Monday, Wes called with the news. "Indeterminate fall / presumed suicide, self-harm," was the wording on the Egyptian death certificate.

"So that's it?" Cate said. "No one's looking into his death any further?"

"We still are!" Wes's shallow breathing made that promise sound as wishful as his chances of a full recovery.

*　　*　　*

That evening she left work early and walked south, cutting across the lawns of Central Park. The nights had begun to leave an aching chill, the kind of cold that clung like cigarette smoke to hair and skin. There were sections of the city named after the industries that once thrived there—the Diamond District, the Flower District,

Curry Hill. Cate headed to a street just below the south side of Central Park that by right should be christened Piano Way. A slew of glass-fronted piano stores collected along the street. Some were named after German composers, others went by multihyphenates that sounded like WASPy boarding schools. The tiniest of these shops had the least ambitious name, Regent Fine Tuning. But Regent was the oldest—and only—Puerto Rican–run piano store in Manhattan, "Est. 1986" according to its awning. As Cate turned down West Fifty-Eighth Street, it was nearing seven o'clock and she knew that Luis would be sitting in Regent's showroom, visible through the plate-glass window. He always visited his uncle's shop on Monday evenings. Regent was where he'd first learned to play.

The uncle—a squat, red-cheeked man with hairy forearms— was known primarily for his adroit fingers. He'd been a child prodigy growing up in San Juan and toured a turbulent Latin America in the 1970s and '80s as an apolitical dignitary, playing for dictators and rebel leaders alike. A star in Puerto Rico, he became one of thousands on the prodigy-crawling streets of Manhattan and bought the music shop from an old Jewish couple who had lost their enthusiasm for the ivory trade. Luis, the nearest thing to a protégé in the family, disappointed his uncle by mostly turning his back on classical sonatas and spending his twenties playing keyboards in several doomed-to-obscurity indie bands (his old tour T-shirts were used as cleaning rags in the apartment). Still, watching Luis at the piano, his face electrified to near salvation, was the closest Cate had ever gotten to a secondhand high. That's what she wanted to see tonight, the face of someone she loved in a city of so many strangers.

What was it that had always attracted her to musicians? New York was full of power players who owned palaces or masterpieces or people's time, but only musicians could crawl into your head and take temporary possession, mind and body. Early on, Cate had cultivated a "type" among her friends as a serial musician dater. Two of her boyfriends had even achieved a modicum of fame (one of them, a scrawny singer-songwriter whose first album went platinum, still haunted her at unexpected moments, his face staring out from the covers of scratched jewel cases at Brooklyn stoop sales). Luis, for all his talent, had never achieved an ounce of popular appreciation. Fame had interested him about as much as life on a distant planet. He worked three days a week as a web designer. The rest of the time he freelanced for his uncle at Regent as a piano tuner and emergency repairman.

Cate approached the glow of the shop. She only wanted a peek at Luis. At night, Regent's stadium-bright wattage converted the window into a one-way mirror, and she knew he wouldn't easily spot her on the sidewalk. Every inch of the showroom was crowded with pianos—grands and uprights, Steinways, Yamahas, and Baldwins. Some were lacquered black, others opalescent, many with their lids hitched open like caskets, and for a second Cate was overcome by a vision of her mother touring coffins in a funeral home in Great Barrington.

Luis sat at a rosewood baby grand. He faced the window, not ten feet away from her—he only needed to look up and focus through the glare to find her. She couldn't see his hands, only the movement of his shoulders and his eyes following the gallop of his fingers. The stores on West Fifty-Eighth were fitted with a special sound-absorbing glass, so Cate couldn't even make out the song he was playing, but she watched the way his lips rumpled as he wound the melody around the chords. It had been two weeks since they broke up, and yet he looked younger than she remembered. He smiled as he reached a challenging section, his dark-red gums amplifying the whiteness of his teeth. He looked so beautiful to her that she stepped forward automatically, her nose almost touching the glass. She had been so happy with Luis, as safe as she'd ever been with anyone in her life, and she had ruined it, blown it up in an act of self-sabotage.

"Are you fucking around?" he'd asked her in their kitchen two Tuesdays ago, his body trembling. The lead expression on his face told her that he already knew the answer. He must have come across some damning evidence, a text or an email. "Answer me!" he demanded, refusing to allow her the time to concoct a lie. She'd been preparing dinner, her fingers stained green in her attempt to master a pesto sauce, because Luis loved the taste of pesto. As she wiped her hands on a dish towel, it struck her that the wickedest part of cheating was the hollow virtue of coming clean with the truth at the end, the confession of guilt that inflicts the most damage and lays waste to all the peace and security that came before it. She had worked every day of their relationship to maintain that illusion of peace and security. She had become so adept at deceiving Luis, she wouldn't even need a minute to concoct a convincing lie. Yet she decided to answer him honestly.

"For how long? How many men?" Fair questions.

There weren't that many men, but not that few either. She couldn't tell Luis the more difficult part of the truth. She'd picked older men, not very kind or attractive, ones she was certain never to care about. Here was the truth she couldn't explain to him: she had used these men as a means of escape—from the claustrophobia of happiness she'd found with Luis, or her own headachy desire to store all her hope in him. Something told her to hold a part of herself back, a self-destructive secret that worked as a hiding place. Her mother had been right about her obsession with escape. As a teenager she'd twisted her ankle to get out of the house. In New York, the escape was easier to accomplish. A flirtation at a bar, an innocuous phone number stored on her phone or a DM on her Instagram account, then a subway ride to an apartment across town. The chief purpose of those men had been a means for her to disappear, to shed emotions, to let her become, every month or two for an hour, a stranger even to herself.

Whatever her reasons, within two minutes of her confession in the kitchen, they both reached the same conclusion: Cate did not deserve Luis Ruiz in her life. "You're selfish," Luis had said, his eyes wide as if seeing her correctly for the first time. "But you know that."

Luis's uncle emerged from the back office, his hairy arms crossed. Luis lifted his head to speak to him, probably asking for a few more minutes at the piano. But Cate couldn't wait any longer. The uncle began turning off the lights, track by track across the ceiling, and soon she'd be visible through the glass. She pulled herself from the window and hurried down the sidewalk toward Seventh Avenue.

On the corner, a drugged-out woman wearing a balding mink coat jostled past her. In a fit of city paranoia, Cate checked that she still had her wallet and phone. But no one had stolen anything from her.

*   *   *

It arrived the next day in her mailbox, a paper-thin piece of dynamite stuffed among credit-card offers, store flyers, and bank statements addressed to a previous tenant. Cate nearly overlooked it. In fact, she almost threw it in the trash.

She hadn't checked her mail in weeks. Facing the grid of brass mailboxes in the lobby, she spotted the one labeled RUIZ & CASTLE and wondered whether it was her duty to cross out the first name. Releasing the stack of mail from its metal cell, she flipped through it absentmindedly as she climbed the stairs. On the second floor, she tossed the entire pile into one of the building's recycling bins.

A flutter of red. The gleam of a sea. A postcard slipped from a clothing catalog and fell in two parrot-like swoops toward the floor. Cate had to perform a small dance to step on it before it continued its flight down the stairwell. Picking it up, she was about to lob it back into the bin when the picture on the front caught her eye. A paradise beach with white sand like ground porcelain disappearing into a turquoise sea. A few hairy palm fronds framed the view. The postcard looked old, speckled in water stains and its top half faded, as if it had sat on a rack for decades under a hot sun. At the bottom of the picture, in tilted red letters, ran the greeting: *The Only Thing Missing in Jamaica Is You.*

Walking down the hallway, she turned the card over. The note on the back was short, its scrawl a lazy melding of print and cursive.

Dear Cate,

See, you were right.

Love, Eric

She froze in the hallway, her heart hammering, and she scanned the eight tiny words again, not one of them long enough to hold two syllables. "Love, Eric." That much she understood. She recognized her brother's handwriting; she'd seen it only a few days ago on the disturbing note found in his hotel room. But the central line, *you were right*, what in the world did that mean? She flipped the postcard over, staring again at the white beach and turquoise sea. When had Eric taken a vacation to Jamaica?

Cate checked the postmark in the upper right corner. That's when her vision began to swim. On the stamp was the picture of the broken, wide-eyed face of the Sphinx. Further, amid the inky swirls of postage in Arabic and English, Cate could make out the date and location of its mailing. Eric hadn't sent this tropical brag on some long-past trip to Montego Bay, but from a post office in downtown Cairo on the day of his death. *The Only Thing Missing in Jamaica Is You.* But Cate wasn't the only thing missing from Jamaica. So was Eric.

Queasily, she wondered whether this postcard was proof that Eric really had lost his mind. A Jamaican postcard sent from Egypt with a nonsense message scribbled on the back? *You were right.* Was that an admission of failure, tantamount to a suicide note? *You were right that my job made the world a more horrific place, that I spent my days doing more harm than good.* No, she couldn't believe that was what he meant. For fifteen years, he had sent her postcards to prove he was safe. This message couldn't be the way her brother would say goodbye.

Inside the apartment Cate shook off her coat, dropped her purse on the kitchen floor, and hurried into the bedroom. Dragging a stool to her closet, she dug through the top shelf of sweaters and books to locate the shoebox of old postcards from her brother. She knelt on the living-room floor and dealt them out, one by one like a game of Concentration, thirty-eight in total. The majority hailed from the Middle East, a few from North Africa, three from Southeast Asia, and two from post-Soviet nations. All of them featured images of sunsets, and their backsides were filled with prosaic descriptions of the things Eric had eaten, seen, or climbed. Each time he wrote at the end, in increasingly crammed letters as he ran out of space, "See, I'm fine!" Not one of the postcards had been sent from the wrong country.

Cate sat on the floor, staring at a grid of setting suns and one Caribbean beach under bright blue skies. These were her brother's final words to her: *See, you were right.* Her whole life, she'd never been right about anything, according to Eric. But on his last day, he'd changed his mind. *See.* But Cate didn't see. Right about what?

Fuck you, Eric. Why did you send this to me? She hated him for saddling her with this last obligation. Why not their mother, or

Willie, or Wes, any of the family he'd grown close to in recent years while the two of them had drifted apart?

As evening fell, she sat on the floor flipping the postcard over and over. It seemed to her that it worked like a ticket. She could submit it as evidence of Eric's obvious mental distress in the last days of his life, or she could trust that he'd reached out to her for a reason. *Which will it be, Cate?*, she could hear him asking. *Was I crazy or not? How well did you know me?*

Chapter 5

NEW YORK CITY

"May I speak to Dr. Yang?"

It had been Cate's idea to hire an expert to double-check the findings of the Cairo autopsy. If there was something suspicious about Eric's death, and the Egyptian police were bent on covering it up, an independent autopsy might uncover the answer. Wes's lawyer in Great Barrington had recommended Dr. Cynthia Yang as the go-to forensic pathologist for mysterious deaths. Undoubtedly the doctor had an impressive résumé. She had served as the chief medical examiner for the City of New York in the 1990s, and for the past twenty-five years, consulted on high-profile cases. Joy was initially opposed to the plan, reluctant to agree to a second dissection of a son who'd already been floating around in Egyptian cold storage for more than a week. She was finally worn into acquiescence by the tag-team bullying of her husband (next to her in the kitchen) and daughter (on speakerphone). Or maybe it took Cate swearing in exasperation that she'd pay for the autopsy herself.

"By the way," Cate asked on that same call home, "you didn't get anything in the mail from Eric, did you? A letter or a postcard?"

"No," her mother retorted. "I never get any letters from my children. Why do you ask?"

As Cate suspected, she was the only one he had written. Postcards, after all, had always been their method of correspondence. "No reason."

The lawyer had briefed the pathologist on Eric's case before Cate called her New York office. ("Did you tell Dr. Yang we think it's murder?" she asked the lawyer, imagining that pathologists were like fortune tellers; you fed them too much information in advance, and they regurgitated your hopes back to you as conclusions for a fee.) But once on the phone, Yang proved reassuringly serious. She didn't waste her breath on condolences. The doctor named her price up front: $12,000 for an autopsy with a full report and a follow-up consultation. Cate did the math in her head. She had roughly $63,000 in her savings.

Cate scribbled down the details of Yang's PayPal account, and the doctor walked her through the next steps. Now that the body was released from the coroner in Egypt, it would be prepared for transport. "Eric will be shipped in a lead container," Yang explained. "We reroute the container through New York, open it up, and have a look. Then we send it on its way to the funeral home in the Berkshires." Cate's task was to submit the request in writing to her contact at the US embassy. "Hurry! Send the email right away!" the doctor urged. "We want to stop them from embalming the body if it isn't too late!"

At her desk at Upper East, Cate composed the email to the embassy attaché, Elizabeth Skyler, and proceeded to transfer one-fifth of her life savings into the pathologist's PayPal account. Cate's job involved coaxing sums far greater than $12,000 from a class of people who dropped that kind of money in a single afternoon on

Madison Avenue. But pressing send on the transfer gave her a wave of vertigo and a bout of self-doubt. Was her mother right? Was she wasting twelve thousand hard-earned dollars on a macabre whim?

When an unknown call came in on her cell later that afternoon, Cate was wrapping up a call with a donor: "Well, Mukesh, for an additional two hundred thousand, we could discuss having your name on prominent signage for the run of *Imperial Vessels*. But don't get too married to the idea. Sarita's been putting me in a headlock about giving too much away to friends. She'd probably expect you to buy a table at the spring gala. Should I tell her you'd be interested?"

The call had a Berkshire area code. "Mukesh, let me call you back. Go ask your wife about the benefit table." She hung up the desk phone and pressed accept on her cell.

"Hi, Cate. What is this about a second autopsy?"

Cate snorted. She had expected blowback from Polestar about the autopsy, but she hadn't anticipated such a rapid response—it had only been three hours since she'd sent the request to the attaché. She pictured Elizabeth Skyler forwarding the email to Theresa Alvarez before she even sent it to the Cairo coroner. The American embassy and its chief missile supplier must be sharing information.

"We're ordering one," Cate replied nonchalantly. "Here in New York."

"May I ask why?" When Cate didn't reply—the answer seemed obvious—Theresa changed tactics. "It puts us in an extremely uncomfortable position. I want you to be aware of that. It indicates that you lack faith in the Egyptian government *and* in our handling of employees overseas."

Cate suppressed the urge to say *Yes, that's accurate.*

"Good faith is what we foster abroad," Polestar's head of HR continued. "It was our good faith that ensured Eric's death was properly investigated. And let me remind you, we worked night and day to clear the obstacles in bringing his body home as soon as possible. I've been negotiating around the clock, *pulling a lot of strings*, for your family. So I want to ask you, *honestly*"—that word oozed with ire— "what has Polestar done to make you distrust us? Please tell me! I really would like to know how we've betrayed your trust."

It was a clever tactic, and it left Cate momentarily speechless. Another tremor of doubt coursed through her about the autopsy. But she thought of Eric's postcard. *You were right.* The matter she might have been right about was Polestar. Hadn't his job been the root of so many of their arguments?

"It's very simple, Theresa. I'm sorry if it's confusing to you. We don't think Eric killed himself. You do. Thus, we want a second opinion."

"I'm stumped. We've gone out of our way. But, no, we can't control everything. We can't hide evidence. We can't force the Egyptian investigators to draw the conclusions that the family wants to hear. We can't amend the cause of death until you're satisfied. And neither can Cynthia Yang."

"I'm impressed you heard who we hired so quickly. You must have extraordinary ears." Cate was about to ask who had informed her, but right then her boss walked past her desk. Sarita might catch the tone in her voice and know she wasn't trying to save *Imperial Vessels* from extinction.

"I don't need to remind you," Theresa said, "that we're not only paying for Eric's remains to be returned but covering the cost of his funeral."

"And by reminding me of that, you are implying what, exactly?"

"I'm implying that we're supporting your family at every turn. We've done nothing but offer support from day one. What I mean is, we would hate to withdraw our support."

"What would that look like?" Cate asked. "Withdrawing your support?"

"We want you to feel you can depend on us. I don't want to consider the alternative, of your *not being able* to depend on us, of your *not being treated* like a member of the Polestar family. Do you understand?"

"I have to go, Theresa. I'm at work."

After Cate hung up, she swiveled in half circles in her chair, trying to keep calm. She tried to imagine what not being treated like Polestar family might entail. A gas pipe left on in her apartment? A random mugging that ended in a stabbing on the East River? The house on Foxglove Lane set on fire? Maybe she was overreacting to Theresa's threat. How dangerous was a private arms firm whose biggest clients were the world's most human-rights-abusing dictators and mercenaries? Cate took comfort in the illusion that she was safe as a resident of the biggest city in the United States. They couldn't kill two siblings, first Eric and then his sister, and expect to get away with it. Could they?

A half hour later her phone buzzed with a text from Wes. He sent a photo of a bouquet of white roses, followed by a message: Just delivered. Card reads "From your family at Polestar." Why are they sending us flowers?

Cate texted back, Because they know we have a strong case against them.

*   *   *

That night, when Cate walked home on the dark streets of Far Midtown East, she could just make out the ghostly contrails of her breath. Christmas lights blinked arrhythmically on the fire escapes of passing apartment buildings. Most of the stores had closed for the night, a few railroad-thin bars loud with jukeboxes but drained of customers. The windows in many of the town houses were shuttered, as if their owners had prematurely fled the city's harsh winter. Not for the first time since her breakup, Cate missed the overpopulation of downtown Manhattan and the consolation of strangers rushing around her, life wailing from all directions, and the constant, small emergencies of neighbors. She crossed from Second Avenue to First on East Fiftieth Street, two rats darting around her feet.

Halfway down the block, she became aware of a second set of footsteps on the pavement behind her. East Fiftieth Street was deserted. Her eyes fled to a lit basement window; behind its metal bars and rusted grating, an old woman folded towels in a laundry room. The pace of the footsteps on the sidewalk behind her matched her own. Glancing back, she could only discern a thin male-ish figure bundled in a puffer jacket twenty feet down the block in the shadows of an awning.

Cate took a few more steps and abruptly stopped. The person behind her stopped as well, the footsteps no longer echoing. Crime had spiked in the city in the past few years, her generation's rash wish for a rougher, grittier Manhattan coming true with little of the attendant romance they'd mythologized. But Cate thought of Theresa's threat that afternoon and of the flowers that had been delivered within an hour to her family's door. Surely Polestar knew where Cate worked and lived. Ahead, she could see the traffic rushing along First Avenue. On the other side of the avenue, two blocks down, stood her building, guarded by the night doorman, Jimmy, with his bluebird tattoos on the top of each hand. She heard the footsteps start up behind her, narrowing the distance, the scuffing beat of a determined purpose.

Cate bolted. She ran down the block, her heart racing, her purse clenched to her chest, her own feet so loud on the cement they interfered with her echolocation of the pursuer behind her. She kept expecting a blow to the head, an arm wreathing around her waist, a tackle into empty garbage cans, an attack in the front garden of a vacant row house. The walk light had already turned red, but Cate sprinted across the avenue and didn't stop, not until, out of breath, she reached the steps of her building. Rude Steve, the substitute doorman, was filling in for Jimmy, and even he seemed alarmed by her frantic state. "Are you okay?" he asked, straightening up on his stool as if he'd been caught napping.

"Yes," she wheezed, and turned to search the sidewalk through the safety of the glass doors. No one lingered there. No danger. Only Theresa's invisible threat, which was far more effective than flowers. It didn't wilt. It couldn't be thrown away.

"I'm sorry to hear about Luis," Rude Steve said. "He was one of the nicest tenants in this building. Any chance he'll come back?"

*   *   *

Five days later, Dr. Yang called. "Your brother is on my table," she announced in lieu of a greeting. "The bad news is that he isn't in the shape I'd hoped. I'll have some preliminary findings soon. Say, tomorrow afternoon at my office?"

Until recently Cynthia Yang's office, on the twenty-sixth floor of a Midtown West skyscraper, must have enjoyed panoramic views of the Hudson River. Now her office windows were blocked by a phalanx of West Side construction sites, needle-thin towers covered in thick mesh nets that shimmered like chain mail in the cold sunlight. Yang followed Cate's gaze out the window and shrugged. "No more New Jersey." The doctor's gray bob framed a lively, weathered face. The room smelled not of astringent death, as Cate had expected, but of lavender.

"We were either too late or Cairo ignored our request," Yang reported from behind her desk. "Your brother came back embalmed, and rather sloppily. I'm going to have to give more credibility than I'd like to Egypt's toxicology tests. Nothing out of the ordinary there. No suspicious narcotics, although he certainly had been drinking. The blood alcohol level they recorded is quite high." Cate wondered whether that result alone was enough to discredit the theory of delirium tremens. "Of course we're going to verify that with our own tests," Yang added. "We took some samples from the eye, which the embalming fluid doesn't touch. Those results won't be back until next week. But I know your family has been waiting for answers, and in this circumstance, I don't need the lab work to give you some hope." As Yang smiled, Cate tried to imagine what constituted hopeful news from a forensic pathologist—a verdict of foul play was the worst good news she could think of. "I've already sent an email to the Cairo medical examiner and your contact at the State Department, refuting their findings. For the most part, it's not their autopsy report that's flawed. It was the *interpretation* of it that's negligent."

Cate squeezed her hands together. "So you're saying it wasn't a suicide?"

"Exactly! I'll save you the razzle-dazzle of pathology jargon. Your brother fell from the third floor, an approximate drop of no more than thirty-five feet. That's a survivable fall. But let's presume he went headfirst over the balcony, which by the way, jumpers never do. But let's presume the blunt-force trauma to his skull was due to the impact of hitting the ground. Even then, he would have sustained single-impact injuries. Judging from the scans I've done, he clearly suffered multiple impact. Are you following me?" Yang's smile froze as she assessed the aptitude of her audience.

Cate nodded eagerly, although her nerves and adrenaline were making a tangle of even the simplest dot-connecting.

Yang leaned forward. "Eric experienced multiple fractures to the skull. That means multiple trauma, not single impact." She took a breath and spoke more slowly, like a school-bus driver braking over speed bumps so the children don't get rattled in their seats.

"He was likely struck on the head—bludgeoned would be my guess—*before* he fell. A lone jump from a forty-foot drop cannot account for the compound blunt-force trauma to his skull." The pathologist reached across the desk and gripped Cate's hand. "Listen. There is no doubt, in my opinion, of foul play. Your brother did not leave that balcony voluntarily. This has all the indicators of a homicide."

Cate couldn't believe that Dr. Yang had just substantiated her suspicions. Eric's death hadn't been a suicide. Someone had entered his hotel room that night and bashed his head in before throwing his body over the balcony to make it look like he'd killed himself. She felt both extremely cold and unbearably hot, as if shivering while in need of fresh air. One horror was ending, and a new one was opening in front of her. Someone had murdered her brother in cold blood. And judging from the bizarre message Eric had sent her, he knew that some sort of danger was awaiting him.

"Now, I warn you," Yang cautioned, lifting a file from her desk, "they might try to explain away those multiple fractures. Eric could have hit his head on some obstruction on the way down—a balcony railing, for example. Although one leaps to one's death, right? They don't jackknife straight down. Or they could claim that someone mutilated his body while he lay dying in the alley. He'd been dead for several hours before he was discovered." Cate felt tricked. A second ago she had been offered indisputable evidence, and now it was being yanked from her grip. "But don't worry. We have an ace up our sleeve."

"We do?"

Yang swept open the file, and Cate caught a glimpse of the autopsy photographs—a glossy patchwork of green and purple flesh. A photo of Eric's face peeked out. Cate shut her eyes, but the image coalesced in her mind despite her efforts to block it. In the photo, Eric's mouth hung open, and a metal rod had been inserted behind his upper teeth. She had seen enough of the face to confirm that it was her brother. There would be no miraculous case of mistaken identity, no proxy Eric lying dead in Dr. Yang's freezer.

"Sorry," Yang said, not very apologetically. "Can you tolerate this one? It's of his right hand. He was right-handed, yes?" Cate nodded and forced herself to look at it through fluttering eyelids. Yang pointed to the undersides of swollen fingers and the peeling, blood-stippled palm. "Contusions. Cuts and bruises. Those are defensive wounds. Have you ever heard of a suicide that tried to stave off an attack right before he jumped? The Cairo authorities failed to note these wounds in their report."

Cate couldn't contain the hope swelling inside her. "Oh my god, this changes everything. Now they can't deny it was murder. They'll have no choice but to reopen the investigation."

Dr. Yang's smile faded. "I'm afraid that's a matter for your friends at the State Department." She wished Cate luck.

Chapter 6

THE BERKSHIRES, WESTERN MASSACHUSETTS

Burning leaves filled the November air in New Marlborough. It was the smell of endings, of a season on the brink. Cate couldn't stay at the family house for the funeral. Willie had reclaimed her old bedroom, which left only Eric's room (out of the question) or a blow-up mattress in the den. Cate booked a tiny garret room at the old colonial inn on the village green, stuffy with too much chintz and radiator heat.

Although Polestar was making good on its promise to pay the funeral expenses, her mother insisted on doing the floral arrangements herself. Cate stopped by the house on the morning of the funeral to help bring the weedy bouquets of marigolds and daisies to the church. In the mudroom, two giant foam-core boards greeted her, glued with thirty-nine years of pictures of her brother. The kitchen was empty, her family still getting ready in separate parts of the house. A dog dish sat upturned on the floor, the only trace of Moose that remained. After Cate returned to New York on her last visit, Willie had swooped in to claim Eric's puppy as her own, taking the dog back with her to Smith and using it as an excuse to move off campus with her new girlfriend. Willie really was the golden child, saving her mother from her lifelong phobia of dogs. No doubt with her brains and sterling education, she could be counted on to rescue her parents from dire poverty in their retirement years. Cate could at least clean the dishes, and she soaped and sponged three dirty Smith College mugs that had been left in the sink. Smith College had replaced the Patriots in brand loyalty on Foxglove Lane. Out the window, Cate watched a FedEx van pull into the driveway.

"Sign here, ma'am." She swirled her fingertip across the electronic screen. Carrying the package into the kitchen, Cate saw that it had been sent from the US embassy in Cairo. At the table, she pushed aside the stems and wilted petals of Joy's floral arranging and sliced the package open with a pair of gardening shears.

The thick plastic-cocooned bundle inside couldn't have arrived on a worse morning. A typewritten list documented the inventory of personal items belonging to the deceased, Eric Arthur Castle. Cate was holding her brother's last effects, the possessions left in his hotel room. How dare they send this package on the day of his funeral, without any explanation or soft hands to guide them toward accepting these tokens of a lost brother and son. Cate had learned, though, that there were no soft hands when dealing with a death overseas.

As she ripped open the plastic, she saw that the contents consisted primarily of neatly folded clothes. Each piece—shirts, pants, underwear—appeared to have been professionally laundered, right down to the folded canvas duffel at the bottom of the pile. Cate unzipped a green leather toiletry kit that contained a comb, a bar of Egyptian soap, American condoms, a stick of deodorant, and a spool of dental floss. It was as if the authorities were mocking them: You really want everything back?

Still, there were items missing. As Polestar had warned, there were no electronics: no cell phone or laptop or even so much as a charger cord. Eric's wallet and passport were also absent. There was no sign of the work notebook from which the police had obtained her brother's screed about paying for sex, either. But as Cate ran her hand through Eric's shirts, her fingers fell upon a tiny white envelope. Inside lay a small silver pendant on a thin gold chain. She couldn't remember Eric wearing jewelry, and certainly not a necklace. The pendant was a St. Anthony, the front bearing the image of a bearded saint clutching an infant to his chest. Anthony, Cate recalled, was the patron saint of lost things. Flipping it over, she saw a word engraved on the back: HUXLEY, in crooked block letters. It wasn't a manufacturer's stamp. The inscription had been added by a previous owner. *Huxley.* The name meant nothing to her.

"What are you doing?" Joy was glaring at Cate from the door frame while trying to button a sleeve of her wrinkled midnight-blue dress.

"It's Eric's stuff from Egypt," Cate said. "It was just delivered."

"And you opened it?" Her mother's face flushed with rage. "Without—"

"Mom, it's his pants and socks. I don't think we need to build an altar to open the box they came in."

Joy hurried to the table, her sleeve left unbuttoned. She began to sift through the pile of clothes as if taking her own inventory. "You should have waited," she reprimanded. "You could have at least . . ." She sputtered into silence, perhaps realizing what a marathon of grief lay ahead of her. There could be no sprints of anger or bench press of tears at 9:00 a.m. if she planned to get through the afternoon without collapsing.

Cate placed her hand on her mother's shoulder. "I can take it up in the attic for another time."

"No," Joy said. "I'll put it away later. We need to get the flowers into your car."

Cate dangled the saint's medal in front of her eyes. "This came too. Did Eric wear a pendant?"

"A St. Anthony?" Joy asked as she caught the pendant in her palm.

"With 'Huxley' inscribed on the back. Who's Huxley?"

Joy shook her head. "I don't know anyone by that name. And I'm fairly certain your brother didn't wear a chain."

"What's that?" Wes asked from the doorway, swimming in a baggy suit that used to fit him snugly. He walked over and examined the pendant, his thumb pressing over the figure on the front.

"Do you remember him having a chain?" Cate asked him.

"I don't think so. He told me he didn't even like to wear his wedding ring." Wes shook his head and let it fall from his grip. "Maybe it's just some good-luck charm he picked up on a work trip?"

Joy raised her exclamatory finger and beckoned Cate into the mudroom to scan the photo collages. In a picture from the previous summer, Eric stood in swim trunks by Spectacle Lake. No pendant hung from his neck.

The sound of a crash echoed from the kitchen, and Cate and her mother returned to find Wes trying to climb from the floor, his lungs and legs giving out on him, the oxygen machine overturned. Joy rushed to her husband's side. Cate had a premonition of a second funeral within the year, another family member reduced to pictures glued to a posterboard. As Cate hurried over to help, she slipped the St. Anthony into her pocket. *Huxley*. It must somehow belong to Eric's time in Cairo. Maybe he'd been wearing it when he died. Or maybe it had been found in his hotel room and the police mistook it for a precious heirloom, figuring the Castles would raise hell if it wasn't included in the FedEx shipment. Whatever the case, it was the closest thing Cate had to a physical clue.

*   *   *

Cate sat on a stone bench on the top of a hill. Below her, the Steigerwalds were still gathered around Eric's grave. A few car engines started up, headlights blinking on in the gray daylight. She had come up here alone to say a few words to her brother, but for the past five minutes she'd been watching an unfamiliar young woman in heels climb the slippery grass slope toward her.

Nearly a hundred guests had attended the mass, packing into the white clapboard church in a valley ringed with mountains. Halfway through the priest's homily, a horrifying idea struck Cate, one that should have occurred to her before: Jason Castle might have learned of his estranged son's death and driven the three hours from Boston to show up at the funeral. She slowly rotated in her seat to search the pews for that unwanted face—the most unwanted face in her history of faces—but to her relief spotted no one who vaguely resembled her father.

"Excuse me," the young woman said when she reached the bench. She pointed to the empty section. "May I sit here?"

Cate nodded. The stranger lowered herself down, sliding her hand down the back of her skirt. She looked to be in her late twenties, with brown hair streaked with caramel highlights, and she wore a salmon-pink blouse that stretched at the buttons at her breasts. There was a tiny diamond stud in her nostril, and even in the cold wind, Cate caught the scent of tobacco and hair products.

"Excuse me," the woman repeated. Her expression was pensive, and she held a fistful of tissues. It occurred to Cate that she might have been Eric's girlfriend, perhaps a new love interest that the family had neglected to contact. Cate studied her more closely. She was pretty, diminutive, and wore too much makeup—a description that matched Eric's ex-wife in New Hampshire. Cate couldn't decide whether it would be kinder to admit her ignorance of the woman's existence or pretend that Eric had gushed about her.

"You don't know me," the woman said, and Cate began the well-meaning chorus of, "Oh, no, I do, I just . . ."

But the woman shook her head. "No. We've never met. I'm Lucas Keulks's fiancée."

"Lucas Keulks?" But as Cate uttered the name, she remembered the sweaty, agitated Polestar worker who had appeared on Theresa's laptop, beamed in from Cairo to tell Eric's family that he had lost his mind. Cate's goodwill evaporated. "I don't know what you want, but I'm not in the mood—"

"Lucas asked me to come here," the young woman blurted. "To talk to you. I'm Nicole. I live over in Lee. I mean, Lucas and I do"—she swallowed—"when he's in the country." Lee was a blue-collar village of hardware stores and gas stations not twenty minutes away. Cate had only seen Lucas in the context of Cairo; but of course, so many of Polestar's overseas workers must have houses and apartments sprinkled across the Berkshires, right around its headquarters. She might be fighting against an international weapons corporation, but it was largely made up of her neighbors.

"It must be hard to date someone who's never here," Cate said coldly.

"It *is* hard," Nicole agreed, as if they'd found some common ground. "But you know what these guys are like. They love to be in war zones, mixing with militaries, getting their hands dirty. Lucas wouldn't know what to do with himself at home twenty-four/seven. I mean, when we met six years ago, he was still serving in Afghanistan, so I'm kinda used to the distance thing. We have an infant, well, she's almost one now—"

"Why did your fiancé want you to talk to me?" Cate interrupted. Lucas had claimed to be Eric's good friend, *like brothers*, and yet he'd sided with Polestar on the suicide verdict and, worse, shared that opinion with the Cairo police. She refused to make small talk with his fiancée about their baby.

Nicole turned to take in the view of trees and lichen-spotted headstones. "He feels terrible," she said, rubbing her knees. "He spoke with your family on a video call?" Cate nodded. "He didn't want to say those things about Eric, but Polestar didn't give him a choice." Nicole leaned forward on the bench and stared intently into the distance, as if driving through thick fog. "Look, I didn't want to come here and tell you any of this. Lucas needs to keep his job. We need the money. We have a baby! But Lucas has been so eaten up about it, I had to promise." She turned and studied Cate's face. "According to Lucas, Eric *was* acting weird the week before he died. On edge. Not himself. Drinking a lot. But Lucas doesn't think that his behavior had anything to do with some mental break. He thinks it was because of something else."

"What?"

Nicole shifted on the bench. "Something he learned, I guess. Or something he witnessed? I don't know, so don't bother asking me. But Polestar pressured Lucas to paint it like Eric was having mental issues. Polestar can be very persuasive. But I suppose you already know that."

"If Lucas feels so bad about it, couldn't he correct his story and tell—"

"No!" Nicole cried, her arm latching around her stomach. "No, he can't! And don't you dare say a word to get him in trouble. It's enough that I agreed to come here and tell you how bad he feels. Lucas thinks Eric was gotten rid of, stopped before he had a chance to talk. That's all I know, and that's all he wanted me to tell you." She let out a ragged sigh and buried her face in her palms. A tiny moan escaped through her fingers. "The problem is, now Lucas is the one acting weird. On edge. Not himself. Drinking too much." Cate wondered whether Nicole was picturing her fiancé falling from a hotel balcony, another murder made to look like a delirium tremens suicide.

"Thank you for coming here and telling me," Cate said. "I appreciate it."

"It's very dangerous work!" Nicole insisted, as if trying to compensate for the fear in her voice. "I know that, and Lucas knows that. And your brother did too. The techs work in missiles and special ops. There's always the threat of some group kidnapping them for their expertise. There's always a risk they learn too much about the way these foreign militaries are run. We live with that fear. We get the risks. But still . . ."

"Maybe when Lucas gets back from Cairo, I could meet up with him to talk about it?"

Nicole shook her head. "He's not coming back," she said bitterly. "His Cairo assignment was extended for another six weeks. Egypt is Polestar's biggest client. That means once they're over there, they usually stay. Could be another three months. Could be even longer."

"Maybe I could talk to him on the phone? I could give you my number—"

Nicole smirked at Cate's obvious gullibility. "The phone? Are you kidding me? He can't talk to you *on the phone* about any of this. Or email or Snapchat or WhatsApp. They monitor everything the techs do over there. You know that, right? They record every word of communication. Tell me you know that!"

Nicole waited for a response. Cate stared down the hill and

watched her mother walk toward the car, Wes and Willie trailing behind her. "No," she said. "I didn't realize it was that extreme."

"Oh my god, it's ridiculously extreme! Polestar watches their techs like a hawk! They say it's for their own protection, but it's really to safeguard the company's trade secrets. It's not like the techs can complain—it's in their contract that Polestar will be monitoring them. But it's not just Polestar spying. It's a safe bet that Egypt's also tracking them with spyware from the minute they land. I mean, the country is spending billions on missiles, right? They're going to try to intercept any information they can from the guys tweaking their defense shields. So, *yeah*, it makes normal communication kinda tricky." Nicole gave a skittering laugh. "You don't even want to know the lengths Lucas has gone to just to send me messages without his bosses eavesdropping. Seriously, it's going to sound insane! It's like when he was working in Saudi Arabia and didn't want Polestar to find out I was pregnant. They don't like to hear their employees are settling down."

Nicole paused to ensure Cate's full attention, as if waiting to deliver a punch line. "Last year Lucas bought a burner phone, but they caught him with it and suspended him without pay for two months. So now he'll sneak off to an internet café if he can find one, or pay a random stranger to use his cell phone for ten minutes, which is how he convinced me to come here today. I swear to God, what I'm about to tell you sounds crazy, but that's exactly why it's so effective. No one would think to look there. If there's something really personal that Lucas doesn't want his bosses reading"—Nicole suppressed another giggle and shook her head—"he'll write it on a postcard and drop it in the mail."

Chapter 7

NEW YORK CITY

Music and news. The first listening option inevitably led to love songs, the second to war reports. Music and news, love and war. Increasingly, Cate chose to forgo her earbuds on her morning run along the East River and simply listened to her own breaths mixing with the sounds of rush-hour traffic.

In the middle of November the lawyer in Great Barrington had lodged a formal appeal with the State Department to open its own investigation into Eric's death. Cate felt confident that the autopsy report alone would be compelling evidence to convince the government to intercede. Overnight temperatures in New York flirted with the freezing point. Frost hung in the air long after dawn. The sky was an intense blue, but the cold wind that skittered trash down the avenues made it hard to keep her eyes open on the streets. On a Tuesday afternoon, Cate was heading up Lexington Avenue to meet a potential Upper East benefactor when she received a call from an unidentified Egyptian number.

She didn't expect an American southern accent to clarinet in her ear. "I'm very sorry," Elizabeth Skyler said. "I know you must be disappointed. I tried my best to convince them, on your brother's behalf, but that's politics for you."

"What are you talking about?" Cate asked the embassy attaché.

"Check your email."

Cate paused midblock to scroll through her phone until she spotted the email from their lawyer. He had forwarded the State Department's response to her and Wes.

No one could deny the elegance of the department's stationery. Even in jpeg form, it exuded an aura of unimpeachable authority. A blue eagle soared across the top, and at the bottom, below the assistant secretary's lassoing signature, the DC address was embossed in gold. "We want to assure the family of Eric Castle that we, too, are troubled by the circumstances surrounding his tragic death, and have offered our assistance to the Egypt authorities. We, however, cannot investigate an incident that occurred on foreign soil without the permission of said host government. We have not received any request for assistance and therefore cannot proceed in any manner without an invitation."

Cate wanted to slink into the nearest doorway and slide down to her knees. That was it, the ultimate bureaucratic runaround—no one would investigate Eric's murder because no one wanted the murder to be investigated. Why had Cate bothered to shell out $12,000 for an autopsy that wouldn't have changed matters had Dr. Yang found a knife jutting out of her brother's back? She stood midblock on Lexington Avenue, her phone pressed to her ear, realizing that all along she'd possessed a naïf's idea of justice—she had believed, inevitably, there was such a thing, as dependable as gravity or the arrival of spring. But justice wouldn't come for Eric. Elizabeth Skyler, with her friendly, lilting voice, made an opportune punching bag.

"My brother did not jump from that balcony!" she yelled into the phone. "We have evidence. There were multiple fractures to his skull. There were defensive wounds to his hands. You didn't know my brother. He wasn't suicidal!"

For a moment Elizabeth didn't speak. A car horn blasted so loudly into Cate's ear that she looked up as a stream of Ubers and taxis rushed past her along Lexington. But that wasn't its source. The attaché must be phoning from the street in Cairo, the noises of that faraway city bleeding onto the sidewalks of New York. "Actually," Elizabeth said in a corrective tone, "I *did* know your brother, in passing. We met once or twice here in Cairo. It's a big city, but there's a small American expat scene. That's why I was assigned his case. I could put a face to a name."

The news that Elizabeth had met Eric made it difficult for Cate to reignite her anger. This woman had seen her brother more recently than she had. "He was an American citizen," Cate said quietly. "Isn't it the State Department's job to protect him?"

"It's not that simple. How well versed are you in US-Egypt relations?" Cate wasn't well versed. She possessed only a *Times*-podcast-while-jogging familiarity with Egypt's political climate. She knew about the Arab Spring uprising in 2011 that had unseated the country's longtime leader. And hadn't there been a second coup that knocked their first elected president out of power only a year or two later? Beyond that, she had no idea.

"Egypt is the second largest recipient of American military aid after Israel," Elizabeth explained. "One point three billion annually, and much of that money is earmarked for weapon stockpiles, which—surprise, surprise—is mandated to be purchased from American defense firms. Enter Polestar in Cairo." Foolish Cate had always pictured US foreign aid being spent on school desks and sacks of grain, but the US government had cleverly ensured that American companies were chief beneficiaries of its own largesse.

"Polestar supplies the Egyptian government with their missiles," the attaché continued, "so it's safe to say they share a common interest. And neither side can afford the noise of opening a murder investigation on an American weapons tech, especially when his death has already been ruled a suicide. That would look like culpability, like the ingredients for a very ugly scandal. Do you see?"

"So what am I supposed to do?" Cate pleaded. She wanted to tell Elizabeth Skyler that her brother had reached out to her in the days before his death, that she had not been a good sister to him, that Eric had been the only family she had left. Cate supposed the attaché had heard these same laments from other bereaved relatives on long-distance calls after tragedies far from home. "He was murdered. Am I supposed to just let it go?"

Elizabeth let out a sigh, as if years of applying her sweet southern accent to brutal politics had drained her. "Write the ambassador in Washington? Or you're in New York. Try to get an appointment at the Egyptian consulate. I'm sorry, Cate. I really wish I could do more."

For five days in a row, Cate tried the consulate. Once in the morning and again in the afternoon, she called the office of the Consulate General of the Arab Republic of Egypt, asking to speak with the consul general. *Mr. Mersal is in a meeting. Mr. Mersal is out of town. Mr. Mersal has stepped away from his desk.* The Egyptian consulate was located a mere five blocks from Cate's apartment, in the minimalist salt-white utopia of the United Nations, but its tight security wouldn't allow her to enter the building uninvited, let alone camp outside Fouad Mersal's door.

It finally dawned on Cate that within Upper East's digital Rolodex of wealthy international philanthropists, she knew one prominent Egyptian. Lina Weleily lived with her American husband Alan Ostrouski in a Federal-style town house on the crooked arm of Commerce Street in the West Village. Alan was a dull,

Maine-born hedge funder, the kind of man who suburbanized Manhattan by walking his two golden retrievers through the Village in the evening. It was Lina and her earnings as the CEO of a paper-pulping company that spawned their generous contributions to Upper East. Lina sat on the board of several New York cultural institutions, and it was a safe bet that she was friendly with Egypt's top dignitary. Cate called Lina under the pretext of asking for a donation for *Imperial Vessels*. After finishing her stump pitch, she swerved toward her intended purpose. "I want to ask a favor," she stammered, "um, about Cairo."

"Are you going?" Lina gasped. "It's heaven! Simply the most remarkable place. You *must* go, Cate. Frankly, it makes New York seem like a starter kit of a city. Mind you, I haven't been back in twenty years. I won't go, not as it is. Not with that current leader stepping on everyone's necks." Lina's voice grew more animated as the subject of Cate faded from focus. Lina had the expat's penchant for monologuing on her homeland any time the chance arose. "My family was part of the ancien régime, Mubarak loyalists. Mubarak was no saint either, but at least he was a gentleman's dictator, do you know what I mean? He had an interest in *appearing* fair. Egypt was once a country with an army. Now it's an army the size of a country. You can get arrested for attending a rock concert or liking a post on Facebook. Not just arrested, *disappeared*. The security police thinks it can do whatever it wants, and the sad part is, it can . . ." Lina trailed off, perhaps realizing she wasn't selling Cairo as an ideal vacation destination. "But don't let that stop you! You'll be absolutely fine as a tourist. And for the love of god, go see more than the Pyramids. I have an idea—why don't you contact my nephew? He could take you around." Lina's voice evaporated from the line, and a text lit up Cate's phone. "I just sent you my nephew's email," she said, resurfacing. "Omar has been studying economics in London, but he's just returned to Cairo and, according to my sister, is doing nothing but floating around with no job prospects. It would be good for him to show you the city."

Lina paused, awaiting due payment in groveling thank-yous. And in truth, Cate had been harboring a secret fantasy of flying to Cairo to corner Lucas Kuelks and demand he tell her everything he knew about Eric's murder that he wouldn't say by phone or text. "Thank you for the contact," she granted. But she hadn't risked calling Lina for a favor only to be pawned off on her idle nephew. "Actually, though, it's a bit more serious than that. I was hoping you could introduce me to the Egyptian consul general."

"Fouad?" Lina cried. "For something serious?" She gave a trilling laugh. "He's utterly useless. Fouad Mersal looks distinguished all right, beautiful suits, speaks seven languages, makes for a wonderful dinner companion. But I'm afraid unless you need your visa extended, he's really just a walking handshake."

*   *   *

Cate should have seen it coming from the start. After all, Polestar wasn't selling weapons simply because it loved to proliferate havoc and human-rights abuses. Despite any lingering ethics, the money was just too good to quit the business. In the end, though, on the sunless December morning when the lawyer from Great Barrington called with the news, it reached Cate as a total surprise.

"Polestar is coming back to us with an offer."

"What kind of offer? What do you mean?"

"Are you sitting down?" he asked. "A settlement somewhere to the tune of four and a half million. We're negotiating. The threat of going to the press worked. Of course, no talking to journalists in the meantime, okay?"

"Wait. I don't understand." But as the shock wore off, she did understand. Four and a half million was the price for keeping silent.

"Polestar wants to preempt a wrongful-death suit," the lawyer explained. "I think we'll find the deal very generous, primarily thanks to the evidence you've gathered. I hinted we had interest from a reporter at the *Boston Globe*, and that brought them right back to the table. We're nailing down a final figure in the coming weeks." The lawyer's voice was so warm it sounded like a call of congratulations rather than defeat. "The family will need to sign a nondisclosure agreement. That's standard."

"But what about Polestar covering up his death? What about getting them to admit they were involved in his murder?" Cate's voice was high and careening, like tires spinning off a highway. "I don't want their money. I want to know what happened to him."

"Cate," the lawyer said, as if waking her from sleep. "They were never going to admit responsibility. This money is the closest thing to an admission of guilt. Think of this settlement as the company saying, 'All right, we didn't look after your brother when he was in Cairo on our watch, we're culpable, we put him in harm's way.' Please realize, this is the only justice we were ever going to get, and we're lucky. Polestar's in a weak position with its foreign contracts, and it can't handle a media shitstorm right now."

"There's no way my mother is going to agree to that!"

"She already has," the lawyer replied. "The settlement will be divided among you, your mom, your sister, and your father—all the beneficiaries of Eric's estate. It's a *very good deal*."

"Wes is not my father!" she screamed, latching on to the most trivial inaccuracy simply to lob an objection at him.

The lawyer hesitated. "I don't mean Wes." Cate heard a rustle of papers. "I'm talking about Jason Castle. He filed a claim. He is your father, isn't he?"

Chapter 8

THE BERKSHIRES, WESTERN MASSACHUSETTS

C ate eased the rental car over the potholes on Foxglove Lane. Snow had already fallen in the mountains. Her mom's front garden was reduced to hardened clumps of dead plants, frozen before they had time to decay. As she let herself into the house, she heard Wes's oxygen machine whirring from the downstairs bedroom.

Joy was sitting at the kitchen table. Cate hadn't called ahead to warn her she was coming. She'd spent the drive rehearsing a speech about the family's obligation to reject the settlement. It was their responsibility to demand that the person who murdered Eric be held responsible. But now, standing in front of her mother, she couldn't remember a single word of her speech.

"Keep your voice down," Joy said preemptively, without lifting her eyes from the shirt she was sewing at the table. "Wes isn't well and needs his rest."

"I spoke with the lawyer."

Joy shrugged. "I don't want to talk about it."

"Don't you care about finding out what happened to Eric?"

For a moment, Joy didn't answer, and the question hung between them like a rabid animal capable of attack. But when Joy did speak, her voice was calm. "He died, is what happened. He was killed doing his job."

"Someone killed him, Mom. Someone attacked him in his hotel room and threw him off a balcony. If Polestar's willing to settle based on the autopsy report, think of all the evidence in Cairo that we never got to see. His killer should be held accountable."

"Held accountable," Joy scoffed. "Who is going to hold this person accountable? Polestar? You think they'll ever tell us the truth? You think the Egyptian government will give us an answer? You're dreaming. I knew from the moment I got the call that we'd never find out what happened. Just as I know that taking Polestar to court won't do anything. Years of fighting them through lawyers. And what would we end up with? A little more or a little less in the bank. I'm not doing that. I'm not going to remember my son that way."

"It isn't about the money, Mom," Cate sniped. "It can't come down to that! Your son, my brother . . ." How could she phrase what she owed Eric? How could she explain not wanting to be selfish for once when it came her family? "Polestar tried to convince us that Eric committed suicide. When that didn't work, they offer us money. It's about holding that company responsible, not letting them shut us up with some cash—"

Joy shushed her, nodding toward the bedroom. "Eric would want us to have that money!" she whispered fiercely. "He'd want to take care of us, to make sure we keep a roof over our heads and pay for your sister's education." Cate rolled her eyes, but she knew her mother was correct. It only took a scan of the kitchen with its warped linoleum floor and gaps between the walls to realize just how close to poverty they skirted.

"You can roll your eyes," Joy said, "but while you were running around in New York, your brother came back, helped us, and made sure we were doing *okay*. He grew up, unlike you."

"I—" But Cate wouldn't do it. She wouldn't take the bait and act like a child by throwing a fit about being an adult. Anyway, she and Joy had different definitions of growing up. For Cate, it meant leaving, going away, striking out alone; for her mother, and maybe also for Eric, it had meant coming back, making peace, taking care.

"Cate, we don't have any money! And"—Joy nodded again toward the bedroom to indicate Wes—"is very sick. He needs treatment, and he's still not going to get better. And don't get me started on Smith College. It's too much for me to carry alone!"

Again, Cate understood. How could her mother refuse that much money? Why take a vow of poverty and condemn her favorite daughter to a lifetime of student debt?

"I get how important money is, Mom. But is it worth selling out Eric's memory?"

Joy dropped her needle and rose from the table. Her whispered voice turned mean. "I am *protecting* his memory. That's exactly what I am doing. Don't you see? Polestar would spread those awful lies about Eric if we went to the press. They'd tell the reporters that he paid for sex with men and women and show them that note. They'd paint him all sorts of ways. I'm not letting them destroy his memory like that!"

Cate had never thought of her mother as proud. Joy had cleaned and tended the country homes of the proud, but she had never been like them. Still, there was enough pride in her to be ashamed of a son who had gotten murdered over sex in a distant country.

"I take it you heard that . . ." It seemed a violation to call Jason Castle her father. "That Dad has reappeared with his hand out."

"I won't do it," Joy sputtered. "I won't see him again. Not ever." She reached for the counter to steady herself. "That's the one thing I'll never forgive Eric for. Reaching out to that man when he moved back from New Hampshire. Why did he feel the need to repair that relationship, along with the ones with Wes and Willie? I suppose that's why he never told me. I would have demanded he cut off contact. Apparently your father has been living right across the New York border in Hillsdale these past few years."

"He's only been an hour away from us?" Cate tried to picture the reunion between Eric and their father. She too couldn't forgive him for letting that man back into his life. It felt like a betrayal. "Are you sure Eric and Dad reconnected? It isn't some trick?"

"I'm sure. Eric left him a small amount in his will. That's the only reason your father has any claim on the estate." Joy shook her head. "The first thing your father does is send a lawyer to Polestar about a wrongful-death suit. He didn't bother to show up to his son's funeral, but he's ready to claim any money he can get." Joy's hands were shaking. "That's the thing. If we refuse to settle, your father can sue the estate, and we'd end up wrangling in court. I won't do it! I won't see that man again! I won't sit across from him in a courtroom!" Her voice had risen to a shout, and through the whir of the oxygen machine, Wes called out to ask if she was okay. Cate saw the scar on her mother's temple, and it occurred to her that after all these years, Joy had never felt safely beyond Jason Castle's reach. She was still running away from him. Even now, while standing in the kitchen, she was running.

"Joy," Wes warbled louder from the bedroom, "are you okay?"

"I'm okay," she called, wiping her eyes.

"No, you're not." Cate stepped forward to embrace her. "But I'll never ask you about the settlement again."

*   *   *

Your father wants to see you. Jason Castle tried reaching out to his daughter through the Great Barrington lawyer. Cate deleted that email. Another arrived the next day. *He's hoping for twenty minutes of your time. Tell me to stop forwarding you these messages, and I will.* That email also went into the trash, but she did not tell him to stop. That evening a final email arrived, containing a photo attachment. It was a color snapshot with white-veined creases running down the center (she suspected her father of artificially manufacturing the sentimental wear). Cate was five years old in the picture, wearing a white dress with a yellow bow, standing in front of a black Corvette that did not belong to her family. A handsome mid-thirties Jason Castle knelt beside her, his shirt unbuttoned to his breastbone, his dark hair slicked back, his left arm sutured around her waist. The most amazing part of the photo was how little it moved her. She might as well have been looking at two strangers who had been dead for thirty years.

Jason Castle was living an hour away, across the New York border. All these years Cate had imagined him in Boston, and it was disorienting to think of him west instead of east. She wondered whether he had sent Eric a photo too—whether that was the method he'd used to worm his way back into her brother's life. Had he also creased that photograph for effect? For an entire day Cate tried to move past the thought of her father, but the question kept returning: What had her brother seen in that man? How drastically could he have changed? When she finally agreed to meet him for ten minutes at a diner in Otis, she too did not tell her mother.

The diner was an old fisherman's hangout straddling a bend in the Farmington River. A cardboard sign was affixed to the window: WE SELL WORMS AND NIGHTCRAWLERS. The diner did a brisk lunch business. Most of the booths were filled with men in plaid shirts bent over sandwich platters, their fingers black from the kind of grime that wouldn't come off in a single washing. Cate chose a set of stools midway down the counter. She already pictured herself swiveling around on the bottle-lid seat and marching to the door at the first nasty remark that Jason Castle dared to utter. Maybe, in the end, that was the reason she'd agreed to meet him: she wanted confirmation of her nightmares, an enemy she could depend on.

"I'll have a coffee," she told the waitress, who was dressed like a librarian from the waist up (purple cardigan, crystal-beaded neck-lace) and like a duck hunter from the waist down (camo pants, mud boots). Cate sipped her coffee and tried to convince herself that this meeting was not a betrayal of her mother.

Jason Castle was shorter than she expected. He wore a dark-green corduroy jacket and slipped into the diner as two fishermen were leaving. He had the smug grin of someone who appreciated a door held open for him, gliding in on other people's politeness. His hair was dyed black and slicked just as it was in the photo he had sent her. He was still handsome, the strong cheekbones, the sharp nose, and when he caught sight of Cate, his wide smile confirmed a naked self-confidence, like it understood its power to charm. He was old now, weathered, but to Cate's irritation, there was still a glamour about him that set him apart from the workers and outdoorsmen crowding the tables. He walked toward her with a slight limp, each step an experiment in whether it would result in pain. Something must have happened to his leg. Or perhaps he was faking an injury to garner instant sympathy.

"Hello!" he crowed, his dark eyes alight with something near to happiness. He seemed to be waiting for her to hug him. She nod-ded toward the empty stool. He climbed onto it, wincing as it took his weight. But once on, he swiveled in half-moons like a child who could make a ride out of any piece of furniture. Propping his elbow on the counter, he took her in.

"What a beauty you are!" he marveled. "Both of my kids turned out so attractive." Cate cringed at the compliment. "Thank you for meeting me today," he said. "I know my invitation might not have been welcome, and it arrives a few decades too late. Let me start by saying that I've wanted to see you since the day your mom and I divorced. It was only out of respect for her that I stayed away."

He was still lightly spinning in half circles.

"Does that also explain why you didn't bother to show up to Eric's funeral?" Cate realized the true reason she had come. She wanted him to know that he hadn't been forgiven—maybe by Eric, but not by her.

Her question didn't seem to faze him. "Exactly!" he replied. "I'm glad you recognize that. It was out of respect for Joy that I didn't attend. I went to the cemetery alone a few days later." The waitress appeared, and Jason Castle stopped swiveling.

"I'll have a coffee, just like my beautiful daughter." The waitress smiled, clearly charmed. "Do you see the family resemblance?" he asked, flicking his thumb back and forth between them.

"I can see it!" the waitress swore, giving Cate only a cursory glance. "Yes, I can!"

"I'm so proud of her. She's a big deal in New York City."

Cate wasn't going to indulge him by playing into his hand. "How dare you try to extort money from your son's death." She glared at him, and the waitress walked quietly away. "We were going to sue Polestar to get to the truth of what happened, but you, who abandoned us, show up and try to shake out as much money as you can. You're disgusting. You're greedy and manipulative and out for yourself!"

Jason didn't flinch. He stared forward and nodded repentantly. "I deserve that," he agreed. "I understand your anger."

"F—" But she let the *uck you* deflate in her mouth. He had endorsed her anger, and she didn't want to give him the upper hand.

"All I can say is that your mom and I had a lot of problems, and you've grown up hearing one side of them. I won't defend myself. I was a terrible husband and too young and ill-prepared to be a father, and I'm sorry every day of my life for that. But there's another side, my side, and one day I hope you'll be willing to listen."

"Did Eric listen?" She laughed hollowly. "You must have told some amazing lies for him to forget the monster you were to us as kids."

"Your brother reached out to me. Last spring, he tracked me down and said he wanted to make amends. It shocked me, seeing him pull up to my house, but Eric felt he needed to address what happened to our family. I think it was his own divorce that made him want to reconcile. It wasn't easy between us. We didn't do things like Eric and Joy's new husband did. What's his name?" He tapped the counter.

"Wes, and he's hardly new."

"Yeah, Wes. He and Eric went hunting, from what I gather. Myself, I don't like to kill animals for sport. That kind of fun doesn't sit well with me." Cate rolled her eyes at his cheap sanctimoniousness. "Eric and I mostly sat in my backyard. We eventually found a way toward peace. That's what a person tries for as they get older and humbler. They forgive. They make the effort to understand. They let go." His hand began to spider across the counter toward her own. She dropped her hand in her lap. "I remember, not long before Eric left for Egypt, he told me that Polestar only cared about its bottom line and not about the safety of its employees. I want you to know, I went to them to demand a settlement for you and your mother. I knew Joy wouldn't have the strength to fight them. Your mother is a wonderful woman, but a backbone has never been her strong suit." Cate wrapped her fingers around her coffee mug and considered bashing it into his temple the way he'd once bashed a flashlight into her mother's head. "You get your grit from me, whether you want to admit it or not. I felt that you and Joy deserved compensation for the danger they put Eric in. I did that for you, so you both would be protected. You're still my daughter."

"I'll be interested to hear which domestic-violence shelter you're donating your portion of the settlement to." Cate swiveled around and pressed her foot on the floor. "I'm afraid you're wasting your time on me, Dad. You won't be able to get much. I'm not as important in New York as you think."

His eyes tightened. "Eric said you were stubborn. You can think what you want, Cate. But that settlement is the best deal you and your mother could have expected, and you have me to thank for it. The truth is, I know Eric was starting to lose his grip over there. He was coming unglued. And that wouldn't have been hard for Polestar to prove in court. As sad as it is, I've got proof that he was suffering from a delusional state right before he jumped. A few days after your brother died, I got something from him in the mail." He reached into his jacket pocket and withdrew a folded card. Cate saw a tropical beach on the front, and at the bottom, in red letters, *The Only Thing Missing in Jamaica Is You.*

"Eric sent me this from Cairo. I mean, look at it. Clearly, he was suffering a break. It says Jamaica! The thing makes no sense—"

She grabbed the postcard from him and flipped it over. The same handwriting scrawled on the back, the same muddy stamp of the Sphinx in the upper right-hand corner.

Dad,

If it all blows up, ask him about Huxley.

Love, Eric

She could almost forgive her father for concluding that Eric had lost his mind. It was an even stranger message than the one she'd received. *If it all blows up.* And it had blown up. But it was the word *Huxley* that ricocheted through her head, bright as lightning, calling up the name on the back of the saint's medal. All of it pointed to his last days in Cairo. He'd written it on a postcard so that Polestar wouldn't see.

"The name Huxley?" she asked pleadingly. For the first time since the age of twelve, she was hoping to receive something of value from her father as if the answer to this single question might redeem him. "Does it mean anything to you?"

"Not a damn thing."

"Come on, Dad. Think! Have you ever heard that name before? He must have sent it to you for a reason."

"There's no heads or tails to it. It doesn't mean anything, period. Jamaica in Egypt? I hate to say it, honey, but your brother had lost his mind. That's the definition of insanity right there on a postcard. Can you imagine how this evidence would have played out if your case against Polestar had gone to court? We're lucky we got the settlement we did." He snatched the postcard from her fingers as if it were a winning lottery ticket. Cate smiled down at him. The poor, pathetic man, now for once in his con-artist life a millionaire, thanks to the death of his son.

"Goodbye," she said as she pulled on her coat.

"Where are you going?" he whimpered, a little boy suddenly afraid of abandonment.

"Cairo," she said.

PART II

Greetings from Egypt

Chapter 9

CAIRO

———————

The customs agents picked off passengers right and left, pulling them aside to swab their laptops or unroll their socks for hidden contraband. But no one bothered to stop the passenger from seat 32D, and Cate continued with her bags toward the exit doors. There had been a time, not too long ago, when she considered it a compliment to be flagged as a suspicious person. It confirmed the outlaw aura she had cultivated in her youth, the glamour of a criminal persona. But Cate was now older, wiser, and far too exhausted from the overnight flight.

She had left Manhattan so abruptly that it was somewhat disheartening to learn how easily she could disentangle herself from her life. She took a leave of absence from Upper East, a break only slightly more extreme than an unpaid vacation, and Sarita couldn't completely lose her mind over the sudden abandonment because Cate had managed to raise the funds for the spring porcelain show. Cate doubted she'd return—after all, in a few months, when the

Polestar settlement was finalized, she might have more than a million in her bank account.

She'd saved the most difficult task for the Uber to the airport. Speeding over the grumbling cantilevered arm of the Fifty-Ninth Street Bridge, she dialed Luis's number. As the rings accumulated, she imagined his phone vibrating in his cousin's Harlem apartment, perhaps even rattling on his piano bench, her name glowing demonically on his screen. To her surprise, Luis answered, and she allowed herself to drift for a moment in the tiny oasis of his voice. In it, she could hear all she had lost. "Why are you calling?" he asked.

Cate offered him their midtown apartment, the rent already paid for the final month of the lease. She didn't tell him where she was going, or why, only that she'd be out of the country and the place would just be sitting empty. Before they hung up, Luis thanked her, twice, the first thank you wary, the second one grateful, and it was only as she heard the call end that she found the courage to say, "I love you."

New York City vanished below her in the plane's sharp ascent, the spilled toy chest of Brooklyn and Queens disappearing into open ocean. Ten hours in economy over the Atlantic. For most of the flight she read through an Egypt guidebook, using the Jamaica postcard as a bookmark. The pendant of St. Anthony dangled from her neck, the coin chilling her skin as she tossed and turned in her cramped seat, the saint of lost things, including, apparently, sleep. She managed to nod off just as dawn light pierced the plane's windows. She drifted in and out of consciousness through breakfast service and the pilot's self-congratulatory PA announcement about their early arrival, as if he'd personally rowed them over the ocean instead of steered the plane.

"Miss, miss!" a guard called as she was exiting customs, and she found her heart racing, fearing that the authorities had realized who her brother was—the murdered tech who worked for the military. But she'd only forgotten to hand over her declaration form.

"*Shukrun,*" she said, practicing her guidebookese. *Thank you, yes, no, goodbye.* These were the phrases with which she had armed herself to navigate an unknown country.

Cate had pictured herself tracking down Lucas Keulks as soon as she landed, but she was so tired she now prayed only for an early check-in to her hotel room, the bed soft and the curtains light-canceling. Her hotel, the Grand Nile, was a satellite of a high-end American chain. She had chosen it because of its proximity to Eric's hotel, a mere two blocks from the Ramses Sands. Officially, Cate was visiting Egypt as a sightseer. That's what she'd written on the airport visa form (*sightseer, vacation*) and how she self-identified at passport control.

The customs doors split open, like a dramatic grand prize reveal on a game show. In the outer terminal strangers collected behind steel barricades—many holding flowers, others balloons, some with babies aloft in their arms. These welcomers stared in heightened anticipation, their eyes washing over Cate before falling away in disappointment.

Staticky pop music blared through the terminal. Cate followed the barricaded path. At its end stood a congregation of men holding signs with the names of arriving passengers scrawled across them.

Cate had emailed Lina Weleily's nephew Omar from JFK, thinking it would be wise to be in contact with at least one person in Cairo. Omar had responded instantly, not only agreeing to show her around but insisting that he pick her up from the airport. She didn't expect him to be standing among the drivers, but she scanned their signs anyway, just in case. Finding Omar Meshref in the commotion of an international airport had seemed a relatively easy proposition right up until the moment she actually had to undertake it. As Cate put her suitcase down, she realized she had no clue what Lina's nephew looked like, or vice versa. She had his email but not his cell phone. Why hadn't she thought to ask for his number before the plane took off?

She turned in circles, trying to advertise herself as a confused, new arrival in case Omar was searching for lost-looking Americans. Some of the friendlier drivers smiled and asked if she needed a lift, even though they held other last names at their chests. She pulled her phone out and thumb-tapped a quick email to Omar: I'm here. My flight landed early. Dark brown hair, yellow shirt, brown jacket, swollen face from lack of sleep. She pressed send and decided to loiter around the arrival hall for five more minutes. Then she'd take a taxi to her hotel and hope he'd accept her apology later.

For a second she thought she spotted her name on a sign—"C. Castle" scribbled in blue ink—but the forest of drivers thickened, and she lost sight of it. A phalanx of Saudi sheikhs in red-checkered headdresses marched through the hall, and she had to wait for the procession of men and overloaded luggage carts to pass. But in their wake, there it was, she couldn't believe it—"C. Castle" and a tall young man with ash-dark eyes holding the paper at his rib cage. She frantically waved her arm.

Omar's face was long and sharp. His cheekbones jutted out, notched almost like knuckles. A black puff of a curly goatee at his chin extended the oval of his face. The goatee must have been an attempt to disguise his youth, because he looked exceedingly young to her, or at least younger than she'd expected Lina's nephew to be. His body was boyishly skeletal. He wore a pale-green shirt, untucked over a pair of tan trousers. The shirttails were frayed, and their tips were discolored with city grit. Omar gave her a very sweet smile, which widened as she approached.

"Omar, it's Cate! I'm so glad to see you!" she cried, hoping to forge a fast friendship.

He nodded vehemently and said, "Cate? Are you Cate Castle?" For a moment she didn't recognize her own name on his tongue. He'd put a musical emphasis on the wrong vowels. She smiled and nodded, mimicking his vehemence, and he gave a sigh of relief.

"You found me!" she exclaimed, letting out a laugh that sounded erratic even to her jet-lagged brain. "I was imagining a nightmare scenario where we were both wandering around the terminal passing by each other for hours. I should have googled you!" Omar's eyebrows scrunched in confusion. "I'm sorry, I'm babbling. I didn't sleep on the flight. Anyway, I'm so relieved to find you."

"I wait for you all morning," he told her in broken English. "I don't leave until I find you."

"Well, thank you," she said sincerely. "I hope it wasn't too much trouble."

"Follow me." He quickly commandeered the handle of her suitcase. "The car is outside. I take you." Before she could acquiesce, he hurried off with her bag, weaving through the terminal around throngs of travelers with their spills of belongings at their feet. The bitter smell of coffee tempted Cate to make a detour, but Omar was zooming so rapidly around columns where soldiers with rifles were stationed that she was scared to lose him. High above, on humming monitors, departures blinked.

"It was so nice of Lina to introduce us," Cate said as she struggled to catch up. Omar nodded, staring ahead at the glass automatic doors that would release them into the orange December sunlight. She dug into her purse for her guidebook to look up the hotel address. "Do you know the Grand Nile?"

He glanced at her again, his eyebrows still knit, and grunted out a "no."

"I can read the—"

"But everything okay. I bring you." Cate had expected Omar to speak perfect English—his email to her, while brief, had been grammatically convincing. And hadn't Lina mentioned that he'd gone to grad school in London? Perhaps he was simply bashful around strangers, or strange women, or even more likely, he'd begun to resent the annoying chore of picking up a friend of his rich aunt's, waiting around for her all morning in the arrival hall. But Cate wasn't willing to drop her manic, sleep-deprived attempt at solidifying a friendship. She was hoping to lean on him for help during her visit.

"Was it economics you studied?" she asked. A man with a tray near the terminal doors offered her a small paper cup filled with yellow liquid that looked like a urine sample, but Omar gallantly shooed him away with a hiss. "You must miss London," she continued. "It's such a great city. I went there a few years ago with a boyfriend. He was playing a concert. We stayed in Knightsbridge, but I can't even tell you where that is because the city is so sprawling—"

She wasn't sure Omar was listening. In fact, she was fairly certain he wasn't. He offered up another adorable smile, but his eyes had slivered in what seemed like annoyance at the speed-talking American in his care. Cate felt her own spasm of annoyance. Omar had volunteered to pick her up. She would have been perfectly happy to take a taxi.

The automatic doors whooshed open, and Cate got her first dose of North African heat, a gust of dry, stale wind blowing over her face. But no, that gust came from a vent in the ground just beyond the terminal doors. The real outside was windless. Omar hurried along the sidewalk past rows of idling cars. She scrambled to keep up with him, feeling the soft sun warm her face. It was perfect weather, like California in winter, and she almost shared that impression with Omar but remembered how uninterested he'd been in her trip to London.

As if sensing another attempt at conversation, Omar moved at an even faster clip. Every joint in Cate's body ached from the ten hours belted in her economy seat, and she focused on the goal of reaching her hotel. She noticed Omar's scuffed sneakers ahead of her. There were visible rips in the leather, and flashes of bare skin winked with each step. The rubber sole of his left sneaker was coming unglued, clapping when his foot struck the sidewalk. Lina had mentioned that her nephew hadn't found a job in Cairo, but it hadn't occurred to Cate that he might be broke. She figured he was living like a prince off his family's largesse as he waited for a cushy post at a bank. But maybe Lina's family had fallen out of favor since Sisi took power. Cate decided to pay Omar's gas money for picking her up. She could even give him a daily retainer as her guide. No, they would not become friends, but they could still be of benefit to each other.

She pulled the guidebook from her purse. "Omar?" she said. "Do you want me to read the address of the hotel?"

"I have it!" he barked, and with visible effort, he turned and gave her a smile. "I am sorry," he said. "Do not worry."

She looked around. Cars honked along the road. On the opposite side, a parking garage blocked out most of the view, leaving only a sliver of pinkish gray sky, tinted from airport smog. Omar clucked his tongue to catch her attention.

"Do not worry," he repeated. "It is right here, our car. You see?" He pointed to a sleek white town car, with only a skirt of dirt along its bottom edge. It was not the vehicle she expected him to own. Maybe it was the style here for wealthy kids to dress slovenly but drive fancy cars—as it had been in her youth. The car admittedly lifted her spirits. It promised a comfortable, upholstered back seat and robust air-conditioning. She couldn't see through the tinted windshield, but she glimpsed a hand dangling from the driver's window. It was a man's hand, with large, hairy fingers and a thin silver ring on the curled pinkie.

"Who's that?" she asked. She assumed Omar had come alone.

"Father."

"Oh, Lina's brother-in-law?" He nodded curtly. Cate felt weary at the thought of having to charm a second relative of Lina's on the long drive to her hotel. Maybe they wouldn't mind if she fell asleep in the back for most of the trip?

Omar lifted her bag off the sidewalk and carried it between the bumpers of the parked cars. Cate trailed behind him, flipping through her guidebook for the hotel's address to read to Omar's father. The Jamaica postcard began to slip from the pages, and she slammed the book shut to keep it in place.

Omar rapped his knuckles on the town car's back window. She heard the click of the door unlocking, and he pulled it open for her. "Get in," he ordered. "We take you to hotel."

Cate peered into the cavern of the luxury car with its hot trapped air and saw dried mud flecking the leather seat. On the floor was a set of rusty tools—a hammer and pliers and a coil of nylon rope. Instinctively she stepped back and looked at Omar for reassurance. He held her suitcase crookedly at his chest.

"Does Lina—"

"Get in!" He pressed a hand against her shoulder.

"Cate?" She thought she heard her name being called from somewhere in the distance. She heard it again—"Cate?"—coming from near the terminal entrance. She squinted toward the flurry of bodies at the automatic doors. A dark-haired man stepped into the road thirty feet away.

"Get in!" Omar demanded. "Now! Please! Hurry!" His hand pushed hard on her shoulder, and she twisted backward to escape it. He grabbed her wrist and squeezed it with his ropy fingers. "In! Now!" he hissed, and she heard the driver's door open and a shoe scrape the pavement. But no head rose on the other side of the roof. Perhaps the driver had spotted the man calling her name, who was now approaching them with his head tilted apprehensively. Omar stopped tugging at her wrist, holding it limply while staring at the interloper.

"Cate Castle?" the man called, all the vowels clicking into place. She could see him more clearly at fifteen feet: his black, untidily parted hair and the manicured scruff of a beard, his brown eyes wide and humorous, as if he were second-guessing his hunch. "Cate?" He was in his mid-twenties and wore a thin gray sweater and dark jeans. A pair of gold-framed sunglasses dangled in his right hand. "It's Omar. Did you find another ride?" He smiled, as if he had interrupted a comical case of mistaken identity. "I'm sorry I'm late. I told you I'd pick you up. You didn't need to find another lift." He paused. "You are Cate Castle, aren't you?"

Cate yanked her arm from the other Omar's grip, but she didn't have time to consult his face. He dropped her suitcase on the ground and shoved his palm into her chest, sending her tripping backward. She nearly hit her head on a car bumper as she fell. The young man jumped into the town car and slammed the door. The vehicle was already tearing toward the exit ramp by the time Cate recalled the set of rusty tools on its floor—a hammer, pliers, nylon cord—along with the horror of their possible applications.

The new Omar ran to her, bending down to help her up.

"Who was that?" he cried. "What just happened?" His eyes were wide, their playfulness gone. Cate's whole body was shaking.

"Tell me your aunt's name?" she insisted. "What is her full name?"

"Lina Weleily Ostrouski," he answered. "My mother's older sister. Why? What just happened?"

"I was almost . . ." But Cate was only five minutes out of the Cairo airport, and she decided it might be wise to keep her mouth shut.

*   *   *

Omar Meshref drove a rusted red Fiat with a rattling stick shift and front seats that jittered whenever the engine dropped below twenty miles per hour. Luckily, Omar's foot was rarely off the gas, the car racing on the highway like a quivering red arrow toward the heart of downtown Cairo. Their speed blurred the already grime-blurred concrete buildings cluttered around the airport. Tricolor flags of red, white, and black fluttered from the tops of domed buildings, while an assortment of bedsheets waved from clotheslines on tenement balconies. Massive digital billboards blinked advertisements for a soap opera, a cell-phone provider, and portraits of reigning politicians. In the first minutes of their drive, Cate tried to convince Omar that the incident outside the airport had just been a misunderstanding—the wrong female traveler arriving on the overnight flight from New York. She was also vainly trying to convince herself of that fiction too. It had all been a terrible mistake.

"You were knocked to the ground," Omar said, swerving out of the left lane to avoid crashing into the back of a delivery van and killing them instantly. "That is not how we treat visitors who have just arrived in our country. So you're aware, pushing foreigners down is not the local custom."

Omar had a deep voice. Purposely deep, Cate thought. She had a theory that most men deepened their voices toward emotionless baritones the same way women lightened theirs into out-of-tune string instruments—an entire artificial human orchestra. Omar's English was indeed faultless. She caught little British shortcuts in his words that matched the background of a man who had studied economics in London. He was also handsome. From straight on, his face held the flatness of a lion, but studying his profile, she saw that his cheeks and jaw were deceptively angular, with a prominent bump halfway down the bridge of his nose. A few faded purple scars flecked his forehead from teenage acne. He had a thin waist that swelled into a muscular back, and he smelled of a cologne that reminded her more of a spice rack than a nightclub. What took her the longest to notice was the clear plastic device hooked over his right ear that ended in a tiny pea-sized receiver nestled in the ear canal. She pulled her eyes away from the hearing aid in case her stare felt intrusive.

"A bike accident," he announced, his eyes fixed on the highway.

"Where?" she asked, glancing through the windshield at the teeming lanes ahead of them. "Is that why there's so much traffic?"

"No, my ear," he said. "When I was a little boy. One summer, when I was eight, my family was vacationing on the Mediterranean up near Alexandria. I fell off my bike and slammed my head against the curb. I'm pretty much deaf in my right ear without my hearing aid."

She nodded. She wouldn't have asked about it but appreciated his openness.

"Are you sure you don't want to file a report?" he asked. "At least with airport security if you don't want to deal with the police?" He'd already brought up this question when they were walking to his car, and she'd refused, concluding it would be unwise to involve the Cairo police. She couldn't explain to Omar why she was so wary of the police. They'd played a key part in covering up Eric's murder, and they might not be disposed to helping the dead man's sister.

She looked out the window, trying to calm her nerves, but her first view of the city offered little in the way of serenity. Tenement buildings morphed into brutalist concrete high-rises looming over the highway like vertical power strips. Beyond were blocks of dilapidated Belle Epoque mansions, many enclosed in palm-topped walls. The city around the highway quickly transformed again, to mosques, to Arabian palaces, to a polo field, to a military academy, to a demolition site with brick dust still rising off it like steam.

Some buildings looked so new and ornate they seemed to have just slipped out of a cake mold; others were gnawed by poverty and time. In the distance entire rooftops served as plate racks for dirty satellites dishes, and nearer, on the zebra-striped median, prickly yellow flowers held their petals against the gale of cars.

Cate had made it to Cairo. That fact kept crashing over her like a dream. But it was panic, not a vacationer's excitement, that pierced through the jet lag. Those men knew she was due to arrive this morning. Someone had been expecting her and decided to grab her as she left the airport. Eric had worked in the international arms trade, and the same people who'd killed him might be after her now. All the American tourists on her flight had given her a false sense of security. She'd been an idiot to assume she could simply turn up in Cairo under the radar.

Her travel information would have been easy to access. The Egyptian government could have found her name on the flight manifest. Polestar, too, must monitor those lists. Didn't it have a whole division devoted to surveillance? There she was, the disruptive sister of a murdered weapons tech flying in on Flight 103. They could be tracking her phone right now, following her movement as innocent Omar drove her to her hotel. Could they monitor her credit-card purchases or read the emails on her phone? Cate had no realistic conception of how far surveillance could pry into the corners of her life, or what secrets they could excavate from the strata of her online existences. As she sat gripping the door handle and trying to breathe like a normal human being, her brain kept skipping like a record needle from one paranoia to the next.

What she couldn't understand—and the only saving grace of the botched airport kidnapping—was the utter clumsiness of the attempt. Certainly the Egyptian police could have taken her into custody at passport control. Surely Polestar could have staged a successful abduction. Or really all Polestar needed to do was arrange for a company representative to meet her at the gate with the promise of answering her questions. No, a bumbling goateed teenager and a faceless father with a silver pinkie ring had been the two men sent to intercept her. In its way, that fact was even more terrifying. Presumably both the Egyptian government and an American defense firm would have qualms about silencing her. A father and his teenage son in a borrowed town car might have no hesitation about a quick disposal.

"Are you okay?" Omar asked, flashing a look of concern. "It sounds like you're having trouble breathing."

She was. She couldn't get air. Her lungs weren't inflating, as if she had swum too far out in a lake and couldn't make it back to shore. "Omar," she said, gasping. "I'm so stupid. I shouldn't be here." She closed her eyes. Her body seemed to be pleading for her to take two separate courses of action simultaneously—to go back to the airport and to lie down at the hotel. When she opened her eyes, they were zipping down a wide boulevard away from the highway. Peach-colored high-rises drifted above the thick green skirts of banyan trees. Cars threaded together, argued, refused to respect lanes, and jockeyed for position at the stop light. The car next to them was so close that Cate could have reached her arm through its open window and changed its radio station. In the claustrophobic heat of traffic and sun, she began to wonder whether this handsome Egyptian man driving her was the real Omar or just a more charming impostor, and whether his hearing aid was a different kind of listening device. But no, of course he was Omar. He'd proven it. The jet lag was making her crazy.

She took a deep breath and scanned the city around her. Her eyes focused on a lone palm tree rising above the tangle of streets, through air pollution so thick its particulates glittered gold. What had she expected Cairo to look like? The Nile, the Pyramids, the Sphinx. That ancient broken face on a muddy postcard stamp.

Before anything else, though, Cairo was the place where Eric had been killed.

"Are you going to tell me what's wrong?" Omar asked.

"It's nothing," she whimpered.

"I'm going to stop so you can calm down." Omar shot the car at a sharp diagonal and ferried them onto a quieter side street. He parked under a leafy canopy. The cool shade spilled over them, and it felt like the first sanctuary she'd found in nearly twenty hours of nonstop travel. But here she couldn't evade Omar's eyes.

He lifted his eyebrows. He didn't smile, but his face—with its liquid brown eyes, soft facial hair, and crooked front teeth—was still inviting. She hadn't let anyone fully into her confidence since the day she'd received Eric's postcard, not even Wes or her mother. This young Egyptian doing a favor for his aunt might not be an ideal confidante. But Cate, who in her Manhattan prime could count several hundreds of people as close friends, didn't know another soul in Cairo. She desperately needed one person on her side.

She unfastened her seat belt and looked at him. "What do you know about the international arms trade?"

*   *   *

The Grand Nile, like the smaller Ramses Sands, was located in the Nile-abutting neighborhood of Garden City. True to its name, lush gardens multiplied, some jailed behind private gates, others flourishing in simple plastic pots that lined the sidewalks or growing like ogres out of tree wells. Nearly every street came jeweled in extravagant nineteenth-century mansions with fossil-colored facades and glass-blown windows thick with grime. The architecture was like some motley attic hybrid of Gothic and Beaux Arts, and it managed the impossible double life of appearing haunted and filled with ordinary activity. Every few blocks a police kiosk poked from the sidewalk, sheltering an officer slumped in a foldout chair, armed with a rifle, eyes watching.

A hum pierced the streets, a few octaves higher than the grumbling traffic. It reached Cate's ear first as a warble, but as she listened, it turned into a mournful song. It was the call to prayer. She'd never been in a city of minarets before. As Omar sped across an intersection, she thought she caught a flash of water at the end of the avenue, and while she craved sleep, she felt the uncontrollable lure of the first-time visitor to set her eyes on the Nile.

Omar broke the silence to read her mind. "The Nile is two blocks away," he said offhandedly, as if it were no big deal. She supposed it was similar to her first years in Manhattan walking through Times Square while on the phone with Berkshires-stranded friends. *Oh my god, you're where?* The lifespan of awe was depressingly short.

She looked at him. "Well?" she asked, wanting a sign of reassurance after everything she'd divulged about Eric. The whole story had come pouring out of her, and paradoxically she felt safer once she said it all out loud. "You haven't told me what you think?"

"To be honest," Omar replied, "I'm a little offended."

"Why? I'm not blaming Egypt. My guess is that Polestar is responsible. Eric wrote 'You were right,' and I think it means—"

"No, that's not what I'm talking about." He smiled. "I mean, I thought my aunt liked me. How could she get me mixed up in a murder connected to weapons dealing?"

"You aren't mixed up in anything," Cate replied and touched his arm in a sign of gratitude. She felt his bicep reflexively harden under his sweater. "Your aunt doesn't know about my brother. Lina only wanted you to show me around."

"I'd really like to help you," he said hesitantly. "But honestly, I don't see what you can gain from asking questions here." The car stopped at a light, and Omar continued to stare forward, lost in thought. "From everything you said, I agree, it does sound like his death was connected to his job. I imagine working for the military, he came in contact with a lot of classified secrets. Maybe he threatened to expose one of those secrets?" He shot her a look. "What was the name of his company again?"

"Polestar." The light turned green. Omar let the car roll backward before shifting it into gear, the vibrating so intense that Cate's teeth rattled. "My plan is to try to talk to some of Eric's coworkers, off the record. I'm not technically allowed to mention Eric being murdered. That was a condition of the settlement." Cate hadn't wanted to tell Omar about her family taking Polestar's money, but he had been such a willing listener, she didn't hold back. "But the nondisclosure doesn't stipulate that I can't travel to Cairo or speak with people who knew him. I'm allowed to come to Egypt. I'm not obligated to pretend that Eric didn't die."

"Yes, but what I mean is—and please don't take offense—what difference will it make? They are arms dealers. They control the world. They are best friends with my country. In fact, they probably help run my country. I don't see what good can come of it. You'll only make them—"

"I want to find out what happened," she erupted, her voice cracking in exasperation. She couldn't take discouragement on top of fear and jet lag. "I just want an explanation, an answer, something more than total uncertainty. He didn't commit suicide, but his death will always be presumed a suicide unless . . ." She squeezed her hands together, too exhausted to articulate what Eric's murder had come to mean to her. *Eric's murder.* It felt more like her murder, *Cate's murder.* The murder of Eric now belonged to her, because the rest of her family had given up on finding an answer to it. She was the last holdout, the murder's sole caretaker, feeding and tending to it, keeping the murder alive while Polestar did its best to bury it. Cate owed that duty to her brother. But trying to express that to Omar right now was beyond her capacity. "It's a pilgrimage, all right? That's what I'm doing. I'm here because Cairo is the place Eric died, and I didn't know where else to go. I just wanted to be here, all right?"

"No, I understand," he entreated. "I have an older sister. I would do the same." He nodded at his own declaration. "I would try to find out what happened." Then a little squeak of laughter escaped his lips. "You know, I never think of Americans as having brothers and sisters. They always seem so alone in the world, so individual, so self, self . . ."

"Self-sufficient?"

"Yes! Like they're hatched from eggs!" He smiled and made a sharp left. Tree branches interlaced high above the street, their shadows slicing the sunlight that filtered through the windshield. "But listen to me," he said. "You should be careful about asking questions here. *I* am scared of the police. I am genuinely frightened of them every day. You should be scared too. Since Sisi took power, you can go to prison for posting a tweet. For having a coffee at the wrong café. For complaining about the rising fares of the buses. Not even prison, but infinite detention with no trial. Women have been arrested for reporting their own rapes. It's dangerous here, Cate. There are no rights but Sisi's rights. It's not good for you to be asking questions about the military."

Cate wondered how many years Omar had been away in London, and whether he'd come back to a homeland so transformed he barely recognized it—more restrictive than the one he'd left.

"The police are not going to sit down with you and have a conversation about the parts of your brother's case that don't make sense. I wouldn't sit down with the police to talk about the weather."

"Got it," she said. "I won't talk to the police."

As if the mere mention of police conjured men in uniform, Omar threaded the car through a gated driveway where they were immediately surrounded by guards. Two held clipboards, and one began circling the car.

"The Grand Nile," Omar announced. He pointed to a large glass sign protruding from a bed of ferns. A fountain head gurgled underneath the *G* and *N*. Omar unrolled his window and spoke in rapid Arabic to the head guard, who stuck his head inside to give Cate a quick appraisal. Another guard searched the trunk, and a third ran a mirror along the underside of the car.

"They're checking for bombs." Omar spoke with the same nonchalance he had used to mention their proximity to the Nile. But she understood. She, too, lived in a city that seemed forever on the verge of a bombing. "At each hotel, it's the same routine. At least, at all the best ones. They write down the license plate, like that would deter me from blowing up my car." The guards finally waved them through. The car lumbered up the brick drive toward the entrance. The hotel was an enormous high-rise of iridescent glass, and the sunlight bounced off it in glints of purple and green like the wobbly bubbles that children blew on summer lawns. It could have been a hotel in Denver or Damascus; its only characteristic was the promise of Western comfort.

As they waited in the line of cars for their turn, Cate realized she only had another minute left with Omar. She wasn't certain she'd cemented their friendship in the drive from the airport. In fact, the tragic story about her brother might have him scrambling for excuses not to see her again. She hadn't even asked him a single question about himself. Maybe he'd been searching for the word *self-absorbed*, rather than *self-sufficient*, to describe Americans.

"Are you glad to be back from London?" she asked.

"Sometimes," he answered, his arm dangling out the window. "It's different here than it was even three years ago. I've been back four months. I'm guessing my aunt told you that I haven't found a job yet."

"She might have mentioned it."

He blushed. "The talk of the family, my idleness after all those years studying finance." Omar didn't sound that regretful about being the family disappointment. "To tell you the truth, I'm not sure I can live in Cairo much longer. Not like it is now. I spent some time in Berlin when I was studying in the UK, and I've been thinking of going back there."

Cate nodded in approval. "Berlin is a lot of fun. Berlin knows what to do with a person's twenties."

"It's not just that. There's someone there I'd like to go back to. A person I'd like to spend more time with, to find out if it clicks." His fingers picked nervously at the window's rubber trim. "That person makes it hard for me to be here, among all the other impossibilities of Egypt right now." He surfaced from his brooding with a smile. "Sorry."

"Don't be." Cate sensed a signal being relayed in Omar's careful ambiguity about this person in Berlin. It reminded her of the way Willie had been ambiguous her senior year of high school about girls she liked, or the way gay friends in New York had spoken a decade ago on the phone to their parents, not daring to make a boyfriend any clearer than a ghost floating through a sentence. The times had changed, but change was not a substance that was evenly distributed around the world, and perhaps times hadn't changed so much for Omar in Egypt.

He pulled the car up to the entrance. Cate retrieved her purse from the footwell. She had waited to show him the postcard, and now she pulled it from the guidebook, the beach side facing him.

"Jamaica," Omar murmured as he took it. "But mailed in Cairo." He flipped it over. "Weird. Cairo is the capital of postcard racks. Why would your brother send one of a Jamaican beach?"

"My guess is that he wanted to make sure I paid attention to it, that I didn't just toss it out. Maybe the point was that it's *not* Egypt."

Omar kept flipping the postcard over in carouseling circles, as if it would eventually revolve into a sensible solution. "Jamaica," he repeated, "Jamaica." The second time there was a twinge of recognition in his voice.

"What?"

He shook his head. "There's something about Jamaica in Cairo that's nagging at me." He sighed. "But I can't get it."

The bellhop opened the passenger-side door and waved his arm toward the entrance. A line of cars awaited their turn behind them.

"Please try to remember," she begged.

"Give me your phone," he said. She took the device from her purse, unlocked it, and handed it to him. He tapped his name and number into her contacts.

"The real Omar, nephew of Lina," she said, checking to make sure it was stored. "I can text you?"

"Of course," he laughed. "I live across the river in Zamalek, right over the bridge." Omar gave her a wink. "So, yeah, text me if you need a tour guide."

Chapter 10

CAIRO

S he woke with a jolt to a pitch-black room, her hands grasping
across the comforter. She felt like she could have been asleep
for twenty minutes or twenty hours, and for the first few seconds
of consciousness, she knew only that she was elsewhere, in a place
nowhere near home. The mattress was warm with her body heat.
There was a bitter taste in her mouth, as if she'd been sucking on
a quarter. Then it came to her: Egypt. Cairo. The Grand Nile.
Room 909. She climbed from bed and staggered over to the window to yank the curtains open. At least it was still daylight; she
hadn't lost the entire afternoon. The Nile—or the direction she
imagined the Nile to be—was blocked by a buffer of gray mu-
nicipal buildings. Her eyes dropped to the hotel's elaborate back
gardens and focused on the pastel-blue squiggle of the swimming
pool. A lone swimmer was doing a lap midway across it. Directly
under her, she spotted an outdoor terrace crowded with tables.

Cate went into the bathroom and turned on the faucet. Her eyes were puffy, and their whites were a marbleized pink. She splashed water on her face. That's when she felt the soreness of her wrist, bruised from where the teenager had grabbed her outside the airport. A hammer, pliers, a coil of rope: she could be dead right now. She had nearly been kidnapped, only a few hours ago; in groggy disbelief she remembered what had happened. She wasn't certain whether she had survived the danger and it had passed, or whether it remained a permanent threat for as long as she remained in Egypt. She checked her phone, ignoring the text from Wes asking if she had landed safely. It was a few minutes past three. She'd slept for an hour.

*　　*　　*

"Room number?" the waiter asked.

"Nine oh nine."

"Name?"

"Castle."

He tapped her answers into an electronic notepad, and the screen brightened in confirmation. The waiter took her order: a glass of white wine. Cate sat amid the orange-clothed tables of tourists—most of them American, a few French and British, and one extended table of Japanese families bickering over Nile cruise brochures. Cate had been lucky to nab the only free table on the terrace, shoved against a window with a view into the lobby. A warm breeze wafted from the garden, strangely odorless despite the lavish flowers and delta grasses. There was only the occasional top note of chlorine fumes from the swimming pool.

As she waited for her drink, she watched the procession of guests arriving in the lobby. Much like the security checkpoint in an airport, entering the hotel required dumping one's belongings into a plastic bin to send through a scanner, and then stepping through a metal detector. Also, much like at an airport, the same brewing impatience and alarm bells over forgotten pocket change applied. By the time Cate's wine arrived with a bowl of mixed nuts, she had grown so accustomed to the entrance routine that she was thrown off when a slender, middle-aged woman breezed through one of the front doors that wasn't equipped with a metal detector. She wore flowing cream linen, and her dark hair was wrapped in a loose bun. A skinny teenager followed behind her, his hair the bright copper of a penny. He, in turn, held the door for a little boy of five or six with olive skin, his lips and eyelids a soft violet, absorbed in the screen in his hands. The security guards nodded amiably to them, and the family disappeared into the bowels of the Grand Nile.

Cate took a sip of wine, hoping the alcohol would steady her nerves. She'd need them for the task ahead of her, confronting Lucas Keulks. Her memory of the tech on the laptop screen was hazy due to the bad lighting and faltering satellite connection, so Cate performed a quick image search of him on her phone. Only one photo materialized. It was from his time in the army a few years back, a goofy kid lounging shirtless on a tank in another soldier's Facebook post. She zoomed in on his boyish face, and mentally added a buzz cut, a few years of sun damage, and a guilty conscience.

It was four o'clock when she finished her drink, still too early to track Lucas down if he observed regular work hours. She raised her hand to catch the waiter's attention, but he darted into the kitchen before noticing her. Instead, her wave drew the attention of a stranger who'd just entered the terrace from the pool. His hair and swim trunks were still dripping, his head tilted to the side as he rubbed a towel against his ear. He stared at her in confusion and tentatively returned her wave.

Cate dropped her arm, but it was too late. The swimmer slung the towel over his shoulder and wove through the tables toward her. He probably mistook her for a member of his tour group. He had a thin face, lightly wrecked with nicks and sunspots, the bent nose suggesting a familiarity with fistfights. Silver-brown stubble collected on his chin. His hair was slicked back, most likely the result of the pool, but it lent him the accidental suaveness of an old film star. There was a large gap in the upper right side of his smile, as if two back teeth were missing. Still, his was a friendly face, slightly unserious, as if he were playing along with a joke.

"We don't know each other, do we?" he said as he reached the table. His accent was harsh, not German, but near to it.

"No," she conceded. "We don't. But to be fair, I also wasn't waving at you. I was trying to flag the waiter."

"Ahhh." He sighed, pulling the towel from his shoulder. He was in decent shape, muscular in his chest and arms, with a little softness creeping around his stomach—the body of a man in his late forties who performed a specific number of laps in the pool but never exerted himself beyond the set amount. A few pitted scars encircled his left shoulder, one deep enough to fit a pinkie tip. He made a show of scanning the terrace for another empty table.

"You're welcome to sit," she said, offering the chair across from her. "I'm only staying for another splash of wine."

"Are you sure I'm not intruding?" When Cate shook her head, he took the seat with a thankful nod. The waiter approach, and Cate ordered a second wine. Her table companion asked for the same.

"On your room, ma'am?" the waiter asked her.

"Put it on eleven-oh-three," her new tablemate said. "Surname Vos." He smiled at her as he picked through the bowl of nuts. "My first name's Matthias."

"Cate."

"Nice to meet you, Cate. What brings you to Cairo? Or is that like asking a stranger what they're doing in an emergency room at four in the morning? The answer is obvious."

She stuck to the official excuse listed on her visa. "Sightseeing." The word struck her as strange when uttered aloud—to travel thousands of miles simply to let your eyes roam, as if all other senses were subordinate to the orbs. She doubled down on the term, committing to it. "I'm here to see sights."

"Djoser over Cheops. But I like to play the contrarian." His fingers returned to the bowl, mining it for the pistachios.

"What's Djoser and Cheops?" But she guessed the meaning as she asked the question. "Oh, pyramids. I just arrived today."

"Alone?" He pried a pistachio shell open with his teeth. "Welcome to the center of the world."

"Actually, I'm from the center of the world, New York."

"Yes, well, that might be the center of the universe, but no, you're wrong," he said with blithe certainty. "New York is definitely not the center of the world." He shook his plunder of pistachios in his fist and noticed the impatience on Cate's face for lectures from strangers who she allowed to share her table. "Sorry," he said less arrogantly. "I can really bore a person with my geopolitical theories. Don't you hate the world-weary? So many grand opinions about the state of affairs while waiting for white wine in a wet bathing suit on a hotel terrace."

Cate was willing to humor him for the duration of a glass of wine. "Okay, I'll hear you out."

Matthias glanced around as if he were dispensing confidential information. "I just mean, where we are, this place, Egypt, no one can make sense of it. I don't mean its past, which is what you and most everyone else is here to see. The past is for tourists. I'm talking about the country right now, the madness of it. Every time I leave Cairo, I think, 'What the hell did I just experience?' It's the Middle East. No, it's North Africa. It's Islamist, no, socialist, no, an American puppet state, no, actually it's a military junta–capitalist dictatorship full of rich new pharaohs bulldozing the oldest neighborhoods to build the next Dubai. Or maybe it is just a fever dream that won't die down. Who knows what Egypt is?" He swept the pistachio shells into a neat pile. "The world is messy. This is the center of the mess. That's all I mean. New York is a terrific city, but it floats too far above the rest of the world."

"I might agree with you on that."

The waiter brought their wine, and Cate raised her glass. Matthias clinked his glass with hers and took a thirsty gulp. "I'm from Amsterdam. Beautiful weather, wonderful people. Not really the center of much anymore. Maybe tulips. Or hashish."

"Are you on vacation?" Somehow she doubted it.

"I come to Cairo for business." He threw his head back and stared up at the Grand Nile's silky wall of glass. "At least they booked me in somewhere nice this time. Although I prefer the Marriott over on Gezira Island, near the old sports club." His head dropped down to face her again. "It's got a nice bar in the evenings, good crowd. That's my travel tip in case you get lonely."

"What kind of work are you in?"

Matthias made the face of a man being garroted, his tongue slung to one side. "Consultation. Alliance building. Trust me, the vaguer I keep it, the more interesting it sounds. On airplanes I usually answer that question with 'abstract painter.' You get the same glazed-over expression, only a few minutes faster." He laughed. "I'm envious of you. Getting to see Cairo with fresh eyes."

The second glass of wine had succeeded where the first hadn't: it softened the edges of the world around her, filling it with sweeter sounds and cooler air. The worry pushed onward like changing weather. She let her mind rove over the possibility of ordering another round with Matthias Vos, maybe even going to the bar he liked on Gezira Island. He didn't wear a wedding ring, not that it had ever mattered to her. Usually she preferred that complication, because it worked like a filter to block any real emotions. The second glass of wine had softened the world only to fill it with a rush of self-disgust. *Selfish*, that's what Luis had called her. Cate didn't believe in an afterlife, but the alcohol engineered a portal to her brother in her head. *Do you see the kind of person I've become, Eric? This is what I do. I wreck people, relationships, the peace others have fought so hard to find. Were we both like this? Did you treat your ex-wife as cruelly as I did Luis? Now that you see me clearly, are you even surprised?*

"A boyfriend?" Matthias asked. Cate refocused her eyes on him, shocked that he could read her thoughts. But she followed his gaze to her phone on the table. The screen hadn't gone dark. It still showed the zoomed-in face of Lucas Keulks from her image search.

"Oh," she exclaimed, fumbling to pick up her phone and click it off. "No, not a boyfriend."

"He looks like he's in the army."

"He's nobody." She'd been careless, and whatever Egypt was, it was not the place to be careless. She set her wineglass down, retrieved her purse, and stood.

"Are you off?" Matthias asked. He bundled his pool towel around his neck. "Sights to see?"

"Thanks for the wine."

"I'd be happy to show you around Cairo. The tentmakers market, some spectacular out-of-the-way mosques, the best Mamluk architecture. How about tomorrow? I'm in room eleven-oh-three. And you're in . . . ?"

But Cate already had Omar as a guide. "Very kind of you," she said, dodging the invitation. "But I'm good for tomorrow. Thanks again."

There was still a yellow wash of daylight in the sky when Cate descended the hotel's brick driveway. She heard the streets before she entered them. The incessant honking seemed to pour from every crack in the architecture. Even to a New York ear, Cairo possessed a furious dissonance. Across from the hotel stood a block-long buffer of spinsterly European cast-iron buildings. Their thin casement windows seemed gritted shut against the noise jittering through them.

The sound was a mere preamble. The real chaos was the traffic. Cate plunged across the first avenue, where a van nearly plowed into her, its driver not even offering the pretense of a tap on the brakes. A dark-haired man in ripped jeans and a 7UP T-shirt smiled at her from the opposite corner, a collection of spray-painted tote bags hanging on his outstretched arms. "Will you buy?" he asked, and when Cate slipped past him, he called after her, in a tone that sounded genuinely earnest, "May god bless you, your family, and your country."

The next block proved less hectic, its buckled sidewalks covered with a dusting of cigarette butts, dried palm fronds, and tire-flattened water bottles. Cate stopped only for a moment to check the map on her phone; she didn't want to identify herself as a lost tourist. Yet as she continued down the sidewalk, vehicles slowed and men leered. They ignored the young Egyptian woman a few steps ahead of her (her cell phone cleverly tucked into her head-scarf so that she didn't need to use her hands to hold it against her ear), concentrating their appetites on foreign Cate. She was used to a lifetime of such looks jackaling out of pickup trucks in Great Barrington as a teenager and from delivery vans in Manhattan as an adult. It was the slowing down of the cars themselves that un-nerved her. It reminded her of the white town car at the airport, and the faceless driver with the pinkie ring. She quickened her pace and jogged across the next avenue.

It was nearing five in the evening, and the sun leaned far in the west, the buildings covered in shadows, their lobbies flickering with pale fluorescents. She watched a black dog skitter along the opposite sidewalk; at the corner it disappeared so entirely into the shadows it was as if it had dissolved upon contact. A few steps later she spotted the Ramses Sands.

Cate had pictured the hotel hundreds of times since Eric's death, but always from the vantage of his balcony. She now appraised it as most visitors did, its five floors of sturdy concrete, its name etched in gold paint on the front window. There was no mistaking the place for five-star accommodations. The Ramses Sands was the kind of clean-and-efficient budget hotel vacationers booked on the excuse that they would be spending most of their waking hours outside its domain. Polestar had probably negotiated a deal on long-term employee stays. At least Cate hoped that was the case, because it was a pure guess that Lucas Keulks would be staying here.

In contrast to the strict security at the Grand Nile, only a skeletal metal detector guarded the front door. The machine beeped meekly as she stepped through it, and no one came running to empty her pockets. The lobby was dim and cramped, with a reception desk nestled off to the side. An older woman with wavy silver hair manned the counter, a phone cradled at her ear as her fingers pecked on a keyboard. Cate tried to picture the receptionist's reaction if she announced who she was: *I'm the sister of the guy who fell to his death a month ago from room 3B.* Would she be met with a hostile stare? Would she be asked to leave? It occurred to Cate that many of the answers she'd come to Cairo to collect might be stored inside this receptionist's head. What Eric's moves had been that night, if he'd made any last calls or had any visitors up to his room. At the least, there must have been staff gossip. This receptionist might be able to solve so many riddles for the grieving sister, but Cate didn't know how to risk such questions.

"May I help you?" the woman asked after finishing her call.

"I'm here to see a guest. Lucas Keulks."

The receptionist's eyes widened, and she glanced into a small back office behind the counter. A young woman was perched on a chair in the doorway. Both were dressed in the staff uniform of a black skirt and white blouse with dark pantyhose and flats, although the young woman had a headset hooked around her ear. She was picking a fork through a tin of rice. The two coworkers spoke in a volley of Arabic, and the young woman made eye contact with Cate, a little shyly, gesturing with her fork.

"He is not in his room," she said.

The older woman repeated the same information in the tone of seniority. "He is not in his room. He is"—she pointed toward a set of mirrored French doors across the lobby—"in there. At the bar. We don't usually . . ."

The young woman stood, dusting rice grains off her blouse. She removed her headset and came to the counter. There was a halting limp to her gait, as if her leg had fallen asleep. "Will you want a drink too?" she asked Cate. "We don't have a bartender on duty. Your friend, when he wants something, I need to go and prepare it. Would you like me to—"

"No, I'm fine," Cate said. "I'll just sit with him. Thank you."

As she crossed the lobby, she caught the two receptionists staring at her through the reflection in the mirrored doors. The hotel's interior was chilly. Cate had expected Cairo to be gruelingly hot even in December, but it was heat, not air-conditioning, that these old buildings lacked. Opening the door, she entered a small slate-tiled vestibule that led into the hotel's wood-walled dining room. The tables in the darkened restaurant were already set for tomorrow's breakfast, the upside-down juice glasses glowing blue from the fading window light. A compact bar occupied one side of the vestibule, with shelves of dusty liquor bottles climbing the wall and a muted television hanging from the ceiling, its screen flashing the bad-frequency greens and grays of a soccer game. The bar had only one customer, slumped on a stool below the television set. His elbow was pinned on the counter, his fist holding up his head. He wore black leather boots, tan fatigues, and a nylon bomber jacket. His dark hair had grown since she'd seen him on the video call a month ago. Cate felt nervous about approaching Lucas—not because he might be drunk or volatile, but because he represented the only clear starting point for her mission. If he refused to talk to her, she didn't know where else to turn.

Lucas didn't look up, even as she stood two feet away. His eyes were focused on his thumb, which rubbed a groove in the wood countertop. His eyelashes were a long black calligraphy. A tumbler of tawny liquid sat in front of him.

"Hi," she chanced. Lucas raised his eyes, glassy brown, with little flames dancing in them from the solitary candle at the other end of the bar.

"Hey there," he slurred. "If you want a drink, you need to fetch the girl with the limp—"

"No," she interrupted. "I was looking for you. For Lucas Keulks? That's you, right?" His back stiffened. "Lucas from Polestar?" Cate asked enthusiastically, like she was a fan hitting up a musician for an autograph. "I know it's you. We've spoken before."

"Okay." His tone was guarded. "Where?"

"I'm Cate Castle. Eric's sister."

His jaw clenched. He swiveled around on his stool, facing the bar as if to ignore her, but he seemed to realize that the move only trapped him in place. He braced his hands on the counter as she continued. "We met over a video call that Polestar set up. You talked to my family about Eric's death?"

He grabbed his glass and took a gulp from it. Then he shook his head furiously. "Oh, fuck," he cursed. "Fuck, fuck. No, I'm not speaking to you."

She kept her voice sunny and warm, the kind of first-date

buoyancy that hid the jagged emotional reefs below the surface. "I came all this way. I flew in this morning, just to talk to you for five minutes. I was hoping—"

"Fuck. No!" He spun around, and his left boot flailed toward the floor.

"I got your message," she said.

He stopped flailing. "What message?" His hand, like any practiced alcoholic's, went for the protection of his glass.

"From your girlfriend, your *fiancée*. From Nicole, who you have a baby with." Cate felt her best chance was to keep talking, no matter his reaction. "She came to the cemetery and gave me your message about . . ."

"Shhhhhhh," he hissed violently, his shoulders lifting to his ears. "Jesus, shut up!"

Cate realized her mistake. Nicole had warned her that Polestar was always listening—or at least that Lucas and his fellow techs thought they were. Lucas lowered his voice to a murmur, filtering his words through his teeth. "I asked Nicole to give you a message. That message did not include an invitation to fly here to interrogate me."

Cate let out a weary sigh. She was losing her patience at the exact moment she needed it. She dropped onto the stool next to him, hooking her foot around the metal ring of his chair. She kept her voice at a whisper.

"What did you expect me to do? Just accept that you lied about Eric so that Polestar could cover up his murder? Of course I came here. He was my brother, and, I thought, your close friend."

Lucas shut his eyes. She assumed he was absorbing the guilt stored in her words. But when he snapped them open, he blurted, "You don't know shit about what we do for work or what it's like over here. So don't feed me a guilt trip." He took a deep breath and chased that gulp of oxygen with whiskey.

Cate dug through her purse and pulled out Eric's postcard. She slapped it on the counter. "Can you at least look at this? It came in the mail a week after he died. Eric sent me postcards for years, but this one's different. I can't figure it out. But I hear that you also send postcards."

Lucas looked around the vestibule, as if assessing whether anyone was monitoring them. Then he stared down at the picture of the Jamaican beach and flipped it over. "A trick of the trade," he muttered with a laugh. "A little loophole when they're watching all of your devices for suspicious communication." He tapped the flimsy rectangle of paper on the counter. "A postcard with no return address. You stick a stamp on it and toss it in a mailbox. Bang, might as well be invisible ink. So obvious no one thinks to look there." He flashed her a sly smirk. "We did the same thing in the army, although we knew so fuck-little about the weapons we were using, it didn't much matter what information we were sharing. You know, I still bet on college football this way, send a postcard to my bookie once a week, because we're not supposed to gamble either. That's another no-no. And I guess Nicole told you that we communicate this way when there's something personal I need to get off my chest. All the techs do it."

"Polestar really monitors you that much?" she asked. "Every call, every email?"

"Not just Polestar. The host country does too. Egypt. We're double-tracked." Lucas had reached the level of drunkenness where his expressions lost subtlety, first a cartoonish smile, now an exaggerated scowl, his head wobbling on the unsteady pedestal of his neck. "You don't get it. You don't understand what your brother did for a living. A tech might sound insignificant, but we're actually the real weapons. We're the priceless hardware. We hold the secrets on how the damn things work, and believe me, that's Polestar's merchandise. So they need to keep us on very tight leashes. Stranglehold leashes. The kind that dig into your neck."

"Do you think those secrets are the reason that Eric—"

But Lucas, so unwilling to talk to her initially, found his drunken love of an audience. "That's what you outside people don't get. It's not as simple as flipping a switch or turning a key. I don't carry my phone on me, but if I had it . . ." He frisked his body, patting his pockets to ensure it wasn't with him. "I have some photos from a few years back of these dudes in Libya right after Gaddafi fell. Suddenly these rebels get their hands on the whole government arsenal. It's a free-for-all, right? You probably saw these images on the news of insurgents posing with rocket launchers or sitting with their legs wrapped around an antitank missile. They look like total badasses, ready to take on the whole world. But it's a joke. They couldn't take on a girls' softball team. Not one of those men could get those weapons to so much as blink. In their hands, they're as harmless as plastic baseball bats. You see, in order to fire them, they need men like your brother and me." He drained what was left in the glass. "So, yeah, you better believe that our bosses are listening. Our little brains are worth billions. They have a whole tracking department following who we talk to, what apps we download, every key stroke, just to make sure those secrets don't get out." He flapped Eric's postcard in front of her. "And so, to be a human being, we, subvert, no, subvent . . . we circumvent! All this rush for the latest encryption services and firewalls, but no one expects anything of value to be written on a postcard. Just don't send one from a hotel, because they steal the stamps."

"If Eric was here in Cairo, why did he send me a postcard of a Jamaican beach on the day he died?"

Lucas shook his head. "That I can't answer. Maybe it just happened to be close at hand when he got the chance to write you.

Although you can't walk a block in this city without falling over a rack of camel postcards." He stared at Eric's note written on the back. "My eyes are shit," he said as he lunged for the candle at the other end of the bar. The effort of grabbing it winded him, and he breathed deeply as he held the postcard near the flickering flame. "What's this about you being right?" he asked.

"I have no idea!" She grabbed the card back before one of the edges could catch fire. "But he also sent one to our father, where he wrote, 'If it all blows up' . . ."

"Everything blows up eventually," Lucas interrupted with a drunk's delight in dispensing simple truths.

"He also wrote, 'Ask him about Huxley.' Who's Huxley?"

He shrugged. "No clue. Never heard the name."

"There must be a Huxley," Cate persisted. "Maybe someone you work with? Or someone out in the desert where you conduct your missile tests? Could there be a friend, a *him*, we're supposed to ask—"

"Stop with the questions!" he shouted. "I don't know! I don't know anything, all right? Anyway, didn't your family a take a settlement? That's the rumor I heard."

"The reason we took it is because they found a note in Eric's hotel room," she said in defense, "about paying for sex, about sleeping with young men and women. My mom couldn't . . ." She stopped herself and tried to keep her voice neutral. "Be honest with me, was that something Eric did?"

"Eric gay?" Lucas rasped. "No. We were close friends. Eric wasn't a—" Cate flinched preemptively, but Lucas swerved away from the slur. "Believe me, if Eric liked boys, Polestar wouldn't have risked sending him to the Middle East. They do background checks, and that's just asking for a firecracker to explode in your face. As for paying for sex, I mean, it happens. I've done that once or twice in other places. I'm not proud of it, but I'm not ashamed either." He shook his head. "But, again, not here. You can't do that kind of stuff in Egypt if you want to stay in breathing condition. Eric wasn't stupid. He fooled around, sure. He had a few women in Cairo he saw. He was quiet about it, as you have to be, because that's another thing Polestar doesn't like. Affairs. Eric had a little place over the bridge in Zamalek that he used."

"A little place?"

"A place," Lucas spat. "A little spot he rented for screwing around. I don't know exactly where it was. The whole point was that it stayed a secret. Ask that chick who works at the American embassy, if you're so interested. She certainly knows."

"The chick?" Cate rummaged through her brain for the name of the embassy attaché. The delay in conjuring Elizabeth Skyler's name gave Lucas too much time for reflection.

"What am I doing?" he cried. He grabbed his glass to take a final swig, only to discover he'd already drunk it. The lack of alcohol seemed to sober him. "Fuck! I can't talk to you. I'm not allowed. I have a child back at home. I need my job. Please," he implored, "leave me alone."

He spun on his stool and lurched to his feet, stretching his arms out for balance as he took his first erratic steps away from the bar, a man pretending to be a doomed airplane. Cate tried to grab his arm, but the doomed airplane soared. Lucas hurried into the dining room, weaving through the maze of tables. Cate followed, skirting the room's edges. "Lucas," she called. "Stop." But he had already reached a set of swinging doors and disappeared through them. Cate rushed after him, entering an empty kitchen. The only way out was a security door. Jamming her hip against it, she stumbled out into the cold night. The sun had set, and she seemed to be standing in a back alley, the concrete wet with hose water.

She saw Lucas running down the alleyway. "Lucas," she yelled.

"Lucas, please stop!" She turned around to get her bearings, and her breath stalled as her eyes traced a line of half-moon balconies ascending like vertebrae up the back of the building. She dropped her gaze to her feet, where the wet concrete glittered. She might be standing in the very spot where Eric had landed. Right here, her brother had lain for hours, dead. She stood on this unexceptional expanse of pavement that, for a brief period, had become the center of her family's world.

"Cate," Lucas whispered, standing ten feet away. "Come here." He must have turned around when he realized where he'd accidentally led her. For a moment she felt glued in place, unable to move. She stared up at the Ramses Sands, counting the balconies to the third floor. She saw the metal railing and the shimmery glass of a sliding door. There was no light on in 3B. She wouldn't have wanted to see it occupied. It was a long way down. And yet her instinct had been correct. No one in their right mind would have picked it for a suicidal leap.

"Cate," Lucas appealed with his arm out. "Get away from there." She forced herself to walk toward him. When she reached him, she pushed his arm aside. She would no longer gently coax Lucas into telling her the truth.

"You told Nicole that Eric found something out, and that's the reason he was killed. What was it?"

Lucas staggered in place, less from drinking, she thought, than from his own failing resolve. "It's Polestar. It had to do with the weapons we were fixing out in the desert. They weren't broken. They worked! But I kept my mouth shut. I'm not careless like Eric was."

"What do you mean, the weapons worked? Isn't that what they're supposed to do?"

"Forget it!" The cautious Lucas had returned. He wiped his mouth as if to remind himself to keep it shut. She reached for him, but he dodged her hand and began walking backward down the alley. "I'm leaving for the desert tomorrow at dawn. We're doing test fires. So don't bother looking for me. I won't be around."

"When are you back? Can't you at least explain what you mean about the weapons working?"

"Ask another tech. Ask his bosses, the Driscolls. They're staying here too. Just don't mention my name. Leave me the hell out of it." He turned and ran, his footsteps echoing down the alley. Cate stood in the darkness as the sound of his feet grew fainter until it merged into the sea of city noises. She reached for the St. Anthony pendant at her neck. She hadn't gotten the chance to ask Lucas if he'd seen it before, and now he too had become one more thing that was lost in the world.

Chapter 11

OMAR

On the wall of Omar's apartment in Zamalek hung a photo of a handsome blond man kissing a Roman statue. Or almost kissing a statue. *Pretending to kiss it.* Omar had taken the photo of his boyfriend last year when they'd spent a rainy afternoon touring the bunker-dark galleries of Berlin's Neues Museum. The kiss had been a joke, Tobias checking to make sure the guard was out of sight before leaning in as if to make out with the white marble bust of a curly-haired, rabid-eyed emperor. Omar had his camera ready and fired off a round of clicks. The result was astonishingly convincing, framing Tobias with his neck muscles straining, his eyes softly shut as if under a spell, his parted lips coming within a hair of the mouth of bloodless stone. "I full-on kissed him," Tobias giggled as they resurfaced into the drizzly gray decadence of Berlin. "No, you did not," Omar countered. "I did! Our lips touched." "No, they didn't!"

Omar spoke no German, Tobias no Arabic. They knew each other only in English. "You don't believe I kissed him? Is that what you're saying?" Tobias's eyes were starting to twitch, which Omar knew to be a sign that his boyfriend was getting overly agitated. "My lips made contact with marble, that's a kiss. I might be the first human to have kissed that emperor in, *what?*, like two thousand years. He was quite sexy, don't you think? Beefy, angry, like he wanted to rip me apart." They climbed the steps to the street, and Omar ransacked his brain for a change of subject. Tobias, tall and thick, a laborer for his father's construction company, was always hungry, and the prospect of food could usually divert his attention. "Do you want falafel?" Omar asked. "There's a good Lebanese place a block away?" Omar didn't want to hear how turned on Tobias was by beefy, angry, or someone who could rip him apart, because that eliminated Omar from the erotic equation. In their two and half years together—on and off—Tobias had established such a firm hold on Omar's heart that he could make him jealous of an ancient piece of stone.

In another time, in another country, Omar would have been content to use this photo of Tobias as the wallpaper on his phone screen. But since returning to Cairo four months ago, he'd been extremely careful not to store any gay content on his device. It was better to be safe than tortured. Omar may have been exercising excess caution, overscrubbing his digital fingerprints, but if rumors were true, Sisi's secret police could use anything—a photo of a shirtless man at a beach who wasn't a relative, a misguided Google search for porn, a flirty post on Facebook, a photo of a shirtless man at a beach who *was* a relative—as grounds for arrest. Over the past four months the rumors had been upgraded to corroborated facts. Men had been tossed into detention for the mere suspicion of "acts of debauchery." Some had been subjected to anal virginity exams (Omar had lived in his body for twenty-six years, but he still couldn't fathom what such a test entailed). Public parks were combed, bathhouses raided, gay hookup apps baited to catch virtual debauchers hoping to rendezvous in real time. Faces of guilty men, some of them members of important families, occasionally appeared on the news or in the papers, and the shame of their crimes broke families apart and even led to suicide. Homosexuality had always been taboo, even in cosmopolitan Cairo. There had been dragnets and crackdowns before (the raid on a Nile cruise boat that cleverly doubled as a floating gay discotheque at the start of the century was an often-cited example). Nevertheless, two regimes back, under Mubarak, homosexuality had been a vice largely ignored as an aberration, banished to the margins of the unmentionable, and thus it lived in its own magical snow globe of secrecy inside straight, snowless Cairo.

It is a universal truth that a person moves through the world only as openly as they're allowed. Omar had used Grindr in his late teens and twenties to fool around with men, and once or twice, during his years at university here, had cruised the strip of riverfront under the 6th of October Bridge where gay men gathered. None of this early experimentation was very serious or fulfilling, but at least it was an option. Omar had returned to his homeland in the prime of his twenties, to find it more provincial and policed than ever. That's what angered him the most. He was under no delusion that Sisi and his henchmen actually cared about the vice of homosexuality; it was merely a convenient lever of distraction whenever a political scandal or a bribery allegation erupted. A judge was discovered to have ruled in favor of a corporation in which he owned considerable stock? Quick, cue the raid of a gymnasium in Madinet Nasr, the uncovering of an all-male sex ring at a club in Dokki. Attention diverted by moral disgust. Hairy, tapioca-bodied men dragged out with towels wrapped around their waists, news-casters demanding their heads. Meanwhile, Tobias kissed a Roman emperor on Omar's living-room wall.

It was hard to remember the excitement he'd felt as a teenager for the uprisings in Tahrir Square. It was like a votive candle that erupted into a bonfire and eventually blazed outward to ignite the entire nation; now it was a circle of ash, its embers stomped on by the boots of the military. Back then he'd been living in his family home, a vine-covered brick terrace house in Zamalek. His mother was a psychology professor—loving, liberal, Western-leaning, with a special zeal for Omar's creative inclinations—while his father was a VP at a company that monopolistically imported the region's steel sheeting and terra-cotta tiles. During the revo-lution, their house was a jittery mix of hopes and fears, excited for new freedoms, tired of the old restrictions and cruelties, and yet terrified by the possibility that the family's strong Mubarak connections—the very government contracts that had made them so affluent—might turn around and sink them. Omar's older sister had already gone to university and was engaged to an engineer. But Omar's future seemed far less certain. He had attended the protests in the square, wanting change, desperate to do more than sit by as Mubarak passed his crown to his son. But Omar also har-bored the desire to taste the freedoms of places that had already been liberated. His dreams tended to drift like smoke toward the nearest window of escape, and for him that meant north across the sea to the patchwork countries of carnal Europe.

Since Omar was the Meshrefs' only son, he didn't have to serve the mandatory eighteen months of military conscription. After four years at the local American university, he convinced his par-ents to let him move to London on the expensive excuse of earning a master's degree in finance. His father, who had barely survived at the top of his steel-and-clay empire, thought it wise for his son to acquire some elite foreign credentials. It was a two-year program that Omar managed to extend to three and a half, thanks chiefly to a procrastination tool called Tobias Schweitzer. One weekend every month, Omar left London to investigate a different city in Europe, exploring its arts by day and its bars and clubs by night. He had never been much of a drinker, and he'd always been too choosy—or shy—for much random sex, but he managed to intoxicate himself on Lisbon, Madrid, Copenhagen, and Dublin before he finally tackled Berlin. On his first night there, on the dance floor of a former munitions factory, he fell alongside a tall, sweaty blond with a rippling body and a doughy, expressionless face. Tobias's tongue tasted like honey in his mouth. They didn't sleep together that night but made a date for the next afternoon at Omar's Airbnb studio in Prenzlauer Berg. Omar waited impatiently for the young man to appear, half convinced he wouldn't show up. But an hour late, the buzzer sounded, and there Tobias stood in the doorway, in denim coveralls, his hair and skin speckled with plaster. He wore a white undershirt underneath his work jumpsuit, but no underwear. From that trip on, it was Berlin, Berlin, Berlin, every other weekend.

Tobias was the most noncommittal human being Omar had ever encountered, the very worst kind of person to fall in love with. He seemed unable to remember which weekends Omar planned to visit from London. He never talked about the future, or about being monogamous, or about what he got up to during his twelve-day Omar-free stretches in Berlin. He also forgot when Omar didn't have his hearing aid in and would whisper words into his dead ear during sex that he refused to repeat afterward. Omar played it cool, pretending to be as indifferent to Tobias's inconsideration as he was to his tedious grad-school seminars on risk management and investment strategies. But for all of Tobias's faults, he was the very first man ever to hold Omar's hand in public, the first to kiss him on a street corner, and the first to introduce him to his parents as "this strange guy from Egypt I'm dating." It was exotic to Omar to experience an adult romance without any wrapper of hiding, going on a date without pretending not to be on a date for the comfort of the strangers around him. Maybe it was that particular freedom of the West that Omar loved the most.

As it usually went for expats, Omar felt most like an Egyptian when out of his homeland. He followed the news of Sisi and his tightening fist on democratic freedoms (press, due process, the speaking of one's mind at an audible volume) from the safe remove of London, and when others labeled the former military general a monstrous autocrat, Omar felt the urge to defend. Sisi was merely blustering, he'd say, showing his political strength. Egyptians notoriously talked out of both sides of their mouths, and every crackdown was really a tented spectacle with a back flap leading out to fresh air. The national state of emergency that Sisi had declared by presidential decree to quash any rebellion couldn't possibly be a permanent condition. Also, the anecdotes of Egyptians putting their phones in their refrigerators to prevent the secret police from eavesdropping was just a testament to the inherent theatricality of the Egyptian character. Like many expats, Omar failed to perceive what his country had become in his absence.

One day, to his genuine surprise, he had received a master's degree in finance, his student visa was set to expire, and Tobias, nearing thirty, had begun flirting with the idea of moving to California. "What if I come with you?" Omar proposed one morning while lying in Tobias's bed. "I mean, once you get settled." It had been a risky suggestion, as Tobias's daydreams of Los Angeles had never included a two-car garage. But Omar was scheduled to return to Cairo in a week's time, and he wanted even a quixotic token of commitment. Tobias rolled over to face him, the blond fuzz that fanned his chest thinning into a line along the ravine of his abdominal muscles before puffing out into pubic hair. Tobias's tongue probed his upper gums as if hunting for stray bits of food lodged there from last night's dinner. For once he checked that Omar's hearing aid was in. "*If* I end up going. . . . For all I know, I may have to stay in Berlin. My father has so much work, how would he manage without me? But *if* I go, then, maybe, yes, it might be nice to have you there." It was the closest Tobias ever got to a declaration of love.

During Omar's extended absence from Egypt, his parents had sold their home in Zamalek and moved into one of the elite gated communities that were popping up in the suburbs west of Giza. Ever since the revolution, the wealthy had left the city in droves, wary of the chaos and the fitful disruptions and the nonsensical caprices of the lawmakers. Omar's boyfriend might have appreciated his family's new residence, tucked into a development called Palm Hills, which consisted of one pink-stucco mini mansion after another, complete with a robin's-egg Jacuzzi and the rapid gunfire of rotating sprinklers on the front lawn. Omar often had to double-check the number plates on his parents' door, so interchangeable were these mansions on curving blacktop lanes patrolled by teams of security guards in pink golf carts. It was exactly how Omar imagined the suburbs of Southern California to look, tacky affluence shellacked onto an inhospitable desert.

To be fair, the new house was comfortable and cool, and his mother and father both appeared trimmer and better rested away from the racket of the city. They had reserved a bedroom for their only son upon his return from London. Adult children in Egypt tended to reside at home until marriage. But obviously that arrangement wasn't going to work, and he used his parents' move an hour outside of the city center as the justification. He explained that he needed to be in Cairo for job interviews, to make connections, to leverage old friendships into financial opportunities. But in truth he was homesick for the wide, shadowy streets of haunted Zamalek, the languorous island in the middle of the Nile. While it was nearly impossible to find an apartment to rent as a young single man—landlords distrusted the motives of young single Egyptian men, suspecting them of all shades of illicit activities—luckily his brother-in-law's cousin rented in a tall, crumbling Beaux Arts building on mid-island, and they could vouch for Omar's decency, integrity, and family pedigree with the widowed landlady. She had one apartment available, reserved for a Japanese banker, but he had been reassigned to Bahrain at the last minute, and Omar, in a tailored suit, managed to flatter Mrs. El Fettah, while mentioning his expensive schooling and bragging of his sister's extravagant wedding, where they'd rented out an entire villa in Obour City.

The apartment was on the sixth floor. The walls were concrete, some stained prune purple, others a vinegar yellow, all of them scarred from decades of wear, as if previous residents had attacked them with an ice pick. The floor was a medley of parquet and concrete, the latter embedded with pieces of colored stone from what must have once been a lavish mosaic. The tinted windows blocked out the sun, but he loved his view of an old embassy and the rooftop patio of a large, laugh-prone family (the cute teenage son did shirtless push-ups in the late afternoons). Mrs. El Fettah swept the sixth-floor landing every morning with her stick broom, and she constantly barraged Omar with questions on when he would marry, as if his bachelordom were meteorological and its forecast were liable to change by the day. Omar never brought men home so he wouldn't have to explain their presence, and Mrs. El Fettah never crowbarred her curiosities beyond his apartment door. In other words, the photo of Tobias tacked on the living-room wall carried little danger of exposure, but just to be safe Omar strung a cord across the corner, which he used to dry his clothes, obstructing a direct view of Tobias and the Roman emperor. It was best to be overly cautious in Cairo.

Lately, he and Tobias had barely spoken. A few emails and phone calls, one or two innocuous photos of the respective rivers that ran through their cities. Tobias habitually chatted on an encrypted social media app that had been banned by the Egyptian authorities as a tool of insurrection, and it was hard to wean him back onto older platforms. But when they spoke two weeks ago, Tobias had mentioned he'd been setting aside two hundred euros each week for California—"I will give myself a year there, to try it." Omar did not like to imagine lusty sunburned Americans getting their hands on his beautiful German, and maybe, hopefully, he wouldn't have to imagine it. An American travel visa had become exceedingly difficult for an Egyptian to acquire. Omar knew several well-connected friends from college whose applications had been flat-out rejected. Undaunted, he'd already filled out most of the electronic application form.

He palm-tested the dryness of his dress shirts draped along the cord in the living room. Most of them were still wet, and worse, he noticed that the soap he'd used to sink-wash them left a filmy residue. Omar had stopped trusting the dry cleaner two streets over, which had lost three of his shirts, including a favorite tailored silk shirt he'd splurged on in London. After bundling the damp shirts in his arms, he put on his hearing aid and grabbed his keys. There was another dry cleaner near his old high school, a ten-minute walk away.

Jamaica. Ever since Cate Castle had shown him the postcard yesterday in the car, something about that Caribbean island kept gnawing at him. *Jamaica, Jamaica.* There had been a Jamaican restaurant down the street from his apartment in Bethnal Green in

London. He'd stayed at a hostel run by a Jamaican family in Dublin. But neither of those associations scratched the itch in his brain. He squeezed his eyes shut and tried to summon a closer-to-home Jamaica from the fog. It was no use.

"Are the shirts for a special occasion?" Mrs. El Fettah inquired. She sat picking glass bottles out of the garbage on the fourth-floor landing, her portable radio beside her spitting static. "Are you meeting a girl?"

"I'm only taking them to be cleaned," he answered with gentle exasperation.

On the final turn of the stairs, he dropped two shirts and regretted not shoving them in a bag. His hands would be too full on his walk to type an email to his aunt in New York, letting her know that he'd collected her friend from the airport. He'd been delighted when Cate emailed him at Aunt Lina's suggestion. Omar's mother had spent most of her life craving the approval of her older sister, and therefore doing his aunt the favor of showing her friend around Cairo was an ideal excuse to delay the week of job interviews that his parents had been badgering him to undertake. But there was a second motive in trying to appease Aunt Lina: she possessed important contacts in New York, the kind that could clear any red flags that might derail a visa, and he was hoping to call on her to repay this favor. It occurred to him as he neared the end of his block that he might not be using the United States to reach Tobias, but Tobias to reach the United States.

He held the shirts against his chest as he crossed the busy intersection, slowing his steps halfway across to wait for a sputtering tuk-tuk to pass. He had expected Cate Castle to be older, a member of his aunt's stuffy society circle. But that was not the woman who turned up yesterday at the airport—or rather, outside it, very nearly entering a stranger's car. She was only about a decade older than he was, and her face still possessed the troubled vulnerability of youth that he recognized from his own face in the mirror. He took an instant liking to Cate, maybe because he was impressed by anyone who could manage to nearly get kidnapped within two minutes of landing in a foreign country. Then she poured her heart out about her brother, and he genuinely felt terrible over what her family had suffered. He wanted to help her—yes, to please his aunt and win her praises and hopefully a visa, but also because he sensed that Cate needed him.

The truth was, he needed Cate too. He hadn't been able to talk to any of his friends in Cairo about Tobias or the panicky identity crisis he suffered every morning in the shower. While he'd been away, most of his friends had married and started families; others had managed to secure jobs overseas. But Cate, from New York, would understand him. He could sense that in her, a kind trust beneath the hard surface. It also helped that as a tourist, she was a safe storehouse for his secrets; they would fly off with her at the end of her trip. Since he had some extra time on his hands, he didn't see the harm in showing her around, beyond the usual tired world wonders and sheesha cafés.

Omar rounded the block near his old private high school. The grounds were a matrix of gardens and football fields, a veritable jewel of green in a city with so few open spaces. A single turn down a street, and he reached a popular tourist thoroughfare, the elevated highway roaring overhead. A few vacationers were still stumbling out of their hotels, shielding their faces from the blinding sunlight. Omar didn't mind the tourists. Most old methods of meeting men had been stripped away under Sisi. But he had hit upon a new one: hanging out in the lobby bars of foreign hotels, the Marriots and Sofitels and Four Seasons, where polished, Western-dressed Egyptians who spoke a crisp English were permitted entry. For young Egyptians who could afford the overpriced drinks, the fancier tourist hotels offered the immunity and asylum of embassies.

There was one hotel in the heart of Zamalek whose bungalow-studded garden proved a notorious cruising zone, particularly for horny visiting Gulfies. But Omar preferred the more diverse visitor pools of the Garden City hotels. He'd met a few businessmen in those lobby bars—no one who could steal his heart from Tobias, but enough to live on for a month, like a kind of sexual bread. Afterward he often lay naked for as long as possible in those hotel beds to remind himself that his body was wired for pleasure as well as frustration.

The lights were off at the dry cleaner. A sign was taped to the door: "Back in one hour," which could easily mean closed for the remainder of the day. Omar used the ball of shirts to mop the sweat on his face. There must be another dry cleaner nearby. He mentally cruised the side streets that ran off the 26th of July Corridor, his memory winding through the labyrinth of stores and markets that he used to pass on his walk to and from school. Suddenly his mind tripped over the image of a Jamaican flag—a rectangular X of black, green, and gold. A stunned smile crept across his face. That was the memory nagging at his brain. A Jamaican flag hung in the window of the shop that sold barrels of nuts and sweets, right off the busiest section of 26th of July. Anyone, even a tourist, would notice it. He should have remembered it as soon as Cate showed him the postcard. It was an oddity in a town chock-full of famous oddities.

He jogged with his bundle of shirts toward the store, worried he'd find the flag in the window gone, proof of his memory failing him. But after veering around a merchant on the corner peddling bananas and incense, Omar spotted the flag in the shop window, sagging across the glass above stock photos of dukkah and chocolate hearts. Because of the flag, his schoolmates used to joke that the owner sold marijuana under the counter. But Omar knew the real reason it hung in the window. Long ago, the shopkeeper had taken a vacation to the Caribbean and had fallen so in love with the island, he'd brought back a treasure trove of mementos to decorate his shop. Jamaica proved such an alien presence in central Cairo, it turned out to be a clever advertising strategy, and the shopkeeper kept adding to the tropical decor. Shoppers always remembered the candy emporium with the Jamaican flag, and easily amused tourists liked to Instagram selfies in front of it. In turn, the flag became something of a de facto landmark—*Turn right at the Jamaican-flag store.*

A bell clanged above the shop entrance as Omar opened the door. The bitter smells of salt and sugar wafted from the barrels. The elderly shopkeeper in a gray djellaba glanced up from the counter, his hair a white halo. "*Ahlan wa sahlan,*" he said. Omar was too laser-focused to reply. He marched down the aisle and, sure enough, spotted a red wire rack in the back, filled with a selection of old Caribbean postcards.

"You like?" the shopkeeper asked. "Twenty-seven years ago, people said I was crazy. I took my very first vacation . . ."

"Yes, I know, sir." Omar tucked the ball of shirts under one arm so he could flick through the postcards. Halfway down the rack—only a few were left, warped and yellowed—he located a stack of postcards boasting a chalky beach with tilted red letters: *The Only Thing Missing in Jamaica Is You.* Omar grabbed one and turned to the clerk, realizing as he did so that he no idea what Cate's brother looked like.

"Sir, did an American man stop in to buy this postcard? A little over a month ago?"

"Americans love those postcards," the shopkeeper swore. On the wall above him hung a framed photo of the pre-doomed World Trade Center. "My postcards are vintage, my son, very rare."

"No, not a tourist. I'm talking about an American who lived in Cairo." Omar tried describing a male version of Cate. "Dark hair, tall, handsome, white skin, American looking. Healthy teeth. His name was Eric."

The shopkeeper raised his finger in exclamation. It took Omar a second to realize that the shopkeeper was, in fact, pointing up. "You mean Eric, my tenant? He used to rent one of the upstairs apartments. I haven't seen him in months. He was such a nice man. How is he?"

Chapter 12

CAIRO

The walls of the Grand Nile's dining room were covered in arcadian French-colonial murals of the river delta, swirling with lotus flowers, palm fronds, and papyrus leaves. To stand bleary-eyed in the entryway for the breakfast buffet was to momentarily forget the hotel's 1980s skyscraper provenance and deem the room's industrial-metal tables and white-plastic chairs a betrayal of the bygone elegance. But of course it was the walls that were the lie, the tables and chairs the truth. As the hostess led Cate toward an empty table near a party of wailing toddlers and red-faced Russians, Cate scanned the room for a quieter option. An arm rose from the sidelines—Matthias Vos alone at a table for two.

He must have just sat down, for he was still holding his sunglasses case while a waiter poured coffee into his cup. It was the promise of coffee and the distance from toddlers, more than the Dutchman's company, that propelled her toward his table. Matthias was wearing a wrinkled light-green linen suit, the color and texture of a wadded American dollar. He looked more handsome dry and dressed. The slicked-back hair turned out to be his style. She could make out the individual grooves of his comb.

"We make a good team," he said as she sat down opposite him. "One procures the table, the other reaps the benefits."

The waiter poured her a coffee and asked if they were opting for the buffet. Cate and Matthias nodded in unison, and the waiter, mistaking them for a couple, asked for their room number. Matthias paused, raising a mischievous eyebrow.

"What is our room number, dear?"

"Room nine-oh-nine," she said, playing along with the joke. "Remember, you specifically requested a room with *no* Nile view."

"Oh, yes, that's right!" He laughed and turned to the waiter, speaking to him in fluent Arabic. Matthias must have explained the mistake, because the waiter nodded with a humorous snort. "Seriously," he said, turning back to Cate. "I'm happy to pay for—"

"No. You got our drinks yesterday. I can buy breakfast." She smiled to the waiter. "Nine-oh-nine. *Shukrun.*"

Together they foraged the buffet table set with steaming chafing dishes, bowls of overripe fruit, and sugary pastry platters. It struck Cate queasily that the only reason she could be so cavalier about buying a stranger breakfast was because of the impending Polestar settlement. For her whole life she'd maintained the necessary habit of mentally recalibrating her checking account after every purchase, and now Eric's death had released her from that compulsion. She wanted to remember that sacrifice, and not grow content by the warm hug of money.

"I wouldn't if I were you," Matthias warned as she scooped fresh salad onto her plate. "That lettuce is pure water. I've witnessed many a vacationer go down for the count after gorging on that lethal substance. Stick with eggs. Or if you like mashed beans, try the *ful.*"

Cate decided to subsist on a few bread rolls. Matthias went heavy on fried eggs and sausage links, and back at the table she watched him cut up all of his food into bite-size chunks before eating. It was a tendency she'd noticed in parents with young children, accustomed to cutting their food for them, and she wondered if Matthias had kids at home in Amsterdam.

"How did it go yesterday?" he asked.

"How did what go?" Frazzled, Cate tried to recall the lie she'd told him on the terrace. All she could picture about yesterday evening was Lucas Keulks running down the alley in the dark.

"Your sightseeing," he reminded her. "What did you get your eyes on?"

She chewed on a roll to stall for time. The risk of a friendship with Matthias meant stretching lies over several days, inventing pyramids she'd climbed. "I messed up the times. Everything was closed."

"You need a guide. I've already offered. I guess I'm offering again, if you're free today."

"Actually, I'm booked. I'm meeting up with a few friends—or really, friends of friends." That sounded like a lie, but it wasn't. Before Cate had come down for breakfast, she'd taken advantage of two pieces of information Lucas had supplied. First, she emailed the attaché at the American embassy, asking if she'd like to meet for coffee. Elizabeth Skyler had admitted knowing Eric "in passing," but Lucas had hinted that they'd been more than mere acquaintances. The second course of action had proved thornier. According to Lucas, Eric's bosses, the Driscolls, were staying at the Ramses Sands. When she googled Kurt Driscoll and found him on the "About Us" page of the Polestar Industries website, he was described as "chief regional executive for the Middle East and North Africa, concentrating on strategy and growth." She also learned that Kurt, his wife, Maura, and their son, Roe, were longtime residents of Lenox, Massachusetts, a thirty-minute drive from Cate's village of New Marlborough. It seemed bizarre to travel halfway around the world to summon the courage to call a Berkshire neighbor.

Cate dialed the Ramses Sands with the nervousness of a dare. It was conceivable that Kurt Driscoll had ordered her kidnapping at the airport. If so, that meant he already knew she was in town. And if he wasn't yet aware of her presence, it wouldn't stay a secret for long.

She asked the hotel operator to connect her to the Driscolls' room. "Hello?" an American woman answered. Cate asked for Kurt and was told he was out. She decided to come clean and identity herself.

"Oh, oh my goodness," Maura Driscoll kept repeating. "You've come all this way! I'm afraid Kurt flew to the desert this morning with his work team. He won't be back for a few days. But he'll certainly want to meet you." There was a pause. "Listen, Cate? Is it Cate? I was fond of your brother. From what I knew of him, he was a good person. I'd love to invite you over for an early lunch. You could come here if you'd like. We have a terrace. Wait, oh my god, of course you don't want to come to this hotel. I'm so sorry. That was incredibly insensitive. Let me think of a restaurant . . ."

Cate assured Maura that meeting at the Ramses Sands wouldn't upset her, and after another dithering round of apologies, it was settled that Cate would come to the hotel at eleven. Before hanging up, Maura paused again and said, "You know, I think Kurt knows you're here."

Such transparency surprised her. "Really?"

"He said something last night about your brother's case, about how it hadn't been resolved to his satisfaction. I mean, in terms of the family—*of you*. He must have learned you were in town."

For a second Cate could almost convince herself that Polestar wasn't the nefarious, cold-blooded organization she'd presumed it to be. Almost.

"See you at eleven," she'd told Maura.

Across the table, Matthias was now finishing his eggs and dropped his napkin on his plate. "A drink this evening?" he proposed. "In the hotel bar?" He stood and slipped on a pair of aviators. He looked less friendly with his eyes blocked out. She didn't trust him.

"What kind of business did you say you were in?" she asked, staring up at her dueling reflections in his brown lenses.

He smiled down at her. "I am an abstract painter. I create possibilities." He pressed his fingers on the edge of the table, their tips turning chalk white from the pressure. "Leave me a message if tonight works for you."

*   *   *

At the front desk of the Ramses Sands, Cate was greeted by the young receptionist who'd helped her the previous evening. She wore her hair back in two silver barrettes and hobbled as she retrieved a fax from the back room. Cate wanted to ask if she'd seen Lucas return to the hotel last night or leave with his work unit this morning. But it seemed unwise to mention the tech in the same breath as the Driscolls, especially since Lucas had demanded she not utter his name at all.

The receptionist called Maura to announce her and instructed Cate to take the elevator to the fifth floor.

"Any room number?"

"It's the penthouse," the receptionist said. "The Driscolls have the whole floor."

There was only one elevator off the lobby, a cramped wooden cabin with a surveillance camera suspended in the corner. As the car ascended past the third floor, Cate held her breath, just as she and Eric had when driving by cemeteries as kids. What had been the logic behind that superstition? An irrational fear of inhaling death? Surely, the hotel had scrubbed down 3B after the police investigation and had rented out the room to dozens of guests in the past month,. Visitors from all over the world had slept and watched television and fucked and ordered room service inside that room, a petri dish of hundreds of human DNA profiles that had dwelled there after Eric's death. There would be no trace of her brother left, no ghosts haunting 3B, nothing to breathe in even if she wanted to.

Maura was waiting for her in the fifth-floor hallway, its beige walls lined with framed Napoleonic sketches of the Pyramids. The woman wore no makeup, her bony, moisturized face glowing with a light suntan. She was probably only five years older than Cate. She had a long, lean body in white jeans and a cream sweater, and her thick brown hair fell over her left shoulder. Cate had the uncanny sense that she'd seen Maura before, recently, but she couldn't pinpoint the circumstance. Lost in the struggle to recall, Cate moved through a hug and a round of condolences without quite taking either action in. Maybe she'd seen this woman in the Berkshires? Maura Driscoll possessed the kind of self-possessed athleticism endemic to women of that region, the long-distance lake swimmers, the year-round root-vegetable gardeners, the women who woke at five to jog the country roads in reflector vests. She belonged to that breed of wealthy, hale, entitled New Englanders who had impressed Cate so much as little girl, the tenacious, pampered women that her mother used to clean for and complain about.

"I've ordered up some sandwiches," Maura said, "but if you don't want to sit outside . . ."

"Outside is perfect."

Maura smiled at Cate's agreeability and opened a security door at the end of the hall. It brought them out onto the tarry roof-top. The dusty city skyline ran in all directions, although needling glass high-rises blocked a view of the river. To the east the sprawl of tawny cement buildings kept going until it ventured beyond the limits of Cate's nearsightedness. Around a corner, a section of the roof had been transformed into a private courtyard for a low-ceilinged penthouse, its living room and kitchen hidden behind sliding glass doors. Persian rugs quilted this section of the roof, their elaborate designs faded by years of sun into stale pinks and beiges, like cartoons leached of their color in old newspapers. Closer to the sliding glass, a long wood table stretched under the shade of a yellow awning. When Cate used her hand to brim her eyes, she saw a copper-haired teenager sitting at the table, fiddling with a piece of rope. The sight of him unlocked the memory of where Cate had previously seen Maura. She and this young man had en-tered the lobby of the Grand Nile yesterday afternoon, bypassing the metal detectors. She remembered the shine of his hair, the color of a penny. The only missing member of their trio was the little boy.

The young man began to rise to his feet, but Cate lifted her voice to stop him. "Please don't get up."

He smiled at her in gratitude, dropping back on the bench. "I'm Roe," he said in a startlingly deep pitch for his boyish frame. "Short for Roosevelt, but no one calls me that." He had his mother's li-oness leanness, with long limbs and sharp darts of shoulders and hipbones. Maura palmed his head with maternal affection as Cate took the empty bench on the other side of the table. Belatedly, as if remembering to play the part of a sullen teenager, Roe swatted his mother's hand away, but Cate could sense that they were close. Perhaps being so far away from home did that to a family—glued them together.

Maura nudged in next to her son and pressed a plate of sand-wiches on Cate. She took one, wary of the lettuce that peeked between the bread slices. Maura glanced somberly at Roe. "You didn't know Eric very well, did you?"

"No, not well," he said, his eyes focused on the complex knot he was constructing halfway along the piece of rope in his hands. "But we talked from time to time. He was a really nice guy." He looked up at Cate. Perhaps she was getting old, but the pimply, angelic face of this boy offering sympathy nearly brought her to tears. "It's so sad what happened. Did Polestar fly you over? Is that why you've come here?"

"No," Cate replied, cautious with her words. She couldn't risk jeopardizing the settlement agreement by accusing Polestar of complicity in his murder. "I came on my own. Just to be here. To see the city where Eric spent his last weeks."

Maura waited for Cate to finish answering Roe's question before she chided him for prying. "Cate doesn't need to explain herself to us," she said. "Unless she wants to. And Roe, I beg you, enough with the knots. You're driving me crazy!"

Roe laughed, a boy's crooked grin breaking across his face. He coiled up the rope and set it on the table. "Sailor's knots," he explained to Cate. "I can do nearly a hundred varieties. But the boatmen on the Nile who sail the feluccas use these really gnarly knots that I haven't been able to master yet. I just started taking lessons in how to sail the feluccas."

"Roe is an expert sailor," Maura bragged.

"Name a knot," he challenged Cate.

"I don't know any," she admitted and caught a brief flare of satisfaction on the teenager's face, as if he'd correctly gauged her limitations.

"It's like learning a language," he said, "the way the locals ride the water. There are crazy currents in the Nile that make it tricky for sailing. Have you been on a felucca yet?"

"I just arrived yesterday."

"Cate is from the Berkshires," Maura said.

"I figured." Roe didn't sound that interested. "We are too, I guess, although it's been so long I don't feel like it's home anymore."

"Did you go to Brightwell?" Cate asked. Roe seemed roughly the same age as Willie. Cate figured he wasn't the type to matriculate at Monument Mountain like she and Eric had. "My sister went there—"

"I went to Bailey's all-boys in Lenox. But I sailed on Brightwell's lake for a few summers as a kid. Fake lake. Training-wheel boats."

"My stepfather is the groundskeeper there," Cate said with a laugh.

Roe blushed and tried to backtrack from his unintended insult. "The grounds are so nice! It's Western Mass that's the problem. There's no real wind there. You need the sea or a river for sailing."

"Don't be such a boat snob," Maura scolded.

"Well, I don't miss home, Mom!" Roe whined with aggrieved sincerity, as if picking up an ongoing argument between them. "I like being out in the world. Can't I be honest about that? If you think I'm a snob, it was Lenox that made me that way." Maura smiled over at Cate in apology, and Roe, aware of his rudeness, gave a checked frown. "I'm sorry. I didn't mean to be so harsh about the Berkshires. I know it's your home."

"Actually, I live in New York now."

The crooked grin returned. "Ahh," he said with appreciation. "Now that's a *real* place. Where exciting things happen and everyone doesn't know each other already!" Cate always experienced a rush of pride whenever a young person acknowledged the eminence of New York City, as if she could claim a hand in its radioactive cool. Willie, who wore her father's Crocs around the house and refused to brush her hair, never took the slightest interest in her stories of living in the wilds of Manhattan. Sometimes it seemed to her that New York remained the center of the universe only so long as the youngest person in the room believed that to be the case—even one like Roe, already sailing feluccas down the Nile in Cairo.

Roe's eyes shifted to the glass doors behind Cate's back, and she heard the doors creak open. She turned to find the little boy from yesterday peering out. "Mom, can I watch—"

"We have a guest, Saad," Maura replied in slow, overinflected syllables.

Cate smiled at Saad. He shyly stared down at his tiny sandals, which he began to kick lightly against the doorframe. "Hello," she tried.

"Cate said hello," Maura prompted. "What do you say in reply?" The boy said nothing, and Maura turned to her older son with a sigh. "Can you turn on a cartoon for your brother? But you both need to leave for the clinic in half an hour, so start the cartoon toward the end of an episode."

"See, Cate, I'm not a snob," Roe said as he climbed from the table. "I babysit my brother. I teach refugees to drive tuk-tuks." Cate nodded approvingly, although she didn't catch the last reference.

"The closing credits rolling in fifteen minutes would be ideal," Maura said. "And help him get changed."

Roe scooped up his coil of sailor's rope. He then turned to his little brother and quickly transformed into a monster with wicked claws raised high and a gremlin's face. Saad, screaming in terrified delight, disappeared inside the penthouse, and Roe chased after him. Things inside toppled; doors slammed. The sounds of boys at play.

Maura waited until they were safely gone before reaching into a fabric purse on the table for a pouch of tobacco and rolling papers.

"Sorry about that. Roe's at that age where I never know which son I'll get in the morning."

"He seems very nice," Cate said.

"He was supposed to attend college back in the States this past September. It's partly my fault he didn't, and Kurt still blames me. We had already deferred his enrollment once." Maura nodded her head as if anticipating a lecture. "*I know.* He's almost twenty. He should be in school." She sprinkled tobacco across the thin strip of paper to fashion a cigarette. "Roe got cold feet about dorm life, and I relented. Okay, I might have encouraged him to stay. But I feel like he has this amazing opportunity to learn about the world firsthand, which no college would ever be able to teach in a classroom. Do you know what I mean? It can be so stiflingly comfortable back in America. And, yes, I'm aware that learning to sail a felucca isn't Intro to Philosophy. Volunteering with refugees isn't a sociology credit. But it's much more nourishing, don't you think?"

Cate couldn't tell whether Maura had simply been abroad for so long that she was starved for idle conversation with a fellow American or whether she was intentionally trying to put Cate at ease by dancing around the subject of Eric. But Cate saw certain advantages in befriending Kurt's wife.

"I wish I had traveled more at Roe's age," she agreed.

"Exactly!" Maura said and licked the edge of the rolling paper. "Kurt accuses me of being a hippie." She rolled the cigarette between her fingers. "Maybe he's right. But honestly, at heart, I think I'm just a born nomad."

"It must be hard to be a hippie when your husband works as a weapons executive." The observation sounded more insulting than Cate had intended, and she rushed to soften its sting. "I mean, it's a sobering career, in terms of war and repercussions."

Maura stuck the cigarette between her lips and clicked her lighter. "I get what you're saying," she mumbled. As she drew on the cigarette, she shut her eyes briefly against the smoke. "If you had told me when I was Roe's age that I would end up marrying an arms contractor, I would have spat in your face. God, I was only a couple years older than Roe . . ." She stared up at the brown sky, smoke streaming from her nostrils as she performed the equation in her head. "Wait, how old was I when I went to Algeria?" She nodded at her own answer. "I was twenty-two when I went over as a volunteer, basically trying to get weapons out of every counter-insurgent's hands. That's how dedicated I was to disarmament back then. It was such a brutal civil war."

"Wow," Cate said, genuinely impressed. "So what happened? When did you stop spitting in faces?"

"I got pregnant," Maura said, "and then I fell in love."

"That's an interesting order," Cate replied with a laugh. "It's usually the other way around."

Maura took a drag from her cigarette. "No, you mean it's usu-ally *told* the other way around. But that's not always the way it goes, is it? I don't know if you have kids, but having one shifts your perspective. I had Roe in a bombed-out hospital right out-side of Algiers. And, yeah, after he came along, I realized, 'Oh, I actually am in love with Kurt.' " She picked a piece of tobacco from her tongue. "Kurt was working for the US government at the time, stationed in Madrid. He was trying to figure out how to stop the violence in Algeria too. We were both invested in ending the bloodshed, just from vastly different angles, and we had a lot of passionate fights about the definition of intervention and foreign aid. Remember when you could fight in bed about the state of the world? We were that young. Anyway, we married, and eventually moved to the Berkshires for Kurt's job, and now here I am, twenty years later, the wife of a weapons executive."

Cate winced. "I didn't mean to imply—"

"To tell you the truth, I've been in more conflict zones than

Kurt ever has. But the thing that's crucial to understand"—Maura leaned in, propping her elbow on the table, her cigarette pinched in her fingers—"and I say this so that you can respect what your brother did for a living as much as to justify myself, is that it's not as black-and-white as you think. It took me a long time to get my head around that fact. But the situation is not as simple as, defense contractors are prowar and antipeace. Sometimes, believe it or not, it's an arms trade that ensures peace. You don't need to look further than Israel and these miraculously solicitous peace treaties that are popping up with the Arab states. Why would a country like the UAE agree to make peace with their enemy? The answer is, for access to Polestar cruise missiles. It's shockingly straightforward—at least, I'm shocked by how straightforward it is. The real currency among all these rulers is weapons. You want a meaningful sign of change from the egomaniacal dictator, you let him buy a fleet of M1 Abrams tanks. Or you threaten an arms embargo where he can't access the infrared lenses he needs for all his radar systems. Suddenly, surprise, they're holding democratic elections and citizens are allowed to congregate in parks again. Suddenly there's a cease-fire conversation that might end in a handshake. That's due to weapons. They don't have to explode to be effective."

Cate couldn't decide whether Maura had been brainwashed into believing that Polestar was an agent of peace or whether there was a sliver of truth to her reasoning. Cate wished she could have replied with the litany of abuses that Polestar had inflicted on her family, starting with their cover-up of Eric's death. But she was not going to make an enemy out of Maura Driscoll. She'd save those accusations for Kurt.

"How did Saad come to join your family?" Cate asked.

Maura allowed herself one last drag before dabbing out the cigarette in a tin ashtray. "That's what I'm most proud of. Polestar isn't a perfect institution. But it really has given back. That includes donating supplies and infrastructure to relief organizations, funding refugee camps and medical clinics, that sort of thing. I've gotten pretty invested in those endeavors over the last years. I pushed my way in, really, 'the boss's wife,' " Maura admitted with a laugh. "In fact, that's where the boys are going this afternoon, to work at a community center here in Cairo that Polestar sponsors for refugees, primarily kids and young adults. We call it the clinic, but it's so much more than that. The Polestar techs volunteer there too. Your brother did. You should come for a visit."

The cynic in Cate admired the proliferating life cycle of Polestar altruism: the company provides the weapons that destroy the villages, and then it helps the survivors who didn't die in the rubble to piece their shattered lives back together again. Soon another season of bombs awaits them, and on and on the cycle goes. It reminded her of the diagrams in grade-school science books: seeds sprouting into flowers, to generate seeds, before the plant wilts into compost to nurture the next budding stem. Still, it gladdened Cate to hear that her brother had volunteered.

"What did Eric do at the clinic?" she asked.

"Oh, a lot of it is just drawing with the kids or playing checkers while practicing English. Basic contact, time shared, refamiliarization. The Polestar workers get a lot out of it too. There's a little bonus every year from the company for those who volunteer, but that's not the incentive. They're not just fixing missiles. Eric was helping the community."

A child's shriek erupted from inside, followed by a rueful teenage laugh.

"You asked about Saad," Maura said. "There are so many children at these camps. You armor your heart the best you can when you visit. I do. I try to. But when we were in Oman two years ago, I visited one of the shelters that Polestar sponsors. I won't get into the horrors of what happened to Saad's parents in Yemen, or how he and his sister managed to flee. The sister later went missing. But I kept returning to this camp to spend time with a quiet little toddler who slept in my lap." Maura reached across the table toward her fabric purse but retracted her hand, balled into a fist, caught in a struggle to forgo a second cigarette. "We adopted him, and that's our Saad. And even though it wasn't the point of our adopting him, Saad brought Kurt and me closer together too. We'd sort of been wandering away from each other before he came along. Maybe that's the reason I pulled Roe out of Bailey's in Lenox and had him come here to live with us. I wanted a full family again."

Cate hadn't been prepared to like Maura. Yet she did. Maura stared at her with focus. "You know, you and Eric look alike. Do people tell you that?"

"More when we were younger."

Maura inhaled deeply. "What are you hoping to find here? I'm guessing you're looking for answers to his suicide. I know you signed an NDA, but you can tell me. We're off the record."

"Okay." Cate decided to take her up on the offer. "Do you really think his death was suicide?"

Maura tilted her head. "I didn't know Eric well enough to say. The news shocked me. But I heard later from some of the techs that he'd been drinking and acting erratically. He was divorced recently, right?"

"That was three years ago. It had nothing to do with his state of mind."

Maura nodded. "I think Lucas Keulks was a close friend. Kurt told me that he was interviewed by the police. Have you spoken to him?"

"Not yet," Cate lied, abiding Lucas's demand not to be implicated. She slipped her fingers under her shirt collar to gather up the St. Anthony. But as she did so, a child's "Mawm!" wailed from inside.

"Oof." Maura rose from the bench. "Let me play sheriff for a moment."

Cate took the opportunity alone to check her phone. She was hoping for an email from Elizabeth Skyler about coffee but instead found a text from Omar. It had arrived only a few minutes ago.

I solved Jamaica. Want me to drop by your hotel?

Her fingers were clumsy in her hurry to respond: I'm at Ramses Sands. Meet me in lobby in ten minutes? She added giddily, Thank u thank u!!!

Maura returned, shaking her head. "Saad managed to strait-jacket himself in a turtleneck."

Cate pulled the pendant from her collar and held it up. "Do you recognize this?" Maura gently took it in her palm, her knuckles grazing Cate's neck.

"Is it a saint?" she asked.

"St. Anthony."

"Oh, lost things. It's beautiful."

Cate knew it wasn't beautiful. It was hardly of any value, per-haps one degree more expensive than the trinkets given out to children. "It was returned with Eric's possessions," she said. "We got so few things back. Not even his phone or wallet. But this medal was returned, which is strange because none of us remem-ber him wearing it. I thought he might have picked it up here in Egypt."

Maura took a closer look, flipping it over. "Huxley," she whis-pered, rubbing the engraved name with her thumb. "You know what? It could have come from the clinic." She gently let it drop onto Cate's chest and stepped back, smiling down with such a ma-ternal expression that Cate half expected the woman to tuck a mis-placed strand of her hair behind her ear. "We get a lot of Christian groups donating books and clothes. They like to sneak in religious

items—a cross, a saint's card, a prayer book. They're always pros-
elytizing. I wouldn't be surprised if Eric picked it up there. That's
my guess."

"It makes sense," Cate agreed. "Maybe I will come for a visit."

Maura's eyes drifted up and froze on a point across the roof.
Cate turned to see a young woman wearing fatigues, standing on
the far edge of the Persian rugs, her brown hair short and wispy,
her black boots gleaming in the sun. She held a notebook in her
hand, and Cate wondered whether it was the same variety of work
notebook that Eric had used to write his damning confession.

"Sorry to interrupt," the woman said in a thin, glassy voice. She
ran her hand nervously through her hair.

"It's no problem, Ivers," Maura replied. "I'm here with a friend.
With Eric Castle's sister, in fact. Have you two met?"

Cate waved to Ivers, unsure whether that was her first or last
name. The woman stared back with a blood-drained face, as if
startled by her presence. "Eric was a friend," Ivers murmured, before revising that assessment. "A coworker. We all miss him." She
quickly redirected her attention back to Maura. "Ma'am. I'm here
because I just got a call from Siwa. They're having trouble locating
a tech, so I need to fly out to handle this afternoon's tests. That
means I can't take Roe and Saad to the clinic."

"Having trouble locating a tech?" Maura repeated, frowning.
"What do you mean? Someone overslept or . . ."

Ivers glanced at Cate before answering, as if acknowledging the
breach in protocol in speaking in front of her. "Lucas Keulks. He
helicoptered out with Mr. Driscoll and the rest of the team at five
this morning. He made it out to the desert all right, but he never
showed up for the drill at ten thirty. No one's seen him since the
hotel in Siwa. They need me to fill in because I know the code
order."

"That's unsettling news." Maura turned to Cate. "And we were just speaking about Lucas. But no problem, Ivers. I'll take the boys over."

Ivers offered a consolatory frown to Cate. "Again," she muttered before leaving, "sorry for your loss."

Maura pressed her palm to her forehead. "I have to get the boys ready." She looked down at Cate and gave a warm smile. "But I hope we can talk again. And please do visit the clinic so I can show you around." Cate nodded as she grabbed her purse. "In the meantime, I'll let Kurt know you're here."

Cate rose from the table and lingered in front of her host. As if on cue, the two lurched toward each other, laughing as they managed a half-formed hug.

"I'm staying at the Grand Nile," Cate said.

"I know it well," Maura replied. "It's so close that we actually have a deal to use the gym and pool. Ramses is a bit short on amenities, as you might have noticed, but we like to stay here with the team. Maybe we can have a lunch there one day. They have a lovely back garden."

Cate crossed the patchwork of rugs. As she waited for the elevator, her head felt crowded with tiny scraps of information that Maura had given her. But all of that paled against the news that Lucas Keulks had gone missing in the desert. It couldn't be a coincidence that he vanished on the morning after their confrontation. *The weapons worked,* he had sworn to her. Cate did not hold her breath as she rode the elevator down.

Chapter 13

CAIRO

Tourists, loud and sunburned, swarmed the lobby of the Ramses Sands. Outside an enormous tour bus idled on the curb, while inside, bellhops struggled to separate mounds of airport-tagged luggage. Cate reached for her phone to text Omar but spotted him standing at the reception desk, leaning against the counter with one foot kicking absentmindedly against the floor. As she crossed the lobby, she realized he was consumed in a conversation with the young receptionist. Not wanting to interrupt, she waited off to the side as the receptionist giggled and blushed through Omar's jokes. The encounter held a current of flirtation, and Cate wondered whether she'd been wrong about Omar's sexuality. When he happened to glance over and notice her, he drew himself up at the desk. "Ah, there you are. I was waiting for you!" He seemed oblivious to the damage he'd just inflicted on the poor receptionist's hopes.

As the young woman sized Cate up with a look of crushed disappointment, Omar turned to offer her a breezy goodbye. "Great to meet you, Farida," he said in English.

"You too!" she replied with too much blatant eagerness. "*So* nice to meet you!" She added a last remark in Arabic, which bought a laugh from Omar.

Outside, the tour bus's motor was rumbling with such ferocity that Cate couldn't hear what Omar was telling her. The call to prayer hummed around them with a distorted crackle, and she had to loop wide on the sidewalk to avoid a stray dog puking up a crust of bread. ". . . the same music school!" she managed to catch Omar saying as he gestured toward his car down the block.

She waited until they were both sealed in the car to ask him what he'd been trying to tell her.

"That receptionist, Farida," he said, "she went to the same music school as my sister. Not at the same time, but they had a summer program in common."

"Well, she definitely had a crush on you," Cate retorted, attempting to pay him a roundabout compliment.

"No, no." He shook his head. "You misunderstand. It's not like that. She was just very nice."

"Omar, I know flirting when I see it, and believe me, she was—" Cate stopped when she caught the pained expression on his face, the look of a man drowning, and realized her compliment had veered far off target.

"It's not like that," he repeated, tightening his hands on the steering wheel. "It's not like that for me. With her. With women."

She nodded. "I understand."

"It's a guy that I want to see again in Berlin. His name is Tobias." Omar gave an involuntary smile when uttering the name, as if even that passing reminder of him conjured pleasure. It was the same reaction Cate used to give when reciting Luis's name. "That's how it is for me. Except, with this guy, it's stupid."

"It usually is," she said. "I would hate for it to feel sensible, though. Wouldn't you?"

He gave a quiet laugh. "Tobias isn't exactly waiting for me. I send a few messages. He doesn't respond. That's mostly been our pattern since I've returned to Cairo."

Omar turned the key in the ignition, and the car began to quake. Cate had to clamp her teeth together to prevent them from jittering. He ground the stick shift into drive, and just then Cate glanced out the window and noticed two teenage boys in green djellabas holding hands as they walked on the sidewalk. She knew to take this gesture as a sign of friendship and not romance, but it saddened her, how comfortable men here were about showing physical tenderness, while homosexuality was condemned. Meanwhile, back in America, even in free-spirited New York, two male friends would never casually hold hands in public; physical contact there always carried the insinuation of sex. The world was a muddle when it came to human contact, every single side of it, a mess.

"Is it hard to be back in Cairo?" she asked him.

Omar cupped the stick shift's jittery knob. "Like turning into a fossil. Something inert and dry. I love this city, but I can't live here any longer." He studied the side mirror, searching for a break in traffic. "I've applied for a visa. Pray they grant it to me."

"To Germany?"

"Maybe to where you're from."

Honking erupted as Omar tried to pull into the street. They waited as the offended car drove by, its driver gesticulating in manic road rage. More cautiously, he nosed out again and sped toward the red light at the end of the block. The car smelled of his bitter cologne, which she'd grown to like, and as he braked, she caught the box of tissues that slid from the dashboard. Her mind was swimming with possible ways she could help Omar secure an American visa. His aunt possessed far more clout in New York than she did. Nevertheless, she pictured the drawer of letterhead at Upper East, and a few power players within the benefactor orbit whom she could tap for a favor. "If you need impressive recommendation letters," she offered, "I could try to collect a few."

"Really?" Omar shot her a glance. "That would be a big help. Yes, I would appreciate it."

"It wouldn't be a problem," Cate said, although she was already mentally compiling a list of the potential obstacles—like returning to her job at Upper East, for one. She defaulted to the only sure offer a New Yorker could bestow. "No matter what, you always have a couch to crash on in my apartment."

The light turned green, and Omar floored the gas. As he wove them through the lanes of a wide boulevard, he used his free hand to dig through the side pocket of his door and extract a glossy rectangle of paper. He held up the familiar image of a Jamaican beach, the exact same postcard Eric had sent, right down to the tilted red letters across the bottom.

"How did you find it?"

Omar smiled, pleased with himself, and tossed the blank postcard on her lap. "It came from a store in Zamalek. Right over the bridge, not far from my apartment." He shifted gears, his feet dancing on the pedals. "It's a store that sells chocolates and candies, but the owner has it decked out in a Caribbean decor. There's a rack of postcards in the back. I'll drive you over so you can see it."

She studied the card, its faded bands of sun damage only slightly less severe than on the one Eric had mailed.

"I'm an idiot for not thinking of it right away," Omar said as he maneuvered around a bicyclist lugging a washing machine on a wooden cart. "It's right off a busy street in the center of a tourist area. Anyone from Cairo would know this shop." He smiled at her. "Jamaica in Egypt."

"It sells candy? Maybe Eric wanted me to visit the store?"

"No, there's another reason." Sunlight flared through the windshield, and Omar flicked the visor down to block it from his eyes. "It was probably just convenience. Your brother rented one of the apartments above the shop. He kept it for about five weeks before he stopped paying the rent more than a month ago. The shopkeeper doesn't know that he died. He figured Eric had just gone back to the States. I asked how often Eric used it, but he wouldn't tell me. 'I respect the privacy of my lodgers.' You see, he rents those apartments to foreigners with the understanding that he'll be discreet. That's why he can charge so much for rent. It's in his interest to keep his eyes and ears shut. He liked Eric, though, called him *amir awi*."

"I think I know what Eric was using the apartment for." She recounted her conversation with Lucas Keulks, about her brother meeting women in a secret spot across the river, away from Polestar's eyes. "There's a woman who works at the embassy, an attaché, who Lucas implied would visit him there." Cate checked her phone, but there was still no response from Elizabeth Skyler. She decided to try a text: Hi, Elizabeth, did you get my email? Coffee? Today? Please! I'm in town!

Out the window, two bronze lions guarded the mouth of a bridge. Cate hadn't yet seen the Nile, and without warning she was soaring over its span on the Qasr El Nil. The water's surface was a snakeskin of yellow and brown, a near-motionless reptile that extended into the orange haze in the distance. Cigarette-shaped boats floated along its marshy edges. Cate searched for the feluccas that Roe Driscoll had told her about; she thought she spotted one, a single giant fin swerving beyond the next bridge.

There was less traffic on the island. They turned down streets under canopies of thick foliage, making tunnels out of their intertwining branches. It was quieter here, at least enough to hear birdsong. Omar wound them through the island's center, along a park of green that was home to an athletic club, with gated swimming pools and plush soccer fields, past a cluster of antique stores, and men kneeling on prayer rugs in the shade of an alley. He abruptly cut onto a side street and pulled into a parking spot. Across the street, a store sat with a Jamaican flag stretched across its window. There it was, like an X on a map.

"Your brother had the apartment right above the sign," Omar said. "I think that's the real reason the owner keeps the flag in the window. A signal to Westerners that he rents to them. It's like an advertisement saying, 'Don't worry about Egyptian moral scruples here.' "

Cate stared up at a set of darkened windows. "I wonder if it's vacant."

"It is," Omar exclaimed. "I went up to have a look."

She darted her eyes at him. "You went up? Without me?"

"I figured you'd want me to check it out. The shopkeeper didn't want to take me, but I insisted. It's a few hundred American dollars to rent, a lot more than it would cost an Egyptian. But he made it clear, foreigners only. Me, who has lived in this neighborhood his whole life, he wouldn't rent to me. I wouldn't be allowed to—"

"Can I go up?" she asked.

Omar gritted his teeth. "I'm sorry to tell you, there's nothing up there. It's completely empty."

"Are you sure?"

"Yes, quite sure. I checked. The shopkeeper waited three weeks for Eric to pay his rent, and when he didn't return, he went up and cleared everything out that was left behind. The shopkeeper swore it was only scraps, nothing of value. Some papers, a few books, a T-shirt. He said it was the standard junk that foreigners always leave behind."

Cate felt like she'd been punched in the chest. "He threw out everything?"

"He bagged it up and put it out for the trash. He said there was nothing worth saving."

She closed her eyes. The shopkeeper might have deemed those items worthless, but Eric's papers might have contained the answers she was looking for. Why had she waited so long to come to Egypt?

"I'm sorry," Omar said. "That's why I insisted on going up and seeing with my own eyes. The place is stripped bare. The shopkeeper even took out the bed and moved it up to another apartment. There's nothing left but window blinds and a few pots and pans. And I checked the pots and pans! But at least you know where Eric was spending his time. And this proves he wasn't crazy for sending you a postcard of Jamaica. He got it right downstairs."

She was about to agree on that point—at least there was a measure of sanity to this news, Eric had grabbed the most convenient postcard that was available—when her phone began to vibrate in her lap. It was Elizabeth Skyler returning her call, and Cate fumbled to pick it up before it fell to voice mail.

"Hello?"

"I don't have time to meet." The southern lilt was recognizable, but there was none of the attendant warmth that Cate had remembered from their previous phone conversation. It was as if the attaché's kindness diminished with proximity. "I'm sorry you've come all this way. Let me say outright, we're no longer treating Eric's case as an open investigation. It was resolved. I thought I made that clear to you when you called me from New York. I'm not in a position to—"

"I'm only asking for a coffee, Elizabeth. A half hour of your time. It isn't about reopening the investigation."

"Then what is it about?" A fair question.

"I'm staying in Garden City. Do you know where that is?"

Omar waved his hand to signal the foolishness of the question, but Elizabeth was quick to pounce on her ignorance of the city. "That's where the embassy is located," she clucked. What followed was a long, unhappy pause. "Are you free right now?" Elizabeth named a street corner, and Cate repeated it out loud so that Omar could take note. "I'll give you five minutes," the attaché said coolly. "I don't drink coffee."

"Thank you," Cate replied. "What are you wearing, so I can recognize you?"

"I know what you look like."

*   *   *

The giant fortress of the American embassy was protected by a moat of machine guns and roadblocks. Streets that once ran straight to its doors were blocked with fat cubes of reinforced concrete. Palm-fronded villas and minor government agencies surrounded it like a medieval village, the soft targets shielding the prize of central command. Still, from a distance, Cate could see the hulking embassy rising above an orchestra of minarets. The enormous rectangular structure gridded with dark windows looked like an outdated stereo speaker. American marines gathered on the sidewalk near its only entry point, their white vinyl hats shining like ketchup-bottle caps in the afternoon sun.

Elizabeth's proposed meeting point was inside a park that ran along the Nile, a few streets south of the embassy. Omar offered to come along, but Cate figured the attaché would be more inclined to speak if she showed up alone.

The park reeked of burning charcoal from vendors waving palm fans over open grills roasting blackened corn. A broken-down bus slumped on the side of the road, its driver smoking a cigarette on the curb while the passengers waited dutifully in their seats. Boat horns rang mournfully on the water. Cate followed a stone path lined in benches. The park's stretch of green was small, more an exaggerated median strip, and she paused near a patch of grass where women in full niqab knelt on a sheet, fussing over an infant.

"Cate?" a voice boomed behind her. Cate spun around and nearly knocked into a shorter woman in high heels. Elizabeth Skyler had large, light-brown eyes, a stylishly unkempt bob, and vaulted pencil-drawn eyebrows. There was a glittery hint of gold foundation on her dark brown skin. She wore a plastic lanyard around her neck with her State Department ID, and a tapered white blouse with a brown skirt and hose. She kept a hand on her wrist-watch, as if she were timing the five minutes she'd allotted Cate.

"Elizabeth?"

The attaché didn't feel the need to acknowledge the obvious. Despite having claimed to know what Cate looked like, she stared at her with curiosity, as if she had either disappointed or exceeded expectations. Or perhaps, like Maura Driscoll, Elizabeth saw a trace of Eric in her face. "This meeting is off the record," she said matter-of-factly, her southern accent no longer a flowery embellishment. "I'm not telling you anything, but even our being within a foot of each other is off the record. Got that?"

"I'm not a reporter. You don't have to worry."

"That's not why I'm worried."

Cate decided to forgo any attempts at befriending the woman. She extracted the blank Jamaican postcard that Omar had given her from her purse. "You told me that you and Eric had met in Cairo."

Elizabeth eyed the card with suspicion. "I also told you, Cairo's a big city, but there's a small group of American expats living here. I think we met at the Greek Club. So what?"

Cate figured she probably had four and a half minutes left. "You knew Eric better than that, didn't you?" she chanced. "I found the shop in Zamalek, the place where Eric kept an apartment."

"So?" Elizabeth took a step backward.

"A colleague of Eric's told me that you used to meet him there."

The attaché shook her head and searched the park for a place to rest her eyes, anywhere other than on Cate. "You've got your facts twisted up. I'm married. I have a husband in Atlanta."

Cate rolled her eyes.

"It wasn't me! It's true that Eric was seeing a woman who worked at the embassy, an intern. It wasn't a big deal. It ended after a couple weeks."

"Who is this other woman? Can I speak with her?"

It fascinated Cate to watch a stranger invent a lie right before her eyes. "She worked for the economic forum," Elizabeth exclaimed. "She transferred to another embassy. The interns rove around, they don't stay in one place! Anyway, it didn't end nicely between them. I'm sure she wouldn't want to talk to you."

"Why didn't it end nicely?"

Elizabeth shrugged. "Beats me. Ask those folks who run that PR stunt of a refugee clinic where Eric was suddenly *so* busy volunteering all his time." She swept aside a lock of hair that had fallen in her eyes. "Eric was hard to get close to. You probably know that better than anyone. He only let you in halfway, and if you took one more step . . ." She waved her hand dismissively. "It's none of my business."

"Look," Cate said as gently as she could, "I don't care who was sleeping with my brother. I'm just trying to get a sense of his mindset in the days before he was killed. He's been written off as suicidal, but you and I both know he wasn't. I'm wondering if he might have told this intern what he knew or if there was something worrying him."

Cate's gentle approach had been a mistake. It allowed Elizabeth to gather her resolve. "What difference does it make what your brother got up to in his free time?" she hissed, a tiny pebble of spit forming at the corner of her lips. "You could line up all the women he invited to that apartment in Zamalek, and you still wouldn't be an inch closer to the reason he was killed. It's clear as daylight why he died. You snooping into his private life doesn't change that." The attaché glanced around the park before stepping closer. She lowered her voice. "I saw Eric one night, maybe three days before his death. He was sitting alone in a hotel bar, drinking. We weren't on good terms at that point because . . ." Elizabeth closed her eyes as if to block the memory of their ruptured affair. "He waved me over and told me he might need to call on me soon, in a professional capacity. That's all he said. Frankly, I thought he was drunk and was working up an excuse to talk to me. Well, he was *definitely* drunk. I told him he had my cell number, and he could use it anytime, although he never did. I didn't press. As I said, we weren't on good terms."

"What did he want to talk to you about?" Cate asked.

Elizabeth scowled, as if Cate were failing to connect the obvious. "My guess would be that he learned something at work, and it frightened him. Why else would he ask to talk to a member of the State Department on a professional matter? You do that when you need protection." She lowered her eyes to the cobblestones. "Do you know why your brother was a bad fit for his job? He was too ethical, and he liked to talk. He thought all sides should follow the rules. Like there are actual rules by which the sides abide."

She snorted. "Let me spell it out for you, since you're having trouble. Eric worked for a billion-dollar industry that props up the government of the country in which you're currently standing. That industry decides world leaders and redraws the borders on the map. It doesn't get fucked with. It doesn't let someone hold a secret over its head. Or, worse, threaten to walk that secret over to the US embassy. I'm not saying Polestar murdered him. But my hunch is that someone connected to their dealings did. Your brother learned something, and he was too loud about it, and it cost him his life."

Lucas Keulks had drawn the same conclusion: Eric had learned something that he wasn't supposed to know.

"So where does that leave me?" Cate asked. "How do I find out who killed him?"

Elizabeth answered her coolly. "It leaves you nowhere. There's nothing you can do but swallow it." She consulted her watch, indicating that she had fulfilled her promise of five minutes. "I say this with your best interest at heart. We're all expendable. You, me, your brother, every single Polestar employee, that man selling food on the corner, even the president of Egypt, if tides and interests change. We're all a bad headache that can be gotten rid of in a few days. Remember that when you keep asking questions. You seem like a well-meaning person and I'm sorry for your loss, but you aren't wanted here."

Elizabeth didn't say goodbye. She simply stepped into the stream of pedestrians funneling in the direction of the enormous stereo speaker. Cate knew that the attaché was most likely correct—the answer to Eric's murder led further into the midnight world of arms sales than she could possibly follow. But wanted or not, Cate was here, and there was one question that Elizabeth could answer simply by virtue of having seen her brother naked.

"A saint's medal!" Cate called to the retreating figure. "It came back with his possessions. Did Eric wear a medal around his neck?"

Elizabeth didn't slow down or even turn her head. "No," she said, "he didn't," and disappeared into the crowd.

Chapter 14

CAIRO

———————

An elderly tour group brandishing nylon Sinai Sights bags blocked the entrance doors to the Grand Nile. Cate had to wait nearly ten minutes to pass through the hotel's metal detector, and in the lobby the congestion was even worse, the front desk overflowing with check-ins and grousing with short tempers. Cate snaked her way through the melee, whispering apologies. At the elevator bank, a security guard asked to see her keycard before letting her pass. When she finally reached the ninth floor, the hush of the gray-carpeted hallway felt like the most luxurious amenity a hotel could offer. A young man wearing a magenta staff jacket sat in a pink club chair, stationed in the hall to ensure no unchecked-in guests wandered the floors.

"It's a zoo down there," she told him.

"It is always so on Friday. The tours return from Luxor and Aswan, and the new guests arrive by plane. Holy day is our Friday," he added, although Cate couldn't tell whether that fact was relevant to the congestion.

She held up her keycard to prove she belonged. He nodded. "I know, ma'am. Room nine oh nine. Your husband remind me when he retrieve his sunglasses."

She paused. "Husband?"

"Yes, ma'am. After you both leave the hotel, he come back for his sunglasses. The front desk was already too busy, so he bring up the waiter from breakfast. I let him in, not a problem."

"The waiter?" she snarled, remembering their charade of a happy marriage at breakfast. She had been right not to trust Matthias. "I'll be right back," she told the guard.

Inside the elevator, she took a mental inventory of her hotel room. There was nothing of consequence that Matthias could have found—even the postcard she carried with her in her purse. On the eleventh floor, a matronly guard in a magenta jacket sat in an identical pink club chair. Cate hurried by her and proceeded down the hall to room 1103.

"Ma'am, ma'am," the guard called, "I need to see key." Cate located Matthias's door and banged her fist against it. He answered, unshaven, wearing a pair of damp swim trunks. Evidently his lap swimming wasn't merely an excuse to linger around the hotel's communal spaces for an opportunity to meet Eric Castle's sister. Matthias leaned out and waved to the guard.

"Did you find your sunglasses?" Cate asked.

He smiled blamelessly. "Yes, I believe they're in my jacket pocket."

"Did you find anything else of interest in my room?"

He opened the door wider, inviting her to continue the conversation inside. She slipped past him and entered a near replica of 909, except for a larger bathroom and a view of the Nile. A single suitcase was splayed open on the luggage rack, its contents of pants, shirts, and socks rolled into militant rows. Two wet pool towels were balled in a corner. Otherwise, there was nothing to indicate that the room was even occupied, no mess of a person anywhere. Cate sat down on the bed and watched Matthias study her from the doorway.

"I'm sorry I went through your stuff," he said, shutting the door. "I didn't think you were going to take me up on that offer of a drink, and I was running out of patience."

"I take it you know why I'm in Cairo."

"Of course," he said as he walked to his suitcase, in no rush to defend himself now that his cover was blown. He selected a thin light-blue undershirt and slipped it over his head. Then he went to the mini-fridge and yanked open the door. "We can still have our drink. One of the perks of Egypt is that they stock the minibar. Most of the countries I work in leave them empty for religious reasons. Thank god for a secular society! Do you want a vodka or . . ." He fiddled with the tiny bottles on the shelf. "Gin?" When she didn't answer, he chose—correctly—vodka, and poured it into a glass. "I'm glad you booked into this hotel. I've stayed in so many dumps in Cairo. Thank you for picking a good one." He handed her the glass, and to her own surprise, she took it.

"Do you work for Polestar?" she asked. "Did they hire you to make sure I didn't find anything out?"

He gave a sigh as he poured himself a drink. "No, no. You're all wrong. I don't work for Polestar. If anything, I work against them."

She couldn't think of an agency *against* Polestar. Countries had enemies, but private defense contractors seemed to glide through a world with no end of friends and allies, the popular playground bullies of the planet. "You're going to have to be more specific."

"I am an abstract painter." The joke had worn thin, and Matthias seemed to realize its diminished effect. The smile shrunk from his face, and a look of exhaustion replaced it. "I'm a scout, is what I am. I'm hired by weapons companies, or by governments, or occasionally by privately funded militias—sometimes I'm hired by all of them at once."

"A scout," Cate repeated. "I don't know what that means either."

Matthias lowered himself onto the floor next to the minibar. A rectangle of sunlight fell over his hairy legs and left the rest of him in shadow.

"I'm hired to assess opportunities," he explained. "So many of the relationships between governments and suppliers are redundant alliances, grandfathered in from a handshake deal half a century ago by leaders whose parties don't even exist anymore. I'm brought in to find toeholds, to look for cracks of discontent or failing friendships or wandering eyes. Let's say that Qatar likes its line of Lockheed Martin fighter jets, but its missile capacities are outdated, and there's a growing dissatisfaction with the prices of its current supplier. I might advise China to make a play for the contract. Or a Russian company that works out of Uzbekistan. Or a German weapons conglomerate with factories right here in North Africa, where they won't face the same embargo hiccups. My job is to gauge an appetite for the new. I broker possibilities."

"You'll work for anyone?"

Matthias took a gulp of his drink. "You make it sound sinister. Yes, I'm apolitical. I'll work for anyone. But it's really the only way to remain honest. Or a-loyal, as less kind souls have called me. I perform a service for hire. I don't do morality checks. I'm afraid that wouldn't work. I know, I know . . ." He nodded perfunctorily. "I work for killers. But every country is a killer. Yours and mine." Matthias took another gulp, and so did she. Watching another person drink was like yawning; it compelled her to do the same.

"What does your job have to do with breaking into my room?"

"Your brother's death," he said bluntly. "I've been interested in it since the day it happened."

"As an opportunity?" she guessed.

"Well, yes. It was so damn suspicious, it really should have been a bigger flashpoint. An American tech falling to his death from a hotel room in Cairo? Why wasn't there more of a fuss? That should have been a red flag to Egypt about Polestar's practices. Or vice versa, depending upon who killed him. I kept waiting for the inevitable shitstorm in the media. I was sure Kurt Driscoll would get the ax for losing one of his men on his watch." Matthias wiped his hair back, using the condensation from his glass. "But, to my amazement, it all got swept under the rug. Your brother's death was a huge, snarling tiger, and somehow they managed to put a rug over that beast and hide it from the world. Had the full details of his death been made public, I have no doubt it would have prompted a—"

"A toehold."

"Yes," he laughed. "A crack in Polestar's grip on the region. An opening."

Cate understood. Eric's murder should have been good business for Matthias, bringing new contractors to the table with Egypt if the heat on Polestar grew too hot.

"Who are you working for?" she asked. "Who wants to take Polestar's place?"

"I'm on retainer for a number of foreign firms interested in courting Mr. Sisi. It really is only a matter of time. Americans have had a phenomenal run in Egypt, but it can't go on forever. It's already fracturing. The Russians are now being awarded contracts for tanks. Egypt has already pivoted to the Chinese for cyber and tech and to France for jets. Polestar still has a corner on missiles and UAVs, but only because it's too expensive to order replacement parts if not from the original manufacturer. I have a young Indian firm that has the capacity to change the playing field. Imagine," he said with genuine awe, "how radically different the Middle East would be if India had a stake in the game. That could literally shift the center of the world a few meters to the east!"

Cate wasn't interested in envisioning new empires. "How did you even know I'd be in this hotel?"

Matthias reached into the fridge to grab another bottle of vodka. "It's called surveillance capitalism. The people I work for happen to be experts. And just so you're aware, you should assume that everyone knows you're here. Polestar, the Egyptian government, *your* government, some bored intelligence analyst in Beijing. There were a lot of parties interested in the potential fallout from your brother's death. If it had played out correctly, it could have brought about so many exciting changes. I admit, Kurt did a fantastic job handling it." Matthias drained the bottle into his glass. "They must have given your family an awful lot of money to keep you quiet."

Cate ignored the insult. "What were you hoping to find in my room?"

Matthias shrugged. "I thought you might have something about your brother or Polestar that could help encourage Egypt to move in a new direction. Believe it or not, Sisi isn't eager to field questions about a murdered US contractor right now." He gave another sigh. "Shameless, clumsy, intrusive, not to mention rude, but I had to check." He looked up, his face brightening. "But if you do have something that you'd be willing to share, it could be our secret."

Cate smiled angrily at him. "You have a fucked-up job, Matthias. You know that?"

He rotated onto his hip and stretched his legs out, his body bent like a jackknife on the carpet. He sipped his drink in that odalisque position, and a few drops fell on his light-blue shirt, expanding like pen ink.

"For your information, helping to break the Middle East's addiction to American weapons isn't universally considered corrupt. Look what your country has wrought on this region for the past fifty years. Warfare, dust and rubble, cities razed. That's the American legacy, the culture of war." Matthias began swirling his fingertips through the carpet's weft, as if he were drawing in sand. "But if it makes you less disgusted, I'm always threatening to get out. Go back to Amsterdam, take a job at a think tank, consult for an NGO. That's what scouts do when they burn out. The problem is, there's just no money in peace. You can't make a proper living off it. You starve when there isn't war around."

Cate got to her feet and wandered over to the window, pressing her forehead against the chilly glass pane. The sun was starting to set, picking up stray pieces of metal in the rooftops and turning them into lightning. It occurred to her that she'd wasted a vast portion of her life in hotel rooms occupied by damaged men, raiding the minibar, pressing her forehead against the window, watching suns go down and often back up again. She didn't trust Matthias, but he'd been forthcoming enough for her to venture the most pressing question.

"What do you think happened to my brother? Honestly."

"You really want to find out?" he asked, in a tone that suggested the real answer might upset her.

"Yeah." Cate wasn't going to tell Matthias that her brother had reached out to her before he died. She said only, "He would expect me to look for answers. I don't want to disappoint him."

"You can't disappoint the dead, Cate."

"Oh, that's not true."

Matthias nodded and stared down at the carpet. "What do I think happened to your brother? He got eaten by the machine, one way or another. He could have discovered something criminal about Polestar's practices. But just as easily, he could have bruised the ego of an officer in the Egyptian army who decided to take revenge. Or what about someone in his own team who lost their temper in a moment of drunken stupidity? It could have been something that trivial. I wish I knew so I could give you some peace of mind. But if anyone has the answer, it's probably Kurt Driscoll."

"Why would he know?"

"Because . . ." Matthias struggled onto his knees and crawled toward the bed. "Because your brother died in the Ramses Sands." He lifted himself up using the corner of the bed, rising tiredly to his feet. There was a brief vision of the old man that Matthias Vos would one day become, hollowed out, legs spread wide to steady his balance, back slumped. His swimming muscles staved off that fate for now, and he quickly snapped back into his age, broadening his shoulders and straightening his spine. He walked to the suitcase and grabbed a dress shirt and pants.

"What's so important about the Ramses Sands?" she asked as he marched into the bathroom.

"What's so important," he grumbled before shutting the bathroom door behind him. She heard the shower run, and a body moving under its spray for only a minute before it turned off again. The rolled-up clothes, the quick shower—it all pointed to military training, and she wondered what Matthias had looked like as a young Dutch officer, with a tooth not yet missing in his smile. He emerged from the bathroom, tucking in the dress shirt and sucking in his stomach to button the waist of his pants.

"What's so important about Eric dying at the Ramses Sands?" she repeated.

"Polestar always stays there," he replied. "For a reason. The elevator, the hallways, the lobby, it's all monitored by surveillance camera. Every incoming and outgoing phone call is recorded. They're serious about keeping track of their employees. It would be a safe bet that Kurt Driscoll reviewed whatever footage existed from the night your brother was killed. Say it was an angry Egyptian soldier that Kurt saw on video hurrying to your brother's room. Now, he might not disclose what he found. He has good reason to keep the Egyptian military out of hot water. Hell, having that on film could improve relations! But it's worth asking him, isn't it?"

"Driscoll's in the desert," she told him.

"I'm aware." He nodded to his suitcase. "I'm going out there tomorrow. The military is conducting test drills. A few of the ministers have invited me to watch."

"Aren't you working for the competition?"

He smiled. "That's why they invited me. They like to keep everyone vying for their affections. And it's their arsenal. They bought the weapons. They can show them off to whoever they want." Matthias rolled up his sleeves. "Why don't you come with me? I fly out tomorrow at noon. There's room on the plane. We'd stay in a little oasis town called Siwa on the Libyan border, if you don't mind sharing a room. You can corner Driscoll there."

Cate couldn't read Matthias's motives. Perhaps he still hoped she might supply him with evidence that he could use in his negotiations. Or perhaps there was leverage in showing up to a military base with the grieving sister of the dead American. Or perhaps he thought she'd be fun company for a few nights in a shared hotel room.

Matthias sat on the bed to put on his shoes. "I'm afraid I have a work dinner this evening. But come with me tomorrow, yeah?"

Cate thought about Lucas Keulks, who had gone missing in that same desert, and Kurt Driscoll out there too, with the answers she was desperate to glean.

"Are you married?" she asked.

Matthias glanced at her wryly. "Yes," he said. "My wife lives in Amsterdam."

"Kids?"

"Two. One's seven and one's four. My little comets."

"Do you and your wife have an understanding?"

The wry smile frayed at the edges. "Aren't all marriages under-standings?" he dodged. "You don't have to worry about my wife."

In the past, a different Cate would have done whatever she wanted without any consequences. But she didn't want to be that person any longer. She envisioned a family of three going about their lives in the Netherlands, oblivious to actions taking place in a faraway hotel room; it was like blowing up a house by drone strike from thousands of miles away.

"Thanks for the invitation," she said as she walked to the door. "I'll wait to talk to Kurt Driscoll when he's back. I'm thinking I'll take tomorrow off to go and see the Pyramids."

"Djoser over Cheops," he reminded her.

She grabbed the doorknob and paused. "Hey?" she said. "Do you think that footage from the Ramses Sands is stored some-where? The videos and recordings? Do they still exist?"

"Hard to say. Depends on whether someone wanted them saved. Or destroyed."

"The police might still have copies."

"You expect them to keep evidence of a murder that they al-ready ruled a suicide?" He smiled ruefully. "Leave the hotel, Cate. Get to know the city you've flown all this way to visit. Walk around. Breathe in the dirty air. Get lost in the magic of the place."

*   *   *

Cate took Matthias's advice. The next morning she woke early, skipped the breakfast buffet, and asked the valet to call her a taxi. She decided not to burden Omar with hometown world-wonder-hopping, figuring it was smarter to spend his goodwill on more difficult favors. The taxi that pulled up to the hotel was an automotive Frankenstein: black doors, yellow-checkered hood, red fenders, and mismatched back seats upholstered in a sticky vinyl. She asked to be taken to Khan el-Khalili, the famous, sprawling medieval bazaar in the historic district. Starred in her guidebook, it was bound to be a tourist logjam. But for a single day, Cate wanted to play the tourist. She was saving the Pyramids for the late afternoon, when their shadows would grow into long, black arrowheads across the sand.

The taxi was soon mired in traffic. Begging children knocked on the window, but the driver expelled them with a shooing hand. For twenty minutes they sat without moving through a psych ward of nonstop belligerent honking while Cate stared at the same view of a marble mosque, men's shoes lined up in a row at the front door. She used the empty minutes to write an overdue message to her stepfather. She'd been ignoring Wes's daily check-in texts, in part because he and Joy had tried so hard to discourage her from making the trip to Cairo. She'd hoped to wait until she had some vital evidence to send them, proving the merit of her visit, but so far there was nothing tangible, and so she took the opposite tack. I'm fine, going to see the Pyramids, she texted Wes to put their minds at ease. Tell Mom to stop worrying.

The taxi didn't so much arrive at the market as slowly become enveloped, block by block, in Khan el-Khalili's clamoring atmosphere. The guidebook explained that the market was divided into specialty sections, and after bypassing storefronts decked out with brass lamps and copper dishes, the driver deposited her in the land of discount luggage. Hawkers descended on her as she exited the taxi—"Please, for my family, please look! Buy, buy!" She zig-zagged through side streets lined with garagelike shops. Luggage morphed into cane furniture and then on into Chinese toilet paper and Bangladeshi socks; ebony camel statues and alabaster cat gods gave way to inlaid backgammon boards and clay scarabs rubbed in dirt to approximate authentic archaeological discoveries. Antique French Empire furnishings, or artful reproductions, moldered in smoke-stale showrooms. Robed vendors sat cross-legged in store entryways, breaking from their conversations to promise good prices. Down a set of brick steps and through an archway, Cate lingered in front of a shop devoted to fezzes.

In the section of the market reserved for bedding and linens, she stopped to examine a set of apricot napkins and decided to buy them for her mother. A little boy about the same age as Saad Driscoll approached her as she paid, tugging on her sleeve and holding up a few softpacks of tissues. "No *shukrun*." In the next aisle, the boy tried again. "*Kleen*-ex?" She glanced around for an adult he might belong to and spotted an eye staring at her through the gap between two hanging bedsheets. The eye blinked and moved away. Cate gave the boy a five-pound Egyptian note and, grabbing her bag of napkins, hurried through stalls, trying to put distance between herself and the watching eye. After a few min-utes, she turned and looked behind her. Throngs of tourists jostled in the souk. It was a normal Saturday morning, hundreds of shop-pers, and no sign of danger. *You are safe*, she told herself. She forced herself to walk at a leisurely pace, as if she could slow her worries by slowing her steps.

In an open arcade devoted to jewelry, she scanned the velvet trays for saint medals in case she spotted any St. Anthonys. The only trinkets on display were gaudy crustations of fake diamonds and silver cartouches spelling out Western names in hieroglyphics. As she glanced over at the next aisle of jewelry, her eyes fell upon a young man standing not ten feet away. He was staring directly at her, boldly, out in the open, not even trying to hide himself, and the recognition of who he was barreled into her with such force that her hands flew to her chest in protection. There was no question that the young man was Fake Omar from the airport, with his long bony face and scraggly goatee. She had been stupid to think the danger was already behind her, left at the airport days ago. She and the teenager stood frozen, glaring at each other, each a hostage to the other's reaction, with only a long table of glittering merchandise separating them. A smile began to break across his face.

Cate stepped backward, desperate for air, for outside, for a taxi back to the hotel with its fortifying shield of security guards and metal detectors. Those zones of safety seemed so dangerously far away. She broke into a run, rushing down the aisle of rings and chains, pushing past a knot of French women trying on bracelets. The young man kept pace with her in a skipping sidestep along the next aisle. He was fast and determined and spoke the local language. Cate slowed down, and he did too, mimicking her movements, the wide smile tightening on his face. She waited for her chance, and when Fake Omar, too focused on her, knocked into a man pushing a metal cart, she bolted. Tearing as fast as she could down the end of the aisle, she sprinted through a stone archway. She found herself in a vast, bustling warehouse of clothes vendors, the entire room cast in a sickly green tint by its corrugated-plastic ceiling. She fled down a corridor, her shoulders whisking the sleeves of jackets that hung from metal partitions.

She'd been clutching the plastic bag that held her mother's napkins. But now the bag was no longer in her hand, dropped somewhere along her frantic, crisscrossing path. Men whistled at her. One tourist she brushed past cursed at her in American English. That sound of her homeland half convinced her to turn around and plead for help from this tourist. But when she risked a glance over her shoulder, the young man was racing down the aisle not twenty feet behind her, closing the distance. He shouted something— maybe he was asking bystanders to stop her, pretending she was a thief. She wove into the next aisle and darted through a passageway. It brought her out onto a narrow road, and she nearly crashed into three young women in headscarves and tight jeans, who snarled at her before giggling to one another. Cate heard the faint thrum of traffic at the end of the road. She plunged toward that sound, running fast, trying not to imagine a white town car parked at the end with its back door open.

She heard a bang of metal behind her, as if Fake Omar had knocked over a display in pursuit. She didn't dare look back. Ahead, though, she began to apprehend her dire situation. An iron gate cut off the narrow lane from the busy thoroughfare, too high to climb, with curls of barbed wire lacing the top. Her legs started to buckle, accepting the dead end, when she heard a *tssst* off to one side. A haggard man with an unruly beard stood in front of an empty storefront. A birthmark stained his left cheek, and he wore canvas pants and a dingy white turtleneck. He was waving her into the garage space, as if he intuited from her panicked state that she needed a place to hide. At any moment, Fake Omar would appear, trapping her in the dead end. She looked at the old man, at his wrinkled black eyes, and in them she read not threat but concern. She had no choice. She hurried into the storefront's dark interior, which stank of grease and engine parts. The old man followed her and quickly pulled down the clanging metal grate to hide them. A single bulb hung from the ceiling, its weak yellow glow barely illuminating the cardboard boxes that loomed around the garage walls.

"Thank you so much," she managed between breaths, as the old man locked the grate with his foot and turned to face her. For the first time, she noticed that he too was out of breath, as if he'd also just weathered a chase through the market. It didn't make sense that this elderly bystander would be as winded as she was. Panic lodged in her throat. The old man tried to say something, and she caught what sounded like a fragment of her name—*Ait Ast el*. Whatever he was trying to tell her, he gesticulated with both hands, and in the dim light she saw a silver ring glinting on his pinkie. He was the driver of the white town car. And like his teenage accomplice on the other side of the grate, he knew her name.

Cate dove into the airless garage, like a child digging into a closet's recesses in the hope that it contained an escape panel. As she fumbled around boxes, she spotted light seeping from a door in the far corner. By some miracle she made it into the small bathroom, with a gurgling toilet and broken pieces of mirror scattered on the floor. She slammed the door shut and secured it with a metal latch. The door came alive just as she fastened it, rattling as a deep voice—*Ait Ast el, Ait Ast el*—penetrated the wood. The frosted window above the toilet glowed with daylight. Standing on the toilet seat, Cate wrenched it open and felt the cool current of a back alley. Her left knee scraped the frame, breaking skin as she crawled out, and she landed on her right shoulder next to a pile of discarded carpet scrolls. Climbing to her feet, she hobbled down the alley toward that untiring wolf of Cairo life, the busy thoroughfare. Cate waved at the passing cars as if she were welcoming them.

It took the taxi forty minutes to make it back to the Grand Nile. Cate didn't wait for the taxi to clear the security gate. She ran up the driveway and saw Matthias sitting in the back of an idling shuttle van, its side door open. He was staring down at his phone, and she had to yell his name twice to catch his attention.

"What are you doing?" he asked, amused.

"I'm coming with you. Give me five minutes." She tried not to limp as she walked toward the hotel entrance. The desert, where bombs were tested, suddenly seemed like the safest place in the world.

*   *   *

Cate dozed for the first twenty minutes of the flight. The last thing she remembered was a Muslim prayer playing over the plane's PA system while they sat on the tarmac. She woke with her cheek pressed against the window and her bruised shoulder pulsing with pain. Matthias sat next to her. He waited until she committed to consciousness before telling her she'd just missed a spectacular view of the Pyramids from the sky.

The private jet belonged to the Egyptian government. On their way to the airport, Matthias had explained that Sisi had retired Mubarak's fleet of American Gulfstreams and replaced it with a luxury flock of French Falcons—the first sign of his wandering eye. Cate worried about a background security check, but Matthias's invitation cleared them with no more than a trifling paper form that she filled out in pen. The only other passengers on the plane were the wife and three daughters of a government minister, who sat at the other end of the cabin. The wife wore a maroon business suit and spent the flight reviewing legal documents, while her daughters, all but the youngest in headscarves, watched a movie on an iPad. Matthias told her about the oasis where they were headed: the pools where Cleopatra had bathed, the ancient oracle visited by Alexander the Great, the recent droves of the European jet-set who had turned Siwa into an unlikely fashionable resort. Cate was only half listening. When she saw the minister's wife talking on her cell phone, she interrupted him. "Do our phones work up here?"

She typed a quick text to Omar:

I'm going to the desert, but I'll be back in a few days. In the meantime, I have a huge favor to ask.

Chapter 15

OMAR

One of the unexpected consequences of Omar's years living abroad was how much louder his hometown now seemed to him at night. Maybe the family house in Zamalek had thicker walls than those demarcating Mrs. El Fettah's dilapidated kingdom. Or maybe London's pillow of quiet—a drowsy fog pressed over its gassy buses and drunken pub brawls—had lullabied him for too long. Cairo was an alarm bell duct-taped to a hyena running through a field of band saws. Even with his hearing aid charging on the nightstand, the noises crept into his head and kept him from sleep. Most nights Omar stayed home, making himself dinner while phoning his mother in Palm Hills. In their nightly chats she cataloged her aches and pains, perpetually impatient for bed—as if it were an hour on the clock rather than a piece of furniture that she could access any time she pleased. He didn't tell her that his body ached for the very opposite, to go out all night and stay up until sunrise. But Cairo didn't offer the same nocturnal buffet as

London had, and anyway, he didn't have the cash for more than one night a week at foreign hotel bars.

Instead, Omar devoted himself to finishing his American visa application, partly motivated by Cate's promise to secure a few Manhattan-grade recommendation letters. He'd googled Cate's name, and the internet churned up a hodgepodge of party pictures from out-of-order years, with Cate standing beside other attractive, expensive-looking people. He'd stumbled upon a blog that mentioned her dating a famous musician—and while Omar had never heard of the singer, it meant Cate was by-association famous, American famous, which meant world-famous, even if not-in-the-slightest Egypt famous. A check of her Instagram account confirmed the more recent glamour of the art world. The point was clear, Cate had serious connections that might persuade immigration officials to approve him. He felt so confident about the prospect that he texted Tobias the news and included a selfie in front of the Nile. The photo was blurry and looked as if Omar had been caught by surprise, his smile lopsided; it had taken him ten minutes to stage-manage that shot. So far, no ping of a response from the German.

Omar wasn't intentionally avoiding his old school friends. He just found it excruciating to talk to people from his past about the present when his future seemed so unsettled. But on Saturday afternoon he received a text from his friend Ihab, inviting him to a party off Talaat Harb Square. Omar's first instinct was to beg off, but with no response from Tobias and with Cate's "huge favor" that she'd texted weighing on him, he accepted. Apparently Cate was headed to the desert and expecting him to undertake an unpleasant errand he'd rather not think about.

At 8:00 p.m., Ihab picked him up with a prolonged, attention-seeking honk in his parents' new Mercedes. "Whoa, sexy beard!" he teased as Omar climbed into the front seat, and tried to rub

Omar's scruff but was beaten back. For most of the drive they engaged in skittering small talk; anything more consequential proved
impossible with Ihab's bass-quaking hip-hop blasting. Ihab her-
alded from a wealthy Cairene family—his father was the head of
the region's natural gas supplies—but despite the greenish-silver
sports car (the exact color, Omar thought, of fresh pigeon shit),
Ihab lived humbly above his sister's garage on the outskirts of Heliopolis. Ihab had been trying to make it as a deejay since college,
but after lowering the volume on the radio, he described his new
job as a project manager at an advertising agency. Omar found that
news distressing. Even reckless, reality-shirking Ihab had begun
to settle down. Ihab turned up the radio, and Omar let the music
pour over him and erase him from the world.

It turned out that he knew the party's hosts from university. The
newlyweds lived on the fifth floor of a neoclassical monolith that
bowed in the center like the side of a cello. The building looked
onto the grim iron statue of a banker in a wrinkled suit, holding a
rolled newspaper. Today the figure appeared less like a heroic na-
tionalist tycoon than a livery-cab driver waiting for a fare outside
the train station. A creaky birdcage elevator took them up to the
party, located in a rambling apartment that had been passed down
from the hostess's great-grandparents. The wood floors wept with
each step, and built-in bookcases lined the rooms, with dust sneez-
ily covering the volumes. These kinds of apartments served as de
facto family repositories, time capsules of heirlooms that went back
more than a century.

Omar barely had time to pull off his jacket before friends hurried over to hug him or quiz him about London. The hostess,
Nawal, greeted him with a glass of whiskey. "I can't believe you
didn't DM me that you were back," she chided. Nawal had always
been a dear friend, and back at university had even tried to set him
up on the sly with a few men from her program. "How long have

you been here?" she asked. Omar felt the obligation to lie, pushing his return date to a mere three weeks prior, which Nawal still found unsatisfactory, running her black fingernails through her long black hair.

"I have big news myself," she announced, and Omar secretly hoped that it wasn't pregnancy, because Nawal was halfway through her medical degree and by far the smartest person in their graduating class. The news turned out to be a summer residency at a research hospital in Vienna. "Can you believe it? I was sure I'd be denied!" As the hash smoke and Lebanese pop wafted through the den, Omar felt a prick of envy at her upcoming summer of European freedoms. He excused himself to refresh his drink.

The kitchen was the only room in the apartment that had been renovated—disappointingly, it had fallen victim to the character-sucking American penchant for granite countertops and some hideous design precept called "open plan." The counter was sloshed in melted ice and alcohol overpour. Omar didn't need a second drink, but he made one anyway to keep his hands occupied. As he poured the whiskey, he spotted a young man leaning against the pantry on the other side of the room, a plastic cup held to his chest, his head an unruly mane of curly black hair. Omar was caught off guard when the young man glanced over at him and a pulse of a smile enlivened his face, his large brown eyes intense in their stare. Omar felt his cheeks turning red. No, this couldn't happen, and he darted out of the kitchen to join his friends. Five minutes later, however, the nagging reminder of the young man brought him scuttling back in the kitchen on the pretense of needing ice.

The young man hadn't changed position, except that he now held his cup between his teeth while his hands dug through his jean pockets in search of a lighter. He handed it to his friend, who proceeded to light a small metal pipe. Omar didn't like hash. The sticky, resinous substance reminded him of the amber rosin he used on his violin bow as a kid, back before he'd lost half his hearing. He was glad when the young man with the curly mane of hair refused the offer of a hit. Suddenly he looked over at Omar, freezing on him. Omar quickly diverted his eyes, as if he'd been caught staring in the gym showers, and took a coward's quick exit, hurrying into the den to find Ihab.

He was sitting on the arm of a leather couch, talking to Ihab, when the young man ventured into the library. He proved courageous, walking right up to them.

"Ali," Ihab chanted, and the two men exchanged a fist bump. "Do you know Omar?"

"No!" Omar answered for him, too excitedly. He was prepping for a fist bump when Ali thrust his hand out for a proper shake. Ali's fingers were strong, his palm warm, and they kept a tight grip on Omar's hand for a few seconds longer than necessary.

"No, we haven't met," Ali said with a grin. "I'm Nawal's cousin. I just moved here from Asyut."

This stomach-swirling flirtation wasn't supposed to happen, not to Omar in Cairo anymore. He hadn't counted on it, and things he didn't count on, events he didn't spend long hours plotting, did not come to pass here—even the occasional hookup at a hotel bar required an entire evening of patience and a football referee's mastery of reading coded signals. And yet here was Ali from Asyut in his scratchy wool sweater and gray cords with his thick hair that hung over his forehead in ringed clusters that reminded Omar of black grapes. When Ihab wandered off, they moved to armchairs by the balcony doors, their legs nearly intertwined in the tight confine of space. A few times their knees tapped together, and the tips of their shoes kissed.

Ali was born in Cairo but had moved with his family to the southern dam town of Asyut at age twelve. He went to college there and stayed after graduation, working for his father. But he'd recently landed a job at a Cairo telecom company and was now living in an apartment with his older brother in Giza's 6th of October City. Pockets of 6th of October City were fancy, but Ali regaled Omar with stories of power outages and garbage mounds and a war veteran who slept using his bicycle as a blanket in his building's vestibule.

"My parents live out that way," Omar blurted. It was an attempt to broadcast that he occasionally frequented Ali's part of town. "A bit farther out, in the suburbs. Palm Hills."

"Ahh, you are a rich kid," Ali surmised, arching his eyebrows.

"It wasn't my idea for them to move out there," Omar said in defense. "They wanted what everyone in Cairo wants now, the brand-new, the easy and convenient and quiet. My mom hates weather."

"The heat or the cold?"

"All weather!" Omar laughed, willing to sacrifice his mother's character to score a few points with this young man. "Weather in general. The outside. She'd be happy if the planet existed under a dome of central AC."

"Blech!" Ali clutched his stomach. "I love the beach too much. The hottest weather, that's my favorite, when the sun practically hurts the skin." Omar pictured Ali shirtless, the sunlight freckling his broad, peeling shoulders. "Where do you go for vacations in the summer?"

Omar could have told Ali that he had spent the past three summers out of the country, mostly commuting to and from Berlin. He could have admitted to finishing his visa application and to the fact that, with any luck, he'd be spending the upcoming summer on a beach in Malibu, watching as Tobias plunged into blue Pacific waves. But Omar didn't want to reveal that part of his life—the elsewhere part—to the young man with the grape clusters of curly black hair. "When I was a kid, my grandparents had a beach house near Marsa Matruh. The whole family would go for July. Even my aunt in New York would come." His grandparents' house had been a minimal concrete slab, but Omar treasured it as the site of so many early pleasures and desires, thanks in part to the older kids who hung out on the strip of sand in front of it. Even now when he couldn't sleep, he toured the rooms of that beach house in his mind, and in his fantasies his grandparents were still alive, cooking fish stew in the kitchen. Marsa Matruh was also the place where the car accident had occurred, which Omar always referred to as a "bike accident" because it downplayed the trauma; in truth, it was a car-and-bike accident, Omar at age eight on the bike, an older man of questionable sobriety driving a rust-colored car, Omar's head slamming into the curb after impact, the world forever sounding half as brilliant as it had before that hot summer day.

"I've never been to Marsa Matruh," Ali said with a whistle. "You see, I was right. Rich family!"

The accusation gave Omar the confidence to grab Ali's hand. "You've got me all wrong," he entreated, squeezing his fingers. "I skipped lunch today to save money. I'm jobless. You're the one who works for a fancy telecom."

Ali snorted but didn't pull his hand away. Omar heard squeaking feet on the hardwood behind him and turned to find Ihab drunkenly trying to climb onto a friend's shoulders for a game of chicken. Nawal, meanwhile, was running around moving vases and picture frames out of harm's way.

"Ihab is my ride home," Omar said. "Should I be worried?"

Ali pursed his lips. "I could take you."

Within fifteen minutes, they had excavated their jackets from the pile on a bed and descended in the birdcage elevator, standing in opposite corners of the tiny creaking box. Omar, with fluttering nerves, held the front door open for Ali, and as they walked down a side street, he scanned the cars, guessing which one might belong to him. He was surprised when Ali stopped at a slender black motorcycle, its worn vinyl seat patched with electrical tape.

"I don't have helmets," Ali cautioned, "but I promise I'm a safe driver."

Ali climbed on the bike, revved the motor, and pushed the kickstand free. Omar tried his balletic best to slip gracefully onto the back, like it was an old habit, his thighs straddling not only the black lozenge of cushion but also Ali's hips. He didn't know where to put his hands, but the forward lurch of the bike decided for him, and he grabbed the driver around the waist to keep from falling. He softened his grip, but didn't let go, and when he felt Ali's muscles clench, it seemed like he was being granted permission to keep his hands there. Omar's nose inched through the thicket of curly hair, and he recited his address in Ali's ear.

Ali was not a safe driver. He sped through red lights and swerved around slow cars, eating up the middle of the road and sometimes slaloming into the opposite lanes. Omar closed his eyes more than once to avoid witnessing their close calls with garbage trucks and minivans. But for all his carelessness—or maybe because of it— the ride was exciting, full of fresh threats and possibilities, sliding through the city's night air as if surfing on black oceanic waves. As they approached the museum of ancient artifacts, Omar worked up the courage to rest his head on Ali's shoulder and hold him more tightly around the stomach. As they sailed along the corniche and across the bridge, Omar glimpsed the lights of party boats bleeding into the water—the aquatic disco of white and green and red—and wished he lived farther away, so they could keep riding like this a little longer.

"Do you want to come up?" Omar asked as he staggered onto the sidewalk in front of his building. Ali smiled and, instead of answering, nudged the bike to the curb and turned off the ignition. Omar hadn't thought this plan through. Mrs. El Fettah would be asleep, but who knew what neighbors lurked at their peepholes? There were potential informers everywhere—the parking attendant who sat at the end of the block, the street sweeper, the Coptic woman who tended the neighbor's garden. Every workaday civilian in Cairo could find themselves in need of a government favor and be willing to share a droplet of information on untoward activities. Right now, though, Omar couldn't bring himself to care. They climbed the steps, taking two at a time, with anxious grins. On the sixth floor Omar accidentally kicked a bag of glass bottles that a neighbor had left on the landing. He hurried to his door to unlock it.

He flicked on the foyer light that illuminated the scarred concrete with its broken mosaic. Across the room, the faint window light brightened the laundry that hung across the line. Omar was relieved that it hid the photo of Tobias. As soon as he closed the door, Ali pressed his lips against his unready mouth. Omar hurried to catch up, sliding his hand around Ali's neck, kissing him forcefully. First Omar's back was against the kitchen wall, and then it was Ali cornered against the counter, as Omar tugged off his jacket. Ali's hand went to stroke Omar's face and nearly knocked out his hearing aid. A look of worry passed over Ali, but Omar laughed and said, "It's fine. Nothing breaks easily on me."

Their hips ground together as they kissed. Omar could feel Ali's cock hardening, trapped in a downward trajectory by the tight confines of his pants. Omar unbuttoned the waist and plunged his hand into the briefs, his knuckles grazing coarse pubic hair. When he released it, it bobbed and thickened in the scant light. Ali pushed his pants down the rest of the way and laughed with a shy smile.

By the time they advanced to the bedroom, Ali was naked except for a single white sock. Omar's pants were puddled at his ankles, but his undershirt and boxers were still on. They crawled onto the bed, Omar kicking free the restraints of his pants. Before he could climb on top of this beautiful nude man, Ali put his hands up in the gesture of fending off a lion attack. "I just want to say," he whispered, as if he wouldn't have a chance to later, "I'm really glad I met you tonight."

The hours raced by after sex, as they fell in and out of sleep. Omar kept waking to find himself a foot away from this miraculous young man, and he quickly bridged the distance with an arm latched over Ali's rib cage. He was exhausted and yet felt robbed every time sleep took him away from this reality. When he next looked at the clock on his nightstand, it was nearing six. Ali's shoulder glowed a purplish yellow as dawn broke, and with the daylight, worries began to creep into Omar's head—particularly, the obsessive early-morning sweeping of Mrs. El Fettah and the puzzle of how to negotiate a strange man leaving his apartment. It felt ridiculous and humiliating at his age to invent a lie to explain himself. And yet his landlady's curious, shriveled face kept floating through his mind. Omar entertained the fantasy of inviting Ali to stay in the apartment for the entire day, where they could eat and watch movies and have more sex. But then he thought of the motorcycle parked right outside the building, which was technically an illegal spot and would not go unnoticed by his neighbors. Plus, there was the "huge favor" that Cate had asked of him in her text.

Ali stretched his arms above his head and opened his eyes with a greedy smile. "Is it late?" he asked.

"No, it's only six twenty." Mrs. El Fettah didn't usually start her brooming until seven. "My landlady, she's going to—"

"I get it." Ali sat up and began scanning the bedroom floor for his clothes. The only item in sight was a solitary white sock.

"I think the rest is—"

Ali laughed and climbed out of bed. Even after his promiscuous years in Europe, Omar was still slightly awed whenever a man walked around naked in front of him. He was still self-conscious about his *own* body in daylight. As Ali walked around the apartment putting on pieces of clothing in the random order that he found them, his shirt before his briefs, Omar followed behind him, simultaneously herding him toward the door and reticent to let him go. There was no need to go over logistics—*Don't talk to anyone about spending the night*—because they both lived under the current laws of Egypt.

"So, um, do you want my number?" Ali asked at the door.

"More than anything," Omar allowed himself to reply, and handed over his phone so that Ali Hamdy could enter his contact information. After Omar shut the door, he was glad to see the line of laundry across the room and not the photo of the man behind it.

* * *

Omar left his apartment at noon. Jogging down the staircase, he didn't encounter Mrs. El Fettah until he reached the lobby. She sat on the tile floor, engaged in one of her many side hustles for extra cash, repotting a neighbor's houseplant with black soil sprinkled around her slippered feet. Omar smiled through braced teeth.

"Omar," she called. "Who was that man who left your apartment this morning?" She didn't even bother to disguise her interest.

"A friend," he replied with overly earnest innocence. "A schoolmate I hadn't seen in a while. He got sick with a stomachache and had to sleep on my sofa."

Mrs. El Fettah nodded in satisfaction. Perhaps Omar had overestimated the extent of the old woman's suspicious imagination; the prospect of two men blissfully fucking might dwell beyond the outskirts of her scandal-ridden mind. "The poor man," she squawked. "Well, he looked very healthy when he left on his motorcycle this morning. The fresh air in your apartment must have done him good!"

Omar decided she was not being sarcastic. "Oh, yes," he agreed. "He felt much better this morning. Very healthy."

She shoved her trowel into the plant basin. "He must have good parents, this friend from school? What is his name?"

If Ali had simply been a one-night stand, Omar would have gladly supplied a false name to match a false biography. But he wanted to see Ali again, regularly, and that meant his coming and going from the apartment. Omar imagined inflicting all manner of sudden, smiting illnesses on poor Ali's body to account for why he had to crash on his sofa on so many future nights.

"Ali Hamdy," he mumbled, then quickly manufactured a distraction, complaining about the lackluster water pressure in his shower, which he knew would send Mrs. El Fettah on a tangent of recriminations and masked apologies. It did the trick, and Omar managed to extract himself from the lobby, hurrying to his car parked a block away.

It had been surprisingly easy to track down the young receptionist at the Ramses Sands. He knew her name, Farida, and where she worked, and she'd mentioned in their brief conversation that she lived in the suburbs by the airport. It took ten minutes to find her on Facebook—they had two "friends" in common—and he tapped out a quick DM to her, riffing on their joke about the music camp that Farida and his sister had attended. Farida responded almost immediately, each sentence an enthusiastic exclamation. Driving east toward Nasr City, he berated himself for agreeing to do this favor. The thought of even a harmless manipulation made him queasy. But the favor would only take an hour, and he didn't want to disappoint Cate. If he failed, he could genuinely tell her he had tried. Cate had suspected Farida of having a crush, and for that reason she had drafted Omar into the task of trying to pry inside information out of her. Judging by her DM response, Farida almost certainly did have a crush, but so what? He had harbored plenty of crushes that had never gone anywhere (the biography of his teenage years could be chaptered by the crushes he'd had on various classmates). All Farida had to do was say no, and he wouldn't badger her any further about Eric Castle's death.

A donkey had been hit by a car. Its owner, an old man in rags, was crying inconsolably on the side of the highway entrance, as the animal lay bleeding on the ground. A few feet beyond the donkey sat a dented black convertible. A chubby young man with gelled hair and a Gucci polo shirt leaned against the car, talking on his cell phone to the police or to his lawyer—or maybe he was simply continuing his roster of work calls. Omar tried to wipe the bleeding donkey from his mind, the animal's shut eyes and the brown meat of its tongue and the flies already buzzing at its nose; he tried to forget that the donkey had likely been its owner's sole means of support. He sped on, into the bland condominium maze of Nasr City, full of extra-wide avenues and sun-scorched shopping complexes. He had to check the location of the coffee shop on his phone three times, because all the corners in Nasr City looked identical to him. It had been Farida's idea to meet at a branch of a popular Western coffee chain midway between their respective homes (and therefore of equal inconvenience to them both). Had this been an actual date, he would have been discouraged by Farida's dull taste in venues.

He arrived first, claiming a table with his jacket, and ordered an espresso at the counter. Just as he was carrying the paper cup to his seat, Farida appeared in the door's tinted glass. She entered with an apologetic frown and a halting limp, which he initially mistook for an injury—had she twisted her ankle? But he saw the slightly turned-in foot, and as a lifetime recipient of overcurious stares at the device strapped to his ear, he quickly converted his alarmed expression into an exaggerated welcoming smile.

"I'm so sorry I'm late," Farida said, unzipping a windbreaker and rearranging a long-sleeved pink blouse with sparkly threads running through its fabric. She carried a black book bag with plastic emeralds and rubies riveted along its shoulder straps. "I took the wrong bus," she said, "the slow one that makes all the stops."

"I could have picked you up," he replied, an offer she had already refused over DM. Omar guessed that Farida might not have wanted him to see where she lived, perhaps embarrassed about her family's financial standing, considering that Omar's own Facebook page must read like one long brag of princely indulgences. Or maybe she hadn't wanted her parents to know that she was meeting up with a member of the opposite sex. They might have forbidden her, or even punished her. He understood the pressure to be good. The threat of shaming one's family was a gun pointed at every young person's head in Egypt. He felt a surge of sympathy for Farida, coming all this way to meet a stranger who would only disappoint her. "Let me buy you a coffee," he implored. "What would you like?"

He ordered her a latte and carried it to the table, mortified by the heart that the barista had drawn with a swirl of foam. Farida lifted the cup to her mouth and took a slurping sip. One of her metal barrettes had come unhooked in her hair, and Omar kept waiting for her to notice, scared to offend her by pointing it out. He considered breaking the silence by relying on their only biographical overlap—the music camp that his sister had attended. But even that incidental connection was misleading, because Farida had gone as part of a citywide youth group, while Omar's sister had taken private piano lessons.

"So," he said, and watched her face redden. Her eyes dropped to the table to study the veins of its faux marble as if it were a chess-board. "How long have you worked at the Ramses Sands?"

Farida's brown eyes never met his as she ran through the details of her life. She was currently studying accounting and bookkeeping at a local college, finishing up a two-year degree. She'd been helming the front desk of an all-women dormitory for the first year, but foreign hotels paid five times as much, and she'd landed the job at the Ramses Sands five months ago, thanks to a professor who knew the manager. "The hotels usually choose Copts if they're going to hire women, so I was really lucky. I guess I looked like I could handle the shock of Westerners!" She repeatedly swore that she loved her job at the hotel, although Omar couldn't decipher whether the devotion was authentic or she was worried he might be connected to higher-ups in the hospitality industry. She particularly enjoyed working in cosmopolitan Garden City and told him that only last week she'd tried sushi for the first time at a nearby restaurant.

"How could you have missed out on sushi for all of these years?" he exclaimed, glad that they had finally discovered a point of intersection, no matter how trivial. "There's a great sushi spot in Dokki, if you're interested."

"Oh," she hummed. "Oh, yes, I'd love to go!"

Omar realized that the invitation sounded exactly like a date. He cringed at misleading her. It was Ali he wanted to take to the sushi restaurant in Dokki, and Ali whom he wished he were sitting with right now in this generic coffee shop playing jazz-infused Christmas carols, likely chosen by a Seattle executive who had never stepped foot on the continent of Africa. For a second he blamed Cate for putting him in this awkward position. She was off exploring the Western Desert while he was forced to ask a cruel favor of a kind, innocent young woman.

"Farida," he said soberly, eager to get the request over with. "I have to ask you something that might be a little sensitive."

The veins of the faux-marble tabletop received another thorough examination. "Of course. What is it?"

"That woman I was with the other day in the lobby, she's a friend of my aunt in New York." This information seemed to please Farida, whose lips flickered with a smile. "She is the sister of the man who died a month ago at your hotel, falling from his balcony."

Her face contorted as if she'd been jabbed with a needle. "I remember," she said. "It was horrible, a nightmare. I wasn't on duty that day, but I'm so glad I wasn't there to see . . ." She clearly didn't want to say the words *the body* aloud. "It was a suicide. He was an American." As if being an American explained the suicide, and maybe, in some ways, it did. "He was a worker for the weapons company. They are always staying in our hotel."

Omar offered a compassionate smile as he carefully framed his next question. "That's just it, the sister doesn't think it's a suicide. She thinks something might have happened in his room, that someone—"

"No!" She shook her head. "Not a suicide? The police said so, my manager told me it was. He fell off his balcony, drunk. They drink so much, especially the men who work for that weapons company. Maybe it was an accident? He could have leaned too far over by mistake . . ."

Omar nodded like he agreed with her. "I'm sure that's correct," he exclaimed. "I think she's just grieving the loss of her brother."

"The poor, sad woman!"

"Do you know what would help set her mind at ease?" He furrowed his brow, as if it pained him to ask. "There are video cameras in the elevator and halls, yes?" Farida's head tilted suspiciously, as if she could finally see through the fog of his request. "From what I understand, the hotel also records the room calls."

"But that's not . . ." She licked her lips and tried again. "That is only for Polestar workers, and they comply. They know about it. It's not for every hotel guest. It's not like we spy—"

"No, of course," he reassured her, and went back to the point on which their thoughts had last harmonized. "I'm sure it was a suicide. But to give her some peace of mind, it would mean a lot to get the video surveillance from that night. When she sees that no one was coming or going on the third floor around the time of his death, she'll have to accept that it wasn't a murder. Imagine the good that would do her." He took a deep breath. "Do you think you could get a copy of that footage? We could show it to her. It would be our secret. We'd never let anyone know, but it would finally give her family some peace."

Farida was already shaking her head, and as the full extent of the request took root in her brain, she shook it more decisively. "I can't! Not just because it is forbidden and I could lose my job. I don't have access. I don't even know if the cameras on the floors work anymore. All the security monitors are in the manager's office, which Mr. ElBaradei keeps locked. If that footage is saved, I don't know where it would be stored!" Her eyes were welling. "His death was over a month ago! I don't know if the footage still exists! And I don't have any access to it if it does!"

She was visibly upset, and he felt terrible for the distress he'd caused, trying to tangle her up in a murder investigation. "Hey," he said soothingly, "don't worry about it. It was a stupid idea. I was just trying to help this sad American woman, but there's no reason to involve you. So please, let's forget it. I knew it was a long shot." He reached across the table and pressed his hand over hers. She glanced up, and he tried to reassure her with a smile. "I'm sure it was a suicide," he said. "It doesn't matter."

She stared at his hand on hers and then at the table in silence. "The calls from the room, though," she said timidly. "Those re-cordings are stored on the computer in the reception office." Omar leaned toward her, sliding his elbows along the table. She looked startled, her eyes wide, as if she were afraid of the words coming out of her mouth. "We take all internal calls from the office. Sometimes I fill in for the operator on slow days. Unless someone went in and erased those audio files, the calls in and out of her brother's room that night would probably still be saved there."

"Could you check?" He was certainly earning his letters of recommendation. A few audio files weren't going to be as definitive as video surveillance footage, but at least Omar wouldn't be going back to Cate empty-handed. And maybe, in the end, he and Farida really were performing a good deed. Maybe the recordings would bring comfort to a grieving family.

Farida bundled her hands up in the cuffs of her pink sleeves. "I . . . I work tonight," she volunteered before shaking her head. But he could see the spark of collusion beginning to kindle in her eyes. They came from totally different backgrounds and led completely different lives. But they did share one trait: they were both willing to risk their own safety for the smallest scrap of love.

Chapter 16

SIWA, THE WESTERN DESERT

The plane landed at a military airstrip a few miles east of the Libyan border. A driver in a black SUV was waiting on the tarmac to transport them forty minutes to the outpost town of Siwa Oasis. As Cate left the plane, she was surprised to find the desert temperature less mercilessly hot than she'd anticipated. Nevertheless, she saw ominous clues to Sahara hazards in the back of the car: pallets of bottled water, nylon tarps, a shovel, two flare-gun kits—survival gear needed in case of breakdown in the Great Sand Sea.

She watched the barren desert scroll past the back-seat window, the sepia horizon broken only by the occasional ragged silhouette of a wild camel, the bulky continent of its body held up on thin spindles of legs. Matthias sat next to her, describing the missiles they would likely see at the range tomorrow. His vocabulary was studded with incomprehensible acronyms—BVR, SAM, SARH—and Cate's attention drifted over the empty desert. When it returned,

Matthias was reciting the current working definition of a weapon as defined by UN arms embargo treaties. "Anything that explodes. Anything that detonates, that fires." Cate stared through the tinted window, trying to think of everyday objects that fulfilled the UN definition. Champagne bottles. Cameras. Childhood.

"My country took some real heat a few years back, when we exported fighting dogs to Israel," Matthias said. "Those dogs ended up being used to attack Palestinians. The question was, did dogs count as weapons? If they did, the Netherlands had just violated a UN embargo agreement. The matter went to the high courts, where it was ultimately decided that no, dogs were not full-time death machines. At best they were considered 'dual-use technology.'" Matthias looked over at her with a grin. "Countries are now free to import all the Dutch fighting dogs they desire."

Cate pictured Eric's puppy back in Massachusetts. "Were they Dobermans?"

"German shepherds, I believe." He squeezed her hand on the seat. Thinking of his two small children in Amsterdam, she pulled her hand away.

Few cars passed on the two-lane highway. Still, in the relatively short distance to Siwa, they encountered three military checkpoints. Each time Cate's chest tightened as the SUV slowed to a surrendering stop at a line of rusty oil barrels blocking the road. Green-fatigued soldiers with machine guns circled the vehicle and asked to see all passports. The soldiers took prolonged, sunglass-lowering stares at Cate, either because she was an American or because she was a woman. Then the lead officer would snap his fingers, and his grunts dragged the barrels from the road. Safe for another twenty miles.

Watching the waves of the desert pass induced a scary hypnotism— a twofold sensation of peace and emergency. Cate wondered how deep the Sahara went. Was it like the ocean? Did it have a floor?

She thought of Lucas Keulks, who had gone missing somewhere in this desert, maybe lost forever in the sand sea. His last words came to her. *It had to do with the weapons. They weren't broken. They worked.*

The green began appearing in rapid bursts, little skids of errant flora amid the flat vista. As vegetation increased, so did human presence, by way of crude cinder-block buildings and corroded gas pumps. Two-wheeled donkey carts created brief traffic jams. Cate admired the long, princely strides of domestic camels (and later spotted a row of their equally princely heads lined up in a butcher's window). Then came the din of real traffic, cars covered in layers of dust, as if the desert put its mark on anything that crossed it. Truck engines lay autopsied in dirt lots, as did entire oak dining room sets, left baking under the rainless sky. Suddenly a miraculous riot of green in the distance, the thick, fertile palms spilling over the city's mud walls.

As they entered Siwa, her phone erupted in a crescendo of chirps, the electronic hallelujah of reestablished connection. Their hotel was called Tranquil Peace Eco Lodge, spelled out on a sign in fat aqua letters, with "Resort" added later in a sleeker, darker font to appeal to a new class of traveler. The single-story structure was surrounded by a walled garden, and a pile of bicycles spilled around the front gate.

"It's the best I could do on short notice," Matthias apologized. "There are much fancier hotels now, but it was impossible to find a room with two beds."

He checked them in, and they carried their bags to a door that matched the number on their key. "I had to tell them we were married to let us share," he said. "In case they call you Mrs. Vos."

"It's like the Grand Nile all over again."

"I promise I won't search your bags this time," he joked. She wasn't sure she believed him.

Inside, two single beds filled the narrow room like an equal sign, with a teak nightstand chastely separating them. The only decorations on the walls were small red smears around the headboards, where previous guests had squashed mosquitos. Cate claimed the nearest bed, dropping onto it. Matthias started to object—apparently it was his habit to take the bed closest to the door—but quickly conceded and took the other bed.

"We can meet for a late dinner?" he suggested as he stepped into the bathroom and clicked on a fluorescent light. She heard him splashing water on his face. When he reemerged, he was already wearing his sunglasses, his cheeks dripping underneath the reflecting lenses. "I have to go. I'm busy with meetings all afternoon." In his aviators and rumpled seersucker, he looked like a gambler stumbling out of a casino at daybreak in an American desert town—having won or lost, it was impossible to tell. She was beginning to doubt the sanity of this arrangement, sharing a room, sleeping in separate beds, bunking with a man whose motives were still unclear to her.

"Dinner sounds good," she said. "I'm going to go for a walk. I need to find Kurt Driscoll."

Matthias placed an extra key on the bureau. "You'll see him tomorrow at the range."

"Thank you," she said, "for letting me come along."

After he left, Cate waited a full minute before dialing the reception desk. Though the attendant answered with a bright "Hello," he didn't speak English, and there was a long interlude before a child's voice came on the line, the in-house English interpreter. Cate asked if there was a single room available for the night. "We are all fully booked, madam. It is the busy season. Best time in oasis is now."

Cate took a shower, bandaged her cut knee, braided her hair back, and slathered her face with sunscreen. It was late afternoon

by the time she grabbed a bike from the communal pile and followed the palm-shaded dirt road into town.

The center of Siwa was a tangle of lanes, more convoluted than
one of Roe Driscoll's sailor's knots. Thatched shacks protruded
from mud-brick buildings the color of stale cake; merchants sat
cross-legged in the shade, their billowing robes and turbans as stark
white as American teeth. She could hear the difference between
the Berber language spoken by the Siwans and the rapid-fire Cairene Arabic. She didn't spot a single local woman in the town, only
a few rich Western women, imperious and demanding in their
gaudy spa costumes of muumuus and embroidered djellabas. She
tried to avoid them and made a concerted effort to take interest in
the shopkeepers' attempts to explain their fabrics and oils, as if she
could atone for the rudeness of her kind.

By the time the afternoon sun began to weaken, Cate was pedaling out through the olive groves in search of Siwa's famous oracle.
A few minutes out of the village, she reached a clutch of egg-white
houses. Here she finally caught sight of local women. Walking in
twos and dressed in thick black burqas, they wore indigo sheets
draped over their shrouded heads. The only visible skin was the
flash of a hand birding through the folds of fabric. Who was she
to them? she wondered, wishing they spoke the same language.
Beyond the bike's handlebars, her body drew a long Giacometti
shadow across the sand.

The Temple of Amun was a vast warren of crumbling corridors,
one whispery passage leading to the next like the granular tunnels
of an anthill. She stumbled through the maze without summoning
the energy to consult her guidebook. There were no guards at the
site, or any other tourists. In a windless passageway, a jolt of fear
needled through her at being so alone. She reminded herself that
there was no conceivable way her kidnappers could have traveled

across the country to reach her here. She climbed to a higher level of the ancient complex, and gazed out from this vantage over the starry heads of the oasis's palms in the late golden-red sun. When she turned, she was so spooked by the presence of a man standing behind her that she nearly screamed.

Lucas Keulks smiled, a hand raised in reassurance. "Hi Cate." He sounded sober. Somehow that made him seem more intimidating. "I saw you in town and figured I'd take the opportunity to catch you alone."

She was relieved to find him alive—unkidnapped, unmurdered. He wore dirty jeans and a gray sweatshirt, and the blue baseball cap on his head reduced his eyes to a tunnel of shade. In the desert light he looked older than he had at the Ramses Sands. His tone was friendly, although she remembered Matthias's theory that Eric could have been killed by a colleague in a drunken rage.

"Lucas," she said. "I was worried about you."

"Is that why you've come out here? You shouldn't have bothered."

"No, that's not why I came. I . . ." But Cate didn't need to explain herself. She glanced around, half hoping to spot some tourists approaching the temple, but there was only an aluminum can rolling along the dirt road in the wind. "I heard you skipped out on your job. I thought something had happened to you."

He shrugged, working his jaw. "I guess you could say I quit. I flew out here with the team, but when we landed that morning I just decided, no more. I'm going home. It's not safe in Egypt, especially not with you reminding everyone about Eric."

Reminding everyone? But Cate wasn't going to argue with Lucas. It wouldn't help her get the answers she needed from him.

"Nicole will be glad to see you," she said enthusiastically. The mention of his fiancée induced only a huff and a cross of his arms, as if he saw through her attempts at a connection. "Why isn't it safe here for you, Lucas? Safe from whom?"

"For the same reasons that your brother was killed," he snapped. "Safe from the people who murdered him. From the Egyptian military, would be my guess."

Finally he was providing concrete information. "You said the other night that Eric realized the weapons worked. What did you mean?" Lucas kicked his feet through the dry dirt, as if debating walking away. But he'd sought her out at the top of a ten-thousand-year-old temple. There must be some part of him that wanted to talk.

"It's too complicated for you to understand."

"Try me."

He sighed. "The last time your brother and I came out here was to conduct maintenance tests. This was only about a week before he was killed. Part of that assignment involved checking a cache of missile launchers, pretty standard Polestar lower-range firers, nothing fancy, about twenty in total." She smiled and nodded, although she was already reaching the limits of her arms knowledge. "Small surface-to-air launchers," he explained. "Portable equipment. Easy to operate. But highly dangerous, because they have the range to shoot a commercial airliner out of the sky. And that's what makes them so desirable and scary."

"Okay," Cate said.

"We get a report from the Egyptian military that none of them work. They sent a scrap order, which means we sign off and report them as junk, to be deleted from the inventory and replaced with some freshies that Polestar sends out in its next shipment." He shrugged again. "Nothing out of the ordinary. I was cool with it. We all are. Polestar says no biggie, sorry for the defects, we'll provide you with some new ones. That's how we keep Sisi and his generals happy. But Eric, *fuck!*" Lucas shook his head. "Your brother wouldn't go along with it. You see, he had inspected that particular cache of launchers the last time he came out, and they were as sound as Swiss clocks. So here I am, on *their* military base, signing off for replacements, surrounded by this unit of Egyptian soldiers whose sole job it is to maintain the weapons. And your brother goes, 'Wait up. Can someone take me to a hardware store?'" Lucas couldn't resist cracking a smile at the memory of Eric's audacity. "These soldiers don't fuck around. They don't like us American techs on their turf. But, swear to Christ, Eric makes one of them drive him to a hardware store near Siwa, and he comes back an hour later with a can of oil and a wrench, and he proceeds to fix the launchers. He gets them all working in fifteen minutes."

"But that's good, isn't it?" Cate asked. "I mean, that's his job, right? To fix them?"

Lucas dipped the brim of his cap on his forehead. "You'd think. But this head soldier—I never could figure out what his rank was—he gets pissed. He walks right up to Eric and threatens him in his garbled English. He says the launchers *still* don't work, and they'll all be broken again the next day. Well, you know Eric. He wouldn't let anyone tell him he was wrong about his job. He knew those weapons inside out, so he snaps back, 'Fuck you, those things are running perfectly.' It was heated. This head soldier gives your brother a death glare. He says that Eric is destroying the operation and he'll be sorry. 'Yull be verrry sarry,' " Lucas tried a flailing imitation of a villainous accent. "Well, guess what? Six days later Eric is dead. We went back to Cairo, and the fear got to him. I think it dawned on him that he'd crossed a line. I think he realized he wasn't in the United States, and soldiers in dictatorships actually do have the muscle to put their threats into action. He drank a lot, way more than usual. He was nervous, not himself, and honestly, in those last days, he was rambling incoherently most of the time. I didn't lie about that. He was depressed and drunk. And sure enough, look what happened. That soldier told your brother he'd be sorry. I bet Eric was very sorry the second he opened his hotel door and saw the soldier standing in the hall that night."

"Wait a minute. I don't understand. Why would soldiers want broken missile launchers?"

"Don't you see?" he exclaimed. "It took me a second to figure out too. They only wanted them to be *reported* as broken. Polestar isn't an appliance store. It's not going to waste its time demanding the return of twenty unrepairable launchers. We'll delete the weapons from the official inventory and replace them at no charge to keep smiles on everyone's faces. But for those soldiers, who are probably paid duck-shit, selling a state-of-the-art portable launcher on the black market would be a gold mine. My guess is they were pissed because Eric was interfering with their money-making scheme. Being in the Egyptian army can't pay much."

Elizabeth Skyler had said that Eric was too ethical for his job. Maybe that was the reason he'd asked to speak with her in an official capacity, to report this threat on his life from a group of rogue soldiers. He must have been terrified once he realized the danger he'd put himself in, stuck in a foreign country that was run by its military without any protection to keep him safe.

"Would you consider reporting—" she began, but Lucas shook his head. He wasn't going to share this story with the State Department and risk putting himself in anyone's crosshairs. Anyway, Eric's death had already been ruled a suicide. What hard evidence did he possess that these soldiers were the killers?

Lucas lifted his sweatshirt, revealing a pistol wedged in the waistband of his jeans, its barrel pressed against his stomach. "Since you've come here, stirring it all up again, it struck me that I'm the only living witness. I was the one who stood there and heard the threat against your brother. I keep looking for that soldier, the one who told Eric he'd be sorry. I'll never forget him." Lucas put his fingers to his cheek. "He had a birthmark right here on his face."

Cate's vision went blurry. The older kidnapper at the market, the driver with the silver pinkie ring who lured her into the storefront, had a red splotch on his cheek, only half covered by his scraggly beard. "I've seen that guy," she wheezed. "He's in Cairo."

"If I were you, I'd try not to see him again. I mean it, Cate. It's not safe for you to be here. Go home! I know you came with good intentions, but there is no way of holding these soldiers responsible. Do you understand that?"

It was the same advice the attaché had given her—do nothing, accept it, move on. "How are you getting back?" she asked. "I could ask my friend if there's any room on the plane to Cairo tomorrow night?"

"Nah. No thanks. I'm waiting to catch a lift from some guys I know who are driving back in a truck. Then, once I pack my stuff, I'm heading home. I'm not getting near a plane in this desert. I told you, those launchers are perfect for swatting down nuisances in the sky. I'm not going to press my luck." He stared past her, gazing out over the darkening oasis. "I'm too old for this shit. I'm tired of being under Polestar's thumb. Christ, I have a baby at home. I can't live like this anymore."

The walls of the ancient ruin were beginning to blue with dusk. It occurred to Cate that the next time she and Lucas ran into each other, it would likely be at a supermarket in Great Barrington. Lucas would be pushing a shopping cart, a toddler on his hip. Cate tried to imagine what she would look like in this scenario, thousands of miles and several months into the future, but she drew a blank.

"I feel guilty," Lucas said, "that I didn't help Eric when I could. I should have been a better friend. He was suffering in those last days, drunk and acting crazy, and he pushed me away, but I should have been there for him."

"That's how I feel too," she said. "That I was never there." Cate thought of the words that Eric had written on their father's post-card. *Ask him about Huxley.* Maybe the *him* was the last friend that her brother had in this part of the world.

"Are you sure you've never heard the name Huxley before?"

"I haven't," he said somberly.

"Why would he write that on a postcard to our father?"

"Your father. Well, that's a different story." Lucas lifted his chin and smirked. "He mentioned your father during those last days, and not very nicely."

"What do you mean?"

"Fuck if I know what Eric was rambling on about. As I said, he wasn't making much sense. He was tanked and wouldn't get out of bed. I went up to his room—this must have been the night before he died—and he was saying what a shit your father was, a man without any ethics, just greedy as fuck like everyone else, and how awful he'd been when you were kids." Lucas shrugged.

That news didn't fit with the brother who had made peace with the man. "If Eric was so filled with hate for our father, why would he send him a postcard right before he died about things blow-ing up?"

"The past must have been weighing on his mind." Lucas sighed. Cate didn't dare ask whether Eric had made any nasty comments about her in his final days. She couldn't take hearing the answer.

Lucas seemed to grasp her worry. "I don't think you should put much stock in what Eric said or wrote. He really was out-of-his-head drunk. He cussed me out too. I didn't lie to the police about his depression. He told me to get the hell out of his room. Told me that everything we worked for was a mistake, and all we did was make things worse." Lucas shook his head. "Those were his last words to me. If I could go back . . ." He rocked on his heels. "You sign up for the military at eighteen, wanting to do something no-ble for your country. Then you look up ten years later and think,

How did I end up working for a defense firm that's trying to put bombs in everyone's hands? For what? A paycheck? To end up lying about my friend's death to his family and the police?"

Two figures appeared on the darkening road below them, and Lucas tensed up. But they were only teenage backpackers with rolled sleeping bags tied to their rucksacks, which eased his fears.

"You know what I hate most about Polestar?" he said. "Their smugness. Their little cult of humanity, forcing us to volunteer at that clinic, just to lighten their conscience about the world they've helped create. I never went. I'd rather have my dignity and remain a heartless asshole weapons tech. It's more honest." He stepped backward toward the corridor that led down to the road. "We used to sell weapons to fight wars. Now we fight wars to sell weapons. The world doesn't seem to care. Maybe Eric cared. Maybe keeping quiet bothered him too much, and that's why he wouldn't let those soldiers walk off with that cache of missile launchers. He didn't want to let more weapons disappear into the desert like a gun that goes missing in a house full of kids." Lucas smiled at her, his eyes glittering. "Maybe he prevented a few people from dying by speaking up. Think of it that way, Cate. What can I say? I'm trying to give your brother a happier ending."

He waved goodbye. "See you in the Berkshires," Cate said.

*　　*　　*

She walked her bike back to the hotel. Night had fallen, and the wind whispered through the olive groves; the maraca rattle of insects shook the trees. Cate tried to summon a feeling of peace in finally uncovering the answer to Eric's murder. Wasn't that the reason she had come here, to learn the truth, even if it wouldn't lead to anything close to justice? Just to know what had happened to him, that's what she'd claimed to be after. At least she could take this answer back home with her and lay it down on her mother's kitchen table. Maybe one day it would bring Joy comfort to know that her son had been killed not by depraved personal choices but by selfless ones.

She dumped the bike in the communal pile at the hotel gate. Heading up the walkway, she spotted Matthias sitting at a table in the garden, half hidden behind the scaly trunks of palm trees. He was waving her over. A strand of white holiday lights suspended over the table illuminated a bucket of ice, two glasses, and a bottle of tequila.

"I smuggled it here in my luggage," he said, tapping the bottle as she sat down next to him. A feeble breeze animated the drooping flowers and high grasses. "I was worried you got lost in the oasis. How was sightseeing?"

"Believe it or not," she said, "I think I figured out who killed Eric. Or found out. I didn't do much figuring."

"Really?" Matthias sounded genuinely surprised. He seemed on the verge of asking her to explain, but caught himself, and instead filled her glass with tequila and ice. "You don't have to tell me."

She smiled. "I'm still processing it." She wanted to believe that Matthias was a friend, and because of that wish, she didn't want to test the limits of their friendship. She didn't want to worry that her information would one day be used to secure a deal.

"I just hope," he said, "that whatever you learned has helped you."

Constellations crowded the sky—not the scattering of isolated stars that appeared in the Berkshire skies, but a thick chalk dusting. The galaxy didn't look as cold and alien here as it did at home. Cate downed the glass of tequila and poured herself another.

"Let me ask you a professional question," she proposed. She could at least use Matthias's expertise to corroborate Lucas's story. "Say someone around here has a stash of weapons that they want to get rid of." He nodded gamely. "Rocket launchers, say." She might have been giving too much away, but the first drink had already softened the tight clamp on her brain. "Would there be a market for spare rocket launchers in these parts? Who would buy them?"

Matthias squinted at her skeptically. "Have you looked at a map recently?" He reached into his jacket pocket and pulled out a pen and a paper napkin. "I'm always collecting cocktail napkins to scribble down my brilliant ideas. Then I forget about them and end up blowing my nose on my brilliance, wiping my sunglasses with my ideas, using my brilliant ideas to pry gum off my shoe." He laid the napkin flat on the table and drew a stitched blue line down the center. A half-centimeter away from it, he added a star. "This is how close we are to the Libyan border. Thirty miles."

"So?"

"So!" He cackled. "There's a civil war going on in Libya right now. A very messy, bloody one, and each side is desperate for weapons. Each side has strong allies around the world, but because of international sanctions, those allies aren't officially allowed to help with supplies." Cate nodded as she drained the tequila in her glass. "No surprise, then," Matthias continued, "that the majority of weapons being used in Libya right now are smuggled in. So, yeah, I'd say there's a rather fertile market for illegal arms these days. Why? Do you have a few rocket launchers you're looking to unload?"

Lucas's story checked out. Cate's would-be kidnapper must have intended to trade the rocket launchers over the border for cash. Those weapons were probably worth a fortune. And then Eric showed up with his inconvenient ethics and threatened to spoil the plan. It seemed a strong motive for murder. Kill Eric, he wouldn't be around to sabotage any future embezzling operations. She really had uncovered the answer to his death.

Cate poured another shot and raised her glass for a celebratory toast. *Cheers, to finding the answer.* But as she started to say "Cheers," the word broke apart in her throat, and the tears washed over her so quickly, it felt as violently uncontrollable as vomiting. She was so tired from the day, from the week, from the past few months, from losing Luis, that there was no fight left in her. She covered her face with her palms and cried into them. Her only brother, who had taught her to swim and drive and listen deeply to music, the first person in her life she ever trusted, was gone forever. He had been murdered, and now he lay buried in a cemetery in western Massachusetts. All she could do was press these horrible facts against her chest and hold them tightly until they stopped stinging.

Matthias slipped his hand across her back. He didn't offer any trite words of sympathy, just let his hand rest on her shoulder in support. Cate wiped her eyes, downed the shot of tequila, and reached for the bottle. Matthias tried to grab it from her, but he wasn't fast enough, and she poured a final drink. "I'm fine," she said with a skittish laugh and drank it.

"We should get you some food," she heard Matthias advise, and with effort, she focused her eyes on his thin face with its pocked cheeks. She leaned toward him and kissed him on the lips. In one of the many mysteries of her own sexual psychology, Cate could always kiss strangers more passionately than boyfriends. In the months before she and Luis had broken up, their kisses had devolved into chaste pecks, whereas strangers felt like wild frontiers. She could fill those kisses with all the many dreams and illusions of herself.

Matthias's palm slid around her waist. She shoved her hand into his crotch and felt a blunt hardening. Cate's chair tipped over as she stood, and Matthias put his arm around her so she could lean on him as they hurried toward the room, the whole world swirling around her. Cate could not think past sex. She wouldn't let her mind run off-leash into the faraway fields of the next morning, with its promise of a hangover and self-disgust. At the door to their room, she nearly bit Matthias's lip while kissing him.

He didn't bother with the light switch as he herded her toward her bed, and she dropped from his arms to lie back on the mattress. Matthias tugged off her shoes and whispered, "I'll be right back," before stepping into the bathroom and flicking on the noxious-green fluorescent light. She heard him rummaging around at the sink and figured he was looking for a condom. She pulled off her jeans, her legs long and skinny in the half light. She took a deep breath and exhaled. As the last of the air drifted from her lips, she saw Matthias walking out of the bathroom toward her with some-thing in his hands. He held a trash can in one hand and a bottle of water in the other.

"In case you get sick," he said, and placed the can beside her on the floor. "Drink this." He twisted the cap before handing her the bottle.

"But . . ." She took the bottle unwillingly and tried to grab hold of him. He eluded her clumsy fingers, peeling the sheet from under her and spreading it over her body.

"Get some sleep," he said. "You've had a tough day."

Matthias was not going to play the role of wild frontier. To-night, it was enough to be her friend.

Chapter 17

SIWA, THE WESTERN DESERT

They woke early to see the explosions.

Cate concentrated on the grueling task of climbing into the back seat of the SUV and buckling her seat belt. Matthias, who had gone to check out of the hotel, appeared a few minutes later carrying two cups of coffee. "I thought you could use one."

As he tried to hand her a cup, she managed to shake her throbbing head. She had gotten up that morning groggy but optimistically lucid. She thought she might have dodged a lethal tequila hangover and had merely been given the reduced sentence of a migraine. The nausea descended on her when she tried to stick her toothbrush in her mouth. A shower might have helped matters, but the water never warmed, and she couldn't withstand the freezing spray long enough to unwork the braid in her hair. Ten minutes after they drove away from Tranquil Peace Eco Lodge Resort, she rummaged her purse for her sunglasses, praying to St.

Anthony that she hadn't left them behind in the hotel room. Matthias's aviators hung from his shirt collar.

"Can . . . I borrow . . . ?" she garbled, scared she might puke if forced to utter a more elaborate sentence. Matthias unhooked his aviators and handed them to her. They darkened the world enough that it didn't look fashioned entirely from jagged, light-glaring glass.

The SUV took a different route out of town, a turbulent zig-zag through rockier terrain that left both passengers bouncing like toddlers on the back seat. It was a three-hour drive to the military range, and Cate tried to steel herself for the disturbing equation of rough roads plus splitting headache plus hot car. Matthias busied himself tapping out work emails on his cell phone. He had been exceptionally kind to her, doubly so because he hadn't mentioned a word about her behavior last night. Only occasionally did a barbed memory of her kissing or grabbing at him flash through her mind. She pressed her temple against the window and let the car's vibration massage her to sleep.

She awoke at the first of a dozen highway checkpoints. The soldiers patrolling these roads used metal-gated barricades instead of oil drums; their guns were leaner and their uniforms a darker camouflage against the beige breakers of Saharan sand. Unlike yesterday, though, the driver simply pressed to the window a neon-yellow card that had come with Matthias's invitation; the soldiers moved the barricades aside and waved them on. After guzzling down two bottles of emergency water and a second nap, Cate began to feel semihuman.

The desert's waves of sand grew tidal, the blacktop road no longer sliding over their surface but shearing through them. Cate could see a diamond sparkle in the distance, like the glitter of the sea.

"The Mediterranean?" she asked. "Aren't we too far from—"

Just as she realized that she was witnessing a mirage, an enormous boom erupted somewhere in the desert, loud and dense, its vibration crawling into the deepest crevices of her internal organs. It was as if the entire SUV had become a tuning fork, capturing that deadening sound.

"We're close," Matthias announced.

"That's from a missile?"

Matthias withdrew two sets of plastic-wrapped earplugs from his seat pocket. Cate watched the driver fit the mushroom-colored plugs into his ears. Matthias tossed a pack in her lap.

"Put those on. You're not at risk of hearing loss—we'll be far enough away from the strikes—but it can feel like walking out of a really bad rock concert."

Cate ripped open the baggie and stuffed the plugs in her ears. They were good quality. The world fell into muffled silence, and without the white noise of ordinary existence, every action—the driver turning the wheel; Matthias glancing over his shoulder; the wave of a soldier's rifle on the roadside—took on a heightened, melancholic choreography.

The driver kept the neon-yellow card pressed to the glass as soldiers guided them toward the parking lot, where a fleet of SUVs was already parked. Two guards escorted Cate and Matthias up a wide metal staircase that led to a cluster of trailers spaced along a steep ridgeline. The trailers were viewing stations, their fronts covered in glass. They were led to the first trailer, and just as the door opened, Cate felt another dense, tooth-rattling boom. A blackish-orange pinprick burst in the distance, followed by a plume of ash, and the observers standing at the trailer's window turned to each other with awed smiles.

Cate and Matthias stood in the back by the door. The trailer was crowded with men: generals wearing green canvas shirts decorated with eagle insignias, a few sporting dark-green baseball caps. Others wore business suits. One harried executive with a smooth bald head and a rumpled forehead had his jacket hooked on a chair in front of him, sweat bleeding down the sides of his shirt as he took notes. The only woman in sight was Ivers, the tech Cate had met on the Driscolls' rooftop. She wore a black flak jacket with a walkie-talkie pressed to her mouth. Ivers appeared to be the one coordinating the strikes, and Cate felt a pinch of pride in finding a woman at the helm.

Kurt Driscoll stood front and center at the window. Cate recognized him from his online photo. He was shorter than she'd expected, wearing a loose navy suit with a red tie. He had a wide stance and a large, handsome head, his cropped hair receding so that it made a horseshoe of his hairline. What was most striking about him, though, was the theater of his face. It seemed bioengineered for easy evaluation of his mood. Right now he wore a huge smile, punctuated by long dimpled creases down his cheeks and animated blue eyes. A prominent vein guttered down his forehead, adding a manic element to his expression. He was directing his enthusiasm for warheads at the white-haired general beside him.

Out the window, a convoy of tanks advanced into the distance of the desert valley, past coronas of charred sand. Matthias plucked out his earplugs, and Cate did the same.

"You see the tanks out there? They're sending out old, expendable models. Desert birds, we call them. Target practice. Polestar is showing off its new line of antitank TOW missiles, which Egypt bought in bulk last spring. They've loaded them with submunitions, so you aren't getting quite their normal blast. But hopefully, if Polestar properly trained the Egyptians in firing procedures, those tanks are going to turn into steel smoothies in about three minutes."

Cate stood on tiptoe to catch sight of a phalanx of helmeted soldiers fifty feet down the ridge, huddled around a giant black tripod. When she looked over at Kurt, he was grinning in antic-ipation. Cate ran his face through the UN criteria of a dangerous weapon: Did it aim, did it fire, did it detonate? The mood of the trailer reminded her of the time she'd been invited to watch a Giants football game from the owner's skybox, the well-dressed men at the window, the violence below them on the field. She half expected a waiter to materialize, carrying a tray of champagne.

"Who is Driscoll talking to?" she whispered.

"Egypt's assistant minister of defense," Matthias replied. "This spectacle has been arranged for his benefit. There's not usually so much show business to missile tests. Driscoll's hoping this demo will result in a nice pre-Christmas shopping order to get his totals up for the year."

The tanks were now gray ants on the horizon, and Matthias in-dicated that it was time to put her earplugs back in. Just as she did, Ivers glanced up from her workstation and locked eyes with Cate. A smile began to form on the tech's face, but it collapsed when she spotted Matthias next to her.

There was a short announcement in Arabic, muted by the ear-plugs. Cate watched Ivers speak into the walkie-talkie, and a mis-sile on a thin wire whistled out from the desert floor, racing at phenomenal speed until it disappeared. Then a red-orange ball engulfed one of the faraway ants. Cheers erupted in the trailer, and there were a few high fives, and there might as well have been champagne. Cate felt sicker than she had when she'd climbed into the SUV this morning. Was she the only one in the trailer imag-ining people inside that gray ant on the horizon? Because that's what these missiles would eventually be used on. That was their purpose, their target. One day the steel ants would be replaced with warm flesh and beating blood.

"I'm going to wait in the car," she told Matthias.

He pulled out an earplug. "Don't you want to talk to Driscoll? There'll be a break in a minute before they bring out some of the new prototypes."

Cate shook her head. She slipped out the door and descended the metal steps. As her foot touched the parking-lot gravel, she felt the boom of another missile hitting its target. Their driver sat in the front seat, watching an American television show on his phone with Arabic subtitles. Cate lay across the back seat, shutting her eyes, but the periodic explosions in the distance made it hard to find sleep. She must have finally dozed off, though, because she awoke to the sound of engines starting and the voices of the first guests returning to their vehicles. She wearily climbed out of the car and spotted Kurt Driscoll at the top of the staircase, chatting with the assistant minister. Ivers was already crossing the parking lot, heading straight toward her. Sweat soaked the top of the tech's shirt, and her flak jacket hung from one shoulder.

"Congratulations," Cate said, trying to sound cheerful. "Did the demonstration go well?"

"It did," Ivers said without smiling. She held a green work notebook at her hip, and Cate thought it must be the same kind that Eric had used to write his sordid confession. Of all the places he could have scrawled that note, why had he chosen a work-issued book that would surely be read by his employers? "Today's program was important for us," Ivers remarked. "I didn't expect to find you here."

"Last minute," Cate said, which wasn't technically an explanation.

Ivers studied her face with curious intent. "I know we hardly know each other," she said, "but would you mind if I gave you some advice? I'd stay away from Matthias Vos. He's a sleazy war profiteer, the definition of zero morals. He cruises war zones looking for loose change. Just a friendly warning from one woman to another: I don't think your brother would have liked to see you in his company."

Cate felt the urge to defend Matthias, who had watched over her and invited her out to this remote desert to find the answers that she'd been looking for. She glanced past Ivers and saw Matthias descending the staircase, holding a paper cup of what looked like ice cream in his hand. Others around him were digging into the dessert with small wooden spoons.

"Thanks for the advice," Cate said, resisting the impulse to ask Ivers how her own morals were holding up after the death spectacular she'd just staged.

"Matthias only brought you here to taunt us. And to shove a little pin in the minister's mind about last month's unfortunate incident."

"By 'unfortunate incident,' you mean my brother's death?" Cate took a step closer to Ivers. Driscoll was now at the bottom of the stairs, giving his goodbyes to the minister. "Listen, could we meet in Cairo to talk privately? You must have spent time with Eric in the days before he died. I'd like to hear—"

Ivers took a step back. "Uh-uh. I'm not allowed to talk to you about that. I've got my orders." She smiled stonily. "That subject is off-limits."

"I'm just asking for—"

The tech's gaze fell to Cate's neck. "Where did you get that?"

Cate looked down and realized that the tech was staring at the saint's medal. "It came back with Eric's possessions. Why? Have you seen it before?"

Ivers spun on her heels and hurried across the parking lot.

"Wait!" Cate grabbed the pendant and held it out on its chain. "Ivers, wait! Please tell me where you've seen this!" She was yelling through a swarm of generals, dignitaries, businessmen, and whatever substrata of military professional attended such horror shows.

Ivers didn't stop. Cate lunged forward, but she lost sight of the tech as a flurry of SUVs began backing out of the lot.

Kurt Driscoll was heading toward his car with an armed bodyguard by his side. He was only ten feet from Cate. She couldn't risk losing this opportunity.

"Hi, Mr. Driscoll," she said loudly, walking toward him with her hand outstretched. The guard stared at her open palm before Kurt shook it, confusion clouding his face. "I'm Cate Castle, Eric's sister."

His expression fell. Her hand was dropped. Belatedly, Cate realized it was only because Maura had been so welcoming that she assumed the hospitality would carry over to her husband. She was wrong.

"I heard you were in Cairo." He made it sound like an accusation. "What on earth are you doing out here?"

"I came to see you."

"Me?" he said mockingly. "I've got nothing to say to you!" He tried to walk away, but she blocked his path. The bodyguard looked uncertain as to how to handle her. "I have nothing to say!" Kurt repeated angrily. "And you have nothing to say to me. Do I need to remind you that you signed a nondisclosure agreement?" He gave her a second to contemplate that fact. "You forfeited your right to speak publicly on any matter pertaining to your brother's suicide. That includes talking to me about it at right here at a business function. Or anywhere, for that matter."

Kurt was correct about the terms of the settlement. But in that instant, with the sun beating down on her and his voice ringing in her ears, she didn't much care. As he stormed off with his bodyguard, she only knew that she wanted to hurt him for all the hurt that his company had inflicted on her family. Or if she couldn't hurt him, at least unsettle him. Anything she had signed in a Great Barrington conference room seemed to have little bearing in an African desert reeking of mortar blast.

"You and I both know Eric was murdered!" she yelled across the lot.

Those magic words stopped him. He turned and marched back toward her with such speed that his guard was left wrong-footed and stumbled to catch up.

"It wasn't a suicide," she said in a more compliant tone now that he had come back. "I know for a fact that Eric got into a fight with a group of Egyptian soldiers on his last trip out here—I can even identify one of them. A week later they went to his hotel room and killed him as payback for disrupting their smuggling operation. My guess is that you've seen the footage from the hotel cameras that proves I'm right. You're protecting them out of your own self-interest. That's why Polestar was so quick to dump all that money on us. You wanted to shut us up so we'd stop asking questions."

Kurt's Adam's apple bobbed. His blue eyes took her in. His face was as gifted in communicating hatred as it was delight. "You're out of your goddamned mind," he said. "You have no idea what you're talking about." A gust of wind batted his tie into the air, and he slapped it against his chest, the strike seeming to double his anger. "Be very careful before you make that kind of accusation again."

Cate could never resist a dare. "You're a coward. Eric worked under you, and you did nothing to protect him. Instead you covered up his death. You're a piece of shit."

His eyes widened, but he didn't take the bait. He gestured to his guard and stalked off toward his idling SUV, the guard glaring back at her as if retroactively fulfilling his job of intimidation. Cate was left standing in the lot, swaying off balance by her own anger. Another gust of wind sent a few used dessert cups skipping across the gravel.

Back at the car, Matthias was already buckled in the back seat, finishing off the remains of what turned out to be peach sherbet. The driver revved the engine.

She slumped against her window. "That didn't go well."

"It's a four-hour drive to the airport," Matthias announced. "I'm afraid that gives you a lot of time to play your conversation with Driscoll over in your head."

Matthias turned out to be correct. Nothing grew in the desert but regret. As they made their way through the flat, sun-bleached Sahara, she played and replayed the confrontation, wondering at what point she'd inflicted the kind of damage that could not be repaired.

Chapter 18

OMAR

Omar hadn't expected Ali Hamdy to call so soon.

"Did I catch you at a bad time?" the young man from Asyut asked.

"No, um, this is . . ." Omar stumbled. Veering nervously away from *a perfect time,* he overcorrected. "As a good a time as any." He was sorely out of practice.

"I can call back later," Ali offered.

"No, no. Don't!"

In the past forty-eight hours, Omar had drafted and deleted several texts to Ali without sending a single one. It was all Tobias's fault. The German had weaned him on a romantic sensibility not unlike the grad-school economic concept of artificial scarcity— the fewer phone calls, heart emojis, and what-are-you-up-to texts Omar sent, the stronger Tobias's desire grew. He'd become so accustomed to chasing a resistant boyfriend, he didn't know how to behave on the receiving end of interest.

"It's really nice to hear from you," Omar said, then defaulted to perhaps the dumbest filler question in the human arsenal. "Did you make it home okay on Sunday morning?"

"Yeah, the roads were empty at that hour. Although the bike has been giving me trouble. I had to take it into the shop. They think there might be a pinch in the fuel line."

Omar couldn't improvise an intelligent follow-up question, and they dipped into a lull of silence. But Ali proved brave. "The mechanic promised it will be fixed by Saturday. I was wondering if you were free that night."

"Really?" The word had slipped out before he could stop it. Wincing, Omar laughed. Ali did too.

"Yeah, really. Why, is there some reason I shouldn't want to see you again?"

"None!" Omar promised. He would worry later about devising a strategy to get around Mrs. El Fettah. "Let's definitely do something Saturday."

"Were you cold on the bike? We could take your car. Or I could meet you in the center—"

"No," Omar countered. "I love your bike." He wanted to be as brave as Ali. "I get to put my arms around you."

After they hung up, Omar crossed the living room and ducked under the laundry line. He was careful with the edges of Tobias's photograph, trying not to rip the corners when he pulled it from the wall.

He spent the next hour sending out emails to the contacts that his father had provided, introducing himself to CEOs and bank managers who had promised to grant his son a job interview. He still yearned for the escape hatch of an American visa, but the dreaminess of California had lost its sheen. It was worth at least humoring the option of staying.

When he glanced at the clock it was already after twelve, and he was horrified to realize he was on the verge of standing up Farida. Cursing himself, he sprinted around the apartment to gather his wallet, keys, and hearing aid. Farida had taken a huge risk on his behalf. He bolted down the stairs, conveniently free of Mrs. El Fettah the one time he could honestly announce that he was rushing off to see a young lady.

They'd planned to meet on the corner one avenue away from the Ramses Sands, ten minutes after Farida's work shift ended. She'd been on duty the past two nights, but on neither occasion could she safely access the computer in the reception office. This morning, however, she'd covered the phones while the operator took a break. She hadn't indicated in her Facebook DM whether she'd found anything on the computer, only that she would be waiting at their planned meeting spot.

Omar hopped into his car and drove with fury, already thirteen minutes late according to his dashboard clock. He blew through Zamalek, making excellent time, but as he crossed over the 6th of October Bridge, he got stuck behind the motorcade of a government official—two stretch limos requiring fifteen security vehicles, which, even in Omar's nostalgic adolescent mind, harkened to the Mubarak days of pageantry. By the time he located a parking spot half a block away, he was thirty-seven minutes late.

At the corner, Farida was nowhere in sight. He pictured her already on her way home, staring forlornly out the bus window. He pulled his phone from his pocket; he wouldn't badger her about meeting up again after her next work shift, he'd only tell her how sorry he was. But then he caught a glimpse of a bejeweled backpack peeking from behind a utility box a few feet from the corner, and there she was, still wearing her reception uniform with her name tag pinned over her heart. Her face was puffy, her eyes pink. Omar hoped it was due to work exhaustion and not to the heartbreak of waiting for the past thirty-seven minutes.

"I'm so sorry, Farida," he said and nearly gave her a hug to make amends, but physical contact might be construed as leading her on, even more so than he already had. He wondered whether she had drafted and deleted texts to him, just as he had to Ali.

"It's okay," she said unconvincingly. Her eyes skirted the curb.

"I was late because of one of those stupid motorcades," he explained. "It had me waiting at the bridge forever." He gripped his hair to mime frustration, which drew the smallest grin from her. "I'll make it up to you."

"Sushi?" she suggested. He looked at her, confused. "You mentioned a sushi place in Dokki. We could go there one night."

"Oh, yes. I did!" He'd completely forgotten. "We should! Do you like sushi?" Then he remembered how she'd proclaimed her newfound love of sushi at the coffeeshop. There was no rescuing him from this lapse, and thus, as he routinely did when making unwanted plans, he pushed the obligation of dinner off into the far-flung galaxy of the next week. "Let's go any day after Saturday. I'm free most of next week." That halfhearted plan didn't seem to redeem him in Farida's eyes, and he stepped forward to squeeze her shoulder. "I'm really sorry, Farida. Forgive me. It was rude to make you wait so long."

She nodded like she agreed with him and swung her book bag around to access the front pocket. Taking a deep breath, she pulled out a tiny black thumb drive. She glanced around and clumsily foisted it, like the world's worst drug dealer, into his palm.

"There," she said. "What you wanted."

He was caught off guard. He had expected the search for phone recordings to be futile, more a test of loyalty—Farida to him, him to Cate, Cate to his letters of recommendation—than a means of acquiring solid evidence pertaining to Eric's death.

"There really were calls from his room that night?" Omar sounded astonished even to his own ears. "Did you listen to them?"

Reluctantly, she nodded. "There's just one call. It's him calling down to the hotel operator. But it's . . ." She dropped her eyes to the ground to fight back tears. "It's a call asking for help. It's weird. He gets cut off." She shook her head as if warding off the memory of listening to it. Then she looked at him with urgency. "But I'm not the first person to listen to that call. I could see on the computer that it had already been downloaded once before."

"By who?"

She shrugged. "Who knows? Someone. The computer notes every time the file is downloaded. So it must have been the hotel manager? Or the police?" She pressed her lips together, as if to suppress uttering more fearful possibilities. It dawned on Omar that her tears weren't the result of his showing up forty minutes late; it was the call itself that had upset her. "If that man was asking for help like that"—her voice cracked—"it doesn't seem like a suicide, does it?"

"Oh, Farida, don't worry," he said, as tears began to flow from her eyes. "Please don't be upset." He put his hand on her shoulder and patted her synthetic work blazer. "I'm sorry I asked you to do this."

"But . . ." She gulped, strands of saliva hanging from her teeth. "If he was murdered, and they find out that I downloaded the file . . . the computer marks the time of each download—"

"No one is going to find out! It's a closed case. It's over and settled. Don't let that haunt your mind." She didn't seem swayed, her eyes studying the concrete between their feet. "Think about it. Have the police come back once to ask questions since the man died?"

"No," she admitted.

"See?" He brought his head close to hers, trying to catch her gaze. "Don't worry. Let's go for sushi next Monday, okay? Does that work for you?" He meant it. He would take Farida out for sushi every Monday until spring if it relieved the distress he'd put her through.

He walked her to the bus stop and saw her onto the express, waving as her ghostly shape floated down the center aisle. After the bus pulled away, he jogged back to his car. Rummaging through the glove box for an adapter, he plugged it in, rolled up the windows, and cranked up the volume on his car speakers. The first seconds of the call crackled around him.

"Hello? Can you hear me?" It was a man's voice, deep and urgent, bordering on hostile. It was a little slurred from drinking, but not to the point of witlessness. "I need you to connect me to the American embassy. The American em—"

There was an inaudible response from the female operator.

"Yes, please hurry," the man said, his voice growing more panicked.

The operator told him it was almost midnight, and that the embassy might not be reachable so late.

"I know it's after hours, but they must have an emergency hotline. They must have somewhere to call." The voice grew frantic. "I'm an American citizen. I need help! I heard things, about what they're planning to do with the weapons, and . . ." There was a pause, as if Eric regretted sharing that last detail. The phone seemed to fumble from one ear to the other. "Listen. Can you tell the front desk not to let anyone up to my room? No visitors, under any circumstances. Not even if they say I invited them. Hello? Are you putting me through? Hello? Hello?"

The call went dead. The recording stopped.

Omar sat gripping the steering wheel as if he were racing down a highway. He understood why the call had frightened Farida to the core. Eric sounded desperate and determined to protect himself, the exact opposite of a man planning on taking his own life. Omar had listened to Cate's story, and he'd been persuaded by the autopsy findings, and he'd agreed that no suicide would leap from a third-floor balcony. Yet listening to this fifteen-second call brought the grisly fact of murder home in a way that none of that abstract evidence had managed. Cate was right. Her brother had been killed, and these were his last recorded words, a man groping for any help he could find, a voice alone in the dark.

Omar started the engine and headed toward Cate's hotel. She had texted him the night before that she was back from the desert, and he knew she'd want to hear her brother's call as soon as possible. Already, as he sped west, he could see a giant yellow party tent erected on the Grand Nile's skyscraper rooftop. As Omar drove closer, the thick knot of cars around the hotel's entrance confirmed that a private reception must be taking place. The security team at the gate was swamped, and several glamorous Cairene women in sequins, refusing to wait, had left their cars to walk up the brick driveway. Omar decided to park around the corner. As he steered past the gate, he noticed a white town car idling on the opposite side of the street. It looked disturbingly similar to the one that had tried to take Cate at the airport. As Omar drove past it, he thought he could make out the bony face of the young man through the glare of the passenger-side window. He glanced in his rearview mirror. A hand hung from the driver's side, a ball of hairy knuckles with a silver pinkie ring. It looked as if they were waiting for Cate to emerge from her hotel to try their luck again.

Omar pulled over and turned on his hazards. Nothing dangerous could happen on a busy street in the middle of the afternoon in Garden City. He climbed out and walked toward the white town car, its windshield smeared in half-moons of dry, wipered dirt. Omar stopped in front of the passenger-side window, rapping his knuckles on the glass.

The window lowered, and the long, bony face of the young man with a stringy goatee stared up at him, smiling widely, as if exceptionally happy to see him.

Chapter 19

CAIRO

Cate sat on her hotel bed with her open laptop warming her thighs. For the past hour, she'd been trying—and failing—to compose an email to her mother and Wes. She wanted it to sound celebratory, rehabilitating Eric's image from a drunk, suicidal divorcee with a sordid sex life into a conscientious objector who'd sacrificed his life to his higher principles. That was all true, no gilding of the facts required; it should have been a moment of pride to report that to her family. Yet the memory of yesterday's fight with Kurt Driscoll in the desert kept falling like a shadow over the screen. *Coward. Piece of shit.* Every insult she'd hurled at him underscored her violation of the nondisclosure agreement. Had she put the family's settlement in jeopardy? How could she break the news to them that an entire predator class of financial problems might not have gone extinct like they thought? Eric's death mattered. But suddenly so too did the money, to the tune of several million dollars. The money. Eric's murder. Cate decided to take a break from the guilt trip of the email and go down to the terrace to plot her next move.

She grabbed her purse and took the elevator to the lobby, only to find it swarming with guests. Egyptians dressed in velvet tuxedos and long beaded gowns funneled toward the rooftop elevator. It must be some party, a wedding or an anniversary reception. By comparison, Cate felt like a slovenly American in her wrinkled shirt and khaki pants. As she wove around clots of partygoers, she spotted Roe Driscoll standing off to the side, fiddling with a piece of rope notched down its length like a rosary. In madras shorts and a T-shirt, he stuck out as much as she did. She swerved toward him, hoping the teenager might shed a clue to his father's motivations since his return from the desert. Perhaps Kurt had already warned his wife and son never to talk to her again.

"How are the knots going?" she said in greeting. Roe turned with a look of surprise, and she thought, *Oh, that's the answer, I'm verboten.* But the teenager's crooked grin quickly flared, and his shoulders slouched with the lazy posture of conviviality.

"Bad habit," he said, balling the rope up in his hand.

"We all have them."

"It beats smoking. I've been trying to get Mom to quit. I noticed when I looked in the ashtray that she had a cigarette when you two were outside talking the other day." He shook his head in mock disappointment.

Cate laughed. "Sorry. I'm not good at policing habits. But, yes, don't start smoking. Stick with the knots."

"The trick is to get so accustomed to doing them that you don't have to think twice when you're on the boat."

She was about to ask how the felucca classes were going, but Roe had turned to talk to a young man standing next to him, half hidden behind a column. Roe spoke warmly to him in broken but impressive Arabic. The guy was Middle Eastern, muscular and compact, with close-cropped wavy hair and a large, hawkish nose. Like Roe, he looked in his late teens, but unlike the American, he'd already completed the transformation into manhood, with a thick neck and the kind of clean, blue-tinted jawline that came from regular shaving.

"Hello," Cate said to the young man.

"Oh, sorry, this is Firas," Roe introduced. Cate repeated her hello and received a shy half nod in return. "He doesn't speak much English," Roe explained. "He's staying at the clinic for a few weeks. From Syria originally, although he's been in a few different countries before arriving here."

"I see," Cate said. Firas was a refugee. His clothes bore the telltale trace of Western charity hand-me-downs; his jeans boasted the repeating faux-graffiti logo of a discount denim brand; his shirt promoted a hockey team from Minnesota with a cartoon rooster mascot. He refused to make eye contact with Cate, staring almost belligerently into the lobby of swanning party guests. A lot of men in Cairo, she had noticed, avoided her altogether with their eyes. Cate turned to Roe. "It's nice of you to look out for him."

"Well," Roe drawled shyly, suggesting a catch, "it comes with a favor I have to ask you." He scrunched his nose. "I'm supposed to be teaching Firas how to drive a tuk-tuk, but it gets *soooo boring*. Firas told me how much he loved to swim as a kid, and Saad was begging for the pool, so I just brought them here to let them do laps." Roe grabbed Cate's hand, and she felt the tiny barbs of knots from the coiled cord in his palm. "But Mom and Dad would kill me, because it's breaking hotel rules. We're not allowed to bring friends from the clinic here. It's disgustingly elitist. Racist really. No Firas in *their* pool. Saad is only allowed because he's family."

Cate liked that Roe called Firas a friend rather than an assignment. She couldn't imagine that Maura would disapprove of this infringement on hotel privileges, but as for his father, she'd witnessed his anger up close.

"I won't say a word."

He smiled. "We're just waiting for Saad. He went to use the bathroom. My brother has the bladder of a gerbil."

Cate tried a casual shift in subjects, to glean Kurt Driscoll's state of mind. "Has your father returned from the desert?"

"Oh, yeah," Roe said with a roll of his eyes. "He got in last night."

"Did he say anything—"

"He was in such a crappy mood. He uses up all his charm on his clients, and Mom and I get what's left. He's demanding that I go to college back in America next semester. I know I have to go eventually, but I'm not ready yet." He puffed out a stream of air. "Now he wants me to enroll at some awful military school in the South. Can you believe that? He's obsessed with war, even when it comes to me."

"You've been so lucky to have these world adventures," she said noncommittally, afraid of incurring more bad will by speaking against his father.

"You're right," he agreed with a snort. "But I'm selfish. I want to be lucky forever."

Firas tapped Roe's shoulder. "I wait, I wait—" Unable to summon the words, he gave up and slipped past them toward the entrance.

"You'd think Dad would at least be pleased by my volunteering. He doesn't care. The clinic doesn't mean anything to him. But do you want to know the secret to being a successful tuk-tuk driver? Tuk-tuks are a tourist trade, so the most important lesson is the sales pitch. I teach the students to pull up to tourists in these slow-moving tin cans and say"—he mimed holding a steering wheel—"'You want a ride in a Ferrari?'"

Cate laughed. "Maybe I'll sit in on your class. Your mom invited me to visit the clinic."

"Yeah, you should come."

In the midst of his invitation, Saad appeared, pattering across the lobby, his sandals smacking the marble floor, his tiny body pinballing between the legs of the partygoers. He wore oversize plastic sunglasses and had a thick towel around his shoulders. His hair was a glossy black, dripping wet, and Cate could smell the chlorine on him as he launched straight into his brother.

"Hi, Saad," she said, and the giant sunglasses gazed up at her. "Do you remember me?"

He nodded sheepishly. "From the roof. You're Eric's sister."

"Yes, I am," Cate replied.

"Your brother was a favorite of the kids at the clinic," Roe told her. "They always gathered around him in art class, and he'd give them subjects to draw."

"I love to draw," Saad declared. "Will you tell Eric hi for me? I miss him. How is he?"

All Cate could manage was to smile through the heartbreak of the little boy's question.

"Sorry," Roe murmured. "Death's not something . . ."

"It's okay." She turned her smile on Roe, who pried the towel from around his brother's shoulders and began to dry the boy's head. Cate's phone vibrated with an incoming text. It was from Omar. Meet me as soon as you can, it read. I'm at a restaurant near your hotel. I have important news about Eric. Omar had included a map pinned with a location a ten-minute walk away. It seemed odd that he hadn't simply come to the hotel if the news was so important. But it was likely that the rooftop party had jammed the front gate, and maybe the guards hadn't let Omar through.

"Everything okay?" Roe asked as he folded the towel into a square.

"Yeah," she said. "I've got to go. I'm meeting a friend."

Roe hesitated in his goodbye. "I guess I should tell you that my father did have a few not-very-nice words to say about you when he got home last night."

She nodded in defeat. "I figured."

"He tends to overshare his work problems with us. But really, I should thank you. It took the heat off me for a night. At least he can't banish you to a four-year military college in rural Alabama."

Cate hurried down the hotel driveway, looping around the bumper-to-bumper congestion. But at the security gate she paused. Beyond the perimeter of the hotel, a vast ocean of threats lurked. Her brother's killers were still roaming free, and they'd already tried to silence her on two occasions. She double-checked the distance to the restaurant on Omar's map. Would ten minutes alone on the crowded sidewalks be safe? She scanned the street for a white town car but found no trace of one. If she walked fast enough, she could probably make it in seven. Omar wouldn't have written if the news hadn't been important. Glancing back at the hotel and its flurry of arrivals lining up at the metal detector, she told herself that it was too late to go back and ask Matthias or Roe to escort her. Before she could think wiser of it, she plunged into the flow of late-afternoon pedestrians. I'm on my way, she texted Omar.

It was the hour of domestic workers finishing their shifts. Cate traversed a crooked sidewalk dotted with exhausted bodies, beaten like rugs from a long day's work, some still dressed in their uniforms, others in street clothes, carrying plastic bags of groceries or laundry. Following the map, she turned at the corner onto a broad avenue reeking of bus diesel. Fluorescent lights in atriums began to blink on in preparation for night. She passed an old perfumery and a repair shop where a sewing machine was running unattended at the front table, punching stitches into thin air. The next storefront corresponded to the pin on Omar's map. There were no windows, only a heavy oak door with an unreadable sign in Arabic above it. Cate grabbed the door handle and went inside.

The space was dimly lit, with lacquered-wood panels covering the walls. The dining room hummed with customers. Cate passed through a green-carpeted bar where chubby men in suits lounged over drinks while Dubaian horse races flickered on flat screens. Tables were littered with scraps of paper and miniature pencils for the placing of bets. She gave Omar's name to the host, and he led her through a maze of peach-clothed tables and down a narrow hallway, where a few private rooms were situated behind closed pocket doors. The host stopped at the last door and drew it open. Cate spotted Omar sitting at a table. In front of him was a copper cup filled with red tea. At the sight of her he rose from his chair, his hand lifting in an open-palmed gesture that read like a warning. That's when she saw the two other men in the room.

"Cate, don't panic," Omar cautioned. "It's okay."

But his words failed to stem the alarm coursing through her as she recognized the men. So unexpected was the sight of the bearded soldier with the red birthmark and his bony-faced teenage accomplice that she froze, not in obedience but in fear.

"They aren't trying to hurt you," Omar swore. For a split second she wondered whether Omar had purposely lured her into their hands. He let out a soft laugh as if guessing her suspicion. "You're going to want to hear what they have to say. Trust me, okay?"

The boy with the goatee was smiling at her, just as he had at the airport. The older man was gazing at her with a mix of pity and apprehension.

"Omar," she cried, her whole body shaking, "these men are the killers. I found that out in the desert. They're lying to you! You're the one who's been tricked!"

"Ait Ast el," the older man erupted, and slapped his palm against his chest. "Your brother, no, I did not hurt."

"My father wants," the boy tried, "to make plain to you, to let you hear—"

"Please, Cate." Omar calmly gestured to an empty chair. "They didn't kill Eric. Listen to what they have to say. Although maybe it's best if I do the translating."

*　　*　　*

Her tea was cold by the time she went to sip it. Her tea was cold, and she was sitting in the back of a restaurant with two strangers who were not her brother's murderers. She gripped the arms of her chair to stop her mind from spinning. Omar had recounted their testimony, and the old man interrupted only occasionally with a complaint or clarification in Arabic.

The man's name was Gasser. She didn't catch his son's name, but the young man's commitment to his smile was so unnerving that she nearly asked him to stop. Omar already knew their story; he'd talked to them for an hour before she showed up. He trusted it. His English translation didn't include verb tenses that allowed for doubt.

Gasser had served as a career soldier in the Egyptian military. For the first twenty-five years of enlistment, his primary duty entailed "standing in the sun holding a rifle for fourteen hours a day." Six years ago, he had been promoted to corporal, and his new assignment involved overseeing one of the units entrusted to safeguard Egypt's foreign-made missiles. (Cate imagined these missiles like bottles of wine, stored in subterranean cellars on terracotta racks, Gasser rotating them and checking their vintage like a proud sommelier.) He was stationed in the Western Desert and often worked with defense contractors and weapons techs. Gasser admitted getting into a heated argument with Eric during a recent weapons check. He had lost his temper and threatened Eric, telling him he would be sorry for reporting that cache of equipment as operational. (It was at this point in the story that Cate whispered to Omar in lightning-fast English, "That's the motive, a threat on his life from this soldier a week before Eric was killed. How can you believe him?" But Omar held up a calming hand. "Just listen, Cate. He's come to you with his account voluntarily. Hear him out.") Gasser confessed that his squadron had tampered with the missile launchers so they would appear defective. But he was only following orders.

As Omar divulged this part of the story, the old man twisted his shirt anxiously at his chest. According to Gasser, the Egyptian military had an ongoing arrangement with Polestar to write off periodic caches of weapons as faulty and scuttle them from the official records. Those twenty launchers were slated to be sent across the border to Libyan fighters, which Sisi's government backed. This arrangement was routine to sidestep sanctions and covertly arm allies. According to Gasser, the Polestar tech was supposed to be aware of the agreement and sign off on the damaged goods. But due to some assignment mix-up, Eric showed up instead and fixed each launcher one by one.

"Gasser says that he always dealt with a different tech, a woman." Cate assumed it must be Ivers. "Apparently she was trusted to follow orders, and the arrangement had gone smoothly several times in the past. But Gasser had never dealt with Eric before, and when your brother failed to cooperate, he got angry."

Gasser nodded at Cate. "I am sorry for what I said to him. I paid."

Omar explained the price. Eric had reported the threat to Polestar, and Gasser had received a harsh reprimand from his superiors. That should have been the end of it. But not a week later, Eric was found dead behind his hotel, and in an effort to tie up loose ends, Gasser was formally discharged from the military—fired without explanation, given a small severance, and told to keep his mouth shut if he wanted to hold on to his pension.

"I have not killed anyone!" Gasser cried, his palm now beating against the table. "I have not!"

"For the past month Gasser has been working as a driver for a wealthy family in Heliopolis—hence the white town car," Omar continued. "He heard that Eric's death was ruled a suicide. But then one of Gasser's military friends tipped him off to the fact that you were coming to Cairo, the sister of the dead man whose life he had threatened, and he got scared. He figured you were going to raise a fuss and demand answers, and the government might feel the need to offer you a murderer." Omar waved at the old man at the end of the table. "Gasser wanted to talk to you before the police did, so he could explain what happened. Because once the police pointed their finger at him, he was sure to be—"

"Ask the tech!" Gasser cried. "The woman. Ask her if we don't always—" Struggling to find the words in English, he could only finish the sentence in Arabic.

"They didn't have to kidnap me to talk to me!" Cate snapped.

Omar nodded. "They thought I was a member of the security police running to rescue you. Me!" He laughed. "But to be fair, they figured you were going straight to the police, so they tried to corner you as soon as they could."

"Nothing's fair about any of this." Cate didn't want to give up her murderers. Gasser and his son had seemed convincing villains, and it hurt to release them back into the world of the innocent. Doing so meant that Cate had no clue what had happened to Eric that night in his hotel room. She tried one last time to force them to be guilty.

"Come on, Omar, the threat on his life. And Elizabeth Skyler said Eric was going to talk to her about a professional matter. It had to have been about their smuggling operation. He was scared for his life right before he died." She looked at Omar pleadingly, as if he were a judge.

"Maybe he was going to talk to her about the smuggling operation. Or maybe it was about something else. Either way, Cate, they didn't kill him."

"I am very sorry," Gasser said and reached his hands across the table. It was an offering, small and frail, and she took it.

"I'm sorry too," she said.

*　*　*

She didn't need Omar to escort her back to the hotel. Apparently no one in Cairo was trying to abduct her. She could run through the city screaming and flailing her arms, and no one would blink an eye. She and Omar walked together in silence for a few blocks. Only when the Grand Nile loomed ahead did he ask how she was feeling.

"Not great," she admitted. "I might as well have been sightseeing every day for the past week. I'm back to square one."

"That's not true. Gasser said that your brother lodged a complaint about their fight, which means he raised a red flag with Polestar about the incident. I don't know the protocols of the defense industry, but it's got to be illegal for a weapons company to help a government sidestep arms sanctions. Maybe your brother did more than raise a red flag. Maybe he threatened to report it to the US embassy, and that's why he wanted to talk to the attaché. I can't imagine that would have sat well with Polestar or the Egyptian government."

"Maybe, maybe, maybe," she echoed wearily. They were nearing the hotel gate, and Cate pictured her next steps involving only a hot bath, two sleeping pills, and booking a flight back to New York. "I can't vacation on maybes any longer." She squeezed Omar's arm in preparation for goodbye.

"Wait," he said. "I have evidence that Eric was killed over what he knew about those weapons."

"What evidence?"

He dug into his pocket and brandished a thumb drive as if it were a lit match. "I couldn't get any surveillance videos from the Ramses Sands. But I got the recording of a call Eric made from his room on the night he died. There was only one call. It was down to the hotel receptionist."

"Oh," she said dismissively. "I know about that call. They told us about it early on."

"They did?"

"Yeah. The operator told the police that he called down around midnight asking not to be disturbed. No one told us it was recorded."

"They probably hoped you'd never hear it, because it doesn't make a strong case for suicide. Cate, there's so much more to it than asking not to be disturbed. Your brother sounds terrified. And he specifically mentions a plan involving weapons."

"What?" She couldn't trace back the initial mention of the call. It had been offered as a fact from the very start to help establish his time of death. She hadn't even considered the call in all the discussions about hotel surveillance.

Cate practically dragged Omar up the Grand Nile driveway. Rushing through the metal detector and punching the elevator button, they could have been mistaken for honeymooners desperate for an hour in their room.

The idea of hearing her brother's voice frightened her. But she was also grateful for the chance to listen to him once more, alive for a moment in her ears, even if it was a voice in pain.

Cate sat on the edge of her bed and inserted the thumb drive into her laptop, turning up the volume. Omar leaned against the bureau.

Static. *"Hello? Can you hear me? I need you to connect me to the American embassy. The American em— Yes, please hurry. I know it's after hours, but they must have an emergency hotline."*

Cate paused the recording and stared at the floor. She squeezed her eyes shut, trying to retune her brain. She started the recording over from the beginning.

"Hello? Can you hear me? I need you to connect me to the American embassy."

She hit pause, took a breath, and glanced at Omar in distress. "Just listen to it all of it," he said.

"They must have somewhere to call. I'm an American citizen. I need help! I heard things, about what they're planning to do with the weapons and . . ." Cate's hands tightened into fists. She couldn't believe what she was hearing. *"Listen. Can you tell the front desk not to let anyone up to my room? No visitors, under any circumstances. Not even if they say I invited them. Hello? Are you putting me through? Hello? Hello?"*

The room went silent. "Well?" Omar exclaimed. "Did you hear him mention the weapons?"

Cate's face crumpled, and she started to laugh. "Yeah, I heard that part." Then she looked up at him and stopped laughing. "The problem is, that's not Eric on the call."

Chapter 20

CAIRO

At the center of the world, you can get everything except a Dutch newspaper. Matthias had to settle for an English edition. When Cate entered the dining room to join him for breakfast, he sat reading its pink-hued pages over a plate of half-eaten eggs.

"Never any news from home," he grumbled. "Always news of *your* home, of course. They can never get enough of the States. Tell me, what's it like to come from a land of consequence?" Cate didn't respond. She'd warned him when he rang her room that morning that she wouldn't be pleasant breakfast company. "I won't laugh at any of your stupid jokes." Determined to keep her promise, she signaled to the waiter for coffee.

Matthias continued scanning the news. "Sisi rounded up eighteen journalists and human-rights leaders yesterday," he reported. "He's made his quarterly sweep of insurgents, and away they go into the Tora prison complex, never to be heard from again. The amazing part is that it even made it into the paper. It must have been the English censor's day off."

Cate watched a blond Italian couple at a nearby table. They looked happy, sated by each other. The man read aloud the entry for *la città dei morti* in his guidebook.

"Hey." She turned back to Matthias. "Remember in Siwa when I asked you about soldiers selling weapons over the border?"

"Were they soldiers?" he retorted as he resumed eating his eggs. "I don't think we got that far."

"What about governments?" She leaned toward him and lowered her voice. "What about Egypt? Would they sneak weapons from their own arsenal to support the side they're backing in Libya?"

"The Myth of the End User," Matthias said as if he were quoting a movie title. "Legally, weapons have end users, meaning Egypt is supposed to retain all the arms it purchases. But that's just smoke and mirrors to keep the UN off your back. Of course they invent little ways to get around that stipulation. Every country does. If those embargos were effective, why are there still bombs exploding over Tripoli all these years later? They aren't being made in Libya."

Matthias's answer substantiated Gasser's story. She already knew in her gut that the corporal hadn't killed Eric. After all, neither Gasser nor his son could have faked Eric's American accent so convincingly in that late-night call to the Ramses Sands operator.

The voice on the recording hadn't belonged to Eric. It was most likely the voice of his killer, and equally likely that Eric was already dead—bludgeoned in the head—when the call came from room 3B to the night operator. The speaker must have known the conversation would be recorded. Its intention wasn't to beg for help but to be heard begging for it when Polestar and the Cairo police listened to the call later. It gave the needed false impression of a terrified defense tech rambling on about weapons and trying to contact his embassy. She and Omar had listened to it six, then seven, then eight times in her hotel room. The voice—disguised, muffled, hysterical, slightly slurred—belonged to the person she'd come to Cairo to find. "Are you sure that isn't your brother's voice?" Omar asked. Of course she was sure. She'd grown up with Eric's voice. Her entire life she'd heard it. She knew its tones and pitches by heart.

But even if the voice had been more convincing, the killer had made a small yet crucial error. Eric didn't need to rely on a hotel operator to contact the US embassy. He had a direct line via Elizabeth Skyler's personal cell phone number. The attaché had told her that fact. He could have called her at any time for help. No, the call was a ruse, a fire alarm pulled to draw attention away from the real motive for his murder. It was entirely possible that Eric's death had nothing to do with his job fixing warheads.

"Huxley!" Cate exclaimed to Matthias over the breakfast table. "Does that name mean anything to you?"

All she had left were the clues that she knew for certain had come from Eric: two postcards he'd mailed on the day of his death, and a cheap saint's pendant.

Matthias wiped yolk from his lips. "No, I've never heard that name."

"Have you ever visited a chocolate shop in Zamalek? It has a Jamaican flag in the window."

His face brightened. "Yes, I know where you mean! That flag in the window right after you cross the bridge. It sells sweets? I've never gone inside."

She pulled the pendant from her neck, and Matthias leaned forward to examine it.

"I'm not religious," he confessed. "What is that little man on it doing?"

"He's holding a baby boy to his chest. It's St. Anthony. Does that ring a bell?"

Matthias looked at her with bewildered sympathy. "How can I help you?" he asked. "Tell me what's troubling you. I thought you had found your answers. But now I don't even understand your questions."

She rose from the table. Matthias couldn't help her. She didn't understand her own questions either.

"I have to go," she said.

"Would you like to have dinner tonight?"

She wanted to remind him of his wife and kids in Amsterdam. But it wasn't Matthias who had been trying to wreck his family for the past week. It was Cate. "Maybe. I'll leave you a message at the front desk."

"I've come," he said, smiling, "to put a lot of hope in your maybes."

*　*　*

The first two taxis refused to take her to the neighborhood of Hay Al Asher. The hotel valet apologized and asked once again whether she was certain she had the correct address. "Tourists do not go there, ma'am. It is not a place to see." She wished she could ask Omar to drive her, but he was off visiting his parents in the suburbs today, and her destination lay east instead of west.

"I'll pay double," she told the valet.

Cate had tried reaching out to both Ivers and Maura Driscoll that morning. Neither had been in at the Ramses Sands. She wondered whether Maura would be less hospitable after hearing of her confrontation with her husband in the desert. Cate might very well need to make amends with Kurt Driscoll too. While Polestar had good reason to eliminate Eric for threatening to report their part in the smuggling operation, why purposefully incriminate itself by faking a recorded phone call about weapons plots? Why not let her brother be a drunken, paranoid suicide, leaving no final trace? It didn't make sense.

The third taxi drove her through a sprawl of car dealerships and weather-beaten housing complexes. Hay Al Asher emerged on the city's smoke-choked periphery. Bands of cables and extension cords hung like bunting between buildings. Kids ran giddily across gapped asphalt rooftops. Cars decomposed in empty lots, their doors and engines stripped. The smell of garbage pervaded the air. Hay Al Asher, according to the scant information she'd found online, was a refugee neighborhood, settled by various East African communities fleeing a half century's worth of war. Here and there on store awnings and windows hung small flags of Sudan, Eritrea, Ethiopia, and Tigray. True to the valet's word, there was no trace of tourism. Although the same question sprung to mind in this wrecked, poverty-struck neighborhood that arose when staring at the great wonders of Giza: How did this come to be?

In the blink of a single city block, the neighborhood transformed again into an ordinary congestion of strip malls and high rises. Aside from a proliferation of mosques, Cate could have been taking a taxi through mid-borough Queens. Out the window, competing car radios made a dissonant duet, one side all soupy treble, the other a leaden bass. The taxi ducked down a narrow side street and stopped in front of the clinic, a rectangular tan-brick complex that reminded Cate of Monument Mountain Regional. A series of brass plaques decorated the wall by the door. Cate spotted the Polestar Industries logo prominently placed under UNHRC and two other global peacekeeping organizations. A parking lot extended from one side, the perimeter enclosed in double-weaved chain-link. Cate glimpsed a sputtering tin vehicle at the far end of the lot. Orange traffic cones made an improvised course. The penny of Roe's hair was visible among the young bodies standing around the tuk-tuk. At least she knew one volunteer on duty today.

At the front desk, a lanky receptionist with an orange head-wrap notified Cate that Maura wasn't in. Gazing through an inner window, Cate caught a glimpse of a classroom filled with students mutely reciting words in unison. "Might Ivers be here?" she chanced, and the receptionist reached for the phone.

Cate would have preferred Maura, especially after the tense interaction with the tech on the military range. But when Ivers appeared at reception, Cate gave her a warm, sorority-worthy smile and was relieved to receive one in return.

"Sorry to bother you," Cate said meekly. "Maura invited me on a tour of the facilities. I thought she would be here . . ."

"She's off today. But I'm happy to show you around. It won't be the Driscoll five-star donor tour, but I'll do my best."

As Ivers held the inner door open, Cate decided to banish any lingering resentment. "Let me just say, if I was rude to you the other day, I hope you'll forgive me. I think all the explosions did something to my head." Cate was rehearsing for her potential bigger apology to Kurt.

"No need to apologize," Ivers replied. "Although"—she made a point of sustaining eye contact as Cate slipped by—"I do hope you took my advice."

Cate gave an indeterminate smile and charted the subject away from Matthias. "Do you live in the Berkshires too, like all the other Polestar techs?"

Ivers let out a small laugh. "I spend time there, but I've actually kept my place in Pittsburgh. I'm the one holdout from tight-knit Western Mass, the exotic Pennsylvanian." She beckoned Cate to follow her down a hall. "I'm afraid I can't show you any of the *active* rooms," Ivers said. "We don't want members to feel they're on display, forced to perform *need* for visitors. But you're in luck.

Today's pretty quiet." Ivers took Cate through a computer lab and modest paperback library, a game room of air hockey and Ping-Pong tables, a woodshop studio, and a "mental health lounge" with giant baseball-glove chairs ready to catch distraught teens. Ivers paused at the doorway to a wing devoted to women's health. "This is the section I'm most proud of. Many of the displaced have suffered sexual violence before they fled. Polestar funds this unit. We're able to provide a service that, frankly, offers more resources for young women than I had access to growing up in rural Pennsylvania."

Cate had been skeptical of the tangible good a team of weapons specialists could provide war-torn refugees. She'd thought of the clinic the way Elizabeth and Lucas had: something between a conscience-reliever and a PR stunt. During the tour, however, Cate became a convert. What tangible good had she ever effected back in New York? Yes, Ivers organized missile demos, but she also devoted her free hours to helping refugee women. Which stance proved more beneficial, Ivers with her thumbs on both sides of the scale, or Cate with her hands nowhere near it, arms permanently crossed in judgment? Cate had played a bystander her entire life.

The clinic, Ivers explained, was founded in the early 1990s to aid the influx of Sudanese refugees. But with the new century, the pattern of refugee migration no longer followed the predictable flow of the Nile, south to north. Asylum seekers poured in from every direction—Syria, Yemen, Libya, and Afghanistan. Ivers called it "the tornado effect," as if it were a freak weather event rather than a result of human agency. Polestar began its sponsorship in 2005, and in recent years the clinic had expanded its mission to include education and job training for young adults.

"Say what you want about Egypt's current government," Ivers said, "the country has proven a safe haven for refugees. I wouldn't say it welcomes them with open arms, but who does? It tolerates them and gives them opportunity, which is more than Europe is willing to do. Or us. Egypt is stable. And when you're from a place that's always teetering, stability is gold." She pointed across the courtyard to a small dormitory, home to a few of the most recently arrived until apartments could be secured for them. "We're not a camp," Ivers emphasized as she opened the door to a series of dark, interconnecting classrooms, "we're a communal building block. Do you see the difference?"

Cate waited until they reached the second classroom, terrarium-lined and devoted to science, to ask, "What did Eric do on the days he volunteered here?"

If Ivers noticed the calculated swerve in the conversation, she didn't wince. "Oh, Eric was terrific with the kids," she effused. "Here was this strapping, tall American who looked intimidating, but he was so patient and kind with the children. They really responded to him. Eric and I often volunteered on the same days."

Who do you think murdered my brother? Cate posed a softer, adjacent question. "Did he come here that last week? In the days before he was killed?"

Ivers narrowed her eyes. "Before he committed suicide, you mean."

"Okay," Cate relented. "That last week, after he returned from the desert. Did he volunteer here with you?"

Ivers stared at the ceiling as if memories from a month ago collected there. "No," she said. "He didn't."

"You're sure?"

"I'm very sure. He was in terrible shape that last week, drinking, lashing out, acting nothing like the friendly Eric I knew. I stopped by his hotel room and asked if he wanted a ride here." Ivers shook her head as if still offended by Eric's response. "He was rambling on about how he'd wasted his time volunteering. That all of us had. That we were just making things worse. Your brother was really depressed. If you want to blame Polestar for something, blame them for not addressing the obvious signs of mental illness that brought him to take his life."

Cate took her chance. "Not everyone thinks he killed himself." Ivers's expression hardened. "People other than my family believe he was murdered. People who work for Polestar *know* he was murdered."

"You're talking about Lucas," she retorted. "You can't trust a word he says."

"That's the second man in the weapons business you've warned me about."

Ivers smirked. "No. Unlike your Dutch friend, Lucas is harmless. Careless is more his style. Sloppy. Stupid. We wasted nearly a week of resources looking for him in the desert. For what it's worth, he was jealous of your brother. He never had the skills for the job, and he always leaned on your brother for help. He's back, you know. I saw him at the hotel this morning packing his bag. I'm shocked he quit."

"Why?"

She rolled her eyes. "It's good money, and Lucas should have been fired years ago. I never understood why Polestar kept him on. Loyalty, I guess." Cate knew the reason: Lucas told the requisite number of lies to the police. Cate also knew that Ivers was the tech that Polestar relied on to forge reports and let soldiers slip into the desert with illicit arms. Maybe Ivers believed that such duplicity served a larger purpose. Maybe arming Libyan rebels helped to preserve the precious stability that kept the war zone far away from Hay Al Asher and the women's health unit. No matter, it was clear to Cate that Ivers wasn't going to betray Polestar to help her.

"One favor," Cate pleaded and pulled the pendant from her

neck. "Just tell me where you've seen this before. That's all I'm asking, and then I'll go."

Ivers gave the medal only a cursory glance.

Cate's eyes stung with tears. "I'm not asking you to—" She took a breath and tried a different tack. "Maura thought it might have come from the clinic. She said a lot of Christian groups donate religious items along with supplies."

"Is that what Maura said?" Ivers blinked in astonishment. "Well, then, I guess you have your answer. Let me walk you back to reception. I have—"

"The pendant came back in a box of Eric's possessions. We received so little, not even his wallet. Just this medal of St. Anthony that none of us can account for."

"Ask Maura!" The tech's face flushed. "She knew your brother better than anyone. She would know what he wore under his clothes." The implication hung between them, hovering in the classroom air like chalk dust from clapped erasers.

"What are you saying?" Cate asked.

"It's not a huge secret!" Ivers wailed, as if trying to convince herself that she hadn't just broken a confidence. "I don't know how long it went on for. Or when it stopped."

Maura and Eric. Cate recalled Elizabeth Skyler's comment in the park: *You could line up all the women he invited to that apartment in Zamalek.* Of course there had been other women. One of them was Maura Driscoll, who'd gone out of her way to tell Cate how close she and her husband had gotten since Saad's adoption, as if to keep such suspicions at bay.

The tech's phone rang, and she answered it. "Yes. We're in classroom E. I'll tell her." She gave Cate a warning look as she hung up. "That's Roe. He wants to say hi to you."

In a minute they heard the thrum of sneakers along the hall.

Roe appeared in the doorway, his face damp with sweat, his chest heaving from the run. He looked embarrassed by his own eagerness, but as he walked into the room, he recovered his relaxed, nineteen-year-old demeanor.

"I saw you from the parking lot," he said. "I wanted to catch you before you left."

"I'm about to take her up to the front," Ivers informed him.

"I'll take her. I want to show her the dogs first."

Ivers waved a flailing hand, refuting responsibility for the burden of Cate, and left without a goodbye.

"Poor Kayleigh."

"That's her first name?" Cate refused to accept a world that could be blown to pieces by a person named Kayleigh.

"She hates when I call her that," Roe giggled. "She never seems to realize she's only a volunteer here. She and Mom are constantly butting heads. Kayleigh always knows how to do things better than anyone else. Honestly, if you hadn't shown up today, she'd be out monitoring my driving class." Cate was about to ask how Firas, the Syrian swimmer, was doing on the tuk-tuk, but Roe snapped his fingers. "The dogs! I thought they'd mean something to you."

He led her through the classrooms. Cate kept expecting to hear barking, but the rooms kept their silence. The last classroom was devoted to art, with tables covered in dried paint spills. Children's drawings papered one wall. Roe led her to a section at the far end. For a second, she couldn't recognize their subject—hairy embryos of black and brown splotches, eraser-pink tongues, and curlicued tails. But the longer she stared at the drawings, the more they congealed into a specific form, each white rectangle a crate that kenneled a baby Doberman.

"Eric's puppy?" Cate guessed. "But Moose is in the Berkshires with my sister . . ."

"Eric had a bunch of photos on his phone," Roe explained, "and the kids would crowd around to look at them. It kind of became an art project to draw Eric's puppy." Roe tapped a particularly messy drawing on the top row. "Saad did this one. He *loved* that puppy. He still asks all the time if he can get one. *A puppy just like Eric's.* Saad idolized your brother. Did my mom tell you that?"

Cate shook her head. She wanted to ask Roe whether he knew of Eric's affair with his mother. But there was no way to broach that subject without hurting him. When he looked over at her, he saw the worry on her face and misread it. "I'm sorry. I thought it would make you happy to see how much the kids admired Eric."

"It does make me happy, thank you," she said and paused. "Did you and Eric ever talk?"

"A little." He went quiet for a minute, and they both stared ahead, as if peering out a picture window rather than into a wall of children's scribbles. "He would listen to me when I was having trouble with my dad. My father and I don't get along so well, maybe you caught that? We've always been distant. And I guess Eric had a tough time with his father too."

"Yeah," Cate said. "To be honest, our father could hardly be called a father. He left us when we were little."

"Oh," Roe said in surprise. "I got the impression that Eric and your dad were close. Eric spoke so highly of him."

"Oh, well, yeah." Cate had spent so many decades thinking of Jason Castle as their common enemy, she kept forgetting that Eric had made amends with him. "You're right. They patched things up toward the end. I guess I should tell you it's never too late. Although it is for me. But Eric spoke of our father to you?"

"Yeah. A few times. Always good things."

Always good things, Cate thought, but according to Lucas, he'd made nasty remarks about their father the night before his death, only to send him a postcard the very next day. Why was it that even here, far across the ocean, reminders of that man kept barging back into her life? Was he somehow involved in Eric's death? No, Cate could blame Jason Castle for any number of crimes—not least of all, making a payday out of Eric's end. But she could not accuse him of murder from five thousand miles away.

"Are you okay?" Roe asked, staring over in concern. "Did I say something wrong?"

"No. I was just thinking about fathers."

Cate wondered whether Roe's father had learned of the affair between Maura and Eric. Her mind returned to the most crucial fact she'd learned from her visit to the clinic: Maura was one of the women who frequented Eric's apartment in Zamalek. What if the point of the postcard had never been the gibberish message on the back? What if, all along, the real meaning was the picture on the front? It was the place that mattered, the store with the Jamaican flag in the window and the apartment above it where Eric conducted his affairs.

"Roe?" she asked. The teenager was practicing his sailor's knots, tying them on an invisible string. He pulled at the air tightly. "I need to talk to your mom. Where can I find her today?"

*   *   *

In a taxi back to the Grand Nile, Cate texted Omar, asking for one more favor. Would he take her back to the shop on Zamalek, and this time she would go inside and speak with the clerk?

I'm visiting my family today, Omar replied, but let's meet tomorrow morning, say at eleven, in front of the Egyptian Museum? Cate asked if he could pick her up earlier from her hotel. He wrote back that the shop didn't open until noon, and in the meantime, couldn't she spend five minutes looking at ONE ANCIENT MASTERPIECE so I can tell my aunt I took you somewhere besides a Jamaican candy store? Five minutes. Then we go straight to Zamalek. They're moving all the treasures to a brand-new museum in the desert that looks like an airport terminal. This is your last chance!

Fine! she agreed. See you there.

Maura Driscoll might have been anywhere in Cairo, but according to Roe, she was spending her free day relaxing at Cate's hotel. "She goes there sometimes when Dad's in town," Roe admitted. "I do too. We even have a special deal where we can take a room for a few hours, just to get away from home." In that moment, staring at the young man, Cate recognized a fellow runaway. "Now you know," he said, "why I like being out on boats so much. No one can reach you out there."

The Grand Nile's five-star amenities included a gym, yoga studio, and spa, but Cate found Maura in the mazelike gardens beyond the swimming pool. She was alone reading a book on a quiet square of grass, lying on a blue batik. A few dirty dishes were stacked next to her, the top one having served as an ashtray for the butts of two rolled cigarettes. Maura wore a pair of jeans and a loose cotton shirt, her hair tucked into a Panama hat. It was Cate's advancing shadow, a black compass needle creeping over the grass, that caused her to glance up with a start.

"Cate!" she cried, her hand on her chest. She lifted herself to her knees and gave the kind of involuntary smile that comes after a sudden fright.

"Hi Maura." Cate couldn't generate much warmth in her greeting, and the chill seemed to grow between them as they lapsed into quiet.

"Kurt told me that he saw you in the desert," Maura finally said. "It sounds like it wasn't a friendly encounter." She closed her book and took off her hat, letting her long hair fall down her back. "I'm afraid I might have given you the wrong impression about Kurt. He can sell you the sky, but he's not so terrific when it comes to compassion."

"I wish you had told me about you and Eric."

Maura didn't flinch. She merely tilted her head up so her face caught more of the sun. "I didn't feel it was necessary to share that with you. I still don't see how it's pertinent."

"It might help to explain the mood he was in before he died. Drinking, depressed, acting out. You must have been witness to that."

"Our . . ." She fumbled for the right words. "Our *time together* didn't last long. A couple of weeks. I wasn't going to leave Kurt, and Eric didn't want that either. Even so, it was a messy situation, hardly ideal with Kurt being his boss. That's why I didn't tell you. I don't want our marital problems to be the subject of gossip, and I don't mean just here in Cairo. We live in the Berkshires too, and you know how small that community is, everyone on top of each other." She brought her leg to her chest and hugged it. "It was a minor fling. Eric had an apartment he rented in a separate part of town, safe from the surveillance of the Ramses Sands. There had been other women before me." She let out a pained breath, and Cate reminded herself that Maura had lost someone too, no matter how minor the affair. "I cared about Eric," Maura said. "And yes, I was worried about him in those days leading up to his suicide."

"It wasn't a suicide!" Cate pulled the St. Anthony from her neck. "You lied to me about this. You have seen it before."

Maura's jaw tightened, and she gathered her book and sunglasses. Cate dropped onto the batik, her knees feeling the damp grass below the fabric. "I'm going to need an answer from you."

Maura gripped her book to her chest. It was a hardback on the history of modern Yemen. Cate thought of Saad and what he'd experienced back in his home country. There must have been women sitting on a sheet in a garden there, bickering over a love affair, just as she and Maura were doing right now, when the sky opened up and five-hundred-pound bombs rained down on them.

"I'll tell you about that pendant," Maura said. "But you can't be mad at me for what you hear." Cate nodded, and Maura took a steadying breath. "I *have* seen it before, and I didn't lie to you, it was at the clinic. It was worn by a young woman, a refugee, who was briefly dorming there. She couldn't have been older than seventeen. No parents or siblings. All alone. A vulnerable girl." Maura's voice shrank into a soft monotone. Like a patient under hypnotism, the fight went out of her words. "Eric had just come back from the desert, and I remember I was so excited to see him. He'd given me a spare key to the apartment he rented, so I went there to wait for him. That's where I found it. Felt it really, a cold spot like a dime in the bedsheets. It was that girl's pendant. And that's when I knew what Eric had been using the apartment for when I wasn't around."

Cate's immediate impulse was to defend her brother, but she kept quiet, staring at Maura with a neutral expression.

"I confronted him about it," Maura continued. "He denied it at first. *No, no, no.* But it was clear that he'd taken advantage of the girl, and she wasn't the only one. Who knew how many others there had been? I was disgusted by what he'd done. I banned him from ever stepping foot in the clinic again. I threatened to go to Kurt or to the police." Maura shut her eyes. "Honestly, I was so shocked that I hadn't decided what action to take. But that's the reason for your brother's erratic behavior in those final days. He got caught, and the fear and guilt took its toll."

Maura reached for her phone. She opened an email, holding it up for Cate to read. It was the note that the police had found in Eric's hotel room. "I'm guessing you've already seen this?"

It's sick to be taking advantage of those young men and women. I won't make any more excuses. Exploiting a crisis, paying for sex, and they have to take the money. What choice do they have? Disgusting! I can't stomach it anymore.

"I think," Maura said somberly, "it explains why he decided to end his life."

"I don't believe you," Cate replied matter-of-factly. "Eric didn't kill himself. He had defensive wounds on his hands. He had multiple fractures on his skull that couldn't be explained by a fall from a third-floor balcony."

Maura sighed and rose to her feet.

"He was dead before he went over the railing," Cate said, staring up at her. "It was murder. No matter what you think he got up to at the clinic, he didn't commit suicide."

Maura gave an indulging nod. "Perhaps you're right," she said. "I'm not the police. You asked me about the medal and his state of mind. I told you the truth. In all honesty, I blame myself. I should have reported him right away." She gathered up the dirty dishes. "If it really was murder, maybe it was carried out by one of those young people he abused. Did that possibility ever occur to you, that he died because of his own bad choices?" A cruelness ran through her voice. "Maybe they confronted him in his hotel room that night, and the fight got out of hand. We'll never know."

Maura was clever. For a moment that scenario seemed disturbingly feasible. The only snag was the voice on the recorded call to the hotel operator, the patriotic twang of a frightened, babbling American that seemed near impossible for a foreigner to imitate with authenticity. It was the flimsiest hitch in Maura's convincing theory, but Cate clung to that American voice for dear life.

"Where's the girl now?" Cate asked. "I'd like to give her medal back to her."

"I don't know. She's gone." Maura balanced the stack of plates against her hip and put her hand out to take the pendant. "I could try to return it to her."

Cate smiled and shook her head.

"Look," Maura said sincerely. "I'm sorry that what I told you hurts. I wish we both could go back and save him."

They walked in silence through the garden. As they passed the swimming pool and approached the terrace, Maura stopped and squinted at Cate. "I would appreciate if you didn't mention the affair to Kurt. He doesn't know, and we've been trying to get back on track."

"Of course," Cate said.

"Oh, damn, I forgot my hat in the garden."

"Let me take those," Cate said, grabbing the plates. But before Maura could make her escape, Cate posed one last question. "If you don't mind, the apartment that Eric rented, the one where you two met up. Where is it in Cairo?"

Once again, Maura didn't flinch. "Oh, it's far from here. Eric rented a hole-in-the-wall in the southern part of the city. Impossible to find, in a nothing of a neighborhood." She laughed, as if marveling at her own lie. "I never understood why Eric chose such a dingy, forgettable place. Honestly, I can't even remember the street it's on."

Chapter 21

OMAR

O mar was lying on his back in his parents' backyard, his arms folded behind his head. Through his sunglasses he saw his mother hovering over him, her shadowed face peering down with a mix of apprehension and amusement.

The two had spent the past hour walking in long rectangles around the backyard, trying to determine the best spot to dig the swimming pool. Should it go near the robin's-egg Jacuzzi? Or farther out in the strip of imported Bermuda grass? Omar endorsed a compromise location in the limbo of the patio region, an idea his mother at first vetoed because it had cost too much money to have the concrete poured there. To convince her, Omar sprawled out on the ground, pretending to float on the surface of a pool, while his mother walked around him in a broad circumference.

"Okay, get up!" she finally demanded, worried the neighbors might catch her only son lying on the ground like a lunatic. Omar smiled and tried to enjoy a few more seconds of drifting in the imaginary deep end. "Omar!" she cried and clapped her hands. He laughed as he sprang to his feet. "My, aren't you in a good mood today!" she said almost hostilely. "I haven't seen you in such high spirits since you returned from London."

His mother was right. For the first time in so long, he was in a wildly good mood, and a part of him ached to tell her the reason: a second date with Ali Hamdy on Saturday night. On his drive out to Palm Hills that morning, he'd received a text: Excited for Saturday! It had come entirely unprompted, free and unguilted from the fingers of the young man in telecommunications whom he would meet for dinner and hopefully take to bed again. After he read that message, every love song that played on the radio should have come with its own trigger warning.

"Gwami made lunch," his mother said. "You're staying, aren't you?" Gwami (whose real name was Galila, but who had adopted the nickname due to his sister's lisping mispronunciation as a toddler) had been the family's nanny, then its cook and housekeeper, and, god willing, would end up playing his parents' nurse and angel of death. Gwami was deeply religious and abhorred the current government for its anti-Islamic policies. Yet she adored Omar's mother, who herself disliked religion in any form and hated the predominance of the veil but in turn pretended to keep fast during Ramadan for Gwami's sake, stashing granola bars in her underwear drawer to eat in secret throughout the day. His was a family built on gentle deceptions.

"Of course I'm staying for lunch, Mom. I've come all this way to spend time with you."

"You make it sound like you flew in from another country! We're not *that* far away. You could come more often!" His mother shook her head, her wavy hair molded into place by all the hair spray she used. To Omar, home smelled like hair spray; it sounded like a particular French-Arab radio station beamed in from Paris that his parents always played in the background. Home, however, did not taste like the flaky white fish with sweet mango chutney that Gwami had prepared for them in the dining nook.

"We bought her an international cookbook," his mother bragged. "She's trying a variety of new cuisines."

"At gunpoint, I'm guessing," Omar retorted.

"The world's changing," his mother said lightly as she picked out fish bones with her fork. "Even Gwami is excited about it."

The world was changing, even in Egypt, but it hadn't caught up to Omar yet. He tried to picture bringing Ali home to this pink-stucco villa, pulling into the driveway on the back of his motorcycle, his arms around Ali's waist. That vision seemed as far away from reality as life on the moon.

His father had already grilled him on his job search before driving off to his club for the afternoon. The stern paternal lecture meant that his mother was giving him a pass on a second round of employment hectoring over lunch. When his phone rattled on the table, she frowned at the bad manners of it. But the text was from Cate, which gave him an excuse to answer it—after all, he was still technically doing his aunt a favor by escorting this lost American around Cairo. Omar was in such a good mood that he insisted on meeting Cate tomorrow at the steps of the Egyptian Museum before they drove to the shop in Zamalek. He would drag her on a quick tour so that she could see at least a few ancient wonders of his city. As he typed, his mother began to glare impatiently. "Omar! Not while we're eating."

"It's a text from Aunt Lina's American friend."

"What's this young woman like?" His mother began scraping the chutney off her fish. He knew that she missed Gwami's lentils.

"She's nice. Smart. A real New Yorker."

"I never think of New Yorkers as nice. Is she married?" Even though his mother declared herself a staunch feminist, she stubbornly subscribed to the usual arcane domestic traditions.

"No, Mom. Not everyone needs to get married."

"Is she pretty?"

"Yes, quite."

"How old?"

"Mid-thirties?"

His mother shivered, not from the cold of the house's year-round AC, but from the idea of Cate Castle, pretty and unmarried in her mid-thirties, all alone in the world.

"I'm taking her to the museum tomorrow. Aunt Lina's going to owe us big-time for all the tour-guiding I've been doing."

"Be kind to her," his mother pleaded, as if pretty single American women were a persecuted class. "And please shave that beard you're growing. You're so handsome, Omar. Why do you insist on hiding your face from the world?"

On the drive back to Zamalek from Palm Hills, Omar decided to line up a few job interviews for next week. It wouldn't hurt to explore the option of staying, and it would keep his father from barking at him. He could still submit Cate Castle's recommendation letters for his visa, playing at two different futures, making a lottery out of the year ahead. Lying in bed that night he thought of Ali, the bundled muscles at his shoulders like those on a rower, the fine nodes of his spine where his waist narrowed, and the soft black hair that fleeced his ass and thighs.

The next morning Omar made coffee, did his seven-minute YouTube abs workout, and wrote a few more groveling letters of introduction to the contacts that his father had supplied. It was almost 10:30 when he checked his phone and realized he had to meet Cate at the museum. He snapped on his hearing aid and grabbed his keys. Switching his phone's keyboard to English, he typed a message to Cate as he jogged down the stairs—On my way, I'll be on time for once, don't buy museum tickets, my treat. He pressed send as he reached the lobby.

Surprisingly, Mrs. El Fettah wasn't sorting through her daily trove of glass bottles. He yanked open the building's front door, entering the yellow diesel-scented light of Zamalek. Mrs. El Fettah was standing on the sidewalk, her stick broom pressed to her chest. Her furrowed face held an alarmed expression, as if she'd just been notified that her husband wasn't dead from cancer all these years, but alive and snorkeling off Sharm el-Sheikh. Never at a loss for words, she struggled to speak, her tongue a useless rudder, her mouth moving in gnashing circles. That's when Omar noticed the two men standing a few feet away. One was chubby and short, the other less chubby and less short, both wearing the conspicuously inconspicuous plainclothes of a navy sweater and black nylon jacket. Mrs. El Fettah wrestled her hand from her broom and pointed her finger at Omar. The two men sprang on him so quickly he didn't catch their first words to him. But their identity was clear from Mrs. El Fettah's terrified eyes: members of the security police.

"No," Omar wailed weakly. His heart was beating in his throat, and the worst part was the smoothness of his extraction. He had somehow already been led to their car, parked in the street, and he hadn't yet made any committed act of resistance. No one was intervening in this abduction, not even himself, because he and everyone else had been raised to live in mortal fear of the security police. "No," he said more decisively, finding some depth in his voice, although it was still too meek. "Why? Why are you taking me? I've done nothing."

"We are arresting you by order of the government," the shorter man said, squeezing his arm tightly, and that was the only explanation he provided.

Mrs. El Fettah. Her stick broom with its gnarled handle at her chest. That was the last he saw of his neighborhood, for plastic shades covered the car's back windows, like motel blinds pulled down for privacy. He could have tugged one up, except that he was ordered to sit on his hands and keep his head down, or they would be forced to handcuff and hood him. The officers climbed into the front seat, the taller one driving. Omar felt the eyes of the shorter man on him, but he was carefully examining the blue floor mat, scared to lift his eyes above the horizon of the front seats. His heart was hammering so hard he thought he might pass out; his mind was flooding with rumors and stories and fragmentary nightmare accounts of what Egypt's secret military police did to those who were detained—young or old, man or woman, rich or poor, powerful or weak, anyone, *everyone*, for the crime of high treason or for no reason, all of them disappearing into the same black box.

Simply to break the awful silence, he repeated, "I have done nothing wrong."

The shorter man replied doubtfully, "Then you have nothing to worry about."

They killed people. They tortured them. They shaved their heads. They gave them packets of cookies to eat while the sounds of other detainees being beaten could be heard through the walls. They released them without any incident in three hours. They apologized profusely for the misunderstanding and gave them cab fare home. The prisoners were never heard from again. There was no routine or logic to the detentions. The berserk unpredictability of an arrest was a key ingredient of the terror. Prisoners went two years without seeing a judge. They were allowed to call their lawyers within an hour. Their names were erased from public record. They received a small compensation for their trouble. Their photo was put in the newspaper, they were listed as a sexual deviant, and a news camera filmed them in the courtroom's metal cage as their crime was read by the judge. It was all orchestrated for maximum shame.

The car slipped underground, the interior submerged in darkness. The tires rolled over grates with a steely muffled echo that suggested they'd entered a parking garage. The officers climbed out, Omar's door opened, and there was a squeeze on his arm. His phone vibrated with an incoming message in his pocket. "Please, can I make a phone call?" he begged as he got out of the car. He'd call his father—he would suffer the shame of explaining his arrest later, but for now it was urgent that someone in his family knew where he was.

"Let me see your phone," the agent said.

Omar was shocked that he still possessed the freedom to move his arms. He pulled his phone from his pocket. The agent took it. "Thank you."

They waited to be buzzed through a set of glass doors. Down a long white corridor were more doors, each one buzzing open. Omar's legs shook as they approached a steel desk where a uniformed guard sat stationed. But they sailed by the desk without stopping. Maybe he was only being brought in for a light grilling, some tough questions thrown at him as a scare tactic, followed by a lecture on his deviant behavior destroying the moral fabric of society. He'd promise to change his ways and be released. For a moment Omar allowed himself to believe that his privilege would save him. He had gone to elite schools, studied abroad, and belonged to a wealthy, respectable family. Only the day before, he and his mother had been walking around a backyard in Palm Hills, consumed with the question of where to put a swimming pool.

More hallways, and the grip on his arms tightened. Omar felt it wouldn't matter if he continued walking or dragged his feet or lifted his knees to his chest; there was no slowing down their progress. They were a part of the system now, the way small fish were part of the sea.

Doors with portal windows lined a narrow hall. There was no natural light, only the hot glow of fluorescent tubes striping the ceiling. Most of the doors were shut, but as they turned a corner, the officers purposely slowed their pace, allowing Omar a glance into a room with its door open wide. He spied a young woman sitting in a chair, her face covered in tears, her hand against her cheek, while a guard stood next to her. The crying girl wore a bright purple hijab, and that's why it took him so long to recognize Farida. "Why is she here?" he cried as they continued down the hall, dragging him by the arms. "Why have you arrested her? She didn't do anything!"

Omar wasn't here because of his sexual depravity. Now he knew the nature of his crime.

* * *

He was seated in a metal chair behind a wood table. This room was larger than the ones he'd passed, its walls an eggshell white. The bright overhead light illuminated the strokes of the paint roller, fanning out like frond leaves. There was a single window in the corner, covered in thick smoked glass. No light emanated through it, but it was secured with an iron grille painted such a soft turquoise, the shade of the first shallow steps into the Mediterranean, that it interrupted the steady flow of his fear. Surely torture couldn't take place in a room that contained such a pretty shade of blue.

He had been left alone for several minutes when the door opened and a man shuffled in, stocky like his colleagues, also wearing a navy sweater, but with a black vest snapped over it. He was bald except for a single iceberg of white hair floating above his forehead. His features were rounded—round nose, round eyes, rounded corners of his lips, as if their edges had been worn down by years of detention-center bureaucracy. He didn't look particularly cruel to Omar, even with the small scar running through his eyebrow.

"Omar Meshref?"

"Yes."

"My name is Ahmed."

Ahmed stood on the other side of the table and reached his hand toward Omar's face. Omar instinctively jerked his head back. Ahmed retracted his hand to offer a trusting open-palm gesture, as if trying to convince a dog to let him pet it. Ahmed reached out again, and Omar didn't jerk his head back. He gently unhooked the hearing aid from Omar's ear. The officer studied the device for a moment before delicately placing it on the table as if it were a fragile glass ornament. Then he opened his hand wide and, in a lightning-fast motion, smacked his palm hard against Omar's ear. He hit him two more times, each strike eliciting an involuntary shriek. The entire right side of Omar's head rang with a dull ache at its center, radiating out in hairline cracks. He tried to yawn the ringing away. His whole life he'd been so careful with his right ear, even though the doctors had never told him he needed to be. Now he couldn't clear the ringing, and when he dared to look up at Ahmed with tears in his eyes, the man softly pressed two cold fingers against his cheek.

"You saw the girl in the other room." That was not a question. "The receptionist at the Ramses Sands." A stalemate of silence followed, not only because Omar was too scared to answer but because it took effort to hear Ahmed through the ringing. "Why did you ask her to retrieve the recording of the American worker from the night he killed himself?"

"I didn't realize . . ."

"The hotel keeps a record of anyone downloading surveillance material. Please cooperate. I will have to choke you if you don't."

"Choke me?"

"What were your plans for that recording? Did you hope to embarrass your country with it? Are you a traitor? Did you want to share details of that man's death on social media?"

"No, I—"

"You must be aware that his company is a strong ally of our government, that they work in close partnership on a matter of national security, and anything that threatens them also threatens us. Was that your intention, to humiliate your country?"

Ahmed kept leapfrogging from one accusation to the next without letting Omar answer. It seemed as if he had been brought here not for an interrogation but rather for his sentencing. And he knew that the punishment for treason was death.

"No!" Omar shouted. "I never meant to betray anybody. And Farida, she didn't do anything—"

But Ahmed had introduced a thin black cord onto the desk, as long and sleek as a piece of licorice.

"Did you plot with the American worker's sister? We know you have been in constant communication with her. You have been helping her during her visit. Was the plan to give her the recording so that she could take it to the Western media? Is that what she is planning to do?"

"No." Omar shook his head. Ahmed touched the black cord on the table, and that's all it took to render him obedient. "She just wanted to hear her brother's voice?" he pleaded. "She wanted to hear him one last time? I was only trying to give her some comfort?" Under the threat of torture, every answer was a question.

"And what was she planning to do with the recording?"

"I don't know!"

"You had arranged to meet her today, yes."

"At the museum!" They must have already read their text exchanges on his phone, and he pounced on their meeting point as evidence of his tour-guiding innocence. "I was taking her to the antiquities museum. And then to shops in Zamalek. I was showing her around!"

Ahmed looked disappointed. "Try harder to keep your answers to the matter of the audio recording. Is there someone else who has been aiding her? This Ali Hamdy who you've been texting, does he know what she was going to do with the file? Was he part of your and Farida's plot?" Omar's body went slack. He couldn't tell whether Ahmed was being disingenuous, or he really did believe Ali was wrapped up in this mess. "Why was Ali excited for Saturday, Omar? What were you planning?"

"Nothing."

"Should we bring him down and ask him?"

This threat cracked him. "Cate thought her brother had been murdered. That's all I know. Honestly."

"It was ruled a suicide by our own investigators. Why would you take her side?"

"I wasn't taking a side. I was only helping—"

His right ear rang violently before he realized he'd been struck again. Was Ahmed targeting his bad ear on purpose?

Omar began to sob, his head bent toward his chest. "Why don't you ask Cate Castle? I don't know what she was going to do with the recording." As he said it, the idea took root in his head, wild and beautiful as a flower. Why had they arrested him and Farida but not Cate? He glanced up at Ahmed defiantly. "Why don't you ask her these questions? She knows these answers. I don't."

Ahmed's mouth opened like an opera singer holding a note. "Omar, what a question! This woman doesn't belong to us. She's a tourist, a sightseer, she comes, she goes. She is our guest and is protected." Ahmed walked around the table, moving out of sight behind his back. Omar noticed that the black cord was no longer on the table. "You are ours. You belong to us. Do you understand? You are not going to America. No visa. You are staying here, in your country, with your own people."

"I love my country," he swore.

"Then stop protecting this American's sister!" Ahmed shouted. "She is Western and believes in nothing. That is so much more dangerous than believing in anything. Please, don't lose your faith in your people." The voice turned paternal, almost loving. "I won't hit your ear again."

"How long will I have to stay here?" In this room, in this prison, in this country, in this interval without sleep, in this body, in this republic, in this chair.

There was a friendly pat on his shoulders. "A long time. We will start over, okay? When were you first contacted about stealing security data and betraying your country's secrets? Was it before or after the arrival of this American woman at the airport?"

The licorice was cold around his throat. Light blue bars on the window. He was at his grandparents' beach house, pedaling away from the sea on his bike, and when the car crashed into him, he hit his head on the curb and half the world's music poured out.

Chapter 22

CAIRO

Cate went up to her room after her confrontation with Maura Driscoll and tried to turn the world off. She lay in bed with the curtains closed, the lights out, and her cell phone smothered under a towel in the bathroom. At 8:00 p.m. the landline began ringing, bothering her every ten minutes, but she didn't answer. At nine, there was a knock at the door, and Matthias's voice called from the hall: "Just checking if you want to have dinner." After receiving no response, Matthias and the rest of Egypt finally left her alone for the night.

What was unforgivable? That was the question that kept circling in Cate's head. What if, despite Maura's lie about the apartment's location, her story about Eric taking advantage of young refugees at the clinic was true? What if the note he scribbled in his workbook really did amount to a confession of guilt, and Cate had been fooling herself to think it was otherwise? She knew her brother was loyal, kind, and caring, but that didn't mean he'd been decent in all parts of his life. Who is so clean that they don't contain a few monsters far from family eyes? Cate hadn't been decent; she'd become so attuned to hiding her own demons that the very notion of loving Luis had been contingent on lying to him. But cheating was a pardonable sin. Eric's alleged crimes were of a different magnitude. If Maura's accusations proved true, could Cate forgive her brother? Could she hate him for committing such heinous acts and still find a way to make peace with his memory? Or were such acts beyond forgiveness, and Eric had deserved the death he met? As a little girl Cate had idolized her brother; she'd followed him around the house and into the woods. All these years later she'd followed him to Egypt, but she couldn't account for the person he'd become.

If Eric had committed those crimes, the world would never forgive him. But her question wasn't about the world. Could she, his sister, forgive him? Eric had managed to forgive a monster once. Last summer he had driven to a house in Hillsdale and confronted their father after twenty years of silence. Eric had made peace with Jason Castle. Could she do the same with him? It seemed her duty as his sister, no matter the evil, to claim him as family, to say: *Yes, he is mine, this monster, he belongs to me.*

Cate climbed from bed, stumbled into the bathroom, and grabbed her phone from the towel. It took five long transatlantic rings, but Luis answered.

"Hi," she said. "I need to tell you something."

"Cate, you don't need to—"

"Please, just listen. And then you can hang up and I promise I'll never bother you again." She closed her eyes in the darkness to summon the apology she had never properly given.

Strange that it should take her brother's murder to make her a better person.

*   *   *

The next morning Cate ordered coffee up to her room. Since she wasn't meeting Omar until eleven, she decided to try her luck with Kurt Driscoll. She googled the phone number for the local Polestar Industries office, and when a secretary answered, she asked to speak to his boss. The secretary's loud, stilted manner of repeating her request back to her suggested that Kurt was within earshot. "I'm Eric Castle's sister." She knew that information was more likely to slam the door than open it, so she quickly added the irresistible lure: "Tell him I want to apologize."

Kurt agreed to meet her for a few minutes at 10:00 a.m. His office was in a dilapidated cast-iron building within walking distance of the museum. Cate climbed two flights of narrow stairs, their brass treads polished by a century of feet. In the office's front room a thin young Egyptian man stood over a desk, organizing a set of binders. He wore a short-sleeved white Oxford shirt with a green tie tossed over one shoulder to keep it out of his way. He looked up as she entered, eyebrows arched quizzically.

"I'm here to see Mr. Driscoll. I called this morning."

"Ah, the sister." He spoke with a posh British accent. "He's waiting for you." He gestured toward a connecting doorway. "We have to leave in fifteen minutes, so I'm afraid he hasn't much time."

Cate entered the inner office with thick golf-course-green carpeting that left faint footprints in her wake. Along the walls hung minimalist Bedouin weavings, which she guessed had been chosen by Maura. It was likely she had also been the curator responsible for the collection of family photographs arranged in brass frames along the windowsill—Maura, Maura, Maura with Roe, Roe, Roe with Saad, Roe with Maura. None costarred the man she'd come to see. Kurt Driscoll sat behind two open laptops at his desk. The only photo of him in the office was tacked to the wall behind his chair; in it he was stuffed in the cockpit of a fighter jet, smiling like a hyena and giving a thumbs-up. The current Kurt Driscoll wore a much more somber expression, with the glow of the computer screens radiating his jaw like stage lights. He glanced up at her, and his eyes ticked an invitation to an empty chair by the windowsill.

"Hi," she said dumbly and sat down, her purse scrunched against her stomach, the way she carried it on the subway to avoid being pickpocketed. "Thank you for meeting with me."

His face showed no emotion. She wondered whether he'd already contacted the lawyers back home about blocking the settlement. "I'm sorry for my behavior in the desert," she said with sincerity. "I wasn't thinking straight. Maybe because of the explosions, or the jet lag, or because I traveled all the way here and was afraid that it was my only chance to talk to you." He was on the verge of responding, but she held up her hand to finish. "You might think I violated the agreement you made with my family, but it's not their fault. It's mine. I was upset and said unacceptable things." Cate was not by nature an artful groveler. But apologies were a strange art—the smoother you were at them, the less effective they tended to be.

"Piece of shit, wasn't it?" he grumbled. "Coward. Spineless too, no?"

"I don't think I used—" She didn't recall *spineless*. "I'm sorry, Mr. Driscoll."

"Kurt."

"It was a mistake. Even the idea that Eric was killed by Egyptian soldiers. I was wrong. I realize that now."

"It was quite an imaginative leap," he scoffed. It took Cate every ounce of self-control to let that remark go unchallenged. It hadn't been much of a leap; it had hardly amounted to an extra step. Kurt was undoubtedly the one who had arranged for the missile launchers to be marked as defective so that they could be smuggled over the border. Eric's fight with Gasser stemmed from an error in assignment, meant for Ivers instead of her brother.

"Was the demonstration in the desert a success?" she asked to change the subject. "Did it win over the Egyptian minister?"

"He's already been won over," Kurt replied. "The Egyptian government has been a loyal Polestar client for two decades. It's a very close partnership. We're valued." As if to share the warmth of that embrace, he added, "Your brother's work was valued in this country."

"I thought some of the American contracts were at risk. I was told Egypt was switching to Russian tanks and—"

"Tanks!" Kurt hissed. "That's not our specialty." He leaned back in his seat. "Military dictatorships love their tanks, don't they? They appreciate the spectacle of rolling them through the center of cities. It's great optics for control. Countries like ours, Western democracies, on the other hand, we don't have a taste for tanks. It gives citizens the jitters, makes them feel like they're being invaded, conjures up China or the Soviet Union. We prefer the spectacle of air and sea. Hell, we salute jets when they're flying overhead. Those are optics of freedom, not oppression." Kurt rolled a pen between his fingers. His voice grew thoughtful. "It's ironic. You should be far more afraid of missiles than tanks, but there's a lot of showmanship in this business. I think countries find the defense that fits their character." He looked over to make sure she was listening. Cate was getting a hint of the oversharing work lectures that Roe endured at family dinners. "My point is, don't make a bogeyman out of Egypt's president. He's doing the same thing every leader does. Ensuring stability as best he can. And we're here to help him. I've worked with his ministers to guarantee a long-term investment."

Cate thought of Matthias's theory that Kurt was in jeopardy of losing his job over Eric's death and had only saved it by quashing any scandal. Cate's family had done its part in guaranteeing that long-term investment. Kurt checked his watch. "Okay," he said to

someone behind her. She turned to catch the secretary disappearing from the doorway.

"Look," he said calmly. "I'm sorry we got off on the wrong foot.
I respected your brother. He was an incredible worker, nothing
he couldn't fix. Just a good guy in every sense of the word." It
seemed safe to presume that Kurt had not learned of Eric's affair
with Maura. "But these kind of tragedies, especially when they
happen overseas, always trigger a fleet of unanswerable questions.
And I get that," he said with an actorly grimace. "Sometimes the
family needs the questions because it gives them something to do,
a way that they can be useful, a means of channeling their pain. I
don't blame you. I'd be in Cairo if it were my brother, too." He
nestled further into his seat. "But suicides are tragedies that don't
have easy answers, whether they happen in a hotel room in the
Middle East or in a hay barn back home."

"But—"

He raised a finger. "We have settled with your family. We are
about to pay you a substantial sum. And I will remind you that you
are contractually obliged not to mention Eric's death in any capacity other than suicide, which Polestar could not have prevented.
I'm sorry, I've forgiven you once, but I must insist on keeping to
the terms. Otherwise, what's the point of the settlement?"

Cate shifted her eyes to the window, trying to figure out a way of
getting the truth of out him. She stared at a picture of Roe on the
sill, back when he was a boy of nine or ten, his copper hair a newer,
shinier penny at that age. In the shot he stood on a Sunfish boat, his
chin lifted proudly. A white sail puffed behind him, and beyond it
she could make out a calm green lake and a row of beech trees lining the opposite shore. That forest was unmistakably the land of her
youth. "Is that the Berkshires?" she asked, nodding to the picture.

"Yeah, one of our local lakes. How did you know?" He slapped
his hand on the desk. "So far from home, I'm always assuming

everyone's a stranger. But of course, we're neighbors, plucked from the same mountains!"

The moment of neighborly warmth allowed Cate to dive toward the question she had come to ask. "Kurt," she said amicably, "off the record, settlements aside . . ." She paused, but he didn't stop her from continuing. "Even if you call it suicide, you must have read the findings of our autopsy report. I know there are surveillance cameras in the Ramses Sands. I just want to ask whether anyone checked the footage of the third floor on the night Eric died. Was there any unusual activity?"

Kurt took a leveling breath. "Most of those cameras are bunk," he admitted with what sounded like genuine irritation. "They break and no one reports it, and you only find out months later when you need to review the footage. I will tell you, in confidence, that I examined the elevator surveillance from that night. There was nothing out of the ordinary. The problem is, your brother's body was found at seven the next morning. No one knows when he went over the balcony. The last time he was accounted for was a call to the operator around midnight, which we have on record. So we're talking a pretty big window of time to look at guests coming and going."

"He called down to the operator?" Cate feigned surprise. She would use the question as a lie-detector test. "What did he say?"

"He sounded extremely anguished. He asked not to be disturbed and that no guests be allowed up to his room." Kurt shrugged. "You draw his state of mind from that request." Kurt had supplied just enough of the truth. Maybe he genuinely believed that the voice on the call was Eric's, but he had omitted the part about a suspicious weapons deal or asking to be connected to the embassy. "Eric didn't name a murderer, if that's what you're hoping," Kurt added with a smirk. "There aren't going to be any simple answers for you, except for the one you don't want to hear."

"What about the note found in his room?" she pressed. "You must realize its implications, since Eric volunteered at the clinic." Kurt froze, his breathing stalled. She had poked a sorer subject than lackluster hotel security. "We were only shown a snippet of text. Is there any chance we can see the original page to make sure there wasn't more that he'd written?"

Kurt shook his head with a theatrical sigh. "That's all we got too. The police were the ones to recover that evidence. There's no reason to presume they redacted anything, but if they did, the Egyptian authorities might have their own reasons. Eric was handling delicate security material. If he mentioned anything sensitive to Egypt's interests, I doubt that page still exists." Kurt shook his head again. Then, with a jolt, he gripped the armrests of his chair, as if he were experiencing a sudden bout of turbulence. He looked up at her with such an unraveled expression that she almost felt sympathy for him. "I won't lie to you. That note knocked the wind out of me. You can bet I had no idea that kind of behavior was going on at the clinic. And you can also bet I've ordered an internal investigation to get to the bottom of it. My hope is that it was simply a product of your brother's deteriorating mind." Kurt placed his palms on the desk. "It would have been extremely ugly for your family and for Polestar if that note had been leaked to the public. That's why I pushed so hard to get you a generous settlement. Honestly, it's best for everyone that Eric's death was ruled a suicide. If those allegations had come to light, it would have damaged a lot of people who put their trust in Polestar's goodwill efforts around the world. I don't think your family realizes how commendable the Egyptian police were to keep that note buried."

Cate tried to smile through the notion that a verdict of suicide was a cause for family gratitude. "But between us," she whispered, leaning toward him, "you do know that Eric was murdered, right? You're aware that someone bashed him in the head and threw him off the balcony?" She would accept even this tiny acknowledgment as restitution.

Kurt responded by reaching for his briefcase on the floor and filling it with files. Their meeting had come to an end. But Cate wasn't ready to accept failure. Her eyes fled to the photographs of the happy Driscolls on the windowsill. In the nearest photo Maura and Roe stood together on a dock that looked like Cape Cod. Even with their zinc-white noses, she could see the strong resemblance. Roe was giving an extra-wide grin in the shot, and for once she could see his father in him.

"You and Roe have the same smile," she said, nodding toward the frame.

Kurt paused to glance at the photo. "No," he said emphatically, as if to showcase how often Cate jumped to the wrong conclusion. "That's not possible."

"Why not?"

"He's not biologically mine. Neither of my children are."

Cate recalled the strange phrasing that Maura had used in their first meeting. *I got pregnant, and then I fell in love.*

"Maura told me you two met while she was working in Algeria, and then she got pregnant with Roe."

"You've got your facts in reverse order," he said snidely. "Roe's father was an Austrian aid worker. Some flaky hippie do-gooder that Maura met in Algiers." Kurt shut his eyes for a second to retrieve a memory of the man. "For a year or two Huxley tried to see Roe, but you don't let someone that lost help raise your child."

"Excuse me?" Cate tried not to show her shock. "His name was Huxley?"

"Yes, Roe's father. It's a sad story, really. He died in Algeria in a bombing. Wars are dangerous, Cate." He looked at her from across the desk as if she needed to learn that basic lesson.

The air had gone out of the room. She stared over at the framed photo of Roe as a shirtless boy on a sailboat in the Berkshires, her eyes circling his scrawny neck until she spotted a pendant on a thin gold chain. Roe's father had lost his son. He must have left the St. Anthony medal to Roe as a keepsake. A man holding an infant to his chest, the saint of lost things.

"Are you all right?" Kurt asked as he stood to leave. "You don't look well. Can Mohamed bring you a bottle of water?"

* * *

Cate sprinted across four lanes, dodging trucks. There were no breaks in the endless slurry of traffic. She reached the island of Tahrir Square, only to realize she had to recross the street to reach the salmon-pink museum farther up the avenue. She ran in a diagonal, was nearly taken out by a van, and continued up the sidewalk, bypassing a cement stretch of park studded with steel planters and scrawny saplings.

The Egyptian flag waved from the museum's crown. As she climbed the front steps, breathless and dizzy, she scanned the crowd for Omar. She wanted to tell him everything she'd learned so he could help piece together the answer. It was eleven o'clock, and, checking her phone, she found a message from him sent twenty minutes ago: On my way, I'll be on time for once, don't buy museum tickets, my treat.

A tourist bus pulled to the curb, and a delegation of suit-and-sari Indians funneled through the gates and up the museum steps, disappearing into its visitors' hall. Cate leaned against a column at the entrance, just out of the raw sunlight. Her brain was spinning so fast it was hard to keep her body still: Roe, Huxley, a gift from a father to a son, a medal for the lost. She wiped the sweat from her eyes. *If it all blows up, ask him about Huxley,* Eric had written on a postcard. Ask *who* about Huxley? Maybe the *him* was Eric's boss, Kurt Driscoll, who had just supplied her with the answer. But what did Roe's biological father have to do with Eric's murder? She needed to calm down and think clearly. She slipped out of the shade and walked toward the fountain near the road. So much didn't make sense to her, but there was one reassuring conclusion already: the medal belonged to Roe. That fact refuted Maura's story about Eric exploiting a vulnerable refugee girl. Maura had been so warm and welcoming, and also such a manipulative liar in leading Cate away from the truth. Why would Maura have told her such a vicious lie, unless it concealed something even worse?

Two stone sphinxes guarded the fountain, sinuous lion bodies with cracked human heads. She searched the road for Omar's red car.

At twenty minutes after eleven she texted him. Are you near? I'm by the fountain. A boy selling tissues walked by, and Cate bought a packet to wipe her dripping face. At eleven thirty she tried calling. Omar's phone must be off, because the call went straight to voicemail. She left a message, its tone toggling between irritated and concerned. At eleven forty-five she called again. When noon came, irritation gave way to worry. She returned to the shaded refuge of the entrance and stared into the cool darkness of the museum's interior. She called again, listened to Omar's voicemail message in Arabic, and waited for the beep. "Omar, what's wrong? Where are you? I'm here! I've been here for an hour! You said you were on your way."

At twelve fifteen she knew he wasn't coming. A non-life-threatening car accident became preferrable to the other horrifying scenarios to explain his absence. She didn't know what to do or who to call. She knew only that Omar lived somewhere in Zamalek. She had no contacts for his friends or family in Cairo. It was too early in New York to phone his aunt; Cate didn't want to wake the woman unnecessarily with her paranoia about Omar being an hour late to meet her at a museum. She fought the urge to try his phone again. What good would one more message do?

At twelve thirty Cate left. She walked past the two sphinxes and, stepping onto the street, hailed a taxi. She didn't know where else to go except to keep to the plan they'd made. Climbing into the backseat, she realized she didn't have the shop's address. The young driver kept shaking his head when she tried to describe the store in English. Finally she resorted to the pictograms of Google searches: A bowl of chocolates. The island of Zamalek. The Jamaican flag. His face lit up. "Yes, I know! Jamaica!" He put the car in gear.

She watched the asphalt city melt into brown Nile water as they crossed the bridge. She wanted to focus all her attention on the terrible truth that Maura Driscoll was concealing, but her mind kept skipping back to Omar and his unaccountable absence. She prayed that he was just being irresponsible. She tapped out an email to his aunt Lina in New York: Sorry to bother you. Can you contact your sister in Cairo ASAP? Omar was supposed to meet me an hour and a half ago and didn't show up. I'm worried. He said he was on his way but never arrived. Cate marked the email URGENT and pressed send. As the island rose into view, she wondered how to interrogate the shopkeeper without Omar there to translate. What questions could she ask?

The Jamaican flag crisscrossed the front window. As she pushed the shop's door open, a bell clanged above her head. The scent of sweet and savory wafted from the open barrels.

"Ahlan wa sahlan," an elderly shopkeeper said in greeting as he rose from his stool behind the counter. He wore a tan djellaba, and stray white hairs sprouted around the collar. He studied her with a sly smile. "Might you be American?" he asked in faltering but— blessedly—operational English.

"Yes, I am." Her eye caught the rack of postcards in the back, and she went toward it, the third card down flaunting a pristine beach with tilted red lettering.

"You like?" The shopkeeper followed her. "Twenty-seven years ago, people said I was crazy, I took my first vacation to—"

"I know," she interrupted. She fumbled through her bag for Eric's postcard and held it up. He took it from her in amazement and studied the back.

"Ah, Eric! Is this Eric Castle? My old tenant!" The shopkeeper pointed his finger toward the ceiling.

"That's right," she said with relief. "I'm his sister from New York. I'm Cate."

"New York?" He motioned toward the photo of the doomed World Trade Center that hung above his cash register.

"Sir?" she said, mimicking his gesture at the ceiling. "When Eric rented the apartment"—she didn't know how to be subtle without Omar here to finesse the negotiation—"did many people come and go? Many women? Or men?" She worried that the last addition might offend his propriety, but the shopkeeper didn't seem fazed.

"One or two women, yes. Friends of Eric's, foreigners like him who would go up—" He seemed to catch himself, his fingers balling into fists. He shook his head. "I cannot say more. Please understand. You are Eric's sister. But it is Eric who rented the apartment. I am a discreet man for my tenants. Why don't you ask Eric yourself, yes? He can tell you all about it." He smiled as if he'd solved their dilemma.

"Can I look at the apartment?" she asked. "Can you take me up to see it?" His smile faded. "It hasn't been rented since he stayed there, has it?"

"No, but . . ." He dusted his palms together. "You didn't come for his things, did you? There were only papers and books! I throw out! Nothing left. I keep for three weeks. I cannot keep forever." His face hardened in suspicion.

"I understand. I'm not here for his stuff. But I'd like to see the apartment anyway." The request seemed vital only because she had nowhere else to look. "Maybe I could rent it? I have money."

He grabbed the keys from under the counter, and they went outside. The upper floors were accessed through a steel door next to the X of the Jamaican flag. Together they trudged up a crooked flight of stairs. "Just papers," the shopkeeper muttered. "A few emails printed out. Maybe a shirt. Nothing of value, or I would have saved it. I like Eric, very much."

She nodded. "It's okay," she said with a heavy heart.

"There is not even a bed left," he warned as he unlocked the door in the hallway. "I took it upstairs for new renter. You would need to order a new one."

The apartment was musty but spacious, its floor a water-damaged herringbone, its walls a peeling cream. A bank of tall windows, which were crowned at their tops with crooked blinds, brought in copious sunlight. Cate's evaluation of apartments had been compromised by two decades of living in Manhattan. For a second she forgot her mission and deemed the apartment a rare jewel, with tons of character. "Prewar," she whispered.

The shopkeeper stood in the doorway, his arms folded. "I told you. I threw everything out. Papers, bottles. Your brother liked bottles," he snickered. "All my days, there were so many."

"Yes, the Castles like their bottles," she agreed.

She wandered the rooms anyway, her feet streaking the dust that filmed the floor. She checked the kitchen cabinets and found a few rusty pots and pans. Omar had searched the apartment already, examining the same closets and cabinets for any remains. As he had reported, there was nothing left but pots and pans and window blinds. She walked into the bedroom, with its two windows looking out on the shaggy trees across the street, each window capped with tangled wood blinds. The bed must have been against the bare wall. It was in this room that Eric and Maura had conducted their affair.

"What do you think? Do you want it?" the shopkeeper asked, impatient to return to his store.

Cate stood at the bedroom window. Had she let her brother down by not coming here a month before, as soon as she received the postcard? Maybe there had been evidence left in the apartment that the shopkeeper had unwittingly thrown away. Cate felt so close to discovering the answer. She recalled Maura mentioning that she'd been given her own spare key to this apartment, and claiming to have found the St. Anthony medal in the bedsheets.

Cate turned to the shopkeeper at the door. "One final question, sir. Did anyone else use this apartment when Eric was off working in the desert?"

The shopkeeper shrugged. "At the end, sometimes, yes, his cousin borrowed it."

"Cousin?"

"He must be your cousin too, no? American cousin. He took young friends up here to make a party. Other foreigners, not Egyptians."

Cate stared out the window, trying to make sense of this damning information. Lost in thought, she almost missed the clue dangling right in front of her face. Stirred by the current of air running from the open door, it tapped against the window glass. A cord hung from the blinds, notched down its length in sailor's knots.

Chapter 23

CAIRO

The metal detector at the Ramses Sands beeped in warning, but no one stopped Cate from rushing into the lobby. She glanced at the front desk; the young receptionist who had the crush on Omar wasn't on duty. Cate hurried toward the elevator bank, each surveillance camera in the lobby beating a tiny red heartbeat under its open eye. Did the cameras work? Did it matter if your father controlled the footage?

In the elevator she pushed the button for the penthouse. She didn't hold her breath as the elevator shot past the third floor, although it was undeniably inside room 3B that Eric had been murdered. Roe must have killed him with a blow to the head before placing the midnight call to the receptionist. Roe knew that any communication from Eric's room would be recorded, and he'd summoned his best Berkshire brogue, disguising it with a slurred voice as he impersonated a man who'd come unhinged. Roe had been smart. Merely making Eric's death look like a suicide might have resulted in a legitimate police investigation. The Cairo detectives might have wondered why a man chose to jump from a third-story balcony; the Cairo coroner might have reached the same conclusions about Eric's injuries as Dr. Yang had. Roe needed to ensure that the death would be covered up, and he knew precisely how to guarantee it. His father must have mentioned Eric's fight with Egyptian soldiers in the desert, for Roe had peppered the call with just enough suggestion of a weapons plot to force Polestar to intervene. He knew that his father, fearing a scandal, would pressure the Egyptian authorities to rule the death a suicide and close the case.

The elevator doors opened onto a hallway decorated in drawings of the last surviving world wonder. Cate rang the buzzer, and after a few seconds, she pounded her fist on the penthouse door. "Roe!" she screamed. "Maura!" There was no answer. But she knew another way in. She opened the rooftop door. The hinges squealed, and the sun temporarily blinded her. She was here to return the pendant to its rightful owner.

Was it the St. Anthony medal that Eric had found in the bedsheets that alerted him to Roe's use of the apartment? Maura had her own key to the place, and her son must have borrowed it when Eric was safely off in the desert. Or had Eric caught his "American cousin" red-handed with one of the clinic's young asylum seekers? The note that her brother had scrawled in his daybook wasn't a confession; Eric was wrangling over what action to take after uncovering the habits of his boss's son. *It's sick to be taking advantage of those young men and women. . . . I can't stomach it anymore.* Roe shut Eric up before he could report him. He must have foreseen the damage ahead if his behavior came to light—not least of all the end of his father's career. But Cate guessed that first and foremost, it threatened to curb his life of pleasure. *I'm selfish*, he'd once admitted to her. *I want to be lucky forever.* That fear of getting caught must have brought him to knock on Eric's hotel door that night, worming his way in on the premise of coming clean. Roe's wounded-bird sweetness had been a smokescreen. She recalled him only a few days ago standing in the lobby of the Grand Nile, the uncomfortable Firas next to him, and later bragging that he could get a room there for a few hours whenever he wanted. Roe had moved on from the apartment in Zamalek. It was clear that Maura knew of Roe's sins and tried to cover them up by shifting the blame onto Eric. Kurt probably had no idea. But what difference did it make? The father fuels the war; his son finds exciting new victims stuck in the rubble.

She marched across the rooftop, its tar sticky on her shoes. A helicopter swirled high overhead in the smog-yellow sky, so far up it looked like a housefly drowning in soup. As she rounded the corner, she couldn't gauge any movement through the shine on the sliding doors. Only when her shadow fell against the glass did she spot Saad sitting at the kitchen table. He appeared to be alone, the tabletop covered in a spill of crayons. He was watching her approach. Cate tried the door handle. It was locked.

"Can you?" she yelled, pointing to the handle. He continued to stare at her, distrust in his eyes. Perhaps he correctly assessed who she was: a person who had come to destroy the safety of the family he had found. She was here to demolish his little kingdom of peace.

"Please!" she called through the door. "Please let me in! It's me, Saad. You remember me! Eric's sister!"

Saad dropped his crayon and climbed from his chair. He stood on the other side of the glass, as if at a zoo, observing her wild-animal-like movements. Then he reached up to unclick the lock. Cate slid the door open.

"Where is your brother?" she asked, trying to hide her breathlessness. "Or your mother? Where are they?"

He shook his head. "Not here."

Cate surveyed the stillness of the kitchen and the dark halls leading to the bedrooms. She had been running on pure adrenaline, hungry for a confrontation, desperate to point a finger at her brother's killer. But, like Eric, she had not come without leaving a little piece of life insurance behind. At the shop in Zamalek, she had typed an email to her stepfather with a brief account of all she had learned, marking it URGENT. She'd considered cc'ing Omar in the email to Wes, but his sudden disappearance had made her wary of sending him any further electronic messages; she wouldn't risk putting him in deeper trouble. Instead she scribbled out a note to him and left it with the shopkeeper. "Please give this to my friend if he comes in and asks for me," she'd said, hoping it wouldn't be necessary, that she and Omar would see each other soon. At the time those small precautions seemed like reassuring safeguards. Only now, in the quiet of the Driscoll penthouse, did fear begin to grow inside her. Even with a little boy in the room, she felt alone.

"They couldn't have left you by yourself," she said to Saad as he returned to his chair. "Where are they?" He didn't respond. She stared into the interior of the apartment. "Roe!" she yelled. A faint muffled noise issued from down the hall—someone stirring in the bedrooms, Roe or Maura? Fear made it hard to swallow. There was a butcher block on the kitchen counter. Cate hurried over to it and pulled out a carving knife. Gripping the handle, she hid the knife behind her leg so that Saad wouldn't see it. As she peered down the hall, her ears identified the noise: the tumble of a clothes dryer.

A scraping sound caused her to jump, but it was only Saad scooting in his chair at the table.

"How is Eric?" he asked in a hopeful soprano. "When is he coming back?"

"Soon," she said absently, staring into the hallway's darkness. But then she recalled Saad's continual questions about Eric's well-being and studied him more carefully, with his silky black hair and violet eyelids. She walked to the table, glancing down at his drawing of a house surrounded by a flower garden and a wavy blue stream. Why were children so obsessed with drawing houses? Some kids were obsessed with drawing houses on fire, but that was not Saad's vision of a perfect home.

"Saad?" She squatted down next to him. "Where is your brother?" He ignored her, focused on his drawing. "Saad?"

She nearly gave up when he reluctantly shook his head and offered a tight frown. "He left. He saw you coming up on the monitor for the elevator. It beeps when someone presses the top floor. He didn't want to answer the door when you were pounding on it." Roe must have sensed that she'd put the pieces together and slipped out as she crossed the rooftop.

"Do you know where he went?"

"To the river. He likes to sail the boats with the big fins. That's where he goes to be by himself."

She smiled in gratitude. "I see."

"How is Eric's puppy?" he asked. "Is she with your family, your dad and your mom?"

"Moose is fine," she replied. "She's with my sister at college. But listen to me, Saad, okay?" Now that she had the boy's attention, she didn't want him to get distracted. She palmed his tiny shoulder, hoping he might confirm her theory. "This is important. Did you ever see Roe get into an argument with Eric?"

Saad picked up a light-blue crayon and used the white space above the house to draw a set of giant eyes. She thought she had lost him again. But after a few seconds he tilted his head, looking at her as he chewed his lip. "Yes. Eric came up here one day to talk to Mom and Roe. I stayed inside, but they went out—" He pointed to the stretch of rooftop out the window. "They had a fight, lots of yelling."

"Do you know what they were fighting about?"

He shook his head. "Mom had her phone, and she made a call and gave the phone to Eric. He got even madder."

"Do you know who Eric was talking to on your mom's phone?"

Again Saad shook his head, returning his attention to his drawing. He continued to work on the giant blue eyes hovering over the rooftop, bright as glaciers.

"Did you see Eric after that fight?" she asked.

"No. A few days later he left, and I wasn't allowed to go downstairs to say goodbye. Mom says he had to do a job somewhere else. My dad's people work all over the world."

"That's right," Cate said. "They work all over the world."

She felt dizzy. The knife nearly fell from her grip as she stood up. There was still so much she didn't understand—the *him* they were supposed to ask about Huxley, the identity of the person Eric had spoken to on Maura's phone a few days before his murder, even the point of his sending a postcard to their father. But it didn't matter. Saad had confirmed her theory. Roe was the killer, and his mom cleaned up his mess.

Cate didn't say goodbye to Saad. She simply walked out onto the rooftop in a daze, the sun blazing down on her as she crossed the quilt of rugs. She felt the urgent need to call her mother, to tell her that they'd gotten it all wrong from the very beginning. The truth was so much worse than their suspicions. It wasn't a weapons company or a foreign government that had murdered Eric, but a selfish teenage boy. How could such news bring Joy any peace? In the end, it might only shame her into returning the settlement money.

If it all blows up, Eric had written on a vacation postcard. *If it all blows up, then what?* she desperately wanted to ask her brother now. People keep going. They find a way to live with the grief that terrorizes them. At best, they try to stop it from striking someone else. Eric would never know how far she had come to find the answers, but he clearly had trusted her to try. Her next task would be to phone Omar's aunt, ask for his address, and check whether he was safe. If he wasn't, she'd go straight to the American embassy and beg Elizabeth Skyler for help. She'd use the dirt she had on Polestar and the Driscolls as leverage if she needed to.

Cate yanked open the door to the hallway, her eyes blinded by little suns as they adjusted to the dark. She punched the elevator button, but the indicator above the doors didn't move from three. After a minute of thumbing the button, Cate saw the sign for the emergency staircase. She opened the security door and began her descent along the hotel's cinder-block spine. Her fear returned as she reached the fourth-floor landing. This must have been the route Roe had taken that night to evade the elevator's surveillance camera. His father probably never saw his son on the footage. Cate steeled herself as she neared the next landing. She didn't want to be afraid anymore.

He must have been waiting just inside the access door. He sprang on her from behind, wrapping a forearm around her neck. Cate fought, her legs kicking against the wall and sending them both hurtling off balance, his hold on her throat so tight she couldn't produce a scream. In another life, Roe would have made an excellent soldier. They fell against the steps, with her landing on top of him, and she felt the cold coin of a gun against her temple.

"Open your mouth," he demanded. But she wouldn't help him make her death look like a suicide. "Open your mouth!" He slackened his arm to let her speak.

"It was you. You killed him," she said.

"I don't know what you're talking about." Even holding a gun to her head, he wouldn't admit he'd done anything wrong.

"Don't you feel guilty enough?"

He paused as if considering his answer. "Sometimes. Sometimes not."

Cate knew he wouldn't stop on his own. She plunged the knife into his ribs, and he let out a scream to prove he did feel something. He pulled the trigger.

PART III

Greetings from
the United States of America

Chapter 24

OMAR

Omar had been lost for twenty miles. The last time he'd been certain of his location he had stopped to fill up on gas and to squeegee his windshield in a town called Canaan. He now stared through that crystal-clean trapezoid of glass, trying to decide which direction to take.

His aunt had warned him to keep to the highway. Laughing in the garden of her West Village town house, she told him, "Darling, if you want to see the *real* America, your only choice is the highway. Outside the city, that's really all there is to this country, strip malls and infrastructure." Aunt Lina proved as much of a snob as he'd remembered. Omar still insisted on taking the country back roads. He wanted to see New England, and once he got the hang of his aunt's BMW, he loved tearing through the quaint Connecticut villages, each one a chipped china teacup that seemed to wobble from the roar of his engine.

His GPS only failed when he crossed into the wilds of Massachusetts, the phone screen reverting to a rotating wheel of doubt. Ten minutes back he'd slowed the car beside two shivering, blue-lipped girls in swimsuits, walking away from a lake. "Which way to New Marlborough?" he asked them. The girls promptly pointed in opposite directions. "It's kinda both ways, mister," the taller one said.

Omar turned left and pressed on the gas, speed masquerading as confidence. A cornfield shimmered in the August sunlight, with the *shic-shic-shic* of insects in the crops. He rolled the windows down to be drenched in the warm breeze. Wildflower meadows stretched into the distance, and huge, buffalo-shaped mountains gathered on the horizon. Aunt Lina had shrugged off the Berkshires as subpar. (Already during his brief stay in her town house, Aunt Lina had shrugged off the Frick Collection, a Soho restaurant called Balthazar, and the entire borough of Brooklyn, yet Omar had visited each one and returned with rave reviews.) But the Berkshires, buggy and drowsy and deep green in late summer, had been Cate's home. That was the purpose of his trip today.

After he landed in New York City, Aunt Lina brought him to an uptown ear institute, where doctors took scans of his head and fit him with a new hearing aid. It was a tiny tan slug of a device that fit into the canal, no hooking around the outer ear required, almost unnoticeable—you'd really have to stare to notice it. The sounds of the world instantly sharpened with this new device. Omar had lost his old hearing aid in the detention center. He imagined it still there, in one of the guard's drawers, collecting horrible noises.

He had remained in detention—not in the notorious Tora complex, as he'd suspected, but in a prison for petty criminals and political insurgents in the far west of the city—for five weeks. He might still be there today, sleeping on a steel bed in a room of thirty men, had it not been for Aunt Lina enlisting the help of Egypt's consul general, Fouad Mersal. Officially, Omar's crime was moral debauchery, although he knew that his homosexuality played no part in his arrest. It took five weeks to get him out— Aunt Lina banging her gong of outrage, his mother and father in perpetual panic, his lawyer (whom he met once during his second week in detention) flip-flopping between optimism and despair. Ultimately, he was held for precisely the amount of time it took to ensure that all his wounds had healed. His skin, it turned out, had an annoyingly long memory for abuse. The bruises to his ear and cheek had yellowed by the second week and vanished by the third. It was the ligature marks around his neck—the rash-red line that ran above his Adam's apple, as if a child had drawn his portrait and decided with a cruel swipe of a red marker that he should lose his head—that took the longest to fade. They released him in the same clothes he'd worn on the day of his arrest, his hair longer, his beard scragglier, but otherwise in one piece. *You see, we didn't lay a finger on him, not even for his sin of sodomy.* The officers also returned his phone, with all its contents erased. He would never see the messages that Cate had likely sent him when he failed to show up to the museum that morning. Only after he returned to his parents' house in Palm Hills did he learn that she had died.

By that point, Cate had already been buried in a cemetery in Western Massachusetts. By that point, her death—she was found shot in the stairwell of the Ramses Sands—had moved through the usual dead ends of a Cairo police investigation. Like her brother's death, it had initially been deemed a suicide. But when it was discovered that a critically injured young man was rushed to a private hospital that same afternoon with a stab wound to the stomach, her death had been upgraded to "suspicious circumstances." Roosevelt Driscoll managed to relay in the ambulance that he had been attacked in the stairwell—presumably, according to the police, by the same assailant who shot Cate. The next day, against the advice of doctors, Roe was airlifted by his family to a hospital in Italy.

Omar learned later that Roe's father had resigned from Polestar, but he never discovered what happened to the family after they left Egypt, disappearing into whatever corner of the world rich people hide to lick their consciences clean. Aunt Lina said the Castle family had tried to petition for answers, but there were only two elderly parents left, and the Egyptian authorities stonewalled them. All these months later, Cate's murder was still considered an open investigation—Omar imagined a folder marked "Cate Castle" open on the top of a filing cabinet, so no one could accuse the police of lying.

Farida was MIA. She no longer worked at the hotel, her Facebook page had been deleted, and her enrollment at the local college withdrawn. All he could do was hope she was okay. After his release, Omar hadn't dared to contact Ali, or even consider dialing his number, for fear that the call would be traced. One afternoon in May Omar was driving across the bridge when he got stuck in traffic. He looked over and saw Ali straddling his motorcycle, his curly black hair hanging in clusters over his forehead. He was such a gorgeous man. But when Ali glanced over at him in recognition, Omar turned away, his eyes glued on the Nile. He waited until the roar of the motorcycle faded into the city before he turned his head back to the road.

Hay bales. A broken-down wood cart serving as a vegetable stand. Lakes glistening like aluminum foil in the sun. Stone walls gridding a sheep pasture. Finally, at a three-way intersection he saw a signpost, arrows pointing every which way. There it was: NEW MARLBOROUGH, 3 MI.

He had phoned Cate's parents yesterday, introducing himself and asking if they would be amenable to his visit. Her stepfather, Wes, answered, friendly and sugar-voiced: "Oh, yes, we'd love for you to stop by. How kind of you to think of us." Cate had told Omar all about Wes Steigerwald, how she had spent most of her life quietly despising him, but that they had grown surprisingly close after Eric's death.

"I'll only stay for an hour," Omar promised. "I have some information that Cate uncovered about Eric's murder. The Cairo police wouldn't listen, but I thought you would want to know."

It was Aunt Lina who secured Omar's visa to the United States. By the time he'd gotten out of detention, she had turned him into her own one-woman cause célèbre. "Omar, you will never be safe in Egypt," she lectured over the phone, "not until the government changes. Not until they think forward instead of backward. I know your mother won't accept that fact. Thank god you have one rational family member!" His mother had driven him to the airport. Although she had given no more tender a hug than if he were going on a long summer vacation, Omar felt they both knew that he would never come back. It hurt to abandon the country he loved, but his aunt was right.

He'd been so busy preparing for his departure that he'd neglected to stop by the chocolate shop that Cate had planned to visit on the day of his arrest. One morning in June, he spotted the Jamaican X in the window and out of curiosity, went inside.

The postcard that Cate had left for him now rested on the passenger seat of his aunt's BMW. On its front was the sandy white beach with tilted red letters declaring that he was the only thing missing in Jamaica. Next to it, his phone returned from the dead, loading a map of the village of New Marlborough. A woman's American computer voice instructed him to take the next left onto Foxglove Lane.

It was a shotgun-narrow road, rutted with potholes. Thin, branchless pines lined both sides, their trunks as smooth and gray as alien skin. Just beyond the next hill, the Castle-Steigerwald house came into view, sitting close to the road on a furry pelt of green lawn. A metal sign staked out front listed the contractor responsible for its extensive makeover. The roof was shingled in raw cedar, not yet gray with age, and a coat of butter-yellow paint covered the house like a membrane of happiness. Explosions of flowering shrubs—orange, red, apricot—dotted the front garden and wrapped around what looked to be a new sunroom addition off the side. From Cate's description, Omar had imagined a small, leaky, ramshackle cottage barely hanging together. He steered the BMW onto a driveway of crushed seashells.

As soon as he opened the car door, he heard ferocious barking. Omar hesitated, letting his foot dangle out as if to tempt the vicious animal into showing itself. The barking continued, neither growing louder nor fading away, and yet no dog materialized. The color of the house was so ruthlessly cheerful, it took Omar a minute to realize that its windows were dark. Did he have the wrong address? He heard a faint knocking on glass, and glancing around, traced the sound to a toolshed across the lawn. The shed also seemed to be the source of the barking. As Omar walked toward it, he belatedly noticed the sign hanging on its door: BEWARE OF DOG.

The door creaked open, and the silhouette of an old man appeared. Before Omar could say hello, the door slammed shut as the man struggled to restrain the dog inside.

"Moose, stop!" the man snarled. "Sit!" The dog went silent. The door swung wide.

"Are you Wes?" Omar asked with a warm smile. "I'm sorry I'm late. I got lost." He was about to offer his hand, but the gray-haired man swayed backward, off balance. He stabilized himself against a wood desk.

"Not a problem," the old man said in the friendly voice that Omar recognized from the phone call yesterday. "I'm glad you

managed to find us." His eyes were such a luminous blue, so dis-
armingly beautiful, Omar was left momentarily speechless. Those
eyes were the only signs of health on a face ravaged by illness.
Wes Steigerwald's forehead was ash gray, his cheeks jaundiced and
splotched with broken blood vessels, and he clasped an oxygen
mask near his mouth the way a truck driver grips a CB radio. He
appeared so unwell that Omar almost asked if he should come back
another day. But he sensed that there wouldn't be any healthier
days ahead of the old man.

"Come in, please," Wes wheezed. "It's nice to meet you." He
nodded toward the dog still out of sight behind the door. "Beware
of puppy," he mumbled in jest.

Omar stepped into the office. The walls were covered in peg-
boards from which hung sharp tools and wreaths of bright-orange
extension cords. The desk took up most of the space, its surface
strewn with gears and dismembered appliances. Omar's eyes slid
down three slender shotguns leaning in the corner. But it was
the collection of photographs tacked to the wall that commanded
his attention. It was undoubtably a proud-dad shrine, and Omar
squinted to locate an image of Cate among the snapshots. Instead,
a ruddy, round-faced girl with red hair made a repeated appearance; in the most recent photos, she wore a Smith College sweatshirt.

Only when Omar's foot passed the border of the door did he
hear the growl. "Moose!" Wes cautioned. The dog in no way resembled a puppy. It looked full-grown, sitting in rigid obedience.
The breed was the definition of intimidation, its body lean, its head
shaped like a cocked handgun, its front paws lined up militantly in
front of its haunches, like the disciplined feet of an Olympic diver.
This dog could kill in a single leap.

"What breed is he?" Omar asked as the old man shuffled around
the desk to his chair.

Wes motioned for Omar to shut the door. "*She*'s a Doberman pinscher. Most people are afraid of them. But you don't have to worry about Moose. She's as sweet as they come and loves her daddy."

Wes's oxygen mask was leashed to a long blue tube that ran in circles on the floor and sprouted from a purring machine. Omar moved with slow, deliberate steps toward an empty chair so as not to provoke the dog. Once sitting, he waited as Wes took several greedy inhales from his oxygen mask, as if the effort of opening the toolshed door had worn him out. It was painful to hear the scraping breaths, each one like a tightrope walker struggling to find the next step on the line. But a tightrope walker eventually reaches the other side. Wes had to keep breathing until he couldn't anymore. Breathing would be his sole vocation for the remainder of his existence.

Omar smiled. "Is this the dog that belonged to Cate's brother?"

Wes pulled the mask from his mouth. "Yes. She mostly stays in here with me because Catelin's mother doesn't like dogs. You could say Moose is my fault." He laughed feebly, which devolved into a coughing fit, comets of spittle shooting from his lips. He cleared his throat with an agonized squeeze of his face. "We had Dobermans on the grounds at Brightwell, the school where I worked as director of facilities. When Catelin's brother moved back to the Berkshires from New Hampshire, well, I nudged him toward the breed. They're terrific companions!"

Wes clicked his tongue, and the dog's head whiplashed toward its master. "After Eric passed, my daughter took Moose for a while. Not Catelin, I mean my real daughter, biological," he clarified. "She's at Smith College. She's just starting her sophomore year." He paused as if inviting Omar to be awed by such a prestigious institution. "Willie has all the brains in the family. There's no end to what she's going to accomplish. She's decided on premed.

A doctor! That's what every parent wants, isn't it?" He grinned proudly. "That's probably what parents want for their kids even in Egypt!" *It was true*, Omar thought, *they did*. "But Willie is still a teenager, and even the best kids can't handle the responsibility of a dog. So I had to step in, as dads do. That's the job of parents, to clear obstacles, to smooth a path." He looked at Omar with interest. "Did you go to college in the Middle East?"

"Yes," Omar replied. "Then grad school in London, which was something of an expensive misstep."

Wes dipped his head. "Well, as awful as Polestar has been, they did give us a generous settlement. It means Willie won't have to go into debt with school loans. It means we could fix up this house, and Catelin's mother didn't have to keep working for all the weekend people." He cleared his throat. "Anyway, you didn't come all this way to talk about dogs and colleges."

They drifted into an uncomfortable silence, the only sounds the dog's heavy panting and the soft whir of the oxygen machine. Wes studied Omar with a nervous intensity, his lips twitching, but when their eyes met, he abruptly shifted his gaze to the floor. Out the window behind the old man, the new sunroom gleamed, framed with copper gutters, bright as an American penny. Cate had always maintained that it was her greedy biological father who had pushed for a settlement. But here was another father, sitting in the shadow of his newly renovated house, bragging about his daughter's expensive education, who had also been a beneficiary of Polestar's largesse.

"You were close to Eric, yes?" Omar asked.

Wes nodded. "Oh, yes. We became very close the past few years. He was almost like a son." He caught himself. "He was a son! But even more so at the end."

Cate had mentioned the oddity of Eric sending a final SOS to his unreliable, con-artist father. Why, Omar wondered, had he not chosen to send one instead to this kind, trustworthy man? It must have been a conscious decision, for Eric surely knew his own childhood address on Foxglove Lane by heart.

Wes gulped fresh oxygen, his blue eyes trained anxiously on his guest. "Well?" he sputtered, yanking at the long oxygen tube to give it slack. A curl of the tube lassoed around Omar's shoe, and he discreetly shook it free. "You mentioned on the phone that Cate had learned something in Cairo about Eric's death?"

Omar nodded. "Yes, of course." But Wes's eyes had shrunk into angry slivers, as if daring this stranger to make an accusation. Omar had driven a hundred miles to convey Cate's suspicions to her parents, but he suddenly felt uneasy about handing over the postcard she'd left for him—the only solid shred of evidence against Roe Driscoll that remained.

Omar glanced at the dog sitting a few feet from his chair, its bullet eyes trained on him. He turned to gaze out the window. There were no other cars near the darkened house, only his aunt's BMW in the driveway. Where was Cate's mother? Why wasn't she here to greet him? Wouldn't she be eager to meet the young man from Cairo who claimed to have information on the deaths of her children? Strange, too, that Omar had been invited to sit not in the house but in a toolshed. It occurred to him that when he'd called yesterday, he had only spoken with Wes.

"I thought I'd meet Cate's mom," he said.

"I'm very sorry." Wes's eyes dropped to his desk. "Joy wasn't up for it. As you can imagine, she's been having a hard time. She does thank you for coming. Whatever you have to say, I'll be sure to share it with her."

Claustrophobia began to swell inside of him. The toolshed was too small, the dog only a few feet away, and the bleak hum of the breathing machine filling the silence. But something else hung between him and Wes in this small enclosure, something inexplicably heavier. He suppressed the urge to jump from the chair and step outside. Wes was staring at him carefully, two unblinking blue eyes above a plastic mask.

"If you don't mind, I'd really like to speak to Cate's mom."

"No," Wes said flatly. "As I said, it isn't possible. I will listen for her."

Omar gave a guileless smile to hide the fluttering suspicion. He wondered what lie Wes had told Cate's mother to keep her away from the house this morning.

Outside, crickets chittered. Omar pictured the miles of forest that separated this property from its nearest neighbor. He was panicking for no reason, he told himself. The old man could barely get out of his chair. He had been on the opposite side of the planet when his stepchildren were killed. There was no possible way he could have had anything to do with two murders in Cairo.

"Tell me," Wes prompted, "what exactly did Catelin learn in Egypt?"

Omar gave a meek, indeterminate shrug.

"She didn't"—Wes grimaced—"learn of any additional assailants? We know for a fact that Eric died because of something he discovered about Polestar. That's why they covered up his murder. Catelin and I were always of the same mind on that point. We were very close at the end—"

"Cate believed the Driscoll kid was involved in Eric's death," Omar blurted.

Wes choked out a cough. "That's not possible. How could that poor boy be involved?" He shoved the mask over his mouth and took a few hard breaths. "He lost his life too, don't forget. It was a shock to learn he died in that Italian hospital. I like to think he was trying to protect Catelin from whoever attacked her in the hotel."

Omar almost laughed at that ludicrous version of events. It had been ten months since Cate's death, and in that time, Wes had

revised Roe into the role of martyr. It was the kind of prepos-
terous scenario that the Egyptian government would invent to
explain away a death at the hands of the police. But the question
bothered him: Why would Wes be so eager to defend the motives
of a faceless teenager, when weighing the death of his own stepdaughter?

"It's our fault." Wes's shoulders slumped. "We should never have
let Catelin go over there. Joy won't forgive herself. We both tried
to talk her out of it. Leave it alone, we said. It's a black hole that
has no bottom. Nothing but violence in that part of the world."

Omar gave an offended smirk. He thought of the message that
Eric had written to his biological father. *Ask him about Huxley.*
What harm would it do to follow a hunch? "What about Huxley?"

Wes's eyes shot up, jittery with life in his otherwise bloodless
face.

"Cate had hoped to ask you that question," Omar said.

"You're talking about that pendant Eric found in his apartment?" Wes shook his head. "Now you sound just like my stepson,
making too much out of too little. Is that what Catelin learned in
Cairo? Is that what you've come all the way up here to tell me?
Listen, Eric was killed because of his job at Polestar. That's why
his company paid us so much money. It had nothing to do with
poor Roe—"

"You knew Roe Driscoll, then?"

"Barely, but so what? He was the son of a prominent local family. I know a lot of the better families around here due to my work
at the school. Roe sailed boats at Brightwell as a kid, and I managed the grounds. His mom would come and watch him from the
picnic benches. So yes, I knew who he was, but I didn't know him
well. The Driscolls moved overseas years ago. What did Roe tell
Catelin? Did he mention me to her?"

He cannot hurt you, Omar thought. His aunt's BMW was parked right outside, its doors unlocked. The long blue tube that carried Wes's oxygen snaked an inch from Omar's shoe. He could step on it, block the flow, leave the man gasping, if he needed. Yes, there was the dog, but even it had lost interest, sniffing at its paws. He owed it to Cate to push further.

"Yes," he bluffed. "Roe told Cate everything. Including the part about you."

"Then he must have given her the wrong idea!" the old man cried, banging his hand on the desk. The Doberman's head swiveled toward its master. "Is that the reason you've driven up here? To accuse me of involvement in Eric's death? Jesus Christ, I was only trying to help!" His face had turned crimson. "One day, out of the blue, Roe and his mother reached out to me, asking me to intercede on their behalf. As I told you, I hardly knew them, but apparently Eric had spoken highly of me as a man he trusted and listened to. Frankly, I was flattered. Maura begged me to talk reason to Eric. Roe had gotten into some trouble in Cairo." Although the mask was in his hand, Wes tried to take a full breath on his own, like a child gathering the courage to dive into a pool. "I'm a good person. What was I supposed to do, say no when a family asks for my help? Roe had fallen into . . ." He searched the tools hanging on his walls for the right word. "Roe had made some mistakes. He'd been a typical teenage boy in many ways, experimenting, acting out, not considering consequences. What do you expect? He was stuck all alone in that brutal part of the world. Yes, he behaved improperly. I won't defend him!"

Wes banged his fist a second time, and the dog leaped to its feet, its eyes on its master as if awaiting instruction. Its panting grew heavier, each exhale reaching the harmonic pitch of a whine. "Maura wanted me to talk to Eric about giving the boy another chance, not to report the incident to the embassy. Roe was very sorry, and he didn't want the incident to ruin the rest of his life.

Can you blame him? He wasn't twenty years old! So I agreed to talk to Eric about it. That's all!"

Moose let out a shrill yelp. "Quiet!" Wes chided, his chest heaving. "Maura called me one morning when she was with Eric on their terrace, and she passed the phone to him. We couldn't talk privately on his devices, you see. I told Eric, this is your boss's son! Can't you forgive one mistake? If you can't forgive Roe for his sake, then how about for *ours*? Joy and I were struggling financially. We needed him to keep his job. But Eric was hell-bent. To be honest, I think he'd been drinking. He got all high-and-mighty about the treatment of refugees. This, from a man who fixed warheads for a living! He wouldn't listen to me, and that was the end of it. Eric said a lot of nasty things to me on that call that I'd rather not—"

"You knew from the beginning," Omar said. "You knew from the moment Eric died that he was on the verge of turning Roe in, and you didn't say a word to anyone."

"I, well . . ." Wes struggled to gather his breath. "I didn't know for certain his death had anything to do with Roe. I still don't! That's *your* theory. Maybe it was Catelin's too. But it could as easily have been Polestar or anyone else in your country! It's practically a war zone over there!"

It dawned on Omar that the messages scrawled on Eric's postcards hadn't been meaningless. They had been sent to the two family members who were out of Wes's reach and they were designed to make sense only in the event that something happened to Eric. *See, Cate, you were right about our stepfather. He wasn't the upright, holier-than-thou man he pretended to be.* And *If it all blows up, ask him about Huxley. Ask the last family member I spoke to; he knows the person to blame.* Wes held all the answers to his stepson's death. Eric had naturally assumed that if the worst happened to him, his stepfather would confess what he knew about the Driscolls. The only problem was that when the moment came to talk, Wes Steigerwald kept his mouth shut.

It was clear to Omar the reason he'd remained silent. The evidence was right there in the photo shrine to his daughter at Smith and the sunroom addition out the window. Wes had glimpsed a rare opportunity. Why pin the blame on a teenager when he could cast it on a billion-dollar defense company? Eric was already dead. Blaming Roe wouldn't help the family financially. Eric had been working for Polestar when he was killed. Why shouldn't the company pay? All Wes had to do was keep quiet.

"I haven't done anything wrong!" Wes shouted, his eyes bright with tears. "It's not my fault! How dare you come up here to accuse—"

The Doberman began to bark, drowning out Wes's rambling excuses. Omar could catch only fragments. *Joy is fragile, and it was best . . . By the time I found the lawyer . . .* No, Wes hadn't killed anybody, not with his own hands. His crime was merely one of omission. But how guilty did a person have to be before they took any share of the blame? "Moose, quiet!"

The dog grew louder, each shrill bark broadcasting through Omar's new hearing aid into his head. He closed his eyes, trying to block out the noise. Perhaps it was at that moment that Wes slipped his hand into his desk drawer. Omar wouldn't have noticed had the dog not suddenly gone silent. He opened his eyes in relief, the quiet stinging his ears. Moose's head was cocked toward the window, its ears pricked. Then both Omar and Wes heard the unmistakable sound of a car pulling into the driveway.

Wes yanked his arm from the drawer and shut it. Maybe he was only reaching for a dog treat and not anything more dangerous. Omar would never find out. He quickly stood, opened the shed door, and stepped into the hot August daylight. Moose shot across the lawn, its master's calls—*Come back, come back*—no match for the thrill of a new car in the driveway. Or maybe Wes was calling for Omar.

Moose circled the station wagon that had parked next to the BMW, jumping at the windows, dog slobber streaking across the glass. A frail woman was sitting in the driver's seat. At first it was hard to make her out through the reflection of trees and sky on the windows, but as he rounded the car he could see a faint resemblance to Cate in her face. He tapped on the driver's window, and she stared up distrustfully at him, clearly having no idea what he was doing here, this foreign man walking around her property. Cautiously, she lowered the window a crack. Omar pulled the Jamaican postcard from his pocket and slipped it through the window's gap, as if dropping it into a mailbox. The truth, or at least a good portion of it, landed in Cate's mother's lap.

Omar climbed into his car and reversed onto Foxglove Lane. He sped through the village of New Marlborough and on, through mountains reeking of cow and honeysuckle. His original plan had been to drive to the cemetery to visit Cate's grave. But he'd passed enough forlorn graveyards on his way up here, the cemeteries more frequent than gas stations in this stretch of the world, some of them dating back to the Revolutionary War. But like most immigrants, Omar had come to America for the attractions of the future, not the past. And it felt more in keeping with his lost friend to remember her in the crowded, restless city that she had made her home. He punched the fastest route to Manhattan into his phone.

The highway ran through a purple sloping valley, along a vein of shining river that flowed from the highest mountains. Omar rolled down the car windows. He heard the river fighting the rocks in its fast descent, the locusts chanting in the fields, the wind curling around his ears, warm with sunlight, as free as anything could be. It was all a love song.

Acknowledgments

_____

This novel owes a debt to the Egyptians—friends, acquaintances, friends of friends, and kind strangers—who spoke with me about their experiences, thereby enriching a story that I otherwise would never have been able to tell. In what I only hope can be chalked up to an abundance of writerly paranoia, I've decided not to name them here in the event of any repercussions. But I thank them dearly for their openness, honesty, and trust. It will come as no surprise to readers of this book that several of those conversations dealt with the current government's persecution of the LGBTQ+ community. The events in this novel are fictional. The underlying problems in the United States, in Egypt, and all over the warring world are not. In choosing to set this imperfect vehicle of a novel in Egypt, I do so with a deep respect and tremendous love for the country, and also with a concerned eye for its present and future.

For a book that covers such diverse topics as international arms, overseas autopsies, and even piano tuning, I was lucky to count on the expertise of many sources. Among those who provided information or pointed me toward its discovery are Michael Baden, Bruce Newsome, Jack Jarmon, Noah Mandell, an unnamed operator from the U.S. State Department who humored me on if/ then questions for an hour,, Robert Abrams, Dora Fung, Matthew King, Catherine Chester, and Jeremy Tamanini. The early drafts of this novel were written in the Berkshires during the pandemic, in the New Marlborough–adjacent town of Sandisfield. But much of the rewriting and editing was completed during my stay as the writer in residence on Venice's island of San Servolo for Ca'Foscari's Waterlines Project and at a residency at Cité internationale des arts in Paris. I want to thank both of these magnificent institutions for giving me a room and a desk.

Never could I finish a novel without my trusted first reader, dear friend, and agent Bill Clegg, who always knows how to make the words matter more. Thanks too to Marion Duvert, Simon Toop, Nik Wesson, and everyone at the Bill Clegg Agency. I'm in debt to two editors of enormous talent who steered this book to its final form: the phenomenal Jennifer Barth, who found the story amid the tumult and helped me shape it, and the brilliant Millicent Bennett, who located the holes and missing heartbeats. Thank you to the finest publisher I know, Jonathan Burnham, for his support and friendship, to Liz Velez, Tracy Locke, Tom Hopke, Miranda Ottewell, and everyone at Harper for making me feel like part of the family. Special thanks to Daniela Gugliemino, and to Philippe Robinet, Charlotte LeFevre, and Michael McCaughley, and to Michael Cendejas and Lynn Pleshette.

What a hellish year it was when I wrote this novel. I want to thank my friends for seeing me through it: among the many I owe dearly, Patrik Ervell, Wade Guyton, T. Cole Rachel, Thomas Alexander, Alexander Hertling, Zadie Smith, T. J. Wilcox, James

Haslam, Edmund White, Kelly Brant, Scott Rothkopf, Jack McCullough, Lazaro Hernandez, Joseph Logan, Stephanie LaCava, Lauren Tabach Bank, Olympia Scarry, Adam Kimmel, Mina and Monroe, David Totah, Tiffany Gassouk, Emily Supinger, Suzanne Ackerman, Carolyn Bane, and my family back in Cincinnati.

Finally, this book is partly dedicated to the memories of three individuals who, in vastly different ways, inspired this novel. I never met them, but their lives and ends weighed on me. Sarah Hegazi, Giulio Regeni, and Christopher Cramer. Thank you, too, to the publication, *Mada Masr*, for its brave reporting that kept me close to Egypt.

ABOUT THE AUTHOR

CHRISTOPHER BOLLEN is the author of the critically acclaimed novels *A Beautiful Crime, The Destroyers, Orient,* and *Lightning People.* He is a frequent contributor to various publications, including *Vanity Fair,* the *New York Times,* and *Interview.* He lives in New York City.

READ MORE BY CHRISTOPHER BOLLEN

"Deliciously diabolical. . . . Bollen's wit sparkles on almost every page."
—*Washington Post*

"A seductive and richly atmospheric literary thriller with a sleek Patricia Highsmith surface."
—*New York Times Book Review*

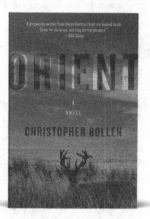

"Rich in literary diversions, moments of keen sociological and emotional insight—often into personal isolation —that transcend the conventions of its story." —*Los Angeles Times*